# LEVITICUS

*Dedicated to Amanda and Sam who always
believed in this book.*

*And to Elizabeth who always believed in me*

I feel exquisite pleasure in dwelling on the recollections of childhood, before misfortune had tainted my mind and changed its bright visions of extensive usefulness into gloomy and narrow reflections upon self.

**Mary Shelley -**
*Frankenstein*

# CHAPTER ONE

*News Update: May 14, 2024. 8:21 p.m. A series of car bombs involving seven vehicles packed with explosives breached the integrity of Baghdad Central Prison, in what appears to be a coordinated attack on the facility. At least a dozen Iraqi soldiers and guards were killed and there were injuries to dozens more.*

The female voice whispering into Clay's ear was neither unpleasant, nor unfamiliar. It spoke with the bubbly playfulness of a young woman; but measured and deliberate, giving it an unnatural cadence. *A female version of the HAL 9000 from Kubrick's 2001: A Space Odyssey,* was his best attempt to compare it to anything.

*The attack is believed to have also killed or injured almost 400 prisoners, and allowed for the escape of an estimated three thousand more, including four top al-Qaeda operatives. The Baghdad Central Prison, formerly known as Abu Ghraib, was the site of the torture and mistreatment of detainees during the Iraq war.*

*Abu Ghraib prison? Jesus,* Clay thought, *I thought that place was knocked down years ago.* A hellhole whose name, two decades later, still evoked rage among many. Clay tried to recall when the tortures occurred. *Was it back in early 2004,* he wondered, *that I first heard about American soldiers torturing Iraqi prisoners?* Back then, the newspapers and internet were filled with the images of some of the horrors that took place within the walls of Abu Ghraib; recurring evidence of man's intolerance toward his fellow man. Now, as then, Clay could not imagine what went on in the minds and lives of those guilty of the worst cruelties that took place.

\* \* \*

The pin-up calendar on the wall showed a voluptuous redhead, lying on her back on a beach, eyes closed, a slight smile emanating from her red lips. Her bathing suit was in tatters, as if she had just washed ashore. Below her, the weeks of December 2003 were laid out in rows. He hated the picture.

The past six months in Iraq had felt like six years. He was not so much bothered by the heat but by the sand. *All the damn sand!* He could not get it out of his mind, his body. It was everywhere. Not the big grains, the ones that crunched between your teeth when you chewed, but the fine sand, almost dust, that would incessantly collect in your mouth, nose, eyes, and ears coating you in a thin layer of gritless sand. And there she was, in all her beauty, left arm, slightly raised, revealing a cake of sand adhering to her damp skin, mocking his predicament.

Second Lieutenant R. George Leeds took to cursing the sand, unsuccessfully attempting to repel the foul material with each hateful expression, and in failing, resorted to spitting a sand-saliva mixture upon the cursed ground.

"God damned country!" he shouted at everybody, at nobody.

"Yes Sir. God-damned country, Sir," Private Niklas Mueller responded, standing guard outside Leeds' office.

Lt. Leeds liked the Private. Mueller was young, just a kid, really, at only seventeen. He was a good soldier. The kind that listens to his commanding officer; that did as he was asked. *One that could watch your back for you, if you ever needed it,* Leeds mused. And in a country like Iraq, you always needed your back watched.

Leeds looked at his watch. It was only ten a.m. but already the temperature and humidity had risen. The air was stagnant and he felt his clothes dampening with a mixture of humid air and sweat. He turned on the fan that stood behind his chair and it quickly began its work of circulating hot air and sand around the room.

"God damned Arabs!" he shouted as he spit again.

"God damned Arabs, yes Sir!" Mueller responded.

Leeds was not someone who would, as his mother would say, use the good Lord's name in vain. She had been a devout Christian, believing every word in the Bible as the spoken truth. Her husband did not believe, and disallowed her from taking Leeds to church. She would resort to reading aloud to her young son from the New Testament on those nights the boy's father was out or incapacitated, in an attempt to instill the Holy Spirit in him. And for a while, the young boy believed.

His father believed in little, other than the knowledge that if one of the local pubs refused to serve him more whiskey, he could always find another that was willing to take his money. It was a rare evening he did not stumble home, loaded, well after 8 o'clock — if he came home at all. Leeds liked the nights his father did not come home. On those nights, he and his mother would share dinner (cold by the time she felt certain her husband was not returning and that it was safe to begin without him), and then he would be allowed to watch thirty minutes of television, usually curled up on the floor, while his mother cleaned up. They would then retire to the couch where his mother would read to him out of the New Testament, stories of forgiveness and Christian charity, and turning the other cheek. He would sit close to his mother, feeling the warmth of her body, the smell of lemon dish soap mingled with talc. This closeness and familiarity, this affection, made these nights special.

The stories, however, did not make sense to Leeds. The pictures of Jesus that his mother hung on the walls revealed a long-haired deity, soft features and kind eyes, his beard oddly out of place. These features did not strike Leeds as male features. He believed his mother misspoke, had turned Jesus into a man in the stories, drawn the beard on the face in the pictures, in an attempt to make it easier for Leeds to relate to this deity. His father, the only man he knew, was not forgiving — would not forgive the untucked shirt, the accidently broken dish, the word spoken out of line. Leeds, himself, was not forgiving. It was his mother, a woman, who, like Jesus, never failed to forgive, to turn the other cheek.

Leeds had difficulty relating to the stories of Jesus, of the slow to anger, selfless, generous God. It was the other god to whom he could relate. On those nights when his father had passed out on the floor, too drunk to raise his hand in violence any longer, his mother would pull young Leeds into his room to read to him from a different book — a book his mother called the Pentateuch. It was filled with stories of seduction and violence and war, of kings and slaves and giants. The God of this book, the Father-god, said he was loving and forgiving, but mostly, Leeds would say, He was jealous and oftentimes wrathful. Leeds would lie awake in bed for hours afterward, struggling to reconcile the all-powerful, everlasting and vengeful Father-god with His forgiving, turn-the-other-cheek Son-god; the Father-god who made man, and the Son-god who died at the hands of man.

It was a warm summer's night, shortly after Leeds had turned twelve years old, when his father did not come home, but instead two police officers did. They spoke briefly with his mother and left. After that she dressed only in black and did little other than read her Bible and go to church. Leeds learned quickly to shop and cook and dress for school, to bathe himself and wash his own clothes. He finished high school and, without a word, left his mother to the musings of the ineffective Son-god—a god who, like his mother, found a place of suffering in the world. And he, R. George Leeds, set out to find his place in the world of the wrathful Father-god, who meted out reward in this lifetime, and not the next.

"God damned Muslims!" he shouted, spitting again. He felt no tinge of regret, no sin, for he did not use the Father-god's name in vain. *Did not the Father-god damn all the peoples who failed to recognize his supreme authority?* he reasoned to himself.

"God damned Muslims, yes Sir!" Mueller responded.

There were worse assignments in Iraq than Abu Ghraib prison. At least here one had the opportunity to gather information from prisoners, perhaps something that could help one's career— information that could lead to the capture of Saddam Hussein, perhaps even lead back to al-Qaeda. Leeds stood up and walked out from behind his desk. He wanted to check on a recent detainee, an Iraqi he called 'Ralph', who had been slinking around the road leading into Abu Ghraib for the past week. Ralph had been wandering around the prison, perhaps spying, when he suddenly started shouting something about Saddam Hussein and attacked one of his troops. *God damned terrorist,* Leeds thought. Private Mueller stood at the door and responded with silence.

* * *

Ismaya had approached Abu Ghraib cautiously. He was both nervous and excited at the same time. He was a poor man, uneducated, hungry. He struggled to feed his family, laboring over a small plot of land and catching an occasional fish from the Tigris. He and his family had always known hunger, and he had never before in his life ventured further from his home near ad-Dawr than Tikrit. His wife and children professed their love for him and he always desired to give them more. He prayed often to Allah to bless him, and to keep his secret safe — that he despised Saddam Hussein and his secular ways. He kept this secret from even his wife. Residing so close to Hussein's hometown of Tikrit caused him to live in constant fear of his secret being discovered by the Republican Guard. Recently, that fear was complimented with a fear of the American soldiers — their healthy bodies, their rough manner, and their guns. But the Americans, who seemed so brutal and uncaring, were supposed to be here to help the Iraqis, to facilitate the work of Allah and, perhaps, to heap blessings upon Ismaya. This gave him the courage to make the journey to Baghdad.

Allah had been smiling upon Ismaya five days ago as he was heading toward the river in the pre-dawn light to fish. He had finished his morning prayers and was walking through a small expanse of trees that ran parallel with the Tigris when he witnessed a lone truck pull over off the side of the road near a small hut to unload several crates. The men who stepped out of the truck were well armed and wearing the red berets of the Republican Guard. Ismaya instinctively had dropped to his knees behind a tree to avoid being seen. A breeze blew gently across the land and carried with it the broken voices of these men as they moved about their business. It appeared they were speaking to someone unseen, asking if he was okay, whether he needed anything. Their voices carried with them a respectful tone. As the two soldiers moved crates into the hut, more than once they stopped their work to look around, seemingly searching for possible witnesses to their actions. Ismaya realized he was sweating profusely and he tried to blend into the trees, make himself invisible. The voices continued, incomprehensible, the wind having temporarily halted. Then, the sound of a new voice — deeper, yet muffled, coming from within the hut. The wind picked up again. Ismaya tilted his head to better hear. Yes, it was definitely a different voice — commanding, confident, gruff and seemingly coming from deep within the hut, deeper than the hut was long or wide. It was the voice he had heard over the radio many times since his youth, a voice, even in its barely audible tone, was as recognizable to him as the morning sun. The sound filled him with dread. It was the voice of Saddam Hussein. The ex-president who had a bounty on his head for $25 million.

It had taken Ismaya three days to walk to Abu Ghraib from his home. For three days he imagined how he would be heralded by the U.S. troops as a great man, as a courageous man who stood up to the dangers of the old regime and turned in his own countryman. For three days he worked up the nerve to approach the foreigners running his country, but as he stood before the gates of the prison and saw the soldiers, he lost his nerve. He cursed himself for his cowardice. *Do you not love your wife and children? Do you not trust Allah, Ismaya?* he asked himself. *Do you not want to reap your due reward?* The fear he felt while hiding in the woods in ad-Dawr only a few days earlier swept back over him as an American soldier came within shouting distance. Ismaya's voice failed him. And did so again several times that day. His shoulders sank with the sun as he slowly walked away from Abu Ghraib. Tomorrow he would speak up. Tomorrow he would find his nerve and reap the fortunes Allah had set before him. He slept near the river that night, and awoke, refreshed and determined to overcome his fear and approach the American soldiers. But on the second day, his nerves again faltered. Fearful, he stalked around the prison, trying to spy a soldier who seemed to be gentle, approachable, but each soldier he saw seemed threatening, dangerous. He kept this routine up for three more days. On the evening of his fourth day, he had a dream.

He was standing in a strange land. Behind him, a road stretched out into a void, a blackness so deep it was as if nothing existed beyond, not even matter itself. Ahead of him, the road reached out toward the sun, yet the light was muted and gave no warmth, a reddish-orange disk floating just above the horizon. Ismaya, fearing the void, walked toward the sun. He continued this way for what seemed like hours, the orb neither rising nor sinking, when at last he came to a fork in the road. To his left, he could see his home far in the distance. He knew his wife and children were inside, tired and hungry and awaiting his return. To his right, the road wound toward a river. The water was blue and cool and the earth partook and brought forth all manner of life. Fish jumped from the waters as gazelle and antelope stood on the banks flush with lotus and papyrus. Just beyond, poplar and willow trees provided shade and safety. And beyond the trees was a light so bright he could not see its source, yet he was drawn to it as a moth to a fire.

As he started toward the river, a feeling of unease swept over his body. To his left he sensed his wife and children, worried over his long absence; yet the light to his right beckoned. As he drew closer to the river, a fear grew up around him. The river seemed not blue, but nearly black. The antelope drinking from the bank took a step back at his approach and Ismaya noticed its ribs showing. The lotus flowers that had filled the air with their sweet aroma were now long past bloom, the petals dry and withered. A pack of jackals stood staring from among the trees, now barren of leaves. He thought of turning back, but the void had followed him and the road behind him had disappeared. Yet the light beyond still held hope. He was overcome with a desire to reach the light, and knew that at its source, his deepest desires would be realized, his yearnings would be fulfilled. He quickened his pace, raising his hand over his nostrils, which were suddenly filled with the odor of rot and decay. The jackals were poised to set chase and Ismaya broke out into a full run. He struggled to catch his breath as the heat and stench rose around him. Until now, he had not noticed how hot it had become. As the pack chased after, he knew that he must reach the light; nothing mattered except the light. Nothing mattered at all — not his wife, not his children, just the light. He could sense the animals at his heels, ready to pounce. They were close, so close he felt the hot breath of one of the jackals on his cheek. Ismaya stumbled forward, and then he was flying. As he soared, he met the light, which fluttered in a bright flash and then darkness. The animals and heat and smells were gone. He was simply floating — absent of fear, of pain. He was overcome with a feeling of calm and peace. Ismaya was free. Freer than he had ever felt before in his life.

Ismaya awoke with a start. The feeling of freedom did not vanish upon waking, but remained. He prepared to pray to Allah, who had shown him a sign, shown him that to return home would mean continual poverty and hunger, but to continue on, to seek his reward, would be difficult, perhaps nearly fatal, but would end with total peace, total happiness. Yes, Allah had offered the difficult path, and promised reward at the end.

With his newly found courage, Ismaya once again sought the gates of Abu Ghraib. Today he would conquer his fears. Today he would deliver information on the location of Saddam Hussein. Today he would realize his dreams. The guardhouse was staffed with two soldiers, both nearly twice the size of Ismaya, but he was not discouraged. He stepped up to the first soldier and stated that he knew where President Hussein was hiding. The guard shouted something at him in English and pushed him back with the butt of his rife, sending Ismaya to the ground. He stood up, yelling that he did not speak English, asking if the soldier spoke Arabic, begging to speak through an interpreter, to share his good fortune with the Americans. He was answered with the butt of the soldier's rifle to his stomach, and he once again fell to the ground. Stars flashed before Ismaya's eyes and he was slow to get up. He reminded himself that, as in his dream, the road to reward would not be easy. It had not occurred to Ismaya that none of the soldiers manning the perimeter would speak Arabic, that America, with so many people and so many resources, would fail to deploy Arabic speaking soldiers in positions with direct contact to the local population.

"Please," he shouted in Arabic, to the soldier, to anyone on the other side of the gate. "Please get an interpreter!" The response from the soldier landed on the side of Ismaya's head.

*How long have I been here?* Ismaya wondered. He had no answer. At first, the Americans had placed Ismaya in a cell. They demanded things from him, yelled at him in English, and Ismaya tried to understand. They shouted at him over and over about 'identification' but the word rang hallow for Ismaya. The soldiers seemed to be looking for something, but he had nothing save for the clothes on his back and the sandals on his feet. Later he had been moved to a different area of the prison. It was here that Ismaya now suffered. His pleas, heard by ears that did not understand Arabic, fell uselessly about.

*Had not the Americans arrived to help the Iraqis?* Ismaya asked, trying to convince himself. Ismaya fought to remember his dream, fought to remember the total calm and peace at the end of the difficult road. He prayed to Allah that the journey would end soon.

Leeds spit as he watched Sgt. Ireland Bingham walk slowly around the prisoner. Leeds hated Ismaya, hated everything about him — his skin the color of wet sand, his eyes so dark Leeds could not tell if they were brown or black, the thick hair covering his head, his face, his body, and his god that Leeds repeatedly accused of calling for jihad against America. Ismaya let out a moan as he started to regain consciousness.

Ismaya stood in the back of a large room, forced to stare at a wall covered with pictures of naked women. Blondes. Brunettes. Redheads. Black. White. Asian. Many posing with naked men or even other naked women. He, too, was naked, his arms uncomfortably bound to ropes strung from the ceiling, a collar around his neck. Leeds gave Sgt. Bingham a nod and she placed a noose around Ismaya's testicles. She gave a slight squeeze as she did so and Ismaya opened his eyes. She motioned him to stand up on a small block as she lashed his legs with a leather strap. Ismaya stood his ground, refusing to move. The Sergeant moved to strike him again, but Leeds held up his hand. He stepped around behind Ismaya and pulled on a rope, increasing the tension on the noose. Ismaya recalled the pain from earlier and immediately stepped onto the block.

"Good dog, Ralph," Leeds spoke as Sgt. Bingham moved to the back of the room and pulled the ropes tied to Ismaya's arms tighter, straining the aching joints of his elbows. Ismaya could feel the exhaustion in his legs already. Ismaya was once again balanced on the small wooden box that obligated him to stand nearly tiptoe as splinters from the roughly hewn wood dug into his toes. Strangely enough, he found himself thankful for the ache in his feet. If he lost feeling in his feet, if he were unable to support his body in its current contorted position, he would risk falling from the block.

*How long ago had it been that I had fallen?* Ismaya tried to sort it out. *Was it only moments earlier, or was it hours?* The female soldier had been screaming at him, gesturing him to remain tiptoed on the block. His body was crying out for relief; his calf muscles protesting the lactic acid building within, his outstretched arms aching at every joint. Then she appeared. That harlot, Sleep, snuck in and tried to seduce Ismaya with her promises of calm and relief. But something inside of Ismaya had warned him to keep standing.

*But to what use?* asked Sleep. *What torture could they inflict that they had not already done?*

He struggled against Sleep's soft caresses, her gentle urgings; battled to keep his eyes open, but his will was no match for her promise of calm, her desire to take control over his broken frame, her offer of opportunity to slip out of this living nightmare and into the heaven of her arms. As his legs gave way, the long-hoped for relief rushing down his legs was met by an unimaginable pain emanating from his groin as his body was literally lifted by the leather noose wrapped around his testicles. The collar around his neck had stiffened with resistance as he fell off the block, and it must have pulled some trigger, some barbaric device that resulted in the immediate tension in the ropes attached to his wrists and his groin.

The strain in his arms redoubled as he hung in a prone position, arms outstretched, legs hanging down at right angles to his now horizontal torso. He thought he might pass out when suddenly the tension eased and his body crashed to the wet floor below. He had landed in his own bodily fluids—blood, sweat, urine and excrement. He had long grown accustomed to the stench beneath him, but now, lying in it, he retched.

"You've been a bad boy, Ralph." Ismaya recognized the voice. Thin. Cold. Accompanied by the sound of spitting. The young lieutenant whose presence always resulted in more pain, more humiliation. Ismaya did not speak. The relief to be off the block, even though lying in his own feces, was almost too much for Ismaya. He wanted to tell the lieutenant something, but he could no longer quite remember what it was. It had something to do with a hut and a man and a truck near a river with jackals and a light, a blinding white light, but each time he tried to put it into words, his thoughts got confused.

"You're a filthy mutt." It was the last thing he heard before the boot came down on the back of his head, before the sleepless dark overtook him.

But now he was once again on the block, once again staring at the pictures of naked women. The ache in his calves was already getting to be too much. Leeds came from behind Ismaya and spoke to the sergeant. She left the room. Leeds took a position beside Ismaya, admiring the women of the photos.

"I like the blonde in the middle there. The one with the two guys. She almost looks like she's going to cry." Leeds spit and stood staring for another moment before he pulled a racquetball from his pocket. He moved to bounce it, but noticing the blood, excrement and teeth littering the floor, refrained.

"You dirty, filthy, Shiite bastard." He spat at Ismaya. "We come over here and free you from that goddammed Hussein, and trying to kill us is the thanks we get?" He spat again. "Where's Muqtada al-Sadr? Where's Hussein?"

*Hussein,* Ismaya remembered. He wanted to tell the lieutenant something about Hussein, and lotus flowers and trucks. He shook his head, trying to clear the confusion.

"You lying bastard, Ralph!" Leeds shouted and then spit. He punched Ismaya in the gut. As Ismaya struggled to regain his breath, the thoughts in his head swirled around again, falling out of order. He had fallen off the block and was, once again, hanging horizontally above the floor, as if he were somehow suddenly capable of flight. The pain was numbing and a wave of nausea passed through him. Leeds reached his arm around the back of Ismaya's head and held tight as he took the racquetball in his other hand and stuffed it into Ismaya's mouth. "You don't want to talk? Fine. Have it your way." Ismaya struggled against the ball jammed into his mouth. He tried to speak, but could only grunt. Leeds smiled widely and placed his hand upon Ismaya's throat and began to squeeze.

As Ismaya's body began to struggle, Lt. Leeds muttered to him. "It is quite different suffocating a man than suffocating an animal." Leeds looked intensely at Ismaya. "When I was in high school, I dated a girl who owned a dog, an old Labrador retriever who did little other than eat and sleep." The pressure on Ismaya's throat eased briefly, and then tightened once again. "One evening when she stepped out of the room to take a phone call, the old dog walked over to me and placed its head onto my lap." A faint smile spread across Leeds' lips. "I had been dating this girl for almost two years and it seems the dog had grown accustomed to my presence in the house, had grown, I believe, to love and trust me." Again the grip eased and tightened. "I placed my hand over the animal's muzzle and, for no reason I can explain, began to squeeze it down. The animal began to struggle, to try to remove its head from my lap, but it was unable." The grip on Ismaya's throat increased. "The whole time I was holding the dog's air passages closed, suffocating the animal, it never once took his eyes off of me. And do you know what the amazing thing was?" Leeds did not wait for an answer. "Never once did that dog's eyes show any hint of anything other than trust and love and, perhaps, mild confusion. Yet now, in my act of suffocating you, I cannot not help but notice the mixture of fear and hate in your eyes. That dog, an animal innocent of any real sin, made no judgment, no accusation whatsoever; but you, a terrorist, a person who has clearly sinned has the nerve, the audacity, to judge me, to condemn my actions?"

"Allahu akbar," he whispered into Ismaya's ear. "But my God is greater." Leeds squeezed tighter as Ismaya's body began to convulse.

The pain was intense and Ismaya began to see dark spots floating before his eyes, his body thrashing about in mid-air, when suddenly he was overcome with the feeling that he actually was flying. The stench from the floor below seemed to fade and among the dark spots, a light began to form before his eyes, a bright light that seemed to hold the promise of comfort. A light he had seen before, but could not remember where. Nothing else mattered anymore, not the hand on his throat or the pulling at his arms and groin, or even the desire to see his wife and children. Nothing mattered except the light. He reached for it. He could still sense the hand of Leeds on his throat, the Lieutenant's face so close he felt Leeds' hot breath on his cheek, but it was all fading, being washed out by the light. Ismaya's body spasmed as he hung in the air, still flying. As he soared closer to the light, it fluttered with a bright flash and then darkness. Lt. Leeds and the burning pain and the smells were all gone. He was simply floating, absent of fear, of pain. He was overcome with a feeling of calm and peace. Ismaya was free — freer in death than he had ever been in life.

Private Mueller entered the room. "They've captured Saddam Hussein, Sir," he said. Leeds released his grip from the dead man's throat. Private Mueller looked from Leeds to the dead man and back. "Would you like me to dispose of the detainee, Sir?"

"Yes. And let's be sure to bring Sgt. Bingham with us."

"Yes Sir," Mueller said as he turned to leave, but Leeds stopped him.

Leeds spit on Ismaya's dead body, hanging above the floor. "And Private, don't forget to bring one of those IEDs we recovered last week. We may have use for it."

"Yes Sir!" Mueller smiled as he quickly left the room.

## CHAPTER TWO

*News Flash: June 6, 2024. 11:30 a.m. Peace negotiations continue in the Middle East*

Although not unexpected, it nevertheless always shocked him somewhat to hear the voice whispering in his ear, not quite loud enough to drown out other sounds occurring around him, but loud enough to be heard and, sometimes, throw him off his train of thought. It had been three years since his fitting, yet Clay continued to be disconcerted by the answers and frequent news updates spoken in his ear.

"More," Clay said. The not unpleasant voice of Clay's iMeme relayed additional information on the peace negotiations.

*An unprecedented twelve weeks of calm has led many world leaders to believe that Hamas' promises of peace and recognition of Israel as the Jewish State may, finally, result in a binding peace treaty between Israel and the Palestinian People. The nightmare predicted after the fall of Fatah three years ago and the aggressive stance assumed by Hamas has never materialized and the recent actions of Hamas to reign in splinter terror groups has lent a certain optimism to the whole conference.*

Clay wondered how many other folks were listening to this news. How many others even cared. The iMeme Notification App allowed users to customize what information would be relayed by the iMeme directly into one's auditory system. Given the scarcity of (and lack of any apparent demand for) real news available in the newspapers, he figured he was one of a very small number not receiving updates only on the latest gossip or entertainment.

Clay had been one of the last of the people he knew to get an iMeme. Most of his friends had been using them for several years, before his wife, after repeated attempts to talk him into getting one, gave him an iMeme as a birthday gift. The decision to actually have the TIN (transceiver interface-nano) implanted in his ear did not come easy for Clay. He could not understand how people were willing to accept the use of tiny cameras and two-way communication tied directly into one's body so quickly. Implanting a device that would not only allow the iMeme to speak directly into one's auditory system, but to listen in on one's thoughts and respond appropriately. He had a lingering fear that he would wake up one day and see himself on the Cloud, having been videoed and published without his knowledge or consent.

\* \* \*

"The technology for TIN has been around for decades actually," said the young man assisting Clay. The lanyard hanging around the youth's neck displayed the words *Rudy* and *Genius.*

It had been almost eight months since his family had purchased him an iMeme as a birthday gift and they had finally worn him down and elicited a promise to have the TIN nanochip fitted today. Rudy was explaining how the process worked and it seemed to Clay the young man knew what he was talking about. Most of the Genius Bar staff did.

"It uses the same technology the physically impaired use to transmit brain signals to a computer to perform specific functions. Your iMeme sits here on your Spot, or wherever you choose to keep it, and as long as it's within a three-foot radius, it can transmit information to, or receive information from, the TIN, which is really just a cochlear nanochip placed in your inner ear. With two-way communication and the iMeme's built-in nanocamera, the iMeme can perform any number of important functions."

Clay was still nervous. "So you're going to stick something in my inner ear? Right here?" he asked, looking around. "No doctor? No specialist?"

"Trust me sir, I'm an Apple trained audiologist. I've done thousands of these. I simply place this device in your ear and the TIN nanochip will be inserted into your cochlea. Takes just a few moments." Rudy put a smile on his face to try to reassure Clay.

"That's the problem, Rudy. I'm not too hip on you puncturing my eardrum with that thing. I mean, don't doctors say that only thing you should put in your ear is your elbow?"

"Sir," Rudy responded. "The PSD will barely enter your outer ear."

"PSD? What's a PSD?" Clay asked.

Rudy was clearly working to retain his patience. "Sir, the PSD is the Placement and Syncing Device," he said, showing Clay the object in his hand. It looked to Clay like an ear thermometer with a small cable hanging off its lower end. Rudy pointed to the small tip protruding from the top of the PSD and continued. "A nano-needle extends from here into your inner ear and to the cochlea. The needle itself is thinner than the proboscis of a mosquito. Not only will you feel absolutely nothing, the procedure is so safe that even if the TIN were misplaced, there would be no harm done to you." He saw the look of doubt on Clay's face and added, "The TIN won't be misplaced. I promise."

Rudy put the PSD to Clay's ear, pressed a button. Clay closed his eyes, expecting the worst. He felt absolutely nothing. A hopeful thought that the PSD was broken crossed his mind. He opened his eyes and turned to Rudy.

"Listen, if there's a problem, I can always come back."

"I'm sorry Sir. What was that you said?" Rudy asked, involved in hooking up Clay's tiny iMeme to the cable dangling off the lower end of the PSD.

"I said," Clay started and then jumped slightly when he heard a gentle whisper in his ear.

*iMeme now activated: November 13, 2021. 5:43 p.m.*

Clay spun around to see who had spoken to him, but quickly realized it was no one, simply his iMeme communicating to him. Clay flushed slightly with embarrassment as he noticed Rudy grinning. Clay wondered whether everyone reacted as surprised or whether Clay was the random oddball. The idea of being looked upon as some sort of fool annoyed him. "What if I want to take the chip out?" Clay asked.

A puzzled look crossed Rudy's face. "Take it out?"

## CHAPTER THREE

*It is June 11, 2024. 2:24 p.m.*

*Listen to the time,* Clay thought. *I wonder how long people have been carrying their iMemes everywhere they went, attached to it like a newborn to her mother's teat?*

The iMeme's use became so ubiquitous that a couple years ago all clothing started to be manufactured with a small, metallic pad, usually located on the left chest area, over the heart, where the iMeme could be attached. The External Docking Interface Spot, or EDI-Spot, was its official name, but everyone simply referred to it as the 'Spot'.

"The third tit," was what Clay most often referred to it as. "An interesting anomaly, but totally useless."

Perhaps not totally useless. The average person held so much of their lives on their iMeme that one seldom went anywhere without it. Being about the same surface area as a large postage stamp, and about as thin, people had complained that iMemes were too easy to misplace. *A conspiracy by Apple!* some alleged, *in order to sell more iMemes.* In addition, so many apps made use of the iMeme's nanocamera that people began to tire of having to continually remove their iMeme from their pockets, purses or wherever they carried them to allow the nanocamera to see. Clay had rightly guessed that it would only be a matter of time before someone came up with a way to solve both the problem of loss and the problem of visibility. The Spot — the place to be and the place to see for your iMeme. But not for Clay. He disliked wearing his iMeme like some type of badge and usually removed it as soon as he arrived at the office.

There was a quick knock on his office door, which opened before Clay could respond.

"Would you get these documents over to City Hall? It's for the O'Donnell project," his boss said as he set a tube of blueprints down upon Clay's desk, knocking over a picture frame. "And try to keep this office a little cleaner. It's a sty," he said, looking around. With that, the door shut and his boss disappeared as quickly as he had come.

Clay picked up the fallen frame and looked at it. It contained a picture of his wife, Lillian. She was wearing a broad smile and her auburn hair flowed loosely over the shoulders of her dress as she danced to music the photograph could not capture. It seemed so long ago. *Had it been a wedding? A New Year's Eve party?* he wondered. He could not recall and it did not matter. He loved this photograph. Lillian's beauty shining out from that moment in time, captured for eternity. Lillian of a time long since past, wearing a simple black dress, pearl earrings and matching necklace. The ubiquitous Spot not yet infecting the styles of the day.

There had been occasional rumors that clothing would soon be manufactured with iMemes built right in, but the current cost to manufacture an iMeme prevented it from becoming a reality. Looking at the photograph of Lillian, he absent-mindedly tapped his finger against his own Spot, feeling its smooth surface. He would need his iMeme. He wanted to stop and pick up some new razor blades while he was out of the office and, as usual, he did not have any cash. But at the moment, his iMeme was lying, buried among the papers, files and personal items that cluttered his desk. He set out to find it.

It took Clay almost fifteen minutes to locate it. On several occasions he had considered giving up, imagining that he had left it at home (a moment of forgetfulness that he, lately, too often experienced), but he had distinctly remembered grabbing it that morning to be sure he could buy the razors. *Besides,* he thought to himself, *it has to be here in the office. It just told me the time.* When at last he discovered it, between the pages of a file he had been attending to earlier that morning, his desk was significantly rearranged, but still disorderly. He placed his iMeme on the Spot as he left his office. It would speed up checkout at the drug store.

The government had made several attempts to remove currency from the marketplace and replace it with government-issued currency cards and an electronic iMeme application called TenderCard. There had been some feeble attempts to prevent the government's actions, but support for such measures crossed both sides of the Congressional aisle. Since the Great Depression II had begun, more and more Americans were reliant on government aid to feed their families and keep roofs over their heads. Estimates were that over 70 million people were reliant on government largess in the form of food stamps or rent subsidies for their very survival. The government announced welfare payments would be quicker with the use of the TenderCard App and too few Americans could afford any delay in their monthly benefits. Even a few days could mean the difference between paying rent and being tossed out onto the streets. The wealthy supported the use of the TenderCard App as a method to ensure that welfare recipients were not gaming the system: using tax dollars to buy expensive clothing and cars rather than live prudently. They rejoiced in knowing the downtrodden were no longer able to purchase the latest iMeme or designer fashions and then claim they were not provided with enough government support to survive. The TenderCard App restricted the use of welfare dollars to basic necessities only.

Additionally, the removal of currency from commerce would, the government claimed, lead to a reduction in gangs and gang violence. Since most Americans had no access to cash, they were unable to purchase illicit drugs. While some dealers initially accepted payment in kind, the barter system became too burdensome for most dealers. Clay had always found it interesting, however, that gangs and the drug trade did not disappear altogether. It appeared that the rich and the depleted middle-class, who managed to retain access to cash, had enough users amongst their ranks to allow some gangs to continue to thrive. Clay did not begrudge the system for limiting the use of illicit drugs. But he was no prude, and in fact, fully supported the public's right to the sin of illicit drug use, provided, however, people did so on their own dime, rather than on public funds.

What Clay could not get over was that, notwithstanding the government's stated intention, there always seemed to be an endless stream of currency. This fact led to rumors suggesting that money was continually being printed and circulated in order to allow politicians to take advantage of keeping certain transactions off the books: gifts, campaign contributions, bribes. *A government of the rich, by the rich and for the rich was alive and well,* he thought. But only in passing.

Stepping out onto Dearborn Street, Clay nearly tripped. The sidewalk in front of his office building had been suffering from an ever-expanding crack for the past several months, yet in the few hours he had been sitting in the office, it seemed to have grown to a small chasm; large enough, perhaps, to swallow a small child, but not yet big enough to warrant repair. He recalled a time not too long ago when the property owner would have corrected the problem, but under current economic conditions he knew nothing would be done until someone was severely injured. Recent judicial decisions had found no fault with defects large enough to break arms and even necks. Even a death was acceptable, provided no one had been previously killed by the same dangerous condition.

Clay turned north and walked, head down, hoping to avoid injury. And the voices. By averting his eyes downward towards the sidewalk, he could walk in relative peace, without being reminded of the identities of his fellow denizens by a whispering in his ear. Clay continued towards the Walgreen's, playing a kind of game he invented in which he would identify people not by name, but by the shoes they wore. He spotted a pair of black dress shoes. *He's someone with a job.* A pair of older suede boots inappropriate for the temperature, but considered by many to be fashionable. *Likely a coed on her way to class.* The upturned toes of shoes held together by duct tape and string. *One of the many homeless.* Every now and then, Clay would spot something out of the ordinary. A pair of expensive open-toed heels belonging to one of the elite. The naked feet of a small child. The rubber-wrapped boots of a city worker hosing down the effects of a heroine addict's latest fix. Clay found peace in not knowing among whom he was walking. Everyone identifiable, but no one identified. He passed a pair of polished-toed wingtips, faded at the vamp, soles worn, riding below the cuff of dark slacks, ankle exposed. *No socks!* Clay thought as he lifted his head, knowing whose face he would confront.

## CHAPTER FOUR

*Update: June 12, 2024. 3:04 p.m. The nanoscience department at the University of Chicago announced today that they've developed a nano-sized battery capable of powering the butyl methyl sulfide molecule nanomotors first developed by Tufts University over a decade ago. Originally powered by electron microscopes, recent advances had reduced the energy source to only microns. The downsizing of the power source to the nanoscale will allow scientists to develop new applications previously prohibited due to size of the microbatteries currently in use.*

Clay had never been much of technophile. When he was young, back near the turn of the millennium, he could distinctly remember the joy his friends experienced in being connected. They loved their smart phones, the 'freedom' it offered to be a phone call, a text, or a tweet away from anyone or anything. He hated it. When he got his first cell phone, he would occasionally leave it at home, pretending it was in error, and enjoying the feeling of being off-line, of being truly free. Freedom was not the power to connect at-will, but the ability to sever himself from the ties to everyone and everything at any time.

On most days, he resented having to carry his iMeme. The expectation that if he had his iMeme, he somehow consented to the frequent interruption of his thoughts in order to answer a call or take note of some business development, or news flash, troubled him. He hated being bound to a professional obligation when he was out of the office, when he should be free from the necessities of work and pursuing other matters, pursuing personal matters. He could recall a time in his youth, before his introduction to social networking, when the Internet was merely a means to answer questions or access games. He had read about a time, not that long before his own, when the Internet was limited to military applications and, later, to some computer nerds in school. That time did not last long. Even now, only a generation younger than he, his own children knew of social networking since their first moment of true cognizance, unable to imagine life without it. By the time Clay was thirty, he had had enough. Friends Facebooking the minutiae of their mediocre lives, tweeting the mundanities of their days.

*I just woke up — can't wait until I have my first cup of coffee.*

*Little Billy kept us up all night last night with his coughing — hope he feels better today.*

*Steaks are marinating and the beers are chilling — can't wait for tonight.*

As if these public declarations meant anything. As if anyone really cared what any particular person was doing at any particular moment in time, or what he or she was having for dinner later that night. It was not that he did not like these people, he did. They were his friends. But the idea that they honestly thought he might be interested in the details of their every action amazed him. He found even his own dietary choices entertaining only insofar as he was the one who got to actually savor and enjoy the meal.

But no, it was not even that. The posters and tweeters knew no one really cared. It was more about them, the tellers, the shouters of the irrelevant, the conveyers of folly. The unspoken contract: *I'll listen to you if you listen to me.* One no longer need be satisfied with his allotted fifteen minutes of fame. Rather, one could now achieve a lifetime of fame, could publish one's entire life for the world to share, to enjoy... or perhaps to suffer along with.

No, he could not understand the whole social networking craze — the meaning of one's life measured by the number of Facebook Friends, or Twitter Followers, rather than one's morals. Nor did he like it. He was disturbed at the willingness to allow oneself to be exploited for fame, or rather, the possibility of fame. A woman giving birth to octuplets, perhaps for the sole purpose of achieving worldwide notoriety, and then making porno films in one of several attempts to cash in on her new-found fame. To trade one's morals, one's self-dignity for money, as more than most seem willing to do, as demonstrated in the popularity of watching, and being watched on, reality television shows, and other forms of social media. As a father, he could not tolerate the indifference with which young women exposed themselves in text messages – in sexting, in emails, on videos – the fact that his children were growing up in a world with no privacy. An entire generation of young girls vying for attention that in an electronic age could not be of any real meaning nor of any real depth; attention that was simply raw exposure of the surfaces of their lives, and their skin. A post-millennium world that placed fame and notoriety over everything else.

\* \* \*

Eli Nakosh could not decide if the year 2000 was going to be a good year or not. President Clinton had just announced the National Nanotechnology Initiative, which would double the funding for nanoscience research to almost a half a billion dollars for the next fiscal year. Nakosh was an assistant professor and researcher at the University of Chicago's nanotechnology department, under the renowned Professor Chin Ho, and this announcement offered the real probability of additional research money for the lab's projects. The downside was that Nakosh had misgivings about nanotechnology, or at least about its newfound identity as a distinct science. The creation of the National Nanotechnology Initiative could only advance the misperception of nanotechnology as a real discipline.

Nakosh had completed a doctorate in chemistry from MIT, and later, a doctorate in engineering from the University of Chicago, both fields for which he possessed a deep passion. Aware of this dual interest, a professor from his undergraduate days at USC turned him on to Richard Feyman's famous lecture, *There's Plenty of Room at the Bottom* and K. Eric Drexler's seminal book, *Engines of Creation: The Coming Era of Nanotechnology*. Nakosh was fascinated at the concepts underlying nanotechnology, but beyond all the hype, recognized it was really nothing new. The essence of scientific understanding holds that scientific fact is nothing more than the best understanding of nature that current methods can reveal, and those understandings are subject to change as technology and knowledge change.

Nanotechnology was still relatively unknown among the

general population.

"And, for good reason," Nakosh would lecture to his *Introduction to Nanotechnology* students. It was a class of mostly freshman that covered enough physics and chemistry to satisfy the University's general science requirement. "Nanotechnology is a paradox. It is both large and small; both ancient and modern; both natural and engineered. Depending upon what you read, nanotechnology will either save our world or destroy the world; it will either enhance our humanity or cause us to cease being human altogether. Nanotechnology is the newest of sciences and one of the oldest of man's foray into science. So what, exactly, is nanotechnology?" He was answered with mostly blank stares from his class.

"Nano is a prefix meaning $10^{-9}$, or one-billionth. In order to grasp the physical insignificance of this scale, you should consider that that average human hair is about 60,000 nanometers in diameter. Yet the scientific significance of manipulating matter at that scale cannot be more important. As a result of the vastly increased surface to volume ratio, even gold, an element which science had believed to be inert, becomes highly reactive at the nanoscale. And while nanotechnology deals with the very small, it is hoped that one day it will be the harbinger of unlimited wealth and prosperity, with the ultimate goal of developing molecular assemblers capable of creating anything atom by atom. Think of it as the Replicator from Star Trek." Here, Nakosh would look around the classroom and watch the expressions from his students. Those whose faces went blank, or leaned over to ask a neighbor what the 'Replicator' was had not grown up on science fiction and the awe of the future. These students seldom possessed the imagination and passion to take any science classes beyond the required minimum.

"Contrary to what you may think, however, nanotechnology is not necessarily a modern science. The Lycurgus Cup, thought to be from 4th century A.D. Rome, is made from a very special type of glass, known as dichroic, which changes color depending upon whether the light is shining on, or through, the glass." If the science itself did not cause several of the students to zone out, the mention of ancient Rome certainly did. Yet Nakosh never failed to regain their attention when his PowerPoint presentation flashed from a picture of an ornate goblet of green glass with the image of King Lycurgus carved in relief to the very same goblet, the background glowing a deep red and King Lycurgus, extremities still green, but his torso glowing a purplish hue, as the image switched to the cup lit from the interior. "This color change is the result of the glass material containing tiny amounts of colloidal gold and silver—that is, nano-sized gold and silver particles—which give the cup these unusual optical properties. But this is not all. Evidence of nano-sized particles has been found in ice-core samplings dating back 10,000 years.

"While naturally occurring, it is only now, with the current advances in science and scientific equipment available, that man has been able to manipulate and manufacture nano-sized materials, rather than make use of those found in nature. Thus, we can differentiate between naturally occurring, or incidental nano-sized particles, such as volcanic ash, ocean spray, magnetotactic bacteria, and purposely-engineered nano-sized particles, or what we call nanotechnology.

"So then, what is nanotechnology? Perhaps everything, perhaps nothing. Nanotechnology is an interdisciplinary science. It is chemistry and physics and medicine and engineering. It is biology and climate and genetics and optics. Nanotechnology is the coming together of a myriad of scientific disciplines, the study of new and strange characteristics of old and previously known materials. Unlike the bulk world, in which the motion of bodies under the action of system forces is described using classical mechanics, in the world of nanotechnology, quantum mechanics rules the day. Nanomaterials will be developed to find and destroy cancer cells, to act as vectors in gene therapy treatments, to extend our lives and affect our health outcomes. Nanotechnology is any scientific field, or any combination thereof, that deals with the deliberate and controlled manufacturing of nano-sized materials. Nanotechnology is, potentially, all science. Or maybe not.

"Perhaps nanotechnology is nothing more than the remarketing of what already exists. Chemistry is the science of matter and the changes it undergoes. The science of chemistry, in one form or another, has been around for thousands of years. As far back as 430 B.C. Greece, Democritis proclaimed that everything was composed of atoms, the simplest unit of matter. In 1789, Antoine-Laurent Lavoisier published *Elements of Chemistry*, which is generally acknowledged to be the first modern chemistry textbook. In fact, scientists have been creating chemical reactions for centuries.

But because chemical reactions occur only at the surfaces of molecules, much of the 'science' of nanotechnology relates to the differences between chemical reactions occurring with bulk materials (small surface to volume ratio) and nanomaterials (large surface to volume ratio), since these large surface to volume ratios greatly affect the reactivity of materials. Ultimately, nanotechnology differs from existing scientific disciplines only insofar as the physical dimensions of the materials have created new possibilities, new rules, for what was previously believed to be known outcomes. And while the materials themselves offer new and exciting properties at the nanoscale, the science itself remains the same.

"So, what is nanotechnology?" Nakosh asked again. "It is chemistry and physics and engineering and biology and, most importantly, what we will be talking about this term."

Professor Chin Ho, Department Head, stood outside the door of the lecture hall. He was a strong proponent of nanotechnology and widely considered by his peers to be the top nanoscientist in the nation. On more than one occasion he had been scheduled to be a featured speaker on a national scientific news story, but each time he had been edited out, his appearance and demeanor unable to compensate for his remarkable achievements. Yet his lack of notoriety did not concern him. What did concern him was the possibility that his research would be slowed by those unwilling to trust his genius. It was through his genius that Ho was able to secure millions of federal research dollars for his Department and the University. Research money for nanotechnology—the most significant field of science in the world. Not, as Nakosh professed, a rehashing of existing fields of science.

"Eli," Ho said, stopping Nakosh as he exited the lecture hall. The two men made an odd couple, Nakosh's handsome face and six-foot frame towering over the childlike height of his superior. "How many times have I asked that you not include your disparaging remarks concerning nanotechnology in your lecture? Your statements threaten the field."

"I'm sorry, Professor Ho," Nakosh replied. "But I think it's important that these students recognize what we're doing is no different than what scientists have been doing for centuries. We're just able to do new things, explore new avenues, because we are now capable of manufacturing nanoparticles."

"If you continue to do this, Professor Nakosh, I will not

hesitate to remove you from the university. I will not tolerate insubordination," Ho cautioned. Ho would have removed Nakosh from his lab months ago, but he could not. Nakosh presented an intelligence that even Ho found quite impressive. On more than one occasion Nakosh had provided insight that solved an issue holding back progress by the Ho Lab. But equally as often, Nakosh had questioned the validity of some of the Dr. Ho Group's findings or questioned his fellow researcher's methods. For the time being, however, Ho felt more comfortable having Nakosh as a junior colleague disrespecting the field, than as a competitor.

*Besides,* Ho thought, *Nakosh just needs to be put into his place. Given time, he will discover that he can advance quite far in this field if he keeps his mouth shut and obeys my demands.*

"You certainly have the right to dismiss me, Professor," Nakosh responded. "But the purpose of University academics is to promote an atmosphere of questioning one's ideas and challenging one's assumptions. Any disagreement we have regarding the validity of nanotechnology as a distinct discipline is healthy and we should promote these discussions among our students."

Ho's face flushed and he clenched his teeth. Nakosh was much older than most first-year assistant professors in his department, having taken considerable time not only to earn two doctorate degrees, but also, unexplainably, taking a couple years off to travel before seeking work in a research lab. Ho had experienced a certain level of defiance during his initial interview of Nakosh, but he had believed that it was simply the need to adjust from the nomadic life to the scientific bench and that it would quickly fade. Ho was wrong.

"I will not allow this department to be run by the concerns of an associate professor regarding the purpose of University academics!" Ho stated firmly and walked away. Dr. Ho returned to his office where one of his post-doctoral research students was waiting.

"Dr. Ho," she said nervously, "can I speak with you one moment?"

It was TeYu Huang, a shy and usually quiet girl, like most of the members of Dr. Ho's lab group. She was holding several sheets of paper and looking down at her feet.

"Yes, TeYu. Come in." He let out a snort, clearly meant to emphasize the disturbance she was creating. She hesitated before following him through the threshold.

"I'm having some issues with the experimental output." With this, she placed a sheet of paper in front of Dr. Ho showing a graph of the output of graphene in relation to time. "You can see by these two points," she began, pointing out two coordinate locations well off the plotted curve, "that the theoretical output of graphene can never be achieved using our current process. It seems that as a result of the atomic force microscope's — "

He cut her off, pulling the graph from her hands. "No, no, no, TeYu. How many times have I told you? Look," he said, taking a pen and marking out the two offending plot points, "it is clear from the remaining data that these two points are anomalies, likely caused by your failure to follow proper protocol. Did you make sure that the cantilever tip was properly cleaned prior to this run?" Dr. Ho did not wait for an answer. "You're not showing the ambient temperature and humidity here." He turned from the sheet to look directly at TeYu. "Take these two points off and use the remaining data. You can modify this graph and use it for the article."

"But, those two plots points are — "

"Listen TeYu," Dr. Ho said, raising his voice, "I will not argue with you on this. I will present this paper to a group of investors at week's end and I need it completed. It is clear that you have made mistakes in the lab. I will not accept this matter being delayed because of your carelessness. Do you understand?" He handed her the graph back.

She nodded, again staring down at her feet.

"Then go re-run this graph without the faulty data and finish the assignment!" With that, he sat down and swiveled his chair so that he faced his computer. She left his office, closing his door behind her, and began to cry as she weighed the consequences of academic misconduct against her fear of displeasing Dr. Ho.

## CHAPTER FIVE

*News Flash: June 13, 2024. 11:16 a.m. The latest jobless claims report shows the number of applications in the U.S. unexpectedly dropped last week to a five-year low, according to the Labor Department. In a statement released Thursday, the Labor Department noted that weekly unemployment benefit applications dropped 6,300 to a seasonally adjusted 470,000, the lowest number since January 2019. The four-week average fell to 481,430, also a new five-year low.*

The Great Depression II was catastrophic to America. When automobile sales ground to a halt and the Big Three all filed for bankruptcy, Congress finally agreed that the people had had enough and proved that no entity was 'too big to fail' by letting Chrysler, GM and Ford cease business. With over two million jobs suddenly gone, unemployment spiked further. Official numbers claimed twelve percent of America's workforce was seeking employment. Unofficial accounts placed the true unemployment rate closer to twenty-two percent. With the loss of the auto industry, manufacturing in America had, for all intents and purposes, come an end. What little manufacturing work was being performed consisted of minimum paying jobs in the food and agricultural sectors. Gas prices forced many farmers to stop using equipment and return to manual labor. Thousands of workers toiled the fields in exchange for enough food to feed themselves and their families. Many more thousands went back to school to learn new skills, living off student loans and government assistance. Credit card debt soared among Americans.

The rich still enjoyed the finer things in life while the middle class not only shrunk, but also adapted to a reduced quality of living. Clay's job in the law firm allowed him to live in what was considered middle class luxury, but compared to his childhood, it would have been referred to as lower-middle class at best. He oftentimes found himself worried that he would not be able to meet his monthly mortgage payment or afford to pay his bills. If it were not for the occasional side job that Clay handled (a will for a friend or a contract review), he was certain he would have been forced to give up his home. These side jobs paid in cash he would not report to the government. At a tax rate of forty percent, even a few thousand dollars of unreported income a year resulted in significant increase in his personal cash flow, allowed him to keep his family above water, to afford the occasional meal out and small vacation. Clay dreaded the thought of what would happen if cash were truly removed from the system.

> *News Flash: June 13, 2024. 1:49 p.m. A six point seven earthquake has been reported in central Turkey. No reports on casualties are available at this time.*

"Enough!" Clay said. He was not in the mood to listen to the recent tragedy. *I'm going to have to ask Katie, again, how to turn off the damn Notification App on my iMeme when I get home,* he thought. Clay decided to power down his iMeme for a little while, to avoid the incessant news updates certain to follow the announcement of a major earthquake. He did this quite regularly since he had difficulty remembering how to turn off the iMeme's notifications. Just as often, he forgot to turn it back on. But the joy of being free from interruption was worth the risk of a missed call.

Or having to remember a name. Lillian had assured Clay that he would love FaceMe, the facial recognition app. He was never very good at names and the FaceMe App would identify people and provide their name and other information. It proved to be worth the cost of the iMeme alone. All the same, while he did find the app helpful, he always cringed a bit, knowing that somewhere, someone else's iMeme was announcing *Levi Clayton Furstman.* He hated his given name.

*Levi, Levi... gonna die.*
*Last man picked is always Furstman.*
*Levi Clayton, friends with Satan.*
*Levi — worthless as a pair of jeans.*

Levi Clayton Furstman was an only child. His parents had moved almost yearly. Each time he had suffered through the adjustment period, began to make friends and finally started to fit in, his parents would sweep him off to another town and another school. By the time he was in fourth grade, he had actually come to expect to be the new kid. He had long since learned not to completely unpack the few items of value he owned, instead, keeping them safely boxed in preparation for his next move. He never failed, however, to unpack his books, and he had many. In the several months it took to become acquainted with the other kids in his new school, he would occupy his time with his books, reading and re-reading novels and stories by Crane, Hemmingway, Cheever, Kafka, Orwell, and many others. He especially liked the works of Cormac McCarthy, novels filled with outsiders struggling to find their place in the world. These books were his friends. And his enemies. Inevitably, he would be picked upon, not only for being the new kid, but also for being a bookworm.

Toward the end of his sophomore year at Alcott High School in Chicago, his father passed away unexpectedly. While making a presentation to an important client in Ohio, he suddenly and inexplicitly stopped mid-sentence, set his laser pointer down and took a seat. He turned toward his audience. "Damn headache," he muttered to himself. Then a little more loudly, "Tell my wife and son I'm sorry," and then slumped over. The doctors told them he did not suffer. The aneurysm had killed him in a matter of seconds. His mother had a job at the time, and a network of friends, and so for the first time in his life, Levi Clayton Furstman did not spend the summer moving. He tried out for the track team and proved to be a decent sprinter. His track coach was aware that some of the kids had made fun of him for being named Levi and so he referred to the young boy as Clayton, or, more often than not, simply as Clay. The name stuck, and Clay's circle of friends slowly grew as he spent less time reading and more time socializing. By the time he graduated he had a sizable group of friends and good enough grades to receive a small scholarship to the University of Illinois, where he was never known by any name other than Clay.

Clay's afternoon continued with minimal interruptions from the telephone, and none from the iMeme (he had forgotten to turn it back on). His job offered him the tedium of repetition and the inability to put his education and skills to work. Clay had earned his degree in English from the University of Illinois and gone on to receive a law degree from John Marshall Law School. He worked for a number of years in a small firm representing real estate developers. Even during the Great Recession building projects continued to come in. With the onset of the Great Depression II, however, most building design and construction halted, even the coveted government projects. But the partners in Clay's law firm were able to keep their doors open. All those years of negotiating the permitting and inspection processes at City Hall resulted in the firm developing solid relationships with a multitude of city employees — employees with the power to move projects forward, or stop them dead in their tracks. Clay had been fortunate enough to be one of the low men on the totem pole in the years running up to the economic collapse and therefore was the one who oftentimes was given the menial task of actually going down to City Hall and dealing with the city workers. He had never minded the task — it was always an opportunity to get out of the office and interact with others — but it had been considered grunt work and had fallen on his lap as the newest employee.

When the economy collapsed, many law firms went under. Those that did not fired their younger employees, thinking that they could lower overhead costs by having senior members do the work themselves. What they did not account for was the loss of contacts with city employees and the resulting inability to move what little work was available efficiently through the system. Whether it was foresight, dumb luck or simply because the firm was never large, only having had five employees — including the two partners — prior to the economic collapse, Clay's firm managed to stay afloat and became one of the only firms capable of continuing to move projects through City Hall. Even so, there was not enough work to keep the firm employees occupied full-time. The partners fired their two junior partners and Clay was kept on, and promoted to the position of Senior Municipal Partner. It was a fictional job title made even more fictional by the label of 'promotion' — it did not even require an law degree — but did recognize that Clay possessed the ability to move paperwork though the entanglement of hoops and ladders set up by City Hall. Perhaps it was not the most ideal situation, but he had to admit it was better than the being unemployed.

At 4:15, Clay shut his computer down. He waited as his day's work was quickly processed — backed-up to some unseen server collecting the thoughts, ideas and labors of the firm—and digitized for future recollection. On his way to the train, he saw a man in a gorilla suit passing out flyers. The ape stepped out in front of Clay and pressed a gold sheet of paper into Clay's hand. It was an offer for a 20% discount off membership to Gold's Gym.

"Hot day to be in a gorilla suit, huh?" Clay asked.

The ape remained silent and Clay noticed the gym's windows perspiring from the cool air inside meeting the hot glass and imagined that the gorilla was faring no better. Clay moved towards the El station, eyes still on the gym and nearly collided with a group of runners, perspiring in the late-June heat, trailing the scent of sweat, or too much perfume.

*It's a horrible thing,* Clay thought. *Men no longer work. They attempt to substitute the basic need to create, to accomplish, with television, the Internet, consumption. But it's not the same.* Clay believed that man has a primordial need to do. Young, firm bodies running on treadmills, going nowhere. Older, muscled men working the dumbbells, lifting pound upon pound of steel, and placing them back upon the racks from which they started. A step class filled with middle-aged women, forever climbing their portable steps but always ending class firmly on the ground. At the end of the day, one was right back where one started, another lap around the track, another circuit in the gym. *But to what did it all amount? Nothing,* he thought. *There was a time when men did not have to exercise. Life itself was exercise—hunting, building, reproducing. Actions meant something, accomplished something. These days, men who work trade PDF documents and exchange digital files, but what does it all mean? What is accomplished by such feats? Those who do real work are the lucky ones.* (Clay did not count among this group those unfortunate individuals who were indentured servants, slaves to want and need, who worked the farms in exchange for food and shelter—such men were not free, were not even men, being forced to assume the role of less than human in order to survive.) Those who do real work dig ditches and build houses. Their life's work is tactile. They can look out upon the world and point to their accomplishments, touch them, see the changes they have made to the physical world. Real changes. Most working men, however, simply punch keyboards, point to their computer screens and smile at their work, but inside they suffer. The work of changing binary zeros and ones is not work at all. To have transferred ownership in real property without ever having seen it, touched it, rolled one's fingers through the soft earth and put up fences or barns or planted a tree is empty, hollow, meaningless. And with each new comfort, with each new modern convenience, man slowly dies. He removes himself from his humanity.

Clay walked past the skeleton of a high-rise building. Scaffolding above the sidewalk, temporary lights blazing throughout, a high chain link fence warning that hardhats and contracts are required. Forty floors. Upscale shopping. Condominium-Hotel units starting in the low $400,000s. It had been like that for a dozen years. More. The developer went bankrupt and all work had ceased. The scaffolding was rusting in its concrete base. He wondered who paid the electric bill. He thought of the men who once worked there, pouring concrete, bending pipe, welding steel. Now they were seeking new employment or sitting in classrooms learning new skills. He looked to his left and spotted the Chicago Temple building, built a century earlier. Hand-carved stone. A lost art. A tear came to his eye. He quickly gazed up toward the sun—giving himself an excuse in case anyone were looking.

## CHAPTER SIX

*It is June 21, 2024. 9:23 a.m.*

*June Twenty-First?* Clay thought. *It's practically July... what the hell happened to June!?* He dug up the small desktop calendar from the back corner of his desk upon which it was hiding. The top few pages were slightly crumpled and held evidence of being the recipients of an untold number of abuses by other items lying upon the desk. Clay tore off the pages of the individual dates, one-by-one, haltingly, as if by this action he could slow the earth's progression around the sun, until he saw June twenty-first. He sighed as he tossed the calendar atop a pile of papers and leaned back in his chair. He looked out his office window onto Dearborn Street below. He felt a ripple of concern pass over him, the sensation of the approaching gloom. It was June twenty-first.

In his home, in the whole of Chicago, in fact, it seemed to Clay that he, and he alone, felt, not that joy and celebration of the solstice that mankind had celebrated for centuries, but rather a tinge of sadness. He was quite certain his children, Katie, Matthew and Elizabeth, still didn't pay much attention to the effects of the earth's tilt as it made its annual trek around the sun and he wasn't really sure his wife was any more aware than the children. Yet the day always brought a certain melancholy. His family would gather around the dinner table, discussing the events of the day. Clay would smile and laugh with the others, but all the same, each June twenty-first he would remain sitting at the dinner table, after his wife and children had left, lost in silent regret. The days would be getting shorter now. His family did not seem to care; the warm weather would last several more months and summer break was just getting underway. But he was aware. And even though the loss of daylight would be imperceptible to even the knowing eye for weeks, the trek toward the winter solstice had begun and he could not help but feel a growing emptiness, a loss; but of exactly what he could not say. It may have been a feeling of the impending loss of summer — the waning of long days, warm weather and that carefree optimism that summer holds. It was silly, of course. His life didn't change much, summer or winter. There was no summer break beckoning him as it once did when he was younger and sat in a classroom, feeling the palpable energy slowly building within the walls of the school from mid-March until the institution, practically bursting at the seams, at last released its wards to the waiting arms of June. And there was no abrupt return to routine when September came back around. That was reserved for others. For the children mostly; but also for some lucky folks who, whether by career or economic means, followed the annual orbit of youthful life from work to leisure to work. Or perhaps it was merely the perception of loss; the loss of youth, of hope and of excitement of the unknown. He would never again experience that feeling of a first love, a first kiss. That warm glow of nervousness, excitement and anticipation that can only be experienced by someone who was still in sole possession of his heart and able to give it to another without guilt, regret, or shame. Yes, he was too old to regain those feelings of innocence, yet, he did not feel old by any means, and certainly not even his age.

Clay was only in his early fifties, still relatively young. He was also in good shape, or at least he had the physical appearance of being in good shape. His true medical health was unknown as he was not in the habit of visiting healthcare professionals; not due to any distaste, mistrust or fear of physicians, but simply because he felt no need to do so, at least not to this point in his life. He had only seen a doctor twice over the past decade. He lived his life unaware of any personal ailments and believed in the old adage: 'If it isn't broken, don't fix it.' He was trim, with a full head of dark hair. He felt good and took that as proof positive enough that his health was good. That, along with comments from friends and acquaintances assuring him that he looked great and hadn't changed a bit.

Clay was, however, simply an optimist, not a fool. He was cognizant of the fact that the absence of bodily aches or pains that can make even the young seem old was no guarantee of good health. The cold truth was he did little to actually stay in shape, other than walking to and from the train and an occasional bike ride.

Given that the two most important factors of good health were exercise and a proper diet, neither of which he practiced, he resigned himself to the simple fact that his body was a temple, and he would play the part of atheist. He gladly ignored the diet and exercise regimen his wife, and many others his age, forced upon themselves in order to hold on to at least some aspects of their vanishing youth. And for him, it worked. Yet the summer solstice always had a way of reminding him that even he was marching forward toward some unknown middle-age calamity, certain to rob him of his vigor.

Clay glanced at the clock on his desk. A relic. He wondered if it even kept accurate time. It did not matter. Today would be a shortened workday. With the economy in the gutter, still attempting to claw its way back from the housing market crash several decades ago and the double dip recession in the late twenty-teens—the beginning of the Great Depression II—businesses often closed early on Fridays. Coupled with that misfortunate statistic was the fact he never got much accomplished on the longest day of the year. The gods had to be appeased and he was not one to deny those powers their proper due.

He wondered what time it was.

*It is June 21, 2024. 12:06 p.m.,* his iMeme whispered in his ear.

*Listen to the time!* he thought to himself. *It's only 12:06? It really is the longest day of the year!*

Usually, even though he may not have much work to do, he would still feel guilty about leaving the office early. But never on Fridays, and certainly not on the longest day of the year. But it was still only noon, too early to leave, even for a Friday, even for the longest day of the year. He decided to walk over to City Hall to check the status of some files, although he knew his contacts would already be gone for the weekend. As he was leaving he remembered the few envelopes he brought to work that morning. He needed to mail them before he left for home and figured as long as he was heading out, he might as well tackle that task as well. It would give him another errand to do, an opportunity to kill a few more minutes of the day. He flipped through them, double-checking to see that they had all been properly sealed and addressed. Only last month he had received notice of a late payment on his mortgage. He had contacted the lender and accused them of poor bookkeeping or oversight, but did assent to making a second payment over the phone. It was not until two weeks later when he received his original payment back via return mail that he discovered the problem. Apparently, he had placed his check in front of the bill, covering up the mailing address in the envelope window, thus making delivery impossible. An error, he knew, which could have easily been avoided by electronic payment. Contrary to his daughter Katie's beliefs, he wasn't a total dinosaur. He did pay some of his bills online, but—and he could not explain why—never his mortgage.

"I'm just doing my part to keep the U.S. Post Office a viable entity," he explained to Katie.

"The Post Office hasn't been a viable entity for at least a decade," she countered.

"Yet it still manages to operate," he replied, smiling.

As Clay stepped out of his office and onto the sidewalk, he noticed the building had placed a construction horse over the ever-expanding crack. He guessed someone had recently fallen and injured himself. As he neared the corner, a dark-haired woman approached him from across the intersection, raised her hand and smiled in his direction. He was just about to look over his shoulder to determine to whom she was waiving when his iMeme chimed in.

*Karen Georges... Business Contact... O'Donnell project...*

*Oh yes. Karen Georges,* he thought to himself as he focused his attention back to her.

"Karen, how are you?" Clay smiled back as she finished crossing the street and was standing in front of him.

*Married to Bill... two children...* his iMeme continued on.

"Hi, Clayton. I was just going to call you this afternoon to follow up on our project."

*James and Hope...* The iMeme continued to drone on its litany of facts. Clay reached for the Spot and tapped his iMeme twice, and the FaceMe app ceased its chatter.

"Yes, yes." The matter was lying atop his to-do pile, having been ignored for the past two days. Clay was not ignoring the work entirely, since he was awaiting final approval from the City of Chicago, but he had meant to follow up since he had not heard from his city contact since late Monday afternoon. "I've had the opportunity to review it again and it's nearly completed. I'm hoping to have it back to you shortly after the holiday. I was pushing to get it completed earlier, but with the Fourth of July Holiday rapidly approaching, and the City closing its fiscal year at the end of the month, I've had some trouble coordinating with Mr. McDermott from the City Licensing Department. I hope that's not a problem."

"Not a problem whatsoever. I'm actually going to be heading out of town this weekend with Bill and the kids, and won't be back until after the Fourth anyway. So sometime thereafter is just fine," Karen responded cheerfully. "We finally decided to take that trip to…" she looked away for a moment. She quickly glanced back, and whispered, "I'm sorry, I've got to take this call." Her hand found its way to her Spot and she tapped her iMeme as she turned away.

"Hi, Phil. No, no interruption at all." She turned her head back toward Clay and smiled as she waived goodbye, engrossed in whatever it was that Phil was telling her from the other end of the line.

He still didn't fully understand how the iMeme managed to recognize individual faces, to determine which of the many faces visible he was focusing on and then transmit the relevant information directly into his brain. He originally had believed that it had something to do with one's social networking apps since FaceMe used to only recognize people he already knew. But sometime over the past year, he discovered his iMeme providing information on nearly everyone with whom he came into eye contact, even those he had never met before. Or, at least some he did not recall having met before. It was during those times that he felt old, felt his brain had lost a step or two. Perhaps the program allowed access to the address books of the friends of one's social networking friends. If that were true, and if we all really were separated from each other by only six degrees, it would seem possible that the FaceMe App would recognize everyone. Or, at least, nearly everyone. For whatever reason, FaceMe failed to recognize certain individuals. Some people, it seemed, lived outside the blanket of social networking, beyond its suffocating enclosure.

One such individual was the older gentleman who Clay would often see downtown. His name was not whispered into Clay's anxiously awaiting ear. Clay called him the Walking Man. Whenever Clay would see him, the Walking Man was inevitably, and seemingly always, walking around the city. He saw the Walking Man regularly during rush hour, but also at odd hours when running an errand, or heading to a business meeting. The Walking Man was a handsome man. Tall, rugged looking, clear eyes. He always wore a sports coat, and seemed relatively well groomed, but he possessed certain oddities. Most strange, he seemed never to be wearing socks. Although his hair was neatly kept and never too long, the style never changed, and the style was of an age long past. His face was always shaven, but never crisp and clean, always the five o'clock shadow clouding his jaw. And there was a certain aimlessness about him, a hint of homelessness. Clay often stared at the Walking Man, but the iMeme never offered a name. He wondered if it were possible that this man knew no one. *Not likely. Even the homeless are known by some name by those who provided him with a little food now and then, and shelter from the weather.*

Clay had surmised that perhaps the iMemes communicated among each other and only recognized the faces and names of others who had an iMeme. He was certain his iMeme identified people who did not have their iMeme on them, or when their iMeme was turned off. But he knew these people did, at least, own an iMeme. Clay had never seen an iMeme on the Walking Man. In fact, he had noticed early on that the Walking Man's clothes were void of the pervasive Spot altogether. Of course, if this man were homeless, then Clay would not expect him to own an iMeme. Perhaps this was the reason, hope as he may, Clay never heard a name associated with the Walking Man. But Clay did not think that this was quite right, either. Clay was unable to place his finger on the definite cause of this oversight in recognition, and it seemed that the Walking Man's true name would remain forever silent. Clay often wondered how the Walking Man had been able to remain below the radar. He imagined him as a sort of specter who had no connection, no history, no obligations. He was unbound and free. Clay wondered what it would be like, and found himself slightly envious of the Walking Man.

## CHAPTER SEVEN

*Update: July 19, 2024. 3:16 p.m. After more than 50 years on the Endangered Species List, environmentalists are hoping scientific work performed by Rejuvenate, a not-for-profit that recently received significant funding from Defense Advanced Research Projects Agency, or DARPA, will help the California condor's numbers begin to soar. While the specific work being performed is still classified, Joan Prendergast, spokesperson for the group, has indicated the recent collaborative effort with DARPA shows promising signs of success. The technology would potentially be transferrable to other endangered species and allow the reintroduction of a wide variety of native species into the wild.*

"Hello, I'm home!" The dog, a German shepherd-golden retriever mix, came running up to greet him. "How are ya', Orion?" he asked as he rubbed the dog's chest. The dog looked up to him and seemed to grin. Tail wagging.

"Hi, Clay. We're down here in the basement." Lillian called.

"Hi, Dad," Katie echoed.

He walked down the stairs into the basement where his wife, Lillian, was folding laundry. Katie was downloading new music onto her iMeme. "Where are Matthew and Elizabeth?"

"Oh, Dad! Did you turn your iMeme off again? I twerped you that Matthew was over at Jason's house and Lizzy had softball practice tonight."

*Twerp. What the hell does that mean, twerp?* Clay asked himself. *It used to mean some punk little kid that always annoyed you.* Clay supposed it still did. Twerp—when tweeting moved from short messages sent to followers to short messages sent to specific people, delivered straight to their iMemes. Short annoying messages. Twerps.

"Yes, I shut it down again. You know, you're going to have to show me again how to turn off the Notification App. I can't handle her damn little voice whispering into my ear constantly." He pulled his iMeme off of the Spot and handed it over to Katie. She powered it up so she could reset his Notification App and the holographic screen went from black to blue—with tiny letters written, row after row, across it over and over: REPREPREPREPREPREPREPREPREPREP.

"You know, Dad, that every time you power off the iMeme and turn it back on, it restarts the Notification App, don't you? If you just put it in sleep mode, you won't have to reset the App." Katie rolled her eyes and added softly, "I don't know why you turn it off anyway. Geez!"

Katie had just completed her junior year of high school. Intelligent and athletic, she still sometimes surprised Clay at how innocent she was. Certainly she had had her fair share of mischief, but in general she had never stepped too far over the line. Growing up, Katie had always been quiet and reserved. Clay and Lillian were both surprised during her freshman year parent-teacher conferences to learn that she was an active participant in her classes and not afraid to voice her opinions in front of her classmates. Even more surprising was her first week of high school when she asked Clay to drive her to the first home football game of the season. Clay had agreed and asked which of her friends they would need to pick up on the way. He was surprised, and a little concerned, when she declared that she was going to the game alone. Katie had a close-knit group of friends, but her circle was never very large.

"So, you've got plans to meet your friends at the game, then?"

"No"

"Then who's going to be there?"

"I don't know, Dad. But I'll know some people there."

Clay could not believe it. "Have you spoken with your friends? Who else is going?"

"Don't worry, Dad. I'll know people there."

His mind filled with images of Katie walking below the stadium stands, wondering alone, seeking out a friendly face in a world gone wrong, like Ambrose in John Barth's *Lost in the Funhouse*.

"Then who are you going to go to the game with?" He could not believe his shy little girl was simply going to mill about the football stadium in hopes of meeting up with her fellow freshman friends, that she was not only going to bank on her friends being there, but also that they would be able to meet up among the mass of students, parents and onlookers without some prearranged plan.

"I don't know, Dad, but I'll be fine." With that, he dropped her off near the stadium and returned home to prepare for any possible tears. They never materialized. To his delight, she had hooked up with several different groups of friends, spending her time between the groups, back and forth, and enjoying herself so much she was unable to even answer who had won the football game. Yet notwithstanding her ever-growing freedom and circle of friends, she continued to possess a seemingly boundless capacity for compassion and spent considerable time volunteering to help any number of local charities.

Katie shut down the Notification App and handed the iMeme back to her father. "Geez, you're getting old, Pops. Why is it so difficult for you to listen to Notifications and do something else at the same time? You know, I could swear I saw you once chewing gum and walking." She was laughing by now. "But seriously, I told you, Dad. If it's bothering you, just open the App and set it to sleep. That way all your other apps work. And, my Twerps will still get through."

"So that means you didn't get my message either, huh?" Lillian said as she walked over to give him a kiss hello.

"What's that?" He kissed her back.

"Matthew is staying at Jason's. Elizabeth is going home with Anne."

Matthew was going to be entering his sophomore year of high school, and like most boys his age, lived a life of sports, eating, video games, and girls. As a child, he had been incredibly affectionate and was not afraid to hold Clay's hand even as a twelve-year-old. But sometime around his fourteenth birthday, he seemed to have disappeared from family life. Clay would occasionally see him, head in the refrigerator digging around for something to try to satiate his voracious appetite, or sitting in front of the television playing the latest video game offering. Otherwise, their only interaction was at the dinner table or after a lacrosse game, when Clay would always congratulate his son, win or lose. Any conversations they had were brief, shortened by the continuous progression of food from plate to mouth, or by the pressing need to return to his teammates for a post-game get-together. He knew less about his son than he would have liked. Matthew's grades were good, so Clay could only presume that he was studying and attending school, although he never seemed to see his son with any books. He borrowed money from Clay occasionally for a date, though Clay could not recall meeting his latest girlfriend, yet he seemed to remember Matthew talking about a girl named Jane. It was not an ideal father-son relationship, but they did not fight and Clay was aware that his son still loved him; the occasional "I love you, dad" spoken as he went to bed, perhaps a smile of pride thrown in Clay's direction after Matthew scored a goal. Clay wondered whether he was he less involved in Matthew's life because he was a son, and not a daughter. Perhaps he was guilty of possessing an underlying chauvinism that boys can take care of themselves better than girls, that there was a lesser need for concern; or perhaps it was evidence of the gender gap resulting from the long-discarded roles of males in the social group, the innate need for a father to remain the alpha male in the household and to fend off the increasing threat from a son who continues to grow stronger each day as the father grows weaker. Clay loved his son, yet remained slightly out of touch with his life.

And then there was Lizzie, who was going to be entering her freshman year in high school. Quiet and intelligent, she took full advantage of the experiences of her older siblings, as well as the more relaxed attitude of her parents, who had by the third child, understood a little better which fights to pick and which to forego. As a result, Lizzie was independent, self-assured and a little bit devious. She managed to cause enough trouble to continually find herself on the verge of dire consequences, yet never quite enough to actually cause real harm. More often than not, Clay would find himself trying to restrain from praising Lizzie for her ability to devise and pull off such intricate plans, rather than actually being angry with her for her transgressions. Such as the time she managed to convince a busload of Korean tourists that she was their docent and walked the entire group around the Loop on her own architectural tour. The group was most gracious for her services and boarded their bus with many thanks and head bowing. Clay supposed there was no real harm done when Lizzie advised them that the Farris wheel at Navy Pier was the original debuted by George Washington Gale Farris, Jr. at the 1893 World's Columbian

Exposition in Chicago. Whether she caused harm when she told the group that Al Capone had been elected mayor in the mid-1930s was debatable. However, when the Chicago Architecture Foundation discovered what she had done, they threatened to contact the police, but after a healthy scolding and the elicitation of a promise by Lizzie to draft a letter of apology to the South Korean Consulate (which was delivered the following day), they let the matter drop. She somehow managed to avoid revealing that she had been tipped handsomely by the Korean group, and was more than happy to suffer the anger of the aging docent and the punishment of a quick apology note in exchange.

Lillian put the last of the folded laundry in the basket. "Katie will be babysitting at the Walters' house tonight. She's planning on staying there overnight because the Walters' are heading to Madison tonight to visit Jim's father. He's in the hospital and they're not sure he's going to make it."

"Oh, Christ. He's taken a turn for the worse, huh?"

"Maybe a turn for the better — he's been battling that cancer for a long time." Clay looked at her, a shocked expression on his face. She paused for a moment. "That wasn't very nice, I guess. But he's been suffering quite some time."

"Yes, I guess you're right. We'll have to send the Walters a note."

Katie got up, handed the iMeme back to her father and hopped up the stairs. "I'm going. I'm taking your car, Dad. Mom said it was alright. Love you. See ya' tomorrow!"

"So, that means we're alone tonight." He smiled and loosened his tie.

"Not so fast, cowboy," Lillian said. "If you hadn't turned off your iMeme, you'd know I made plans to go out with the Diazs tonight. We've got reservations at Morton's at 8:00. They'll be here around 7:00 so we can have a drink before we head out. But if you're a good boy... maybe tonight you'll get lucky." She smiled as she headed toward the stairs. "I'm going to change. They'll be here soon."

Clay had first met Miguel Diaz in the mid-1990s while representing him in the purchase of a home. Miguel had played baseball for the St. Louis Cardinals for several seasons, but moved to Chicago after suffering an injury that left him blind in one eye, effectively ending his career. What started off as a business relationship quickly grew into a strong friendship as Clay and Lillian found themselves going out often with Miguel and his wife Jennifer. They travelled together at least once and year and Clay and Lillian were not surprised to be some of the first to whom Miguel and Jennifer announced the expectancy of their first child. Six months later, their daughter Eva was born. Although it would be several years before Clay and Lillian had their first child, the addition of Eva to the Diaz family did not affect the frequency of their get-togethers or their travels together.

When Miguel and Jennifer arrived, Clay noticed they both seemed to be in an exceptionally good mood.

"Well, well, aren't we a happy bunch today?" Clay said, smiling at both of them.

"We've got some great news," Jennifer said. "Where's Lill?"

"She's finishing getting ready. Want to fill me in in the meantime?" Clay asked.

"Not a chance, friend," Miguel responded.

"Fine then, I'll wait, Clay said, still smiling. "Can I get you something in the meantime? I've got a really interesting IPA from Three Floyds, Miguel—it's new. I haven't tried it yet, but it's supposed to be really tasty. Also some seasonal from Goose Island, and, for the feint of heart, some Lite."

"I'll try the IPA."

"How about you, Jennifer? Beer, wine, something a little more daring?"

"If Lill is having some wine, I'll join her. Otherwise…"

"I'll open some red. Lill brought home a bottle of wine yesterday she said was quite good. A pinot, I think. Or if you prefer, I've got some great malbec."

"I'm not picky. Whatever you think."

Clay pulled a bottle of the pinot from the wine cooler—the malbec was better with food anyway and as they were just going to have a few drinks before dinner, he thought the pinot a better choice. He poured two glasses, one for Jennifer and one for Lillian. He handed Miguel a beer as Lillian came into the room. "Hey, sweets. You look great. I poured you a wine."

"Hi, Jen and Miguel. Sorry, I had to finish getting ready. Clay got you drinks already?" Miguel nodded as he raised his beer. He set it down and gave Lillian a kiss hello. Then Lillian hugged

Jennifer hello as well. Clay handed his wife her glass and grabbed his own — vodka on the rocks with a bleu cheese olive.

"It seems we're about to get some good news," Clay said.

"What are you talking about, Clay? What good news?" Lillian asked, looking around at the others.

"You know that Eva's been looking for a job since she graduated from UCLA with her Ph.D degree in biomedical engineering?" Jennifer explained. Clay and Lillian both nodded. "Well, she was just offered a job working for an environmental activist group seeking to save terrestrial wildlife. The organization is called Rejuvenate."

"That's fantastic," Lillan said.

"Yes. And they just started an ad campaign to raise awareness of the threat of extinction of the California Condor and it features a shot of Eva working in the field," Miguel added, smiling even more. He raised his glass for a toast, "Cheers! To good drink and better friends."

"And to Eva," Clay added. The four of them tapped glasses and took a drink.

Dinner was fantastic: steaks, seafood, drinks. Clay ate more than he should have and they all drank too much. The others were interrupted only a few times by updates from their iMemes, peppering the conversation with stories of the aftershocks from the 7.2 earthquake near Ankara and which Hollywood star was seen at which local eatery.

## CHAPTER EIGHT

*News Flash: July 20, 2024. 12:27 a.m. Al-Qassam Brigades has claimed responsibility for the suicide bombing in Israel that killed fourteen and wounded dozens of others, raising serious questions about the Palestinian promises of security.*

Only the nightstand lamp was on and the room was softly lit. Clay fumbled out of his pants and hung them on the footboard of the bed. He stood there for a moment, naked, thinking he was forgetting something. Lillian walked in, shirt off, skirt partially unzipped.

"Hey, sexy," he said. She turned and removed her earrings, placing them on the dresser before unzipping her skirt all the way and slipping out of it. She was still stunning, he thought. A little bit of a pooch, backside not as firm as ten years ago, but still damn good looking. He smiled at her and crawled under the covers. She joined him in bed and wrapped her arms around him. They kissed. He pulled her away. "I'm sorry," he said, as he got up and pulled his shirt from the basket and removed his iMeme from the Spot and shut it down, the screen fading to light blue and displaying REPREPREPREPREPREPREP across and down the entire holographic screen briefly before turning black. *Prep, prep, prep. Prep for what?* he thought briefly.

"How do we know this damn thing isn't filming us and sending the images into the Cloud?" he asked Lillian. He did not trust the iMeme. It seemed to be too intuitive, too intrusive. Never truly off when it was powered up, just in alternating states of sleep and wake.

"Honey, if folks can't find anything better on the Cloud then the two of us, then let them enjoy the show," she smiled. He knew she wasn't serious. She was not an exhibitionist in any sense of the word, but she had grown weary of his mistrust of the iMeme and used humor to try to calm his fears.

"Okay, then. Perhaps I'll get out the camera and we can make some private films for ourselves?" He wasn't any more afraid to be filmed in the act than he was serious about actually filming it. While it would be pathetic if anyone had any interest in watching the two of them making love, it wouldn't really bother him. What he was bothered by was the loss of separation, the seeming inability to break free from being connected.

"Sure," she said. "As long as the pictures come out okay in the dark." She reached over and shut the light off. The room went dark. "Come back in bed, darling," she said seductively. "I've got something waiting for you."

He got out of bed at 7:45. The alarm had gone off, as it always did, at 6:30 and Lillian had snoozed until 7 a.m. before she left to go workout. He seldom could fall back asleep after she left. This morning, his head was throbbing lightly. *Not enough water last night,* he thought. He pulled on a pair of pants and went down to the kitchen for a glass of water. It was cold and refreshing. He drank another glass.

He went to the front door and got the morning paper. Every few months the Cloud would report the demise of the newspaper—most people receiving their news from other sources and having no time, or more likely no desire, to sit down and read a whole paper. Most of the news the paper contained was local. World and national news had long ago been squeezed onto one page. The op/ed columns were infrequent, and if included, were usually less than one-half a page. Local news consisted mostly of the police blotter and which famous people dined at which local eatery. This 'news' occupied about one quarter of the paper. Sports another quarter and entertainment news the remaining half. Entertainment news was not even news, really. Blabbering about nothing. Still, he enjoyed reading the world and national news—even though most of it was old, having previously read it online or heard it from his iMeme—and perusing the local section for actual news articles, avoiding anything related to the entertainment industry. And the crosswords puzzle. He loved the crossword puzzle.

"Morning, Dad," Mathew said as he walked into the kitchen.

"You're up awful early for a Saturday," Clay said.

Matthew smiled at his dad. "The new *Call of Duty* comes out today. Stores open at nine. I'm going to meet Freddy and we're going to try to get a copy."

"You'll get up for a video game, but you won't get up early to do a little extra studying for school?" Clay asked.

"Yeah, right." Matthew grabbed a cinnamon roll and a banana and headed out the back door. "Wish me luck," he said, taking a huge bite from the cinnamon roll.

"Good luck, son," he called out as the door shut. *Kids and their video games.* Clay just shook his head.

\* \* \*

Clay's first experience with virtual reality was playing *Grand Theft Auto XVI: Washington, D.C.* with his son. With the V-Screen console virtual reality controller, he had difficulty believing that he was only playing a game. Clay found himself running down an unknown street. The oppressive heat from the midday sun beat down upon his head, his back; he felt the heat from the asphalt rising beyond his feet, engulfing his legs, his pelvis, as his shoes continued to pound the blacktop below. The sound of gunshots rang out as he leapt into a waiting car, pulling his arm in tight to his side, feeling the sting of a bullet that just grazed him and which had etched a path across his arm. He slammed the car door shut, moved the gearshift to first and hit the gas. There was music blaring in the car. A classic from a generation before his time that had survived, The Who's *Won't Get Fooled Again*. The adrenaline was pulsing through his blood, and he could discern the sound of more gunshots through the organ crescendo, past the pounding of his own pulse echoing in his ears. His pursuers had fired a couple rounds at his rapidly retreating vehicle and in his rear-view mirror he just caught sight of them getting into their car. Clay thought he saw his son, Matthew, back there. Sweat dripped off his brow. A giggle from the passenger seat. He looked over, surprised that he was not alone. He was sitting next to a dazzlingly beautiful woman, shoulder-length black hair, wide mouth, and emerald green eyes. She was wearing a tank top, midriff, tight, and Clay noticed immediately that she was not wearing a bra. She giggled again and smiled at him. He could just discern the musky scent of her arousal as she lifted her right leg and placed it on the dashboard, causing her too-short skirt to ride up even further. He took a deep breath. The air was thick. He moved his left hand to find the window control, not taking his eyes off her. He could feel the leather trim on the door, the cool steel of the window control, the vibration of the car as they sped along, his ears still ringing to the music of The Who. In stark contrast, he felt and heard nothing as his yellow Lotus Exige S slammed into a brick wall at almost 110 mph.

"Sorry, Matthew." Clay said, removing the virtual reality controller, somewhat surprised to be alive, uninjured. *Had that really been just a game?* Clay wondered. He was still sweating and his pulse had not yet returned to normal. He rubbed his arm, sliding up his sleeve to see if his arm bore any evidence of the bullet that had stung so profoundly only moments earlier. Nothing. "I didn't mean to destroy your car. I told you I never could quite get the hang of this."

"That's okay, Dad. I was only being nice, anyway. I could have shot you easily—you run pretty damn slow. Besides, as you were running I saw Trixie hop into the front seat ahead of you. She had that *look* in her eye and she's been known to distract a few drivers in her day," Matthew laughed. Clay laughed along with his son, wondering if the game could determine the physical characteristics of the user (age, physical ability, female trait preferences) and adjust the graphics and the virtual character's attributes accordingly. And whether Trixie was the same Trixie that would have appeared in the car had Matthew gotten in rather than he. "That was Trixie, huh?"

"Yeah, Dad, that was Trixie. She's something else, but you got to watch out for her. Beautiful, but trouble."

No wonder his 16-year-old son played games incessantly.

It occurred to Clay that his second experience with virtual reality was not much different. Later that same year, his wife bought him Virtual Fantasy for his birthday. It was billed as a couples' game, a sort of sex toy, really. Both people would don a virtual reality mask and then their partner could choose from among dozens of the most beautiful people in the world to transform their loved one into. Mostly, she had purchased it as a joke. He loved his wife and always had. But they decided to try it one night anyway. Clay always had a 'thing' for the famous Columbian-born actress

Sofia Vergara, so that's who Lillian became when he made love to his wife that night. When he touched Lillian, he felt Sofia Vergara's curves where Lillian's would normally be, felt Sofia's hair on his face and neck, the body of his lover that night feeling different, oddly unfamiliar on his. When they had finished and removed their virtual adaptors, they held each other close. She quickly fell asleep. He lay awake for hours. He found it a little disconcerting, and a little distancing. He wasn't even sure if he had actually made love to his wife or whether they simply had lain there, the two of them each in their own virtual fantasy, making love to nothing. He supposed it did not matter. Even if they had physically embraced, it was not as if they really made love to each other. He felt as if they had participated in a simultaneous masturbation game in which they privately shared a personal moment, each in the presence of the other, but blindfolded, lost in their own fantasy. He did not ask who she had chosen him to become and he never offered his choice to her. Nor, after that night, did he ever suggest playing it again.

# CHAPTER NINE

*News Flash: July 22, 2024. 10:07 a.m. Israeli-Palestinian peace talks have broken off as anticipated. Hamas' refusal to be held accountable for off-shoot terrorists groups involved in the recent suicide bombing that killed fourteen people, including four children, was sufficient evidence, the Israeli Prime Minister protested, to demand more secure borders in any new Palestinian state. Hamas leadership stated that the suicide bomber was an Israeli and accused the Zionist government of attempting to gain last minute advantages in the negotiations. While the President has urged calm, Gen. David H. Fallsworth, the recently appointed Chairman of the Joint Chiefs of Staff, has stated that the Hamas terrorist organization would be well-advised to reign in its troops and come to the table prepared to negotiate in good faith. He indicated that the patience of both Israel and the Quartet was wearing thin and he hinted that failure to comply could bring about a serious change in the United States' approach to the peace process.*

As Clay left his office and made his way out into the street, he caught sight of the Walking Man coming toward him on the sidewalk. As always, Clay slowed his pace and tried not to stare at the Walking Man while he thought to himself, *Who is that?* He glanced quickly at the Walking Man's face. *Who is that?* he thought to his iMeme. The Walking Man seemed not to notice Clay, eyes forward, focused on whatever purpose he was pursuing. Clay's iMeme whispered nothing into his waiting ears. As the Walking Man passed, Clay turned and looked down at the Walking man's feet. No socks. Clay looked up, disappointed, and, perhaps, a little jealous of the Walking Man's anonymity. Clay continued walking toward his train. Mentally, he slapped himself. He was blessed with a beautiful family and great friends and he told himself that he should be ashamed at the thought of feeling somehow inferior to a homeless man, a man who likely had nothing. When he had so much.

Clay continued his journey to the El station. He was looking forward to the upcoming weeks. Katie was now a senior in high school and she was beginning to look at colleges. Clay was excited about the prospect of driving around and visiting the various campuses. He continued to hope she would end up at the University of Wisconsin, but he had no qualms with taking her to see two of her other choices: University of Minnesota and Northeastern. Like Wisconsin, these latter two schools were Division I Women's Hockey schools, but Wisconsin was the closest, and while Clay had no desire to interfere with Katie's decision, he did hold out hope that the nearness would translate into more frequent visits home. Minnesota was an easy trip as well, but Northeastern meant having to head to the East Coast. The saving grace would be that Clay always loved Boston and it would give him an excuse to head out there more often than he might otherwise have done. The only school he was not excited about was UC-Davis. Not only was it a Division III school, but also was woefully far and Clay never liked California, though he did have to admit that he liked Northern California much better than Southern California. He had enjoyed quick trips to San Francisco in the past, but the thought of Katie being out there for nine months a year was too much. A weekend was fine, but not anything longer.

He recalled the first time he had ever spent more than a weekend out in California. It was shortly after he graduated from college and he spent ten days visiting a college buddy who was living in Hermosa Beach. While the February weather in California certainly beat that of Chicago, he found the whole experience disorientating. People seemingly out of touch with the going-ons of the world, unaware of even the existence of the area of country that lies between the Rocky Mountains and the Atlantic coast, known as the Midwest. The whole experience in Southern California was so surreal that while he and his friend were driving to the Evergreen Aviation and Space Museum to see the *Spruce Goose*, they happened to pass a Kentucky Fried Chicken. Clay actually turned to his friend, and started. "Hey, I didn't know you had..." and then he caught himself mid-sentence. He had been poised to declare that he was not aware that there were Kentucky Fried Chicken restaurants in California. But of course California had them. This was America, the planet Earth. But it sure did not feel that way to Clay. That disconnection with California, especially Southern California, never left him.

Clay got on the train and sat down. He opened his paper, more out of boredom than interest. He had read it from cover to cover on the way into the city that morning, or at least he had read that portion that actually contained news. The U.S. and International section contained only a small article on the rising tensions with the Middle East and another on the appointment of Gen. Fallsworth to the Joint Chiefs of Staff. The photograph attached to the second article showed three military men sitting at one side of a table. The first was Gen Fallsworth, a small and jovial gentleman with a gray mustache and large, darks eyes.

*Hardly the look of a killer,* Clay had thought. *In fact, the good General looks almost scared.* Clay did not blame the man. Sitting next to him was a tall, thin, balding man with beady and cold blue eyes. Perhaps not blue, but very light, nearly clear; so clear, that the iris' hardly showed up in the black and white photograph, making the black of the soldier's pupils stand out, almost shark-like. He was identified as Col. Leeds. The last soldier was a large youth. Blond hair shortly cropped and even through his uniform, Clay could tell that he possessed the body of a fighter: lean and muscular. He was identified as Staff Sergeant Mueller. Mueller had dark eyes that were hollow, less human than those of Col. Leeds, if such a thing were possible. Both sat next to the General with an air of superiority that made Clay wonder how they had advanced so far in an organization that requires respect and submission to higher-ups. In the background, a small, bespectacled gentleman of far eastern descent and wearing a lab coat sat grinning. He was not facing the camera and Clay wondered what had so amused the unnamed individual. The Local section contained an even smaller article on the latest Chicago City Council meeting. The budget had been approved by a large majority of alderman. Property taxes would remain constant, but a new tax on liquor would be implemented immediately.

What had been a ghost of a paper to begin with kept getting even thinner and thinner. *As perhaps it should,* he thought. With each reduction of honest news, there was a half-fold increase in what passed for news, really nothing more than data on Hollywood personalities or television shows or new gaming devices or iMeme apps. Or worse, simply texts, tweets and twerps sent in by readers. One hundred and sixty characters addressing mostly meaningless topics:

> *How can Apple charge for using virtual iMeme's in virtual reality rooms?*
> *Why can't people pick up after their dogs?*

Or a rant about some perceived wrong in the world that could only be remedied by ignoring facts and common sense and moving forward on a leap of faith. He tried his hand at the NY Times Crossword—at least it seemed unchanged, even if its inclusion was not consistent, as it once was. It was only Tuesday. He usually finished the Tuesday puzzle long before he got home. It was the Wednesday puzzles he struggled to finish before he had to get off the train, if at all. He considered the Thursday and Friday puzzles to be his reality check puzzles. If he could simply complete a respectable number of blanks, perhaps one-third on Thursday and a lucky one or two on Friday, he considered it a personal victory. He looked up at the advertising on the train: *Get a Degree in Photography in only 9 months!* next to an ad that simply had a light blue background with repetitive lettering in a diagonal across the entire foreground:

REPREPREPREPREPREPREPREPREPREP

Clay stared at it a moment, wondering where he had seen that before. *Pre, pre, pre,* he thought. *No. Prep, prep, prep.* But that wasn't right either. Unfamiliar, yet not. Unable to place his finger on where he saw it, he moved on. The next one read only:

> *Are you…*

The balance of the advertisement had been torn down, revealing an old advertisement that someone had apparently forgotten to remove the last time the CTA updated ads:

> *The Chicago Public Library — Reading is Fun.*

The library had closed down several years ago. It had been one of the few non-University libraries still open in the area. The Library Board had been slowly reducing its collection of actual books—preferring that folks 'check out' digital books onto their iMemes and Movebrarys and other readers. At some point, the city simply decided that it would be cheaper to just close down the library altogether since, for all intents and purposes, its entire collection of books could be checked out wirelessly. The City Council found this to be a perfect solution since, they argued, patrons would not need to be bothered to physically go to a library that had few employees and even fewer books. Publishers had long since released books only in electronic format and with the government working on digitizing all previously published works, libraries had run out of work for their employees to actually perform, other than remove books from their shelves to gather them for periodic sales, or in many cases, destruction.

Clay recalled the day the Chicago Main Branch closed. He was passing by the library on a cold January day, the 7th if he recalled correctly. The city was still recovering from the holidays and the traffic was light as many folks were apparently still enjoying their vacation. He had gone down State Street to check out a sale on men's clothes but the shop was still closed for the holidays. He had left his coat at the office, thinking he would only need to walk to the shop, where he would be able to warm up, and then brave the trip back. But it turned out to be colder than he thought it would be and the idea of walking back to the office seemed daunting. He looked up and down the street to see if there were any open stores where he could try to remove the chill from his bones. As he looked south, the library caught his attention. It would be a perfect place to warm up before he headed back to the office. Not only could he stay for as long as he wished without some clerk pestering him to buy something, but he could, perhaps, find a book to read. Most of the library collections had been decimated, save for the math and science sections, which were comprised of a collection of academic works used mostly by students or professionals needing to track down an obscure theory for a project they may be working on. A couple of times, Clay had discovered a book of non-technical literature misfiled among the collections. Neither of any great interest to him: one a Susan Elizabeth Phillips romance novel, the other an adolescent level book from one of the many *Star Wars* novel series. At the time, it had given him hope that at some point he might be able to find a book, a real book, hidden among the dry writings that made up the library's physical collection.

Over the past several years, he was not even able to check out a decent electronic copy of a book. Except for technical books, which seemed to be always available, all other genres seemed to have disappeared. Every time Clay attempted to check out a book, he was advised the particular title was unavailable. Clay placed his name on the waiting lists of numerous titles, yet he never seemed to make it to the top of the list. When he sought explanation, he was told that the publishers only provided for a limited number of electronic copies to be checked out simultaneously. Because most non-technical books were no longer sold in bookstores or available even in university libraries, the number of people seeking to check out a book from the library's collection was extremely long. As such, Clay was directed to practice the virtue of patience by a curt and snippy librarian who had long since tired of Clay's incessant inquires.

As was his habit, Clay headed toward the Classics section first to see if, perhaps, any long-missing volume had shown up from some remiss patron who had been holding on to it for years, collecting dust and overdue fees. Much to Clay's expectation of disappointment, the shelves were empty, except for the note cards intermittently placed upon the empty shelves advising patrons that the collection had been temporarily removed and would be returning soon. The shelves were covered in dust. Even the floor was collecting a layer of dust from disuse and Clay wandered among the empty stacks, well aware the collection was never intended to be returned, but still feeling a little too chilled to make his way back to the office. By apparent stroke of luck, Clay dropped a pen he had been fingering and as he bent down to pick it up, his eye caught the dark binding of a book pushed up alongside the edge of the lowest shelf. He reached over and pulled the thin volume out. He blew the layer of dust from the cover. It was blank, a sea of navy blue cloth worn at the edges. He turned it in his hand. Written in long-faded gold type upon spine of the cloth binding, almost illegible, was the book's title: *Equus*. He considered simply walking out of the library with the book, but did not have his bag or even his coat in which to smuggle the volume out. Clay knew that there was no crime in possessing the book, but he had the distinct feeling that the librarian, upon recognizing it as a non-technical book that should have long been since removed from the shelves, would refuse him the right to check it out, arguing that another patron's name sat atop the wait-list or that rules would not allow the book to be removed from the library. He dusted it off as best he could and proceeded to the Science Collection. He perused the shelves to find several other thin, old volumes to check out, hoping to take any attention away from his discovery.

The checkout desk was being tended by an elderly woman whom Clay recognized. Years ago, when Clay had been a more regular patron of the library, he had conversations with her about forthcoming novels or sought her recommendations of various classics, but lately his visits were less frequent and he had not seen her in many years. She gave no hint of any recognition of Clay as he approached the desk and placed the four volumes down. She did not look up as she began, almost mechanically, to dispense with her duties. She scanned the first two books: *On Being a Scientist: A Guide to Responsible Conduct in Research: Seventh Edition* and *Making Things: 21st Century Manufacturing and Design: Summary of a Forum*, both dated publications from the National Academies Press. Her computer beeped recognition as each was processed from the library database. The third volume was *Equus*. She scanned it, but no beep ensued from her computer. She tried a second time, but again, silence. She picked up the book and examined it closely. Her eyes widened slightly when she saw the title and she looked up at Clay. Her expression changed almost imperceivably.

"Excuse me one moment, please," she said as she slid out from behind the desk and walked into the main collection room, taking the book with her.

Clay wondered where she was going. Thoughts began to race through his mind. He pictured her seeking assistance from her superior, who would, upon discovering the nature of the book, confiscate it. Or perhaps she was seeking help from security to apprehend Clay for some heretofore-unknown violation for possessing such a book. He thought about running out of the library, removing himself from any possible involvement. Although he had done nothing wrong, he felt like he had just been caught in the act of attempting to commit some heinous crime. He dismissed his decision to turn and run when an elderly man with several large volumes of physics books stepped into the checkout line. Clay took a deep breath, trying to appear calm and natural. The librarian returned to the checkout desk. Clay noticed she was carrying two books under her arm.

"I apologize, sir. It appears there is some problem with the barcode on this book." She glanced briefly over at the other patron. "I just went and grabbed a second copy so that it can be properly scanned," she said as she placed a similar looking book under the scanner. It beeped and she placed the new volume to the side, putting *Equus* on top of the two previously scanned books Clay had brought up. She scanned Clay's final book and her printer spit out a receipt. She slid the receipt into the top book and handed them to Clay.

"These books are due back in the library by February 11. I hope you enjoy them." She gave Clay a brief smile.

"Thank you," he muttered as he picked up the volumes and walked away. He slid the receipt out the cover of the top book. He scanned it quickly and noticed that *Equus* was not one of the four books listed. He glanced back to the librarian. She was assisting the other patron, but she looked up briefly at Clay and gave him a knowing look. He returned a brief nod and kept walking.

Clay decided to return to the library the following week. He wanted to return the three books that held no interest for him, as well as to carefully search all the shelves in the Classics Collection to see if any other books had been overlooked. He also wanted to speak to the librarian, but was not sure what he would say. When he arrived, the main entrance doors on State Street were locked. He checked the time.

*'Ten oh seven a.m.,* his iMeme advised.

The hours posted on the door indicated that the library should have opened seven minutes ago. He pressed his face to the glass of the door to see if anyone was inside, but the building was dark. He walked around to the Congress Parkway entrance. A handwritten sign was taped to the inside of the front door: LIBRARY CLOSED PERMANENTLY. Clay pulled on the doors, but they too were locked. He wondered about all the books that had been on the shelves only last week, the possibility of lost treasures among them. He tried to discover what had become of the books, the staff. He never received any response to his inquires other than a twerp several days later indicating the library would not be seeking return of any books recently checked out.

Clay never could get used to reading books on an e-reader. He still enjoyed sitting with a physical book, turning the pages. He was a visual reader. That is, he remembered books, in part, by their physicality. If he needed to find a certain passage, he was usually able to remember approximately where in the book it was located (beginning, middle, end), which side of the open page it was on (left or right), and on which part of the page the passage was located (top, middle or bottom). With the e-reader, the whole book was on the same virtual page. One could not feel the depth of the pages on the left side increase as those of the right side diminished, the gradual progression from beginning to middle to end, the sense of where one stood in the journey of the story. Of course, the e-reader does allow the reader to simply type what he remembered of the passage and then instantly provide matching phrases, but it wasn't the same. Clay still owned many books and would occasionally return to them to re-read. He encouraged his children to read from his collection. They would always agree verbally, but never follow through. *Everyone has their eccentricities,* he guessed, but more than the joy of handling the physical page, he was disappointed to find that while the number of books available for e-reading was continuing to grow by leaps and bounds, the quality and diversity of the materials seemed to be shrinking, with the Classics all but unavailable and except for scientific and mathematical works, and the obligatory entertainment materials, little else from which to choose.

Clay had once possessed a great collection of essays in a volume he was required to buy for an English writing course in college. His professor for that course was an odd man: intellectual, honest and fair. Or perhaps not. Professor Reeves only taught night classes. He admitted that he was demanding and had warned Clay after his first semester that Clay should think twice about recommending him to his friends, as he found many students to be unimpressed by his teaching methods. Clay, however, loved the classes. Clay ignored the warning and recommended Professor Reeves to a friend, who, as foretold, complained to Clay he was not as impressed with Professor Reeves as Clay was. Not nearly so. But Clay loved Professor Reeves' command of literature and keen awareness of the power of language, his love of the simple and powerful language of poetry. Professor Reeves would quote lines from his favorite poems with a knowing grin, and envious smile. It was in Clay's junior year that he, too, became disillusioned, but whether it was with Professor Reeves or himself, he could never decide. He had been writing some poems and short stories and decided to share them with Professor Reeves for an opinion. He was anxious to get feedback from this professor whom he so respected and patiently awaited for a meeting to discuss the works. When, at last, Professor Reeves called him to discuss the works, Clay skipped a class to do so. When Clay entered the office, Professor Reeves had him sit down in his chair while he sat in one of the other chairs usually reserved for visitors. He smiled at Clay and stated that, he too, liked to write. In fact, Professor Reeves had a poem he had written in the top drawer of his desk and he asked Clay to open the desk and read it. Clay slid the drawer open and pulled out a poem. It was short, perhaps only six or eight lines. Clay began to read it and quickly panicked. Here he was, a junior in college, and he did not know the meaning of more than half the words written, had never before even seen many of them. He read it again, unable to decipher any meaning to the poem whatsoever. He looked up at Professor Reeves, who smiled at him and nodded slightly. Clay was embarrassed and could only muster a weak smile.

"That's good," he lied.

Professor Reeves stopped smiling and succinctly told Clay that his work was good, but not of professional quality and that his writing was a bit unpredictable and, ultimately, not impressive. Clay thanked him and left. He had given Professor Reeves a dozen poems and two short stories, and he was dismissed in less than five minutes. He was bitter that he had waited so many months to finally get some feedback, only to receive cursory remarks. He did not take any of the courses Professor Reeves offered during the remainder of his college career.

The event haunted his thoughts. Initially, he blamed himself. Surely, Professor Reeves was rightfully upset Clay did not admit he was unfamiliar with the words, that the poem did not make any sense. Professor Reeves wanted Clay to be honest, and in return, he would be honest to Clay. But Clay failed that test, the test of honesty and openness, a test that would let Professor Reeves know Clay was confident in his abilities, that the two could talk as equals. Years later, in looking back on that event, Clay instead blamed Professor Reeves. *What kind of professor responds to a student who is seeking advice by drafting a clearly unintelligible poem and asking that student for advice? What kind of person plays such a game?* he asked himself. The more he thought about it, the more Clay believed the poem as a hoax. Perhaps he did this to many students. Clay could never know. Clearly Professor Reeves did not, himself, believe the poem had any merit. Clay wondered why he had not recognized it at the time. The poem was filled with large, obscure words. This, from a man who praised the simplicity of language, the joy of a poem that spoke to every man, a poem that conveyed the complexity of life in simple terms. It was a set-up. A cruel enough trick to play on another human being, let alone on a young student eager to please a mentor. But then Clay would blame himself again. Perhaps it really was his fault for not admitting his ignorance, for not being willing to expose his faults before a man he had once deeply respected. *Asshole*, thought Clay, never able to decide whether the description was directed at Professor Reeves or himself.

But that volume, that collection of essays, was fantastic. It contained excerpts of the works of the great thinkers of the ages: Machiavelli, Jefferson, Thoreau, Rawls, Marx and Plato. He had kept it for years afterwards. Referring to it in writing, quoting the greats, re-reading ideologies, and beliefs. His wife had tossed it out with a variety of other books at one time or another. She was adept at preventing the collection of too much clutter, even if Clay refuted her notion of the definition of clutter on a variety of matters. Every other month she seemed to be able to collect several boxes of materials they apparently no longer needed and happily donated it all to a local charity. While many of the items were truly clutter, some held sentimental value, but even these were sent off to new owners. There were, however, some items that Clay, once he discovered they had been given away, felt true disappointment over. The vast majority of which were books. Clay was never able to replace that volume. It was 'out of print,' whatever that meant in a world where nothing was actually printed anymore. Obtaining a copy would simply be a matter of digitizing the work and offering it for sale. Clay resorted to seeking out books at estate sales, garage sales and the occasional antique shop, but it troubled him that the works were unavailable to the vast majority of society. He actually contacted the U.S. Library of Congress once to inquire about accessing copies of various works, but was advised he would have to come to the Library, personally, to view any particular book, and he would not be allowed to copy the work without permission from the copyright holder.

University libraries fared little better. Most of the libraries were fully electronic and, like the public library, the vast majority of the available works were math and science volumes. Since the turn of the millennium, the U.S. Government had been spending millions, and eventually tens of billions, a year on math and science, especially bioengineering, nanotechnology and genetics. Back in the late 1990s and early 2000s there was a constant barrage of reports and studies detailing how Americans were falling behind in math and the sciences, and that the rest of the world was outpacing the U.S. at such a rate that by the mid-2030s, America would be facing a dangerous shortage of engineers and scientists—assets necessary to keep the U.S. as a world leader. The social push for more engineers and scientists worked. However, it was at the expense of the liberal arts. Very few universities offered liberal art degrees and a rapidly growing number of schools were cutting out a majority of the classes that comprise a liberal art education. History, philosophy, even language classes were underfunded and seldom offered. Proponents of the new education system praised the results that showed Americans leading the world in scientific advances. They were also quick to point out, for example, that history, being a series of finite and tangible events, did not need to be studied. With the advent of the microprocessor, and later the nano-processor, coupled with the Internet, and later the Cloud, history was instantly accessible by everyone—each event could be recalled and, if so desired, played back in virtual reality, like films. It was argued that the study of such information did little to advance knowledge or society, and therefore, was treated as irrelevant to the advancement of the Nation. Similar arguments were made as related to philosophy (in a mature, civilized society such as that in the U.S., there was little need to discuss the nuances of 'the good' or 'the right' as the law had grown to encompass and settle all moral questions), literature (entertainment was not a proper subject for university studies) and even basic mathematics (the calculator had become so pervasive in society, that there was no need to teach basic mathematics other than how to properly operate a calculator; the knowledge of why 2 plus 2 equals 4 was irrelevant, only that one knew it did equal 4 was considered important).

*Your stop is approaching,* his iMeme warned. He turned away from the library advertisement.

"Harlem Avenue. Doors open on your left at Harlem," the recorded voice on the El announced. Clay stood up and folded his paper. He exited the train and headed up the ramp toward his home.

# CHAPTER TEN

*News Flash: October 14, 2024. 10:47 a.m. Scientists at the University of Chicago took another step in the Race to the Bottom. While elements of nanotechnology can be found in thousands of consumer products, scientists still seek the Holy Grail of nanoengineering — the molecular factory. In an article to be published in* Nature Nanotechnology *tomorrow, Drs. Ho, Stevens and Yu-Lee have recently discovered how to efficiently program and control massively parallel production processes, which represents a major leap toward the development of a molecular factory. "We have been seeking a method for massive parallel production for a number of years. We stumbled upon our catalyst through Calculated Chance Methodology. Many older scientists complain that Calculated Chance Methodology is the result of a failure to teach the scientific method, but discovery after recent discovery has shown that the method does work. Professor Albert Szent-Gyorgyi stated many years ago that: 'A discovery is said to be an accident meeting a prepared mind.' We have simply taken that idea to its natural and rightful end."*

The ride up to the University of Wisconsin was a pleasant one. While Illinois was dominated by flat and boring landscape occupied by alternating fields of corn and beans, the ride to Wisconsin offered rolling moraines — the last visages of the appearance of the Laurentide Ice Sheet during the previous glacial maximum over 20,000 years ago. When he was younger, Clay used to go to Wisconsin to bike the moraines. Camping with a few close friends, they would spend the day riding along the many trails that crisscross the area west of Lake Michigan, and the evenings by a campfire, sometimes drinking a little too much and laughing a little too loud. For these sins, their fellow campers would awaken with the dawn and begin their breakfast preparations, being certain to bang their pots and pans loudly and then speak even more loudly to each other above the din of their own creation. These types of mornings were always rough, but inevitable as the surrounding campers sought payback for the noise they suffered at the hands of Clay and his friends the previous evening.

Lillian had decided to stay at home with Matthew and Elizabeth, giving Clay and Katie the opportunity to spend a little father-daughter time together while they travelled back and forth from the tour of the University of Wisconsin-Madison. Clay looked forward to touring the college campus. Indian summer had settled in and along with the clear days, the temperature was expected to remain in the lower seventies all week. Clay recalled his own college days, filled with excited dreams of the future, as well as the many good times he enjoyed on campus. He looked forward to his daughter enjoying the boundless opportunities that daily presented themselves to students, from academic to social. To Clay, his undergraduate days always felt like some kind of 'Never-Never Land' where the freedoms of adulthood were suddenly at hand and beckoning while the correlating obligations were somehow diminished, almost as an afterthought that he needed not be concerned with at that particular time. Money remained a hurdle, but whether it was from the small monthly stipend from his mother, dipping into his savings from his summer jobs or from his student loans, he somehow always managed to get by. Oftentimes he would forego a meal or two at the end of the month in order to have enough to go out with his friends on the weekends. And when he did suffer from the occasional zero balance, there was always someone who would lend him a few dollars to go out, knowing that the kindness would be returned in their time of need. Even with a full-load of classes and a part-time job, school never took on the nine-to-five drudgery of true adulthood. There was always time to have a laugh, a nap, or to explore a new interest. Clay couldn't help but smile thinking about how much fun awaited Katie.

When they arrived, the campus was buzzing with activity. A small group of students had gathered around a man dressed in a black suit with a thin tie. He was holding a Bible in his hand and warning the crowd that the price of sin was steep. Purgatory promised an eternity of misery and unless they turned from their evil ways, unless they accepted the word of the Lord Jesus Christ, as written in the Bible, as the gospel truth, they would soon be met with fire and brimstone hailing down from the sky. Several students asked questions meant to rile up the young preacher's ire, but were asked in such a manner he was unable to determine if the questions were genuine inquires of faith or simply attempts to mock him. He answered as best he could, condemning them for studying the words of man rather than the reason of God.

"The good Lord does not suffer the sinner, people. He is an angry God, a jealous God, and your wickedness shall bring you low! You with the sorority shirts!" he shouted as he pointed at a group of Tri-Deltas. "You walk around with pride. Those letters spell whore!" A couple of young men in the group laughed. He immediately turned on them. "You think this is funny? Today you are masturbators, tomorrow you'll be homosexuals! Brothers and sisters, look upon these masturbators, these whores, and help me pray for them. There is hope, sisters and brothers. There is hope of salvation if you seek Him out. Hallelujah! Take this book, brothers and sisters," and with this he held his Bible high over his head. "Take this book and be healed! It is the word of God and it warns that the end is near, my friends! Satan is among us now, even as I speak!" He shuddered and cast his eyes skyward. "Save me, sweet Jesus! You are my shepherd and I am your sheep! Save these sinners, oh Lord, that they shall not succumb to the coming evil!" He dropped to his knees, tears beginning to run down the sides of his cheeks. "Rain Judgement down upon us, Lord, for even as we speak, Satan prepares for battle!"

"Looks like some things never change." Clay rolled his eyes as they walked out of earshot. But some things do. Clay noticed that not a single student carried any books. Back when he was in college, students walked around with loaded backpacks: books, pens, paper, snacks. But all books were electronic these days. All students had iMeme's with which they could listen to their readings or, if they so chose, read them with the aid of the iMeme's holographic screen. In addition, students could easily record their lectures and review them as necessary, making Clay wonder if students still attended classes or whether they got together in the beginning of the semester and appointed each student one day to show up, record the lecture and forward on the remainder of the class.

The young woman leading their campus tour was an attractive blonde with a contagious personality and a matching sense of school pride. She was possessed of that certain amount of exuberance necessary to portray to the young women in the group that Madison was a friendly campus, while donning a Wisconsin sweatshirt and red shorts which revealed enough skin to give the young men the hope that any decision to attend Wisconsin-Madison would not be for naught. She identified herself as Hannah and their tour took them throughout campus, including the ice facilities at the Kohl Center and the various buildings in the College of Letters and Science and the College of Engineering.

"It's been a great tour, everyone! If you have any questions, I'd be happy to answer those for you," Hannah said as she smiled and looked over the group.

Katie looked up at her dad to signal him he should keep his mouth shut and not embarrass her, but she was too late.

"Excuse me," Clay spoke up. "I was looking through the University's Catalogue and I didn't see any of the liberal arts offered. Does the College of Letters and Sciences offer any classes or degrees in the humanities?" Katie rolled her eyes and took a step back, trying to disassociate herself from her father.

Hannah looked briefly at Katie and flashed her a look of understanding. "That's a great question!" she said turning her attention to Clay. "And one I get fairly often," she said. "In an effort to help ensure our graduates have the best chance for securing meaningful employment after graduation, the University no longer offers humanities degrees. Any other questions?" Hannah asked as she scanned the group.

"But doesn't the University believe in the value of History or Sociology and other such classes?" Clay asked. By the reaction of both Katie and Hannah to his question, he guessed that they unanimously had hoped Hannah's initial response would have ended the query.

"The University does offer some classes in the Elementary Education curriculum, such as 'The Teaching of Reading', and 'The Teaching of Language Arts,'" Hannah said. "But for the most part, by the time students get to college, they know how to access history and social studies type questions from the Cloud. It'd be a waste of students' time and money to take classes on things they can access instantly and for free, don't you think?"

*That's just it, I do think.* But Clay held his tongue, finally realizing that he was likely embarrassing Katie. *I think that somehow society is creating a huge hole — a massive lacking in the brains of the next generation, the people who, one day, are supposed to be running this country,* he wanted to say. He was struck with a recurring feeling that something was not quite right. *The future is advancing toward some scientific wonderland, yet the kids who are, and will be, developing these genius ideas and products, as versed as they are in science and math and engineering and technology, could they manage life in an earlier time? Could this future generation have been able to live, to actually survive, in the past?* Clay had serious doubts. New ideas don't come from math and science alone. Ideas require creativity and creativity requires unique thought, thought that comes from independent and questioning minds — minds trained in the liberal arts.

Hannah turned her attention to the group. "Okay, if there are no more questions, we invite the applicants to join us for an ice cream social at Four Lakes Market. There will be representatives from various extra-curricular organizations, including the athletic department and Greek Council to answer any questions. Parents are free to proceed to Bascom Hall where there will be opportunities to review financial aid options, housing options and ask other questions you may have." She looked at Clay as she completed her sentence.

"I'll see you later, Katie," Clay said as she left with the other kids, led by Hannah.

Clay made his way over to Bascom Hall, which was filled with parents seeking information on the campus. He wandered around the building, stopping occasionally to listen to the information provided. He worked his way down the main hall and came to a table not surrounded with parents that held a banner stating: ASSOCIATE DEAN OF STUDENTS, and underneath, CHAIRMAN, CURRICULUM COMMITTEE. The man sitting behind the table was reading something on his e-reader.

"I'm sorry to bother you," Clay said as he tapped lightly on the table to get his attention. "But would you mind if I asked a couple questions?"

The man set his e-reader down and sat up straight in his chair. "No, no problem at all, sir. Please, that is why I'm here," he answered a little sheepishly. He was young, somewhere in his early thirties, Clay guessed.

"Maybe it's not really a question," Clay began. "But don't you think it's detrimental to the educational system to do away with the liberal arts programs?" It turned Clay's stomach to think about what society was doing to its youth.

"I'm sorry, Mr...?" The young man waited for Clay to introduce himself.

"Mr. Furstman." Clay responded.

"Thank you, Mr. Furstman. I'm Paul Newbury, pleasure to meet you," he said offering his hand to Clay. The two shook. "Educational testing has shown that the 'No Child Left Behind' has proven to be wildly successful in increasing the test scores of American students. Are you aware that 98% of American public schools are now matriculating graduates who meet or exceed grade level? This has all been achieved by concentrating on math and science." Paul Newbury smiled proudly at this achievement. "The educational system recognizes that access to the Cloud is available to nearly every person. Given the cost of educating children these days, teaching the liberal arts is a poor use of valuable and limited resources. Our lives have become so interconnected to the Cloud; history, civics, Shakespearian quotes and philosophy are now instantly accessible to everyone. Educators cannot test a student's knowledge of, for example, geography when the student could simply inquire of the Cloud the location of the Yangtze River and receive instantaneous response, and because of this accessibility to information, there is no need to test or even teach the materials."

"But access to information is not the same as teaching," Clay countered. "Students aren't taught how to analyze a problem to reach a solution, but rather, how to respond to specific questions with concrete answers. Students are basically taught answers and then memorize how to apply them to the questions presented on standardized tests. Answers are either 'Right' or 'Wrong'; gone is even the possibility to present an incorrect response, and support the erroneous answer with a well-reasoned argument that would have earned a student in my youth at least some points for reasoning ability, notwithstanding their reliance upon a faulty premise."

"Well, things have changed over the years, Mr. Furstman. As the educational field discovers new methods of teaching, we apply these to the classroom. The fact that public education has become so successful is reason enough to believe we are doing things correctly.

Test scores place American children at the top of the world when it comes to math and science knowledge. And it is math and science that are driving our economy, getting our graduates the best opportunities to secure jobs after they graduate. We have almost a sixty percent employment rate for new graduates."

"Certainly the University looks at education as more than simply knowing the answers, doesn't it? The standardized tests leave no room for the nuances of learning. What about the gray areas?" Clay was shocked. The Chairman of the Curriculum Committee kept referring to standardized tests. 'No Child Left Behind' was proposed by President George W. Bush, a man who had once told the world, 'You're either with us or against us.' A man who saw the world in simple black and white, right and wrong, good and evil. A President whose legacy was a national embodiment of his ideology and a public buy-in of the notion that everything could be broken down into simple 'yes' and 'no' responses. Doubts or concerns were reserved for those unsure of themselves or unwilling to take a stand, those who would waffle on an issue and, thus, those in possession of the serious character flaw of an inability to lead decisively.

"I know this may be difficult for you to understand. You were taught under the old school," Newbury said, a bit condescendingly. "We've gotten rid of the gray areas. There is knowing and not knowing. Things are, or they are not. The goal of education is to allow the students to add to the body of knowledge, to add understanding of what things are or are not. Math and science both provide either correct or incorrect answers. There is no middle ground."

"But the liberal arts allow people to make assumptions, to test those assumptions and to learn from our mistakes," Clay said.

"Yes, that was the old school belief; to learn from the past, and then guess the future," Newbury said, shaking his head slightly. "But we have taken the guesswork out of knowledge and moved directly to the answers. And it is the answers to questions that create knowledge." Newbury pulled a pamphlet from the table showing the many discoveries generated from the University of Wisconsin-Madison graduate labs. "Advancing science is no longer dependent upon scientists developing an educated hypothesis from pre-existing knowledge. Now, we educate students in the standardized processes involved in material manipulation (how to keep track the different material combinations in varied environmental conditions) so that students can test newly combined materials for unique properties. This educational format is based on Calculated Chance Methodology — the theory that the random manipulation of matter using standard methods will result in useful outcomes. Just as the Infinite Monkey theorem postulates the complete works of William Shakespeare could be written by a monkey hitting keys at random on a typewriter keyboard given an infinite amount of time, the Calculated Chance Methodology recognizes probabilities of success using known manipulation methods on random materials over a given time. By churning out thousands of scientists, the United States is fostering a new generation of high-tech workers guaranteed to discover all possibilities simply by the probabilities of chance. Adoption of the Calculated Chance Methodology makes the study of the liberal arts an unnecessary waste of resources.

"Big business also favors Calculated Chance Methodology. With the advent of cheaper and faster methods of creating nanomaterials, it is far more efficient from a cost-basis standpoint to simply try any endless number of combinations on various materials and record the results. The scientific method's reliance on the formulation of a hypothesis greatly increased the time and cost required to generate results while limiting the number of possible discoveries. By use of Calculated Chance Methodology, American scientists are better prepared to realize unexpected reactions and thus, more likely to discover all the potentialities of a process rather than allowing their observations to be limited to preconceived outcomes."

Clay frowned at Newbury.

"Don't you see?" Newbury continued. "Scientists and students are now free to simply do and discover. No longer is a scientist required to spend valuable research time over careful thought and manipulation of common data points and equations. It today's world, a scientist can simply work at the bench manipulating matter. Methods and materials are cheap enough that even duplicative research is no longer considered a waste of time and resources. Like Henry Ford did so long ago, science has finally managed to merge its process with theories of mass production with an end result being that science is booming. Mankind is now racing toward the future and the glory that awaits! And Madison students are helping lead the way!"

*Sprinting onward,* Clay thought. *Or perhaps simply stumbling forward, legs churning at a great pace to prevent from falling headlong onto the path before us.* While scientific discoveries were being touted almost daily, Clay found that very little new was actually being developed. Instead, science was simply producing new and faster versions of existing technology. It reminded Clay of Hollywood's habit of rehashing old television shows into new and exciting blockbuster movies. Clay recalled a time when television was reserved for those ideas, those shows that lacked the luster, intelligence, and sex appeal to make it to the Silver Screen. However, television had now become the source of fodder for current blockbuster features. There were no new ideas in Hollywood, just the ability to pull some television show out of the cobwebs of one's childhood memories, some memory that sparks the feelings of nostalgia, of yearnings for the innocence and love that one had in his youth, whether real or imagined. Hollywood was no longer the seller of dreams and fancy, but the server of cold leftovers seeking to provide crumbs of comfort in a world of change.

"I don't care what you say. It can't be right," Clay responded. He set the pamphlet about Madison's scientific discoveries back on the table. "Thank you anyway, Dean Newbury," Clay said as he left to meet back up with Katie.

## CHAPTER ELEVEN

*News Flash: October 26, 2024. 7:15 a.m. No longer will Wednesday be Prince Spaghetti Night in America. You will soon be eating in style every night—for almost nothing! As well as dressing in the latest styles, driving the best cars and enjoying all the finer things in life. Guaranteed to lower the cost of all products, Americans will once again be the land of opportunity and wealth. With streets paved in gold and a chicken (or perhaps, caviar) in every pot, there will be a new meaning to the phrase, 'Living the American Dream.'*

Clay arose from bed a little after seven a.m., put on his pajama bottoms and headed downstairs. Lillian had left for the gym an hour earlier and the kids were still asleep. He opened the front door and was greeted by the sun, shining brightly and busily working to burn the frost off the neighborhood lawns. Clay took a deep breath of the fresh air. It was crisp and cool, but the clear sky held the promise of warmth and plenty of sunshine. He sought to retrieve the newspaper, but the porch was empty. He stepped down the stairs and onto his front walk to look around, hoping to find the paper lying nearby, hidden from his view, but he had no more luck at the bottom of the stairs than he did at the top. He wondered whether the paperboy—in truth, a grown man who delivered his goods by a car which, although Clay had never seen it, was clearly in need of a new muffler and brake pads, as evidenced by the sound that would, on occasion, awaken him in the wee hours of the morning—was sick, or missed this drop-off. He could, of course, contact the Sun-Times and let them know he did not receive delivery and they would send a paper along later, but there was no point. He simply wanted to read it while he ate breakfast. By the time the paper would be delivered the news would be old—a sad truth about the news even when the paper was delivered on time. It was impossible for a newspaper to keep its readers as up-to-date as the Cloud and while Clay did get a vast majority of his news from the Cloud—he enjoyed flipping the pages of the paper while he ate, reading the Op/Ed letters, if any, and perusing the comics, his fingers, usually greasy from eggs or bacon, staining the pages. But the sun felt warm on the back of his neck, even though his bare feet were nearly frozen on the cold concrete walk, and he resigned himself to enjoy his breakfast in front of his laptop.

### SMALL FACTORY TO YIELD BIG RESULTS

*AP – University of Chicago Scientists working under a DARPA grant, have developed the first fully functional molecular factory. This exciting break-through promises to shake society to its very core. "We now have the capability to create anything from nothing," boasts Professor Peter F. Stevens, spokesperson on the project. "Our molecular machine is capable of aligning and connecting molecules to create anything. Imagine, we'll be able to feed the hungry and provide fresh water to the world at very little cost and using resources available anywhere in the world." The concept of molecular manufacturing has been the holy grail of nanotechnology for decades. The lab is currently disassembling various materials in order to develop the blueprints upon which the molecular machines will be able to create objects. "Once we've run the factory in reverse, so to speak, we have the information needed to run the process forward and re-create the item in endless quantities for no real cost."*

Clay surfed over to the CNN live feed. This was big news! A wide shot of Meredith Betts, host of Weekend Early Start, and two men sitting beside her, one in a military uniform and the other, currently speaking, was a man in thick glasses and wearing a white lab coat.

"...*feed the world's hungry, clothe the naked and eradicate poverty in the world.*"

"*Well Professor, that's quite an accomplishment! When do we expect that these molecular factories would be available to the general public?*"

*"We expect that delivery could begin in less than two weeks. We've—'*

*Did Meredith Betts just scream?* Clay wondered, his fork held inches from his mouth, the soft yolk dripping down to the plate below.

*"Two weeks! I'm sorry, Professor Ho, but you mean to tell me that you expect to get this product to market in two weeks? I don't understand how you can deliver these so quickly, let alone develop the commercial and marketing infrastructure to push this forward in that kind of time frame."*

*"Thank you, Ms. Betts, for raising that point,"* the man in uniform interrupted. *"You see, these molecular factories are, literally, game-changing. We will have these to market so quickly for the very same reason that we expect every household in America to possess one within the next forty-five days. They can create anything—including themselves. While we have been testing these in the labs, we have been programming them to reproduce themselves. They can duplicate themselves in less than 10 minutes. I'm sure you're familiar with the old riddle that offers a choice between one million dollars immediately, or one penny on day one, and doubling it every day for thirty days? One's immediate reaction is to take the Million Dollars and run. But if you do the math, you'll find that getting one penny on day one, and two pennies on day two and four cents on day three, and so on, until thirty days has passed, that by the thirtieth day, that penny, by doubling thirty times, is now worth over five million dollars. So for the past several months, we have been creating millions of these factories which are currently being distributed to facilities across the nation, with the help of the United States military, and within two weeks, we expect to begin distributing them to every American household."*

The camera panned back to Professor Ho, who was sitting back in his seat and smiling stiffly, as the soldier finished his comments. Clay noticed that he was a man of short stature: short arms, short legs, short hair. He seemed to Clay to be a small child pretending to be a scientist in his father's lab coat, which draped his frame like a human Christo and Jeanne-Claude art piece. With each pause in conversation, his confidence seemed to escape, his dark eyes darting back and forth, as if expecting someone or something to leap out and devour him. It was clear that Professor Ho was a person not used to social interaction, a person infinitely more comfortable among computers and lab materials than television cameras and reporters.

Meredith Betts, usually composed and direct, was at a loss. She sat there silently, the camera zoomed in on her face, mouth agape.

"But... but... do you realize what this means? The economy... the... why the social ramifications — "

Professor Ho's demeanor returned to scientific confidence as he began to speak again. "I know this may seem sudden to you, but we have been perfecting this process for years. It is all very detailed and scientific, Ms. Betts. Science has, at last, conquered nature!" At this, Professor Ho began to rise, but stopped himself and settled back into his chair. He gave the camera a sheepish smirk and turned to the soldier, who had again interrupted.

"We've had time to consider all these facets," the soldier said as a graphic across the bottom of the display identified him as Lt. Col. R. George Leeds. "The American economy hasn't produced anything tangible in over a decade. We have long recognized that America is a service society and American workers will continue to provide services. We are all capable of going home and cooking a fancy meal — yet we still go out. But now, it will cost much less because we will not be paying so much for food or gas or linens. Other industries will change more radically, but they will survive. The personal Genesis replicators to be delivered into American households, due to the limits of their physical size, will not be capable of producing many items Americans need, such as cars and major appliances. The individual manufacturers of these items, however, will be provided with industrial replicators capable of manufacturing their goods, which will be sold to the public through normal channels of commerce. You see, it's more than simply wishing for a product and having it manufactured at will.

"Molecular factories are not intelligent, they can only make those items which they have the programming to do so. And these programs will be individual apps that will cost money. Each replicator will be pre-programmed to produce basic food items — hunger will be wiped out from the U.S. immediately. But commercial food products, well they will require programs that will cost individuals real money. As will many items Americans use everyday: light bulbs, socks, laundry detergent, toothpaste. But all *these items will become ever so much cheaper. Currently, the American public pays, let's say, $2.25 for toothpaste. Perhaps $1.25 of that price is for the materials, machinery and upkeep to manufacture the toothpaste. Another fifty-cents is for transportation and storage costs, leaving fifty-cents profit between manufacturer and retailers, who also have their own labor and utility costs. With a molecular factory, they can deliver the same product for much less, all while realizing the same profit margin. Since the cost of doing business will decrease, the product will sell for less. The toothpaste that used to cost the consumer $2.25 may only cost twenty-five cents!*

*"The patent holder of this technology, Replicator, Inc., will create the programming software for all manufactured items, for a reasonable fee, of course. The individual patent owners of all American products can choose to sell their applications through an iMeme app subscription to households who will then have the capability of using the Genesis replicator to reproduce the particular item at home, or the patent owners can replicate their goods on-site and sell them through normal distribution channels, but at greatly reduced prices. The American public will still pay for goods, they will just pay much less than they used to, which will increase the level of living across the nation."*

*"You keep talking about Americans, Colonel Leeds. Will the Genesis be available elsewhere?" Meredith asked.*

*At this question, Professor Ho sat upright and spoke. "As you are aware, Ms. Betts, this was developed, in part, with public funding through DARPA. Under current regulations and guidelines, this technology will not be made available outside the U.S. Since the replicators themselves are manufactured molecule by molecule, we have developed a design so that any attempt to disassemble or reverse engineer the product will be practically impossible. The material components have been programmed to self-destruct with any attempt to disassemble, examine — even via X-ray or MRI technologies — or otherwise tamper with its normal operation. We are confident that any attempt to steal this technology will result in a complete destruction of the Genesis and its component technology," Ho said nervously.*

*"If I may, Ms. Betts." The camera panned to Leeds. He smiled at Meredith Betts, like a wolf grinning at its prey, mouth parted, teeth showing, his demeanor showing little warmth.*

"Please, Colonel. Feel free to expand on this subject." Meredith encouraged him, her expression revealing some discomfort at the way Leeds was staring at her.

"The U.S. Military sponsored this research for a number of strategic defense strategies. Not only will this product increase the standard of living across the U.S., but it will place America in a position of superiority. While the transition to a green energy society has been marginally successful, it has been costly and has placed Middle-Eastern interests in a heightened priority. American society is most successful under a fossil fuel economy, as is the American military, and because a molecular factory can duplicate fossil fuels — gasoline, kerosene, diesel — we have already begun the process of converting the military back to fossil fuel. And we encourage all Americans to return to gas-powered vehicles."

"Am I correct, Colonel Leeds," Meredith asked, "that just because fossil fuels will be readily accessible, that we are going to reverse all the progress we've made on Global Warming?" She turned to the Professor, "Professor Ho, you have spent considerable time and effort in your career trying to improve upon green technologies, and now you're going to turn your back on all that hard work?"

Once again, Professor Ho smiled confidently. "Actually, Ms. Betts, one of the interesting unintended consequences of a molecular factory is that rather than facing the threat of Global Warming, widespread use may result in Global Cooling. Let me explain: almost all products that a molecular factory will reproduce will be carbon-based. That is, materials will be made from carbon bonds — making the reproductions much stronger than the original — and all living things, including our food sources, are carbon based. The Genesis will use $CO_2$ in the atmosphere to harvest carbon for manufacturing purposes. We predict that if every household operates a Genesis, our atmosphere will rapidly be depleted of $CO_2$, resulting in a massive global cooling. As such, it will be necessary to not only burn manufactured carbon fuels to help keep the system in parity, but also to ensure continued consumption and burning of naturally occurring fossil fuels in order to keep up with our expected carbon consumption."

"Morning, Dad," Katie smiled as she walked into the kitchen.

"Oh... huh? Oh yeah. Good morning, sweetie." Clay folded the monitor of his laptop down. The bite of egg still lay upon his fork, uneaten and cold, his bacon glazed in a thin layer of coagulated grease. "I was just listening to this story about—"

"The Genesis. Yeah, I heard about it on my iMeme. Cool, isn't it? Just think, steak and lobster every night! Dad, can we be sure to buy the American Gourmet upgrade when we get our Replicator? It looks like it's only $300 a year." Katie directed her iMeme's holographic screen toward her dad so he could see the American Gourmet download option in the iTunes App Store.

"What? They already have apps up on the App Store? They just announced the damn thing this morning."

Katie laughed. "Dad, they announced it late last night. Don't you ever keep your iMeme on anymore?" Katie rolled her eyes. "The whole world can pass you by and you'd be the last to know."

## CHAPTER TWELVE

*News Flash: October 28, 2024. 8:03 a.m. The President announced today that the U.S. was placing its full backing behind the State of Israel. Recent hostilities in the Middle East have escalated to a point where President Browning has declared that American action is highly likely. The United States' Fifth Fleet in the Persian Gulf was joined earlier today by the United States' Thirteenth Fleet in response to Iranian threats to close the Gulf. FARS reports Iran has accused the U.S. of raising hostilities and has warned all countries that it is shutting down the Strait of Hormuz to all tankers and other commercial traffic. The U.S. Navy has countered by declaring that any Iranian attempt to interfere with commercial shipping lanes will be considered an act of war. The oil markets reacted immediately, with oil rising to over $300 a barrel. This sent the stock market spiraling, with the Dow Jones Industrial down almost seven percent...*

Clay moved to the center of the unusually empty train and took an open seat. He was in a foul mood. He usually enjoyed reading the paper during his commute downtown, but both Sunday and today, Monday, were, like Saturday, absent of any paper delivery. He purchased a copy of the paper from the vending machines located in front of the El stop, swearing under his breath at having to buy a paper for which he was already a subscriber. His ire turned to anger when he sat down and noticed it was last Friday's edition. He stared, red faced, out the window at the passing traffic. The number of cars seemed to be lighter than usual, but there was an abundance of large semis all colored light blue and bearing the same design—the characters REPREPREPREPREPREP diagonally placed and repeated over and over. Clay looked hard at the trucks. He had seen this somewhere before. He tried to remember. *Prep re Prep,* mused Clay. *Rep, rep, rep. Pre, pre, pre.* The expressway disappeared as the train plunged underground as it headed toward the Loop. In the noise and darkness that suddenly surrounded Clay, he realized that his anger had subsided. He turned his head from the darkness outside the train windows. As he did so, he caught sight of his reflection in the glass of the train window slowly fade as the train entered the lighted station.

Clay picked up the phone in his office and dialed the general number to the Sun-Times. He did not want to ride the train home without something to read and he was going to demand the newspaper have today's edition delivered to his office since they were apparently incapable of delivering it to his home, or even the local vending machine near his home. The line transmitted the audible ringtone to his ear six times before it was answered.

"The number you have reached, 312-321-3000, has been disconnected. No forwarding number is available." Clay hung up.

*What the...?* he thought to himself. He checked the number again and saw that he had not misdialed. He Googled SUN-TIMES and searched for recent news.

CHICAGO SUN-TIMES CEASES PUBLICATION. He scanned down the news headlines. SUN-TIMES CALLS IT QUITS. SO LONG, SUN-TIMES. THE END OF AN ERA. The headlines repeated the news over and over. He clicked on the first link. Apparently, the Sun-Times shut its doors for the final time last Friday. Many employees did not find out until the following day, when they tried to show up for work and could not gain access. While everyone was aware that the written newspaper was a dying industry, it seems most believed they would get some type of notice. *So, that's how it ends? No 'final edition' or nostalgic look back. Simply, one day you publish, the next it's over?* Clay asked himself.

The day was otherwise uneventful for Clay. In the late afternoon he decided he needed a book to read on the train, so he grabbed his wallet and left the office. When he exited the building, he was again surprised at the lack of activity on the street. Like his observation earlier on the train, the streets were relatively empty of vehicles, except the seemingly ever-increasing invasion of the light-blue trucks bearing the repetitive design. The city was quiet and, for the first time in ages, he reached over to the Spot and turned on his iMeme without anyone reminding him that he needed to do so. As he made his way toward *Antiques and Oddities,* a little shop that still, on occasion, offered real books for sale, he yearned to see a familiar face. He felt lonely and unattached from the world. His feet impacted the pavement below, but the city seemed distant, void of background conversation and its usual sense of activity. He heard little other than the passing of vehicles. He looked down at his iMeme. The holographic display was blinking on and off and notified Clay that it was automatically downloading system upgrades. The process struck him as odd at that moment. *Is it possible to download upgrades?* he asked himself. *Can you upload downgrades? Why do we not upload upgrades and download downgrades?* The system completed its processes and Clay turned his iMeme off, along with his thoughts.

## CHAPTER THIRTEEN

*Breaking News Flash: Wednesday. 4:17 p.m. In breaking news, the US Government and Replicator, Inc. have revealed that fossil fuel dedicated molecular factories have been operating for over sixty days and the government will begin providing fossil fuels to American consumers for free. The President has announced that the energy situation is a vital national interest and signed an executive order nationalizing all private fueling stations in the United States. By Executive Order, not later than 11:59 p.m. this evening, all employees working at private fueling stations will become government employees at the G7 pay scale. Private owners will be compensated for the value of their property and all fuel products shall be provided to American citizens and businesses free of charge. "The right of Americans to continue a fossil fuel dependent society, when such action is not only possible, but necessary and without cost, is fundamental," Browning said. "From this day forward, the United States will be free from the oppression and indignity of foreign oil suppliers." The President went on to praise the ingenuity of American scientists and stressed that a review of America's current foreign policy initiatives is currently underway. Stocks in the major oil companies initially fell by more than 50% upon the announcement, but have since recovered significantly based on reports that the free-oil technology will not be made available to foreign nations and any projected reduction in fuel sales to Americans will be countered by increased sales overseas.*

"Jesus Christ!" Clay said aloud, stopping in his tracks. He could only begin to grasp at the implications of free fuel. He looked around expecting to see a sudden celebration, a rush of people crowding the streets, a ticker tape parade, but the silence in the city continued and added to Clay's feeling of surrealism. Clay started walking again. He reached down to turn his iMeme off but rather than shutting down, it indicated that it transitioned into Sleep Mode. *Sleep Mode? What the hell is that?* Clay's thoughts were interrupted as when he bumped into someone. "Oh, I'm sorry, I..." he paused as he looked up. He was staring into the face of the Walking Man.

"I'm... excuse me. I wasn't watching where I was going. I..."

The Walking Man nodded his head and smiled. "It's okay. It's been a bit of an odd day today, with so many people taking the day off." His voice was strong and deep. Clay would not be surprised to hear this voice advertising products on television or over the Cloud. What did surprise Clay was not only that the voice was associated with the Walking Man, but also the enunciation, the eloquence of his voice, which revealed a man clearly used to talking, and to being heard.

"Yes, I... I noticed." Clay tried to get a grip on the situation. In his imaginings of speaking to the Walking Man, it was the Walking Man who was unable to speak full sentences, the Walking Man who was tongue-tied, not he.

"I apologize, sir. Have a nice day," said the Walking Man, his voice deep and confident.

Clay stepped aside and quickly continued on his way. He was tempted to look back, to see if the Walking Man was still standing there, watching, but he did not.

As Clay entered *Antiques and Oddities* it was not lost on him that he had just run into an antique and oddity. He tried to shake the feeling of confusion that had come over him and took comfort in the soft tinkle of the ringing bell over the door. The lady behind the counter looked up at the sound and seeing Clay enter, smiled at him. The soft lighting and carpeted floor quickly put Clay back at ease. He smiled back and headed toward the back wall where books, if there were any, would be found. As he approached the back of the store he saw a young woman reaching down to pick up one of the three or four books that were on a low shelf. She had her back to him. Long dark hair pulled back in a ponytail, strong shoulders, curved hips complimenting her nicely shaped figure. As she crouched down and bent forward, her jeans pulled away from her waist and her shirt raised slightly, exposing the small of her back and Dimples of Venus. *Attractive,* Clay thought. Although married and certainly much too old for her, he paused briefly to allow himself a moment longer to gaze before he continued forward, ignorant of her backward glance. As he was about to approach, she stood up and turned. Her face was lit up and she smiled. "Well, hello."

Clay felt himself blush and he spoke a little too loudly. "Hello, Eva. How are you? I wouldn't have thought to see you here." It was Eva Diaz, Miguel and Jennifer Diaz's daughter. He had not seen her in several years, not since she received her BS Degree from the Illinois Institute of Technology. He had hoped that she had not noticed him staring moments earlier.

She gave him a gentle nudge with her elbow. "You know, if you'd actually turn your iMeme on instead of just carrying it around, you would have known it was me when you first approached."

"Clay felt the heat rise in his cheeks again. "I'm sorry. I... I—"

"It's okay. Really. Besides, you're not half bad looking yourself. For an old guy, that is." She smiled. "Anyway, what brings you here?"

"I wanted to find a book to read. I just found out the Sun-Times is no longer in operation and for the life of me I can't get used to reading off of the iMeme hologram screen and I'm not interested in being read to."

"What?! You just found out? The news of the Sun-Times was all over the Notification service this weekend. Let me see your iMeme." She reached to his Spot and pulled the iMeme off. It struck Clay that someone looking on might consider such an action rude, or perhaps, given their age difference, consider Eva brash for reaching over to his Spot like that. But he did not consider it rude and apparently she was not uncomfortable. He had known Eva since she was a little girl.

Eva had always been a bright child. She began reading at an early age and by the time she was in sixth grade, she had devoured many of the classics in literature. A voracious reader, she was always seeking new books to read and would oftentimes seek advice from her parents' friends. Clay was an active reader and would generally offer suggestions, introducing her to Norse mythology and some 20th century authors.

The first time he had recommended a book to Eva he was surprised how quickly she had completed it. Clay and Lillian were having drinks with Miguel and Jennifer before going out and she walked confidently up to him to return the book. She thanked him and, to Clay's surprise, asked if it would be okay to discuss it with him. Clay good-naturedly agreed to sit with her for a few minutes; Jennifer was preparing some appetizers that were not yet ready and the adults would not be leaving to go out for another hour or so. It wasn't long before he realized her perception was well beyond her thirteen years and he actually enjoyed the discussion on an intellectual basis. Thereafter, if he had recommended a book to her, he would be sure to reserve some time to spend with her if she requested a discussion. Usually, Miguel would bring Eva downtown and drop her off at Clay's office where they would talk for awhile, relatively undisturbed, and then meet up with Miguel to share lunch. As a young teenager, she appreciated that Clay took their discussions seriously and always felt a little more grown-up having a real appointment in a downtown office. As she got older, oftentimes she was the one recommending books to Clay. They had, on several occasions, tried to get others to join their little book club, but no one ever took them up on their offer. Clay also discovered as she grew older that he felt less and less like a parent to Eva and more and more like an intellectual equal. Her mind was sharp and they had many good discussions throughout the years.

After she had entered college, their book club disbanded. While he would occasionally email her the name of a book he recently enjoyed, and she emailed him, they no longer met to discuss the materials. As she neared the end of her sophomore year, she would, on occasion, join her parents on evenings out with Clay and Lillian. She and Clay would sometimes talk about one novel or another, but in the company of others, the conversation was too exclusive and was quickly dropped in favor of more general topics. As Eva grew into a mature young woman, she seldom hesitated to speak her mind on any number of subjects, even several Clay would have been embarrassed to speak about in front of his own parents. It was only at this moment, standing at the back of *Antiques and Oddities*, that Clay realized that she had grown to be an attractive woman on top of it all.

"Oh, no wonder. You've got a first generation iMeme. I suppose you still put this thing on sleep?" She pushed on a button and the iMeme hummed to life, briefly flashing the light blue screen with the repeating letters. Eva flashed a puzzled expression at the holograph.

"Huh? What do you mean?" Clay protested. He had not noticed Eva's expression.

"Ever since they introduced the fourth generation, you can't turn the iMeme off. It runs 24/7. It was the introduction of the carbon nanotube fiber generators that allow them to charge off your body movements. You simply keep it on the Spot and as you move, the nanotubes charge the iMeme. But how did you miss the Sun-Times notification? I thought the latest operating system prevented you from turning the Notification Application off. That's why it runs in sleep mode—so you can still stay current with the news, even if you don't want to use the iMeme for any other features."

"I don't know. I've always been able to turn it off." Then Clay recalled his walk over. "That is, I did until just a little while ago. Earlier, it indicated that it was automatically downloading the latest firmware upgrade." He thought for a moment and then, more to himself then Eva. "Come to think of it, I shut it down on the way over, but I did hear about the free fuel." Clay shook his head. *Damn it!* he thought. *Download the latest upgrade, my ass. More like downloading the latest downgrade.* Now he would never be able to shut it down completely.

Clay recognized these things upset him more than they should, so he took a deep breath to avoid stoking the anger and cleared the thought from his mind. "So, are you out here looking for books? I guess I figured you'd grown too old and become much too technically sophisticated for such ancient pleasures."

"There are some ancient pleasures that can never be replaced." Her response did not come out as she intended and it was her turn to blush. She turned away. "I mean, there's nothing like the tactile feeling of a book. The musty smell of old paper, thumbing through the remaining pages left to be read. I think Paul Simon had a song about measuring life's losses with a book." Clay always enjoyed her musical taste and knowledge. His own kids didn't know Paul Simon from Les Paul. But Eva had always exposed herself to all musical genres and enjoyed listening to her father's old CDs. She and Clay would sometimes discuss the merits of classic rock and other artists of the late Twentieth Century whose music continued to be enjoyed even to this day. He had enjoyed introducing her to music she would otherwise have overlooked, such as T-Rex and Taj Mahal.

"Besides," Eva said, "there is so much material that just isn't available electronically. Even at the University there was so much material that I couldn't access. It's a real shame. I really don't know how they expect my generation or later ones to really learn." She paused a moment before continuing. "I originally wanted to get a liberal arts education, but schools weren't offering it. So between math and science, I chose science, as you know." Clay nodded his head. "You know, I really envy you and your generation. You were about the last folks to really have access to material that my professors only referenced. Thanks to you, I was familiar with at least some of the works. I think it really helped me in my classes."

"Surely you were able to, and I'm guessing, still can, borrow some material from some of your professors at UCLA, or at least your undergraduate professors at IIT?" It struck Clay that Eva might be a good source for obtaining books he was no longer able to find.

"Amazingly, no. A lot of professors won't talk about it. I think they're ashamed. But one of my IIT professors, Professor Helen Zelgman, she spoke to me about it once."

"What did she have to say about it?" Clay asked.

"She told me the university had basically ordered the faculty to gather all their books, even from their home libraries, to add to the University Electronic Collection," Eva said.

"And no one thought twice about this?" Clay was surprised.

"Well, I'm sure you know there was a voluntary government initiative to digitize all books and preserve them for posterity," she said.

Clay shook his head. "I thought it was just a money issue. I didn't realize that it was a government initiative."

Eva continued on. "IIT wanted to uphold its duty to advance the preservation of knowledge, so all books were collected from the faculty."

"What duty was it that IIT was trying to uphold?"

"Well," Eva continued. "It seems the government had explained that since most local libraries were seeing vast increases in the checkout of electronic books, and publishers were unwilling to spend the money to digitize books out of copyright protection, it became the duty of the government and universities to promote greater access to important works. The University agreed and asked faculty to cooperate. The University also told faculty that with the reduction of the liberal arts programs, there was going to be a reduction in office sizes and reminded them space could be an issue. Professors were told that once their collections were scanned, they would receive a free electronic copy, as well as the original hardcopy back if they requested. It all seemed quite innocent and most professors were happy to comply since it was going to increase accessibility of some very important works to a much greater audience."

Clay shook his head. "It always seems so innocent, doesn't it?"

"One professor, I think Professor Zelgman said his name was Birkenstein…" Eva paused a moment, trying to remember. "Anyway, this Birkenstein had been at IIT for ages, working in the Humanities Department. Apparently he started a protest against the collection of personal libraries. He had been a young boy when his family managed to escape to Czechoslovakia from Nazi Germany in the late 1930s. He started comparing the government initiative to the Nazi book burnings," Eva said.

*Good for him,* Clay thought.

Eva continued her story. "Many of the IIT professors thought he was reacting too strongly. They argued that this was not Nazi Germany, it was the United States of America and the books were not being collected to be burned, but to be preserved. Professor Birkenstein had little support but the IIT Administration agreed to put it to vote, mostly, Professor Zelgman believed, to appease Birkenstein and try to avoid some negative press he was generating. In the end, the faculty voted almost unanimously to submit to electronic preservation and everyone was required to contribute their personal libraries. But nothing outside of the math and science books has ever been made available for electronic distribution. The last I heard, the faculty was still being told the government is planning to digitize all the collected works, but given the continuing budget crunch from the Great Depression II, the government simply can't afford to digitize anything but the most important works, which apparently are math and science, since they make up the bulk of the higher education system."

"So just like that," Clay said, snapping his fingers, "it's all gone? No complaints or follow-up?"

"Professor Zelgman told me that she was deeply embarrassed about the whole thing," Eva responded. "Obviously she felt betrayed. But also naïve, since they had been warned by

Birkenstein. But, like so many others, she chose to ignore his warnings as the rantings of an old and senile professor." Eva paused, but Clay said nothing. "And now it seems most people don't care anymore," she added.

"I don't believe that for a second, Eva." Clay countered. "I care! And I'm sure plenty of professors still do, too."

"Sure," Eva said. "A few professors do, but when I was out at UCLA, rumor had it professors were advised to keep quiet. There were stories going around that professors who tried to press the issue and either get the books published electronically or have their original volumes returned suddenly found that their department had lost federal funding. I heard of one professor who ignored the warnings anyway. It seems that she suddenly lost her tenure and her job. So, for the most part, professors don't push the issue."

"I can't believe that!" Clay said. "Why don't more people know about this?"

"Who's going to tell? Not any professor hoping to keep his job. And for the most part, no one else knows, and certainly no one else can really prove anything," she responded, disappointed.

There was silence between them. Clay tried to lighten the mood. "I didn't know you were still into older books. Although Lill has managed to donate most of my books, I still have a few you may be interested in that maybe you haven't read. I'd be happy to loan them to you whenever you want. Maybe we can even start up the book club again." Eva gave a little laugh, remembering their meetings. "Next time you're in the area, feel free to stop by the house and take a look," Clay offered.

"Thanks a lot, Clay. That would be great!" Eva raised her arm briefly and wriggled her wrist, as if adjusting the many bracelets she wore. "Oh, snap! Listen to the time! I've gotta run. Hey, it was great seeing you. Tell Lillian and the kids I said hello. Bye." She pressed the book she was holding into Clay's hands and trotted off.

"Will do. Goodbye!" he called after her. And she was gone. He looked at the book. It was the biography of Steve Jobs. Clay had read the book many years ago. He stooped down to look at the several books remaining on the shelf. Two romance paperback novels and a thin hardcover volume. He pulled the thin hardcover book out. The covers and spine of the book were completely blank. He opened it to the title page. *The Road* by Cormac McCarthy. *Hot damn!* he thought. Lillian had tossed his copy out years ago. He took it over to the counter and purchased it.

# CHAPTER FOURTEEN

*News Flash: Saturday. 8:45 a.m. In the largest public works project since the building of the Interstate Highway System, the government has announced that work is nearly complete on the Fully Unified Tunnel Receipt and Extraction ('FUTURE') System. This series of tunnels, really underground pipes, will connect each and every home, apartment, office and building into one unified system which will allow the free-flow of molecules necessary to supply your Genesis with the molecules needed to replicate your desires, and the means to carry away unwanted waste during the deconstruction phase. This complex system of tunnels was created using trillions of nanobots and has been underway for almost a year. Unbeknownst to most everyone, this tunnel system already lies just outside your home, at this very moment. FUTURE will allow you to begin your future today.*

It arrived on a Saturday morning. It was approximately 10 a.m. when a fleet of trucks pulled into the neighborhood and parked at the end of each block. Each truck was identical, light blue with the diagonally printed text REPREPREPREPREPREP Clay had seen so often as of late. And each truck was stacked with light blue boxes with the same diagonally printed text. Clay read the boxes. *Prep, prep, prep, pre . . . pre, pre . . . rep, rep, rep. Replicator! The Genesis replicator,* it suddenly struck Clay. *Though I swear I've been seeing those letters for such a long time now.* Clay watched as two men stepped out of the truck and began to deliver, one-by-one, a single box to each household. Matthew and Elizabeth acted like a couple of six-year-olds in a toy store who were just told by their parents they could choose any item they wanted. Katie was relatively calm, but could not stop smiling. Even Lillian was more curious than Clay would have guessed.

They gathered around as the two men (*Technicians,* they had said when Clay answered the door) entered their home with the light blue box and prepared to open and unpack the Genesis. They were told that they could place the Genesis along any outside wall of the home. The older of the two technicians, identified on his badge as Paul, suggested placement in the kitchen. Paul and his fellow worker, Or, (the family had spent several days thereafter trying to figure out what Or was short for: Orville, Orin . . . Orion?) moved the box into the kitchen, cut the plastic strapping bands holding the box together and lifted the box up to reveal what appeared to be a large cube, exactly the same on each side, except the bottom, which had four small rubber feet attached. There were no other features whatsoever. The Genesis appeared to be a solid piece of black metal, with no seams or bolts or any other indication that it was ever anything than a single solid piece. It was one of the many advantages of building materials molecule by molecule. It would be repeated often in the news and on social media that any attempts to open the Genesis to determine how it operates would be fruitless. Not only would it be almost impossible to gain access to the interior—the Genesis being made of carbon-carbon bonds, similar in strength to diamonds—but any successful breach would cause the Genesis to disassemble itself into many millions of molecule components. It was also reported widely, in no uncertain terms, that anyone caught tampering or attempting to duplicate the technology would be subject to immediate arrest and prosecution.

While the family stared at the Genesis, Or stepped behind the machine and pulled a thin black hose out of his bag. One end had a green band and the opposite had a red band. He placed the green end of the hose along the backside of the Genesis and the hose and machine, as if by magic, melded together. He then placed the red end to the wall behind the Genesis, and just as magically, the hose and house fused together. Or then stepped outside and removed another identical hose from his bag. He held the red end next to the exterior of the house and moved it from side to side in the area where the Genesis stood inside the house. At a point directly behind where the hose had been connected in the house, the hose suddenly resisted Or's motions and fused to the side of the house. Finally, Or placed the green end on the ground within the confines of one of many small metallic rings that encircled the house. Clay leaned closer toward the window. He had never noticed those rings before and was going to ask Matthew about them when the green end of the hose began to move around the circle on its own accord, snake-like, and then appeared to plunge into the soil. The action caught the whole family off guard and the girls let out an amazed "Ooooh."

Paul laughed. "The hoses have been designed to seek out and automatically connect to the FUTURE System to ensure a constant source of molecular building blocks. It still amazes me too. Pretty cool, huh?" He was smiling proudly at them all, as if he were personally responsible for the hoses actions. Paul then peered though the window and Or flashed him a thumbs up sign. Clay gazed out the window again, but except for the metallic ring surrounding the newly attached hose, there was no evidence of any other rings surrounding the house.

By this time Or had returned inside, Paul had folded the box the Genesis came in into a neat square. He then activated the holographic keyboard on his iMeme and punched several buttons. It struck Clay then that he had seen the light blue box with the repeating letters each time he powered up his iMeme. He set that thought aside and continued to observe what was happening. After Paul entered information into his iMeme, the front of the Genesis simply disappeared and Paul placed the empty box into the machine. He pressed buttons on the holographic keyboard again and the front of the Genesis, just as instantly, reappeared.

"This is the Furstman family?" Paul asked, as he typed onto his iMeme.

Clay nodded. "And there are five of you living here, correct?" Again, Clay nodded, seemingly unable to speak. Paul entered more information into his iMeme and the front of the Genesis disappeared a second time, revealing several sheets of paper where the empty box had once stood.

"Welcome to the future," Paul said as he pulled the papers out and handed them to Clay. He flashed his proud smile again before turning and walking out the door, with Or silently behind.

They stood and stared at the sheets of paper. There were five sheets of paper, one with each of their names on it and a unique nineteen-digit number. One by one, their iMeme's began to give notice that a twerp was received and each began to speak.

*Welcome to the Future. Please enter the nineteen-digit number that was included with your Genesis.*

Clay typed the code from his sheet of paper onto the holographic keyboard of his iMeme.

*Thank you. Please state your full name. Speak in a normal tone.*

Clay did as he was told.

*Levi Clayton Furstman. Identification confirmed. Voice recognition activated.*

Lillian went next.

*Welcome to the Future. Please enter the nineteen-digit number that was included with your Genesis.*

Lillian typed in the code. She also stated her full name and received the same confirmations. This procedure was copied by each of their children, in order. Katie, Matthew and then Elizabeth. The Genesis hummed briefly, then stopped. All five received the same iMeme message.

*Your Genesis is now fully functional. You may purchase material applications from the Genesis-App Store. Once you have made your purchase, you may select from your Genesis-App Store menu or simply command Genesis to deliver your selection. The Genesis comes pre-programmed with standard safety and security features that allow only you and any immediate family members living with you to operate the Genesis. If you wish to add others to the usage list, you can list individuals and set preferences at the Genesis-App Store. Usage beyond immediate family members will incur additional charges as indicated in the individual application purchase agreements. Thank you and, once again, Welcome to the Future.*

Clay was still staring at the Genesis when he heard his children squeal with excitement. He looked up and saw his entire family searching the Genesis-App Store, eyes wide open, their tongues practically hanging out of their mouths. He had not seen his kids this excited since Christmas mornings when they were much younger. He grinned from ear to ear and joined them. "Who wants lobster dinner tonight?" Clay asked, smiling. The kids all screamed, but Lillian quieted them down.

"Seriously, shouldn't we make sure this damn thing works first? Let's start slow here." Lillian reviewed the information flashing on her iMeme holographic screen. "Jeez, there are already thousands of choices. Look, here's the BasicApp, Home Supplies. The cost is $25 per year. I'll choose it and let's see what happens." Lillian followed the directions from her iMeme. When she finished, all of their iMemes spoke at once.    *To access your Genesis menu, please choose the Genesis icon.*

Each of them selected the Genesis icon and saw the myriad of products now available. It included: Notebook Paper (lined), Blank Paper, Pencil, Pen, Bags, Plastic (sandwich, quart, gallon, 15 gal., 30 gal.), Bags, Paper (lunch, shopping) and approximately fifty other items. Lillian entered her selection first.

"I'll request some notebook paper."

The Genesis hummed briefly. Slowly the front panel faded into nothing and there, lying in the center of the Genesis was a ream of lined paper. Katie reached in and removed the sheets of paper. She passed the pages out and they each began to inspect the sheets as if it were the first time they had ever seen notebook paper.

*Please confirm your item has been removed,* Lillian's iMeme said.

"Done," Lillian responded. A series of three sharp beeps rang out and then the front of the Genesis gradually reappeared.

"That's amazing!" Matthew shouted. "I bet the nanobots inside assemble and disassemble the front of the Genesis. Kind of open and close it. How cool is that?!"

"I'll give them that. No one's going to figure this thing out too easily, if ever. Certainly most folks won't bother. Americans especially, since they're giving them to us for free anyway," Clay mused.

Lillian spoke again. "Look, every App has a 'dispose' function. It looks like when you are done with anything you made and don't need anymore, you can place it inside and dispose of it." She selected the DISPOSE function and the Genesis softly hummed and the front, once again, disappeared. She placed her coffee cup inside. Nothing happened.

Suddenly her iMeme beeped a warning.

"All clear," Lillian said. "I guess they want to make sure you don't have your hands in it before it starts up," she commented as the front resealed and, again, the Genesis hummed. They all stood there in silence. Nothing happened.

"Hmmm. I wonder if it got rid of the coffee?" Elizabeth asked.

Matthew quickly requested a pencil and almost immediately, the front unsealed and lying inside was a pencil. There was no sign of the coffee cup.

"Oh, damn! That was my favorite coffee cup," Lillian frowned, but just as quickly smiled. "Oh well. I guess it's time to go shopping," she said as she delved deeper into the Genesis-App Store.

By now, all three kids were frantically exploring their options as well, calling out applications they were interested in, and noting to their parents which ones they (as the *breadwinners* and *loving parents*) should purchase for the household.

Clay sat down as he also took stock of the Genesis-App Store offerings. It was going to be an expensive day, but he quickly compared the cost of various packages against the current cost of buying products and realized that he could easily earn only a fraction of his current salary and live like a king. *Unbelievable*, he thought. *Freakin' unbelievable!* as he purchased the Gourmet Dining application.

"Kids! Looks like we're eating lobster for dinner tonight!"

The change was almost as immediate as it was subtle. Not surprisingly, grocery stores such as Whole Foods and other natural food grocers remained almost completely unchanged. They continued to offer organic products and could now offer the added incentive of "Molecular Factory-Free" labels to their wares. Concerns over processed foods continued to be a topic of debate and some people felt that replicated foods were dangerous. Among other stores, however, things were somewhat changed. Rather than supplying the everyday needs of all consumers, stores now carried only those products which the individual manufacturers had decided to continue to produce in their own factories (although now it was done with industrial replicators rather than the old methods) and thus were not available through the Genesis-App Store. This included items from Coca-Cola and Frito-Lay to items which were not practical to replicate in the home, such as major appliances, automobiles and building materials. But because these manufacturers were able to replicate their products for free, retailers were able to sell these products at greatly reduced cost to the consumer. As a result, even selling goods at a mere fraction of their previous costs produced the same profit margins as before. Many companies found that profits were actually better than pre-Genesis days.

Several companies initially attempted to keep prices at their pre-Genesis levels, but ultimately they were forced to come down, or shut down, as the consumer rapidly recognized the Genesis gave them newfound power. The most impressive example was Coca-Cola. Coke, because its cola product outsold all other competitors combined by a margin of over two-to-one, believed that its customer base would remain loyal. It soon discovered otherwise. PepsiCo products and other non-Coca-Cola brands selling at twenty-five cents a twelve-pack quickly outpaced Coca-Cola's products still selling at two dollars and fifty cents a twelve-pack. By the end of the first month of sales, Coke was looking at a serious dilemma. Coke products were still selling; there were some people who simply would not drink alternatives, and given the greatly reduced cost of living, plenty of those people had the extra money to purchase their favorite drink. However, Coke's market-share dropped by more than 60%. Not only would Coke no longer be able to claim itself as the most popular cola product in the world, but a backlash developed against the company's pricing policy in what was considered pure greed. More importantly for Coke's CEO, profits at the company began to slip almost immediately as millions of consumers simply chose to drink other brands in protest. Faced with the prospect of massively reduced sales and further loss of market share, potentially bankrupting the company, Coke was forced to lower its prices to match those of PepsiCo to become competitive again. Most economists who studied the issue agreed that had Coke originally lowered its prices such that it was still twice as expensive as PepsiCo products, its customer base would likely have remained loyal. But its excessive greed turned so many consumers off, that they did not find consumers returning to purchase their products until they matched prices with PepsiCo. Furthermore, the economists found the public became keenly aware of their newfound power and rapidly joined forces to boycott manufacturers who attempted to exploit the system by charging more than what their competitors were charging for similar products. Thus, Coca-Cola and other manufacturers were thereafter unable to charge anything more than minor differences in prices from their competitors. Moreover, increased government regulation and enforcement of anti-trust and price-fixing statutes, supplemented by the fact that the Genesis allowed for the home-manufacture of generic substitutes of any product, prevented manufacturers from charging unreasonable prices for their products and services.

Because of the governmental involvement with the design and production of the Genesis, the U.S. Military was able to persuade Congress to pass strict legislation preventing the export of the Genesis or any molecular manufacturing technology. While much of the world raised serious objections to this move, most critics were forced to admit defeat in instituting change. Although the technology was reserved for Americans, and although it lowered the cost of living in the U.S. to nearly zero while raising the standard of living to levels never before experienced by the majority of Americans, the rest of the world reaped benefits, too. The price changes in America resonated around the world. Americans rapidly took over worldwide manufacturing of most products. Because the cost of manufacture and transportation was zero, American products were sold worldwide at prices significantly lower than previously available in foreign nations—even when such products had been manufactured locally. Even though U.S. manufactured products were priced significantly higher outside the United States, the new costs were simply so low that the mere fact someone lived on less than one dollar a day was no longer a life-sentence into poverty.

Charities were able to distribute humanitarian aid throughout the world and hunger became almost unheard of, except in those despotic nations whose leaders refused to accept, what one country called, "poisoned hand-outs from the Great Satan." Even in the poorest villages, there were movements to open schools and educate the populations. People who spent their lives struggling to gather enough food to eat were now able to acquire all their dietary needs. Clean water was readily available to all. This gave the impoverished of the world time to develop local talents that allowed them to contribute to society. The Luba Tribe of Central Africa, long used to struggling merely to survive, now produced artists of great acclaim, such as the poetry of Kalala Mulunda and the woodworking of Ndaye Kalonji, both of whom were in high demand by the newly rich in America.

# CHAPTER FIFTEEN

*News Brief: Saturday. 8:00 a.m. Police Superintendent McCormick announced today that the Chicago Police Genesis Task Force, in a joint operation with the FBI, have arrested six suspects allegedly tied to Red Star, the group that took responsibility for hacking the Tootsie Roll Candies Genesis-App that put the long-standing Chicago candy manufacturer out of business last year. Government sources fear that Red Star is attempting to distribute replicator technology across international borders, in violation of federal law. Red Star alleges that any such law is contrary to the laws of humanity and claims that until the U.S. government and industry stop the suppression of replicator technology from being shared around the globe and more attention is paid to the third-world poor, it will continue to cause financial harm to targeted industries. Given the sophistication of the process, however, law enforcement suspects that Red Star is funded by either Russia or China, both of whom seek to exploit Genesis technology and regain power on the world stage.*

Clay awoke to the sound of his alarm. He reached over and pressed the reset button. He had already snoozed twice and could not afford another nine minutes of restful bliss. Lillian was gone, out running or at the gym. Her alarm had sounded at its usual time of six-thirty and Clay had hit the snooze button three times for her. It was just before seven, when Lillian rolled out of bed and told him that he could turn her alarm off. It was now seven forty-eight and Clay needed to get moving if he was going to make it in time for a breakfast meeting at 9:00 a.m. with Miguel Diaz. Clay felt great. It had been almost a year since the Genesis first arrived and his life had remained relatively the same, and yet, remarkably changed.

Clay continued to enjoy music and sports and reading. He still loved to cook and prepared meals for his family many evenings, even if what he was preparing was more easily available in ready-to-serve form from the Genesis. Likewise, Genesis' ability to replicate innumerable dishes did not remove the charm of dining out and the restaurant industry continued to thrive. He still helped with laundry, did the dishes and fed the dog, and, on occasion, relaxed in front of the television.

But he no longer worried about money. And he no longer spoke with anyone stressed about paying bills or angry at the cost of rent, or food, or movie ticket prices. Like most Americans, he only worked two days a week. Because the cost of living was reduced so greatly, workers were able to drastically reduce their workload, reduce their income, and still live better than they could ever have imagined. Americans were also healthier. Access to virtually unlimited supplies of foods and medicines reduced almost all the health issues previously associated with poverty. This brought down healthcare costs and allowed physicians and medical personnel to tend to the needs of those whose diseases were not easily remedied with proper diet, nutrition, and medication.

Clay also started driving downtown when he needed to go, rather than taking the train. Driving was promoted as a method of re-supplying the atmosphere with $CO_2$ necessary to sustain the Genesis' need for carbon molecules—one of the reasons fuel and parking were offered for free by the government. But today he decided to take the train. Many people still did not own automobiles, or never bothered to get their licenses during the Great Depression II when many could not afford to buy cars or gasoline. Others were too old or too young to drive and the train provided easy transportation. Clay took the train this morning because he wanted to relax. After breakfast he and Miguel were going to head to the gym for what was becoming his usual workout—lifting, jump rope and then a stationary bike ride, or perhaps the elliptical if no bikes were available. All his newfound free time resulted in a certain level of boredom that, much to Lillian's surprise, Clay occupied with something he had rarely ever done in his life—exercise. Clay was now in the best shape of his life. But even so, Miguel was in better shape and Clay sometimes had difficulty in keeping up with his workout routines.

Clay found an open seat on the train and opened his copy of F. Scott Fitzgerald's *Tender is the Night*. It was the third time he'd read it in as many years, but it was a good novel and it was getting more and more difficult to find books to purchase. More than a few people stared at him. A young teenager, clearly in an attempt to impress the young girl sitting near him, moved closer to him.

"Hey sir. What's that you got there?" he snickered.

"Excuse me?" Clay asked as looked up.

"Is you a bit slow? Don't cha know that your iMeme gots books on it?" He looked back to see if he was amusing the girl. Apparently he was, and she watched, smiling.

"Oh, the book you mean? Yeah, I am well aware I can read on my iMeme. The problem is I can't read *this* on the iMeme." Clay answered, trying to avoid being drawn into the youth's poor attempt at humor.

"Course you can't read *that* on the iMeme! It ain't electronic!" Both he and the girl seemed more amused. The train began slowing as it pulled into the next station. "I got something you can read that ain't electronic. Wanna read it?" he said as he stepped back toward the train doors. The girl stood up and moved next to him. "Here ya go, mister!" he shouted as he raised his middle finger toward Clay. "Read this!" Both he and the girl stepped off the train, laughing hysterically. The doors shut and the train pulled away, leaving the boy and girl still laughing.

When Clay approached Miguel's table at the restaurant he was surprised to see Eva also there. Miguel stood up and held his hand out. "Clay, how are you? I hope you don't mind. I haven't seen Eva in awhile and since Jen and I are headed to Colorado in a couple days, it's the only time we could get together."

"Of course not. You know I always enjoy her company." Clay finished shaking Miguel's hand and turned to Eva. "Good to see you, Eva."

"Yeah, it's been awhile," she laughed.

Miguel gave them both a questioning glance, but brushed his curiosity aside. "Eva was just telling me that Rejuvenate is sending her out to California to work on an experimental project for species preservation. Real interesting stuff." He beamed in pride for his daughter.

"Oh, Dad. I'm not so sure Clay would find it so interesting. He isn't much of a technology buff. Besides, I'm going to have to run in a few minutes. I've got a few things I've got to finish before I head out west." She turned to Clay. "By the way, thank you! That Cheever story was spectacular!" Eva reached down beside her chair and lifted a backpack onto her lap.

"Yeah. *The Swimmer* is one of my favorites. What did you think of Bierce's *An Occurrence at Owl Creek Bridge*?"

"Good," she responded. "But not as good as Barth's piece, *Lost in the Funhouse*. What a story!"

"Did I miss something," Miguel interrupted.

"Sorry, Dad. Clay has been loaning me books again. Do you remember when I was young and you used to take me downtown with you so I could have my *appointments* with Clay? Our little book club?" Miguel nodded at Eva. "Well, I guess we've kind of started it up again." Miguel rolled his eyes, but Eva smiled. "Stop it, Dad! You know how much I wanted to major in the liberal arts in college. These books are impossible to find! I ran into Clay about a year or so ago. We were both in the same shop looking for books, and he offered to loan me some."

"The two of you and your books. I thought that was just phase, Eva." He laughed. "But, no, I'm sorry. I think it's great, Honey." He turned to Clay, eyes opened wide. "You still have books?"

"A few. I kind of collect them. At least until Lill tosses them out." Clay and Miguel laughed.

"I guess you don't keep them long then, do you?" Miguel laughed again.

"Well, here's the book," Eva said pulling the book out of her backpack. "When Dad said he'd be meeting you, I thought I'd better bring it along."

"Thanks. I'm not sure what you're reading now, but I found another box of books stashed in my attic a few weeks ago. It had my copy of Conrad's *The Heart of Darkness* and another great book, *The Comedians*, by Graham Greene. It's a great piece of work."

"Wow, that would be great! If I get that chance, I'll give you or Lill a call and stop by to pick them up, if you don't mind. It'd be nice to have something new for California. I'm not sure how long I'll be there." She raised her arm slightly and twisted her wrist, causing her bracelets to jingle faintly. Eva glanced down at her wrist and as she did so, Clay noticed that among the several bracelets she wore a watch. "Oh, listen to the time! I've gotta run." Eva stood up. Clay glanced at Miguel who had been absent-mindedly spinning a knife while he and Eva were discussing literature, but was now moving his chair back in order to stand. Clay wondered if Miguel had noticed the watch. *Odd,* Clay thought. *When was the last time he saw anyone who was not grey-haired and wrinkled wearing a watch?* He was not even sure any place still sold watches, not when the iMeme could so easily provide the time. He moved his eyes to Eva's spot and he saw that she was not wearing an iMeme. He stood up meaning to ask Eva about it when Miguel spoke.

"Wait a sec, I want to get a picture of you, Eva." Miguel activated the camera app on his iMeme and snapped a photo. "Now the two of you." Clay put his arm around Eva's shoulders and leaned in close to her. He caught a whiff of something. Exotic perhaps, a hint of leather. It reminded him of something from the past and he breathed in deep to try to recall the memory. Miguel finished snapping the photo and Eva pulled away.

"Goodbye, Clay, and thanks again." She kissed him on the cheek and walked around Clay to where her father was standing. "Goodbye, Dad." She gave her father a hug and kiss. "I love you. Thanks for coming out early to meet me. Let me know when you and Mom get back home."

"I will. I love you, too, Honey. Be safe. I'll talk to you later." Miguel said.

Eva walked away and Miguel sat back down. "You would not believe what she's heading to California to do."

"What?" Clay asked, his curiosity over Miguel's comment causing him to forget about the watch.

The waitress came up to the table. "Would you like your check, Sir?"

"That'd be great, thank you. And you can add his meal to the ticket, it'll all be together." Miguel turned to Clay. "I hope you don't mind. I ate with Eva. I didn't want her to eat alone. You, I don't care about." He smiled.

Clay turned to the waitress. "I'll have the Number 4. Over-easy, sausage and rye toast with extra butter. And if you could substitute fries for the hash browns, that'd be great."

"No problem, sir." She took the menu from Clay and walked away.

"Geez, Clay. I still don't get how you can eat like that before working out. But I've been taking it easy on you. Today, we have a real workout."

"What the hell are you talking about, Miguel? You kick my ass every time we work out."

"Ah ha! But today, we're hitting the racquetball courts. Today, you will experience a real ass-kicking!"

"Racquetball? Don't threaten me, Miguel. You're blind in one eye. I'll clean up the floor with you."

"Watch this." Miguel took a knife off the table and tossed it up. He then closed his right eye — his good eye.

Clay nearly dove under the table. "What are you, nuts!" he screamed.

But there was Miguel, holding the knife in his hand. He did it two more times before he set the knife back on the table.

"What the…?" Clay started.

Clay could not believe it. Miguel had not been able to see out of that eye for as long as they knew each other.

It had been a freak accident in Miguel's rookie year in the majors. The Cardinals were playing the Braves and Miguel had been in the on-deck circle, bending over to pick up a bat weight sleeve when his teammate, Clavin Rodriguez, took a swing at a 97 mph fastball. The ball came in on Rodriguez' hands and made contact with the handle of the bat, causing it to shatter. The broken barrel flew down the third base line, striking Miguel in the face, shattering Miguel's orbital bone and puncturing his eye. Miguel lost most of the vision in his left eye as a result.

"I had my eye fixed last week. You wouldn't believe it, Clay. It's a new, experimental procedure, but I managed to get myself in as a test subject. And you're not going to believe this."

"What's that?" Clay asked, still somewhat shocked.

"They did it with nanobots. The same idea that allows the Genesis to build things." Miguel smiled. "They use these things to rebuild body parts, molecule by molecule. My eye is perfect. It's been rebuilt from the bottom-up, so to speak. I still can't believe it."

"Jesus Christ. That's amazing!"

"It is. And that's why I'm so excited. Eva's group is going to try to use the Genesis to duplicate a California condor. An egg, anyway. If it works, they'll be able to duplicate endangered animals. Just think, nothing will be endangered ever again."

"Except maybe humans," Clay mumbled. "What if some idiot tries it on people? Let alone the serious complaints they're going to get from conservative organizations. Can you imagine what the Pope will say? Jesus, he'll be calling for the Apocalypse to come."

Clay found it interesting that, only now, were such experiments being performed. Certainly, the ability to build anything molecule by molecule had made such feats possible over a year ago when the Genesis was first developed. *Why now?* he wondered. *And why the hush-hush?* Of course, the paranoid in Clay told him it is a plan. Allow the public to become comfortable with the idea of molecular manufacturing before you really start to push the limits. Even now, a year later, the idea of molecular manufacturing is probably more than many people could really fathom if they sat down to think about it. Society was numbed with television and movies and reality programming and ever more amazing electronics. Clay was reminded of an article he had found on-line back in the first decade of the 21st Century: *Nanotechnology 1, Assyrian 0.* The author was despairing the quickly vanishing defenders of Culture, the liberal arts faculties, which even then were losing the battle with economics. Professors of philosophy and paleography and history who, due to cuts in British funding, lost their university jobs because their chosen fields of knowledge did not generate income and had no immediate, practical use. The casualties included elementary, secondary, and university liberal arts and humanistic studies which were discontinued because they were, as determined by policymakers, useless frills. Even as he read the article, the U.S. government was increasing spending on math and science. It was pushing ahead with its 'No Child Left Behind' agenda that emphasized STEM education (science, technology, engineering and mathematics), and most importantly, the ability to take tests, rather than to think critically. Yes, nanotechnology brought the U.S. back from the brink after the Great Recession turned into the Great Depression II, but it also, Clay realized, helped Americans continue to get fat and lazy. He mused to himself why any leader would suppress revolutions with guns and machinations of war (ala Assad) when one could suppress them with pleasure. Marx called religion the opiate of the people. But religion died in America with the two Great Wars. Sure, people still believed: fundamentalists spoke of fire and brimstone; true believers preached on college campuses, drank Jim Jones' kool-aid or gave up their worldly bodies so their souls could catch the spaceship following Comet Hale-Bopp, but as an opiate it no longer held sway in America.

No, something much stronger was needed to sedate the masses. So shortly after the Americans rode their courage and strength to the top and defeated Evil in the Second Great War of the 20th Century, consumerism set forth upon this continent, a new nation, conceived in conceit, and dedicated to the proposition that nothing is impossible, that leisure and progress are the destiny of man. And thus it became.

Gone were the days of strength and glory, of robustness and courage. Clay recalled listening to a story on NPR when he was in his teens about a distressed ship in Lake Superior during an ice storm. The men who patrolled the shores of Lake Superior and whose job it was to affect such rescues had a small cannon with which to fire a rope to a troubled ship in order to pull the crew to safety. On this particular day, however, the temperature was so cold and the waters so rough that before they could pull the ship to shore the rope became drenched and frozen solid, turning it into a veritable iron rail, incapable of serving its intended purpose. The rescue crew, having no alternative, jumped into a small dinghy, and using the frozen rope as a towline, ferried the crew in shifts back to shore. Before they were able to rescue the entire crew, however, the rescuers themselves were overcome by the elements and ordinary townspeople took their places in the dinghy to complete the rescue. By the time the last of the distressed crew was towed to the safety of shore, so much water had come onboard the dinghy that several of the volunteer townspeople literally had become frozen to their seats and ice picks were required to remove them. Clay always remembered that tale, wondering how many people would, even in the late 20th Century, jump, unpaid, into a small craft and set sail in an ice storm to rescue complete strangers, and continue doing so until they were frozen in place by wind and water. No, much better to sit back and watch Americans make fools of themselves as they seek to become idols, or to enter a virtual world of war and destruction and still be home for dinner.

"...probably about three months and... and... Clay, are you even listening to me?" Miguel stopped speaking and stared at Clay.

"Oh. I'm sorry, Miguel. I was just... I mean... I just can't believe your eye."

"God damned amazing, isn't it?" Miguel asked, smiling.

## CHAPTER SIXTEEN

*News Brief: Friday. 3:30 p.m. Elma Gartner became the oldest woman to swim from Cuba to Florida. She turned 83 years old last May and finished in 44 hours. She was ecstatic to have completed the adventure. "I never would have been able to do this even 50 years ago, but today, through hard work and the wonders of science, I have done it!" She broke down in sobs, surrounded by her friends and family, including seven grandchildren and 14 great-grandchildren.*

When Clay walked in his front door the house was silent. It had been a long day. All the days seemed long now, with so little work to do and too much free time. He went to the Genesis and retrieved a vodka on the rocks and sat down. At first, of course, it was like a long-needed vacation. The Genesis provided all the necessities of daily living and kept the need to actually earn money to a bare minimum, while the rest of the world continued in their lives, toiling away. It reminded Clay of their family trips to Mexico—waking up whenever he felt, lounging by the pool, sharing a cocktail with his wife, with no particular plans or places to go, yet folks all about him were working: bartenders, pool boys; cab drivers. It was the same now, except the workers were mostly the non-American populations of the world and the vacationers were the American citizens. But work gives one a sense of pleasure, of accomplishment and achievement. Meaning. He did not complain, though, at least not too loudly. He may have been the only one who was concerned—he certainly did not hear any objections from his wife or kids. Nor did any of his friends seem to mind that free time now made up the vast majority of their lives. Of course, many folks frequented one of the many virtual emporiums that seemed to pop up all over the place, or exercised their right to eat out and enjoy a show, but Clay never was much of a virtual reality fan or a movie-goer. He preferred to move about, or build things, do things with his hands. Getting dirty and sweaty and, at the end of the day, looking at something physical, something solid that did not exist earlier. Clay always believed that man needed to create things in order to feel alive. It was a primal need recognized by the earliest of humans, a need so basic it was attributed to God Himself in creating everything, including man. He wondered why the writers of the Bible even felt the need to have God create man. Certainly not to worship Him — man did a pretty piss poor job at that. And God could not have been lonely, for he had the company of all the hosts of heaven. No. Clay decided that when man endowed God with the credit for all creation, it was an acknowledgment of the commonality of such desire, an understanding that the need to create resonates among all thinking creatures. Create for six days, then rest.

Clay found he had too much leisure time and not enough necessity to build. The Genesis ensured that he would never have to fix anything again. He sipped his vodka and tried to think of something he could do to occupy his time, something he could build with his own hands. Something useful he could not simply request from the Genesis. He had tried to build a bookcase several months earlier. An admirable piece, but ultimately, of lesser quality than what was readily available at most any furniture store. Lillian had smiled at Clay and complimented his handiwork, but relegated the shelf to a corner of the basement where it would not be seen by anyone.

*Gone are the days when the ox fall down, he'd take up the yoke and plow the fields around...* Clay got up to turn on his old stereo. He put on the Grateful Dead's *What A Long, Strange Trip It's Been*. It had been a long time since he used his turntable. His father's really. A memento he retained throughout the years, even though his wife thought it was unsightly in the living room. He sat back and listened to the deep, rich sound of vinyl. The pops and hisses couldn't detract from that sound, so real, so rich, the depth that was simply lost in digital formats. The volume was up high enough that he didn't hear Lillian walk in. She had been at the gym working out. She was sweaty, but had that after-run glow. She looked sexy and Clay told her so.

"Yes, sexy and smelly. I'm going to jump in the shower. We're going to meet Miguel and Jennifer Diaz tonight at The Golden Steer. Eva is in town, too and she's going to join us."

Clay hadn't seen Eva since he and Miguel met for breakfast almost ten months ago. A lot had changed since then. Besides the lack of work and accomplishment, the government had begun a program to immunize citizens against disease and illness. While Miguel's eye surgery was quite amazing, the success of it (and many other similar procedures) resulted in FDA approval of PreVentall. The immunization was basically the injection of several millions of self-replicating nanobots that duplicated themselves and migrated into each and every cell of the human body. Once there, they took over control of the cell by manipulating all DNA-RNA replication to ensure that all cells remained healthy. Most diseases and illnesses, and even normal aging, were simply the result of improper DNA or RNA sequencing as cells replicate. Bad cells replicate bad cells while the number of good cells diminishes as minor replication errors multiply themselves and result in disease, illness, breakdown, and all the maladies of age. PreVentall, for adults, was able to process the genome of the host body by averaging the genetic code of approximately one trillion cells and determining the proper, healthy genome for the host body. Once the nanobots have a genetic map to work with, they manipulate all cells in the body to correctly match the healthy genome, resulting in perfect health. The changes included not only the cure of diseases, but also the reversal of the effects of aging and the monitoring of hormone, neurotransmitter, and biochemical levels to reduce abnormal behaviors. All immunized adults physically reverted to their prime. Over one hundred million people were already vaccinated — one hundred million people not only looking, but physically being, in their thirties. Grandmothers, great-grandfathers, middle-aged folks, all thirty again. Immunization of children with StayWell was similar, except the nanobots were programmed to avoid interference with the normal pubescent processes. FetalSafe was being tested to treat birth defects in utero. In as little as one generation, the entire United States would consist of people, physically speaking, thirty years old or younger. Clay's kids had all been vaccinated.

"And young," Clay whispered. "Yes, sexy and smelly... and young!" Clay jumped up and entered the bathroom where Lillian was in the shower. He pulled the curtain aside and stared. Lillian was standing under the showerhead rinsing the shampoo out of her hair. She pulled the curtain back and shouted, "What the hell are you doing!? It's freezing with the curtain open. Stop it!"

"Sorry, it's just that… that…"

The curtain drew open again and Lillian hopped out, dripping with water and shampoo. She stepped around Clay and gazed in the mirror. "Holy shit! Holy, god-damned shit!" She burst into laughter. "Can you fucking believe it?"

There Lillian stood. Thirty years old again. Firm breasts, firm buttocks, smooth skin. The small varicose vein on her left calf was gone. The thick calluses on her heels from years of running were gone. Her gray hairs were back to their original auburn again. "Jesus. I just had the injection this morning. I… I… I don't know what to say." She turned from side to side, admiring her youthful appearance. Clay stood, dumbfounded. He suddenly felt old. He looked at his hands, which showed signs of aging: calloused and dry-skinned. He looked down at his shirt. His belly was not large, but even his recent penchant for exercise did not prevent it from protruding slightly from his midsection and it would not have killed him to add sit-ups to his exercise routine. He looked back at Lillian. Clay had no interest in PreVentall. People aged — it is what nature intended. He used to rail against people who went in for plastic surgery or Botox or tried various cosmetic attempts to stay young. But this was different. Lillian did not only look young, she was physically thirty years old again! She looked great. *But me? Jesus! Why the hell is she going to want to hang out with me?* Clay thought. *Sure, she may love me. But how the hell am I going to keep up with a woman almost half my age?* He hadn't considered the consequences of avoiding PreVentall. *Ok, so I'll get old. But that means eventually I'll become sick or invalid while Lill and the kids remain eternally young. Can I march towards death knowing that my family will remain young and healthy for… for how long? Forever, perhaps. Can I do that to them? Can I simply grow old and die on Lill? Or alone if she chooses not to be burdened with my stubbornness, my refusal to be something other than what I am?* Clay struggled with his conscience. The thought of PreVentall inoculation struck him as an act of vanity. *But is this vanity? This is true youth, true health.* He stepped out of the bathroom. "Well, tonight anyway, it looks like I'll see what it's like to date a much younger woman," he said to himself. *God, I hope Lillian doesn't kill me before I get a chance to get PreVentall.* He smiled at the thought.

The restaurant was filled with youthful faces. Clay sat back and took a drink of his vodka. He felt oddly out of place. There he sat, amongst his wife and best friends, and yet, there was a strange disconnect. They were talking and laughing, the same people he'd known for thirty years, but they were young and vibrant. It was like a strange flashback, like running into yourself in another conversation in another age, yet it was real. He scanned the table. He'd forgotten how pretty Jennifer was when she was younger, and Miguel, having lost the extra weight he'd carried in his mid-section truly was a barrel-chested man. Lillian. Lillian looked great. And young. Perhaps, too young. He remembered having thought only a few weeks ago how beautifully she was aging, but sitting here now, he could barely remember what she looked like last week, this morning. Certainly she was beautiful, but Clay could not say why. *What was it that her maturity revealed and why can't I put my finger on it anymore?* he asked himself.

And then there was Eva. She was already in her prime, and presumably would remain so. Clay imagined that she must certainly have gotten her PreVentall, but it wouldn't show. Not at her age. Not like Lill and Miguel and Jennifer. No, she would simply remain as she was, forever young. It was an odd disconnect for Clay, sitting at a table of his closest friends, yet sitting among strangers. Clay was facing in Eva's direction, but was lost in thought. She was the only one who seemed normal in this fantasy become reality world.

"Earth to Clay. Come in, Clay," Eva said.

"Oh, sorry. I was just…"

"I know exactly what you mean," Eva said, looking over at the others.

Lill, Miguel, and Jennifer were in an animated conversation about some stunt Miguel had pulled. Clay had missed the beginning of the story and wasn't completely aware of what was going on in the tale, and it appeared to him that Eva had either heard the story before, or simply did not care.

Eva turned toward Clay. "It is so weird sitting here with Mom and Dad, and even Lillian, when they look like that. I mean, don't get me wrong, it's great! But… but how weird is it that they're all, like, thirty years old? I've seen plenty of folks out in California undergo the change, but it's not like seeing your own mom and dad suddenly young again. I don't know if I'm supposed to feel like their contemporary or like I'm six years old again."

Clay laughed. "Well, you look the same, anyway." He smiled as he finished his vodka.

"Yes. And so do you."

Clay looked down at himself. "Yes, I guess I do." He frowned. He was not old, but he was not thirty years old anymore either. Graying, wrinkles, backaches, fading vision. All the rewards of age. He looked around the room. He did not spy another ancient body in the restaurant. He slumped a little in his chair. "Christ," he whispered. He looked back at Eva. "Today, I am a man. Tomorrow, I will be a boy."

"Why do you say it like that?" she asked.

"I don't know. I certainly feel old sitting among all the newfound youth. But, somehow... I don't know. I think I may miss it. Don't get me wrong. I can't wait to hit the racquetball court with your dad and have the body of a thirty-year old. To wake up without any aches or pains. But... but, isn't this what life is about? Aren't we supposed to age? Get old?"

"Who told you that? Why are we supposed to get old? Why not just get older?" Eva asked. Laughter arose from the other side of the table as Miguel continued his story. Eva turned to look, but quickly turned back to Clay. "We will all still age. We'll all get older. But why not store all the knowledge and experience in a body that functions at its peak? We aren't our bodies... we're what's inside." Eva placed her hand on Clay's thigh and leaned in close. "Can't you imagine being thirty again, but with all your current knowledge?" Clay could imagine. She leaned back and removed her hand. "Of course, you do look nice with the slight graying around your temples, but hey, you can't have it all, can you?" She looked into Clay's eyes.

"I don't know." He turned toward the others. Miguel had finally finished his story and looked over at Clay and Eva. "So, I think Eva was just about to tell us about the endangered California Condor." Clay turned back toward Eva.

"Correction," she said. "The formerly endangered California Condor." She smiled as she leaned forward. "I'm really not supposed to be saying anything yet because we haven't had the research published, but it looks like it will be accepted to *Nature Nanotechnology* and should be coming out soon."

* * *

Leeds looked around. Above the rocky peaks and shrubbery, the skies over the San Rafael Wilderness were a deep blue, uninterrupted by cloud or bird. "So, Professor Ho, I was expecting to be greeted by a gaggle of condors."

"A scarcity of condors, Colonel," Ho responded.

A scowl crossed Leeds' face. "Yes, Professor. There is a scarcity of condors. That is my point."

"No, no, no, Colonel. It is not a gaggle of condors, it's called a scarcity of condors. A group of condors is a scarcity." Ho smiled at the Colonel, having considered the irony. "Geese come in gaggles," he added a bit sheepishly.

Leeds closed his eyes and turned his head downwards. He took a deep breath. "Well, that is amusing, isn't it?" He lifted his head skyward and smiled. "Nonetheless, am I to understand that all your time and my money have not been able to produce any California Condors?" Leeds asked.

"We are working on that, Colonel. Please, follow me." Leeds removed his eyes from the skies. The two men were standing among the brush and vegetation of the rocky ledges of the Sisquoc Condor Sanctuary, the heat and dry reminding Leeds of Iraq. The area was closed off to the public and except for the low roofed concrete block building which Ho was walking towards, the area was undisturbed by man. As Leeds moved to follow Ho, he noticed that the structure (at least that part visible to him) bore no features except for a large steel door bearing a radiation caution sign and flanked by a retina scanner. Leeds was aware that the facility did not contain any radioactive hazards. The sign was placed there in an attempt to deter anyone who might accidently stumble upon the facility.

Each man in turn placed his eyes to the retina scanner and, after confirming their identities, the protection system deactivated the lock with a loud metallic *click*. The two men stepped out of the hot, dry air of the San Rafael Wilderness into the dark entrance of the facility. The air inside was damp and cool. The smell of mold and ozone mixed with the sour smell of decomposing meat and vaguely, of body odor.

"As you are aware, Colonel, the fertilized eggs which we replicated never hatched. We tested them and found no reason that cell duplication should not have occurred, but the eggs remained exactly as they were at the moment they were replicated. We know it was not an issue with the primary egg, as that egg did fully develop and hatch. We tried the procedure with two more primary eggs, both of which also developed properly, but the replicated eggs themselves failed to develop."

Leeds nodded. While this was his first visit to the site, he had been in almost continuous communication with Ho.

Ho continued speaking. "We gave up on eggs several months ago and, upon your suggestion, Colonel." Here, Ho paused. The two men had reached another steel door marked with another radiation caution sign. *Another lie*, Leeds thought. Ho placed his face to the retina scanner beside this door and, once again, he was answered with the metallic click.

The two men stood on a steel platform overlooking a massive room filled with several large tables covered in computers, tablets and lab equipment. An expansive video monitor took up the majority of the far wall, overlooking a Genesis. Several researchers sat in chairs typing away at their workstations while several others were gathered around the Genesis.

"Mission control, huh Professor?"

"I'm sorry, Sir?"

"Never mind," Leeds answered, as he began his descent down the metal stairs.

"Ah, yes, Colonel. As I was saying, upon your suggestion we have been attempting to replicate a living Condor. So far, though, our results are not encouraging." Ho followed Leeds.

Scattered at the outskirts of the room were multiple cages. The doors were open on most and Leeds put his head near one to look inside. A large bird lay inside, apparently dead. He looked in several more cages and discovered an identical bird occupying each one.

"You've got a lot of dead birds here, Professor." At this comment, the small circle of researchers gathered near the Genesis stopped talking. The only woman of the group, an attractive girl in her late twenties, Leeds guessed, approached.

"Not dead. Non-living," Eva said.

"Pardon?" said Leeds.

"I'm sorry. But the birds aren't really dead... Sir." She glanced over towards Dr. Ho before turning back to Leeds. Although they had never met, Leeds was familiar with Dr. Diaz as a result of the many letters that Dr. Ho had placed in her personnel file. Leeds could immediately see why Dr. Ho felt threatened by the attractive and intelligent young lady.

"Dr. Diaz! If Colonel Leeds had wanted your opinion on the matter, I am sure he would have asked! I have warned you before about your attitude. If you wish to start cleaning cages, I can reassign you," Ho said, his face turning red with anger.

"Now, now, Professor. Let's let the young lady speak," Leeds said, trying to calm Ho down. He turned to Eva. "I'm sorry, Doctor. Please feel free to explain yourself." He gave Eva a reassuring smile.

"I apologize," Eva paused, her facial expression making the reason clear to Leeds.

"Lt. Colonel R. George Leeds," he said, holding out his hand. "A pleasure to meet you, Doctor Diaz." The two shook hands. Dr. Ho gave a brief snort and turned away, pretending to be interested in one of the birds lying in a cage.

"Thank you, Colonel." She released his hand. Leeds noticed Eva leaned in a little closer as she spoke, as if Dr. Ho's apparent displeasure formed a bond between them. She smiled briefly before she continued. "What I was saying was that these Condors aren't really dead. They're simply not alive."

Leeds gave her a confused look. "Say again?"

"I'm sorry. It's a bit of a nuance, but it's important. We have recently begun to," Eva started, but again she paused.

"It's alright, Dr. Diaz, I am well aware of the research taking place here. And I assure you, I possess the highest security clearance," Leeds responded, recognizing the reason for her pause.

Leeds caught a flash of disappointment sweep across Ho's face. Leeds suspected that Ho had hoped to castigate Eva for her indiscretion in speaking so freely and Leeds took silent pleasure in having preventing him, at least temporarily. Leeds knew that Ho would likely add yet another letter to Eva's file.

Eva seemed to relax a little as she began to explain. "We're attempting to replicate the Condor, to be able to repopulate the species in order to preserve them. We have a live, mated pair we have been using as templates for the replicons." Leeds raised his eyebrows and, once again, Eva paused. "I'm sorry, Colonel. The birds we're trying to replicate with Genesis. We call them replicons."

"I see. Thank you. Go on," Leeds said.

"We have been attempting to replicate the condor but, so far, all the replicons have been non-living. Unlike a dead condor, these replicons have every aspect of life: intact cellular structure, cohesion, balanced ribosome and hormone levels. It's like they're in a state of suspended animation, as if we captured a moment of the condor's life and, in replicating it, can only reproduce that exact moment. No past and no future, just that single point in time. So while the replicons are not alive, they cannot be considered dead. No decomposition has started. The cells themselves show no signs of oxygen deprivation or any other indicators that the organelles are not fully functional. It's like the moment between breaths—no longer inhaling and not yet exhaling. So these replicons, at least when the first emerge from the Genesis, are not dead. They are simply non-living. Much like when you replicate a lobster. If you've ever cooked the replicated ones at home, you are aware that they do curl up when they're dropped into the pot. It's just a stimulus response by the central nervous system. The creature is dead, but so recently dead, that the stimuli triggers still react."

"Fascinating," Leeds responded. "So what do you plan to do about that?"

Eva laughed. "That, Colonel, is a great question."

Eva spent a good deal of the day discussing the science with Leeds. She found him to be pleasant, but was somewhat distracted by the fact that Leeds and DARPA were interested in saving the California Condor in the first place. It was after dinner and Eva was sitting on her bed when she heard a knock on her door.

"It's open," she called.

Another young scientist, Ryan Crosby stepped inside. "You doing okay?" he asked.

"What a week, huh? First we start trying to replicate a living animal and then the Colonel shows up," Eva said.

"Yeah. When I was brought on board here, they made it damn clear that we would not be attempting, or even thinking about, replicating living organisms. I was made to understand that it was taboo." Ryan said.

"Can you imagine what would happen if we replicated our pets... or ourselves? The implications are incredible," Eva said.

"I don't know. I think it'd be nice to have the replicon me working here and the real me hanging out on the beach."

"I'm being serious, Ryan."

"So am I. I mean, think about it. Our replicons can be hard at work and the two of us could be doing something else." He put his arm around Eva.

She shoved it off. "Stop it Ryan. I've already told you you're not my type."

He sat down on the chair beside her desk, smiling. "There are only two types of women in this world. Those who want to date me. And those who just don't know it yet." He smiled at her. "It's okay. You've got time to figure it out." His arm had been resting on several books sitting on Eva's desk. He lifted his arm and removed the top volume. "*The Comedians* by Grahame Greene," he read aloud. "So what is this? Some kind of comedy?"

"I've just started it actually. It takes place in Haiti while Baby Doc was still in power there," she explained.

"Baby Doc? Who's that? Was he the comedian?" Ryan asked.

Eva rolled her eyes and tried to grab the book from his grasp, but he held tight.

"What's the matter? A guy can't look at a book?" Ryan asked.

"That's your problem, Ryan. You just want to look. Why don't you try reading some time? You might learn something," Eva said sitting back down on the bed.

"Why the hell do you read these things anyway? They won't help you get anywhere or figure anything out." He tossed the book to her and she set it beside herself on the bed.

"Actually, you can learn a lot from great literature." It was Ryan's turn to roll his eyes. "Oh, never mind," she continued. "You wouldn't understand."

She decided to change tact. "The whole thing with these replicons freaks me out. It reminds me of Stephen King's *Pet Cemetery*," Eva responded. "I suppose you never heard of that book, huh?"

"Nope," he said. "Remember? I don't read," he said condescendingly.

"Yeah, I figured you wouldn't know of it," she trailed off. She sat in silence for a moment. "Does it bother you, Ryan, that we're even attempting this on the condor?"

Ryan thought for a moment. "Not really. Isn't it why we're both here? It's the whole reason I applied for the position. Why wouldn't we do whatever we can?"

"Yeah. Why wouldn't we?" she sighed.

The front of the Genesis dissolved revealing the body of the replicon condor lying on its breast, lifeless. Yet another failure. Eva let out a sigh. *What was it that prevented life in the replicons?* she wondered. The lab was unusually hot and dry. She reached for her tablet computer and was shocked by static electricity. *Odd,* she thought. *I wonder if something's wrong with the climate system.* She adjusted some equations and punched in the code for the Genesis to try again. As the Genesis hummed to life she heard a deep roll of thunder rumble across the sky. The front of the Genesis dissolved once again. She peered inside and saw the body of a condor lying motionless. *Another failure.* Eva reached in to pull it out and felt the sharp prick of a static spark jump from her finger to the beak of the condor. Eva jerked her hand back in surprise. She stepped back towards the Genesis. *Must have been a bigger shock than I imagined* she thought, seeing the replicon no longer on its breast, but now lying on its side. As she reached back into the Genesis to pull out the carcass another peal of thunder rumbled overhead. The lights dimmed and Eva glanced upward. She had been expecting to feel the lifeless body of the replicon, but instead felt a sharp pain. "Ouch!" she screamed as she jumped back. *What the?* She put her finger to her mouth and tasted the saltiness of her own blood. As she did so, the condor poked its head out of the Genesis and focused its yellow eyes upon Eva and then around the room. It flapped its great wings and took flight, circling around the room. Eva was amazed at the agility of the great bird to fly within the confines of the lab. Another roll of thunder boomed overhead and the lights went out. The room became completely silent as the equipment instantly shut down. Eva looked around in the dark. *Where are the emergency lights?* She could not see anything. Suddenly she spotted a yellowish glow moving overhead. She quickly realized it was emanating from the eyes of the circling replicon. Eva tried to feel her way to the exit when the great bird swooped down and tore flesh from the nape of her neck. She fell forward and hit her head on one of the many cages, as the replicon flew just overhead. She felt the warmth of blood dripping down her back. She screamed out.

Eva opened her eyes and blinked. The room was dark except for a faint glow of light from beneath the door and the occasional flash of lightning that reflected through the steel ventilation shaft in her room. The faint smell of rain wafted in from outside and she heard the drip of rain landing somewhere in the ventilation shaft, interrupted only by the sound of thunder. Her breathing began to steady after the shock of her dream. It had felt so real. She closed her eyes and her thoughts returned to her dream: the static shock, the yellow eyes of the replicon, the blood dripping down her back. She opened her eyes and sat up in bed. *The static shock! Maybe it just needs to be shocked!*

Eva quickly got dressed and headed to the lab. It would be empty. The scientists rarely worked late but they were free to access the lab at any hour. *In case,* they were told, *anyone wanted to put in the extra effort to help complete their project.* She grabbed a tablet and started modifying the program sequence for replicating the condor. She searched the database for any apps relating to electricity. She wasn't even sure it was possible to replicate an electric charge. *Why not?* Eva thought. *The system should be able to duplicate the charged state of the electrons and create at least the potential for electricity. All that is needed is to capture something in an excited state.* Her search of the replicator database proved fruitless. "Shit," she sighed. "What can I do to replicate a spark?"

Eva was startled by the voice of Leeds. "That would depend upon what kind of spark you are seeking," he said, stepping out from behind a stack of cages piled on a table.

"Oh, you scared me! I thought I was alone."

"I'm sorry. I was just nosing around." He looked into one of the cages and then turned back to Eva. "So, what kind of spark are you seeking?"

"Any spark, really. I'm trying to capture the potential differential of the electrons. I was thinking that if we could replicate that and then direct it to the heart of the condor, maybe it would act like a defibrillator and sort of shock the birds to life." Eva was speaking with excitement in her voice and she noticed that Leeds' excitement seemed to be growing, too.

"Why not just defib them after you replicate them?" Leeds asked.

"Nice idea, but I think we need to defib them right at the moment of replication," she said.

"Hmmm. What can I do to help?" Leeds offered.

"What can we use to generate a spark?" Eva asked. "Something we can capture in the Genesis so that it can be replicated."

"Spark plug," Leeds mused. "Why not just use a battery and a spark plug?"

Eva smiled at him. "Do you think that would work? I was looking to isolate the spark and program it into the cardio-sequencing unit." Her fingers started typing furiously at the keyboard, while Leeds looked on.

"I used to work on cars as a hobby. Have you ever worked on an ignition system?" he asked.

"I'm afraid that I'm a novice when it comes to auto mechanics."

"It's pretty simple, really," Leeds continued. "The ignition system takes the low voltage, high amp battery power and turns it into a high voltage, low amp system. This is done through the coil, which is fed power to ramp up the voltage. The coil is powered up and intermittently stopped, causing it to release the built up volts, resulting in a spark jumping across the plug gap. Using the proper coil, you can generate whatever voltage you want."

Eva laughed.

"What's so funny?" he asked.

"Sounds like a defibrillator. I guess I'm not such a novice after all." She smiled at him. "Let's give it a try," Eva said.

Leeds, who had been standing beside Eva, nudged her away from the keyboard. "May I?" he asked. She assented and moved aside. He ran his fingers over the keyboard. "How many volts do you need to defib the bird?"

"Good question," she replied. She sat down beside Leeds and worked on a tablet. "Hmmm. How about 50 volts?"

Leeds had the Genesis produce an ignition system, which he removed and configured so that it would produce a spark at a specific interval. "This will give you a 3 millisecond 50 volt spark every 1.5 seconds." He placed it back into the Genesis. The Genesis in the lab not only disposed of objects, but was also capable of storing the disassembly information so that an app could be made to replicate whatever item was placed inside.

After several attempts they were able to capture the disassembly of a spark arcing across the gap. Eva isolated the data and programmed it into the condor replication app.

"Okay. Let's give this a try," Eva said.

The front of the Genesis dissolved. Eva stepped over to the Genesis and looked inside briefly before pulling out the condor. She moved it over to a nearby table and placed it under several different pieces of equipment while Leeds watched in silence.

"Dead," she said, excitedly.

"Dead?" he asked.

"Yes, dead. Not un-living. Dead." She turned to Leeds. "Maybe we're using too many volts, but this bird is different than the others. It's dead. The hormone and ribosome levels are off, like it had been alive and is now dead. I think we're on to something!"

The two continued working together and as morning came around, they were joined by several other researchers. By the time Dr. Ho entered the lab, they were all working on tweaking the voltage to successfully replicate the condor.

"Col. Leeds. Good morning," he said, before turning to the others and frowning. "Have my staff been treating you unkindly?"

Leeds looked around and then at himself. "Oh," he smiled. "No, everything is fine, Professor. I had trouble sleeping last night and I came to the lab to have a look. It seems that Dr. Diaz did too. She came in last night and we've been working on replicating the condor ever since. I guess I'm a little unkempt." He smiled at Ho, who kept his frown.

"And have we made any progress, Dr. Diaz?" Ho asked.

"Yes and no. It struck me last night that if we could defibrillate the birds simultaneously with the replication they might live. We started with 50-volt shocks and the bird presented with evidence of death, rather than non-life. We've adjusted the timing and the voltage and at 38.2 volts at 2.7 seconds into the replication we have managed to create a bird with sustained heartbeats for 3 seconds, but it never lasts beyond that."

Ho looked over the data on a tablet. "You must try adjusting by micro-volts not milli-volts. Keep working on this." He turned to Leeds. "Colonel. Why don't you join me for breakfast. We can discuss the project while my staff tries to find out where they have gone wrong."

"Thank you, Professor. I think I'll freshen up first." He turned to Eva. "I look forward to hearing of any progress, Doctor."

"So, it's back to the proverbial drawing board, is that it?" Leeds asked, speaking to Eva who was seated to his right. It was one of the rare occasions that the entire project staff sat down to eat dinner together. The staff would generally eat together when work did not prevent it. Ho, however, ate in the solitary confinement of his office. The cafeteria had one large bench table and chairs had been placed at the ends of the table for Ho and Leeds. Ho would never consent to sit beside his staff. While Leeds would likely not have objected, the staff felt that his rank and position in the project entitled him to a seat of honor at the other head of the table.

"Well, Colonel," Ho shouted from the far end of the table. Leeds did not take his gaze from Eva and Ho stopped speaking. While his notion of etiquette did not frown upon shouting at the dinner table, he was taken aback at the idea of shouting at, rather than to, Leeds. He cleared his throat but failed at getting Leeds' attention.

Eva looked over briefly to Ho and could see the anger beginning to flush his face. *Nothing I can do about it*, she thought. "We did manage to elicit sustained heartbeats in several replicons, but cellular activity was limited to the cardio system," she responded to Leeds.

"So you were able to shock the heart into life, but nothing else?" Leeds asked, looking around.

"It's not clear what is preventing spontaneous reaction," the man seated to Leeds' left spoke. Michael Henderson was the senior staff researcher. He had graduated from Berkley with a degree in nano-engineering. Tall and broad-shouldered, he had been popular in school, but he, like Ryan, was unable to garner the attention of Eva. Normally, he would have deferred response to Ho, but he was emboldened by the actions of Eva. "We are going to attempt to add a small electrical shock to the brain stem in an effort to kick start activity."

"It's a shame you can't just shock the whole bird. Kind of zap life into it," Leeds mused. A couple of the staff laughed.

Ho saw an opportunity to enter the conversation. "If only it were that easy, Colonel. The complexities of life are beyond even our current knowledge. While my staff represents some of the best talent in the country, I have come to the conclusion this is another dead-end road. I could be wrong." At this Ho gave a slight chuckle. "And I will not interrupt their current experiment, but I believe that what we need to do is isolate the various systems and replicate each in turn to determine what part of the whole is preventing success. No disrespect, Colonel, but the problem is a scientific one and the solution to this issue will be solved by science."

"No disrespect taken," Leeds said a little coldly. "I am not a scientist and was merely making conversation. Had zapping the whole bird had even a chance of success, I'm certain your staff would have attempted it by now."

One young scientist, Kanshay Washington, who had been absent from the conversation came into the room pushing a cart loaded with food. "Sur la table," he said, pronouncing the word table as one would in English. Several other scientists stood to help move the platters on to the table. "Colonel," Kanshay said, holding a platter of stone crab claws before Leeds.

Leeds helped himself to a healthy portion of crab, saving room on his plate for the prime rib he saw making it's way around from the other end of the table. As everyone piled food on their plates, Eva's plate remained empty, her thoughts elsewhere.

"Dr. Diaz, are you going to be joining us in dinner this evening?" Leeds asked.

"Oh, huh?" she responded, breaking her train of thought. "Oh, yes. I'm sorry," she apologized to Leeds and the others. "Let's see, what do we have tonight?" she asked herself, eyeing the various platters on the table.

A low murmur arose as everyone began eating and talking. "I apologize if you found my comment to be condescending. It was meant to be humorous," Leeds said, leaning closer to Eva so she could hear. "Your defibrillation idea seemed to be spot on. And it worked for the heart. I don't mean to make light of your work."

Eva smiled at Leeds. "I didn't take it as an insult, Colonel. Actually, I agree. I think the whole replicon needs to be shocked to life. Not just the heart, but every system, every organ, every cell." Eva's expression suddenly went blank and she blinked several times. Eva popped up from the bench she was sitting on as she shouted, "That's it! Why didn't I think of it before!" She looked at Leeds again. "You're a genius, Colonel! Shock every cell to life." Everyone at the table stopped what they were doing and stared at Eva, who laughed to herself.

Ho stood up from his chair and shouted to Eva. "Dr. Diaz, what are you babbling about now?"

"The Colonel is right, Professor. We can't just shock the cardiovascular system to bring the replicon to life. We've got to shock everything. We're not dealing with cells in the process of dying, but cells in the process of living. The shock worked on the heart, but Colonel Leeds is right, we need to get everything going all at once."

"What are you proposing, Eva?" Henderson asked. "We crank the current up throughout the whole replicon?"

"Forget the defibrillation," Eva said. "It's too clumsy. And we don't need more current, we need less current over more area. What if we adjust the potassium and sodium levels in every cell? Skew them so that at the moment of replication their electric potential is great enough that every cell will spark, kind of defibrillate every cell simultaneously?"

"That's fucking genius!" Ryan interrupted. He turned sheepishly to Leeds. "Sorry Colonel."

Leeds stood up. "Let's try it."

Everyone stood, several grabbing their plates, and they rushed towards the lab. Only Ho remained. For the first time he did not feel in control.

\* \* \*

"So you figured out how to replicate living organisms?" Clay asked, surprised.

Miguel's face went from the concerned citizen to the beaming parent. "Nice job, honey."

"I don't know," Eva said, clearly troubled. "I keep thinking I should never have done it. Maybe no one else would have thought of it, but I got so caught up in the challenge, I guess. God only knows what DARPA wants to do with the knowledge. I'm damn sure, though, it's got nothing to do with endangered species. There is rumor that the government has been considering the development of a teleportation device, like in the *Star Trek* movies, but one of the big questions was whether the disassembly itself would kill the individual. Our process will allow them to move forward on the teleportation device, and it raises some pretty big questions. If you can take a person, disassemble them molecule by molecule and reassemble them someplace else—and stepping away from the question of whether a human replicon would have a soul—then you can not only reassemble them someplace else, but you can reassemble them in multiple places at once. It would be cloning at a bizarre level."

"You can say that again," Clay said. "Can you imagine what war would look like if you could replicate a person? I mean, imagine. Not only would you be able to create a clone army, but you take the soldiers you have, molecularly map them and then, in the event they're killed, you simply replicate them. There would be no such thing as death or injury; the army would become invincible." Clay thought for a moment more and added, "Can you imagine the psychological warfare that could take place? The enemy army finds that they keep killing the same person over, and over, and over again. Really, it's too much."

John seemed less concerned about the ethical ramifications and simply beamed at his daughter's accomplishments. He stood up and raised his glass. "To Eva. May she find continued success in her career." The others joined their glasses to John's and joined in. "Cheers!"

"Yes. Cheers Dr. Diaz." Everyone turned to the source of the strange voice. The smile faded quickly from Eva's face and her cheeks began to flush slightly as she averted her eyes from the tall, thin, balding man standing beside the table, his glass still raised. "I do apologize. It's just that I was sitting across the room and I happened to spot Dr. Diaz sitting here and I could not resist coming over to say hello." At this, he nodded his head slightly to Eva. He looked around the table and continued. "Forgive me, I am coming into this conversation a little blind, but I believe you were just congratulating Dr. Diaz, and I cannot help but join you in your well-wishes." He took a drink from his glass.

At this, Eva rose from her seat. "Forgive me everyone. This is Colonel Leeds. He's the... the..." Eva struggled to complete her sentence, afraid to say the wrong thing.

"One of the benefactors of the California Condor Project." He smiled at Eva.

"Yes, one of the benefactors." She turned back toward Col. Leeds. "Colonel Leeds, this is my father and mother, Miguel and Jennifer." Miguel rose from his seat and shook Col. Leeds' hand.

Jennifer moved to stand, but Colonel Leeds placed his hand gently on her shoulder. "Please ma'am." He bowed as he reached for her hand and gave it a gentle kiss. Jennifer giggled slightly and flushed.

"And these are close family friends, Clay and Lillian Furstman," Eva continued. Lillian merely held out her hand to let the Colonel kiss it while Clay rose from his chair. It struck Clay that he had met the Colonel on another occasion. His face was vaguely familiar, but Clay could not place the connection. Clay held out his hand and as the Colonel grasped it in his own, Clay caught the hint of dissatisfaction in his demeanor.

"Ahh yes, an *old* family friend. My pleasure, Mr. Furstman." Col. Leeds once again bowed his head slightly.

The handshake was a little too firm and Clay noticed that Colonel Leeds' eyes glanced quickly down to Clay's empty Spot before returning to meet Clay's gaze, his eyes seemingly turning a colder shade of blue. Clay had never felt odd about not wearing his iMeme but under the Colonel's gaze he suddenly felt naked, as if he had exposed some weakness in his own character. He managed a smile and replied, "The pleasure is all mine, sir."

The Colonel released Clay's hand and turned back to Eva's parents. "Your daughter is quite an amazing scientist." Both Miguel and Jennifer beamed with pride. "Of course, I wish I could tell you what she has been up to, and how important her work is to the project. But it seems her little group likes to keep secrets of exactly what it is they are doing and I'm afraid that my knowledge of the whole affair is, shall be say, *limited* in scope. But I have been assured by other members of the group that without the brilliant contributions of your daughter, much of the money I have been able to procure for the project would have been for naught. I, as I am sure you too, have made attempts to learn more information, but it seems that the scientific group has adopted the idea that loose lips sink ships, isn't that right, Professor Diaz?" He gave Eva a cold smile. Once again, Eva diverted her eyes from the Colonel's gaze, but Leeds had already turned his head quickly back toward her parents. Clay noticed that Eva's cheeks flushed slightly.

"Please, Colonel, have a seat. We would love you to join us," Miguel offered as he stood up, looking for the waitress so he could ask for another chair.

"Yes, please do," Jennifer pleaded.

"I'd be honored, truly. But I'm afraid I must be leaving. I have an appointment with a dear friend later and I simply wanted to say a quick hello to your daughter. She's quite an individual. And I can tell the two of you must have had a great influence on her. You should both be very proud." He turned toward Eva once again. "Eva," and he bowed his head slightly. He turned and gave the table a small nod of his head as well and left.

"Wow, a colonel, huh?" Miguel smiled at the others. "He seems like an important person. I'm glad he's noticed your work."

"And such a gentleman, too," Jennifer added. "He leaves quite an impression." Lillian nodded in agreement.

"Yes, quite an impression," Clay mumbled to Eva.

She gave Clay a quick look of reproach. "We don't work that closely together. Mostly, it's just the scientists." She looked around but did not see any sign of Colonel Leeds. "I honestly can't believe he even recognized me. It's flattering, but really, I'm sure he was just being nice."

The others were quite taken by Colonel Leeds. While they continued to analyze whether it was simply good manners, or whether Colonel Leeds really admired Eva's work, Clay noticed that Eva was wearing a forced smile. Her eyes hinted at an apprehension that lay just below the surface. Clay felt an emptiness rising in his stomach, the feeling he got when uncertainty took over and his conscience triggered a warning on some heretofore unrealized, but nonetheless impending, disaster. Perhaps it was because they had been speaking of Eva's work when Colonel Leeds approached. *Had Eva sunk any ships?* Clay wondered. But that was not fully it. He showed no signs of anger or discontent with Eva, even if he did seem to make point to mention the secrecy of their work. No, it was the look he received from Colonel Leeds. The silent accusation that his failure to be inoculated was a shortcoming, a sin for which no penance could be had, no salvation could be obtained.

Clay motioned and the waitress approached the table. "Anybody else need a refill?" he asked. Eva was the only one that nodded. "Two of the same, please."

"I'll be back with those shortly," the waitress said and turned to walk away.

Eva stopped her. "Excuse me, can you make mine a double?"

# CHAPTER SEVENTEEN

*Breaking News: Saturday. 10:00 a.m. The President has announced that travel in and out of the country is hereby immediately suspended. "It is the duty of Americans to protect the Homeland, to thwart those intent on destroying the American way of life, and to reach down into our Patriotic selves and stand up to evil. Today, before us, stands the new Greatness of America, the final configuration of the American Dream, our chance to dominate and shine. We shall not be defeated. Continued efforts by enemy states to steal the secrets of molecular manufacturing has resulted in the need to take immediate steps to stop any and all attempts at espionage." While the government has developed the means to prevent the transportation of restricted technology, it is expected to take several days to put into place. The total ban on travel is expected to last for several days. Thereafter, limited travel shall be allowed only when necessary and only if sanctioned by federal security officers. Travelers will be expected to submit full agendas and comply with a series of security procedures developed by the NSA.*

Even the next day, Clay could not shake the feeling of unease from Colonel Leeds's silent accusations. Lillian tried to assure him that he was just being paranoid, but the meeting had left a bitter taste in Clay's mouth. Certainly, Clay would have remembered Colonel Leeds from some previous introduction, and yet he knew that he had seen the Colonel before. He sat at his desk and searched the Cloud for COLONEL LEEDS and came up with over two million hits. He placed his search term in quotes. The results narrowed to a little over four hundred thousand. He clicked on IMAGES and scrolled down the screen. His eyes were immediately drawn to a picture showing Colonel Leeds sitting alongside the Chairman of the

Joint Chiefs of Staff, Gen. Fallsworth, and another soldier. The picture was from a Sun-Times article and Clay recalled having seen the photo, recalled noticing the cold eyes of Colonel Leeds back then. There were also numerous photos from his appearance on CNN's Weekend Early Start, when the Genesis was first announced. He shook his head in disgust. The man had been on national television to announce the introduction of Genesis and Clay could not place the face. *Of course he looked familiar!* His involvement in the California Condor Project made sense to Clay. It also worried him.

He read the transcript from the CNN interview and found what he was looking for. He searched R. GEORGE LEEDS and started to scroll though the results. They all seemed to reference either the Genesis story or the appointment of General Fallsworth, but his eye caught a site that appeared to relate to neither. It was a not-for-profit website that published the full Taguba Report, the official inquiry into the Abu Ghraib prisoner abuse. Clay downloaded the document and searched for the Colonel's name. It came up only two times: the first was in the section labeled Other Findings/Observations:

4. (U) The individual Soldiers and Sailors that we observed and believe should be favorably noted include:

* * *

d. (U) 2LT R. George Leeds, 372nd MP Company, discovered evidence of abuse and turned it over to military law enforcement.

The second instance was under a list of witnesses and suspects and simply read: 'p. (U) 2LT R. George Leeds, 372 MP Company.' Clay continued his search and managed to find a site with summaries of the witness interviews.

The Taguba Report indicated that Lt. Leeds had been off base the morning of December 13, 2003 and, upon return, he discovered apparatus intended to restrain a detainee in an abnormal and unnatural fashion, along with evidence of human excrement and blood in an area of the prison under the responsibility of Sgt. Ireland Bingham. Sgt. Bingham was not available for questioning as a result of mortal injuries she suffered in the early morning hours of December 14, 2003 attempting to disarm an Iraqi citizen in possession of an IED. These findings were reported by Lt. Leeds to his superiors. Clay was unable to find any more information on Colonel Leeds.

It had been two weeks since Lillian had received her PreVentall, but Clay had, again, put off his appointment. After the initial thrill of the prospect of drinking from the fountain of youth, he was still hesitant to give up his normal life — or at least the normal life he had always anticipated living. Lillian was annoyed, but she also understood. She had been married to Clay for long enough to know he did not embrace technology quickly. She was certain that he would come around soon, especially since almost everyone had been inoculated and he was beginning to really be noticed. One could say he stood out in a crowd, but lately, he caused a crowd. Others would stare and whisper, wondering why he had not been inoculated or, if he had, whether there was some error in the process.

Once again, Clay found himself alone in his home wondering where his family was. He guessed Lillian was working out or shopping. He tried to remember the last time he saw his whole family together, but he could not. Clay puttered around, looking for something, anything to do. He went down to the basement where he had his workshop. It was a complete mess. He used to clean it every few months, but it would rapidly fall into disorder and he had stopped trying to stay on top of the clutter years ago. He grabbed the glue gun and the shoebox lid it was sitting upon. He looked it over and noticed that the nozzle was badly rusted. He tossed it into the trashcan under his worktable. There would be plenty of time to dispose of it in the Genesis later. The worktable was a tangle of cords and wires, old electronics and half-finished projects. He lifted an old cassette player from the table and held it between his hands. Lillian had finally assented to letting Clay put the turntable in the living room, but the tape deck had been strictly forbidden. He wondered whether he even could find his old cassettes. Bootlegs, mostly. Jam bands he used to go and see. Phish, My Morning Jacket, several others. He had even managed to see the Grateful Dead a few times before Jerry Garcia passed away. He had been young at the time, but he distinctly remembered the crowds were as entertaining as the performances. He smiled. He set the tape deck down to go look for his tapes in the storage area in the back of his basement. He was pretty sure he last saw it under the stairs. He pulled the cord to the light and had begun moving some boxes around when something caught his eye. It was a ham radio. Ancient. When he was a young boy, probably 10 or 11, his father had taken him to a ham radio class at the local park district. The idea was that the two of them would study for their ham radio operator's license and they would have their own gateway to the world. The class was put on by a couple of old-timers. The registration fee included the parts to build your own telegraph key and sound box. Back then, you were required to pass the Morse Code exam to get the ham license. It wasn't long after, perhaps less than a decade, when the government removed the Morse Code requirement, but at the time, neither Clay nor his father could quite get the Code down fast enough to pass the exam. Somewhere along the way he purchased a ham radio set up, hoping to share it with his kids someday. He had purchased a large antenna shortly after Matthew was born and placed it in the attic, but by the time Matthew was old enough to get involved, ham radio proved a poor alternative to virtual reality video games and the multitude of entertainment options instantly available from the Cloud. Clay had played around with the radio a few times when the kids were young. Mostly he would simply listen in on operators from around the world who transmitted in English. Usually boring, but sometimes not. One night he overheard the tale of an old Russian. Clay never knew if he had interrupted a conversation or whether the Russian was simply confessing his sins to the atmosphere. He sometimes wondered if the conversation had actually occurred.

* * *

The Russian spoke of his youth, his love of his Mother Country, of the Great Soviet Union. The Great War was raging and he was a mere boy of fourteen. Not yet a man. Proud of the Soviet Union's recent successes against the Nazi war machine, he sought to join the Red Army and help carry the Soviets to victory, to beat the Americans to Berlin, and to raise the Red Banner over the defeated remains of Germany. He had begged his mother to allow him to enlist, to lie about his age, to find glory and vengeance, but she refused. His father had been killed by the Germans in the war two years earlier. The Russian had understood his obligations after his father's death and took work up in the cement factory to help support his mother and four younger siblings. His size belied his ability to labor and with his cunningness he proved to be a valuable worker. In the factory, the others spoke of the War, and of the victories. In the village, the soldiers who were returning, injured and wounded, were heroes, given honors and praise. The beating of the war drums would cause his heart to race. For Honor. For Country. For Glory.

When he could no longer ignore the calling, he stole away in the dead of night to a small recruiting center 40 kilometers away. He arrived, cold and wet, an hour before the office opened. When the doors were finally unlocked, he stepped into the space, hoping to look like a man. When the recruiter asked him his age he lied. The recruiter did not believe the lie anymore than the Russian believed it himself, and gave the boy a sour look, but the war had cost the lives of many and the recruiter understood that another body in the war effort was one more body to throw at the Germans. And in war, you can always use more bodies.

The Russian was given a uniform and a weapon and placed on the next available train to the front. On board the train, he was taught how to load the weapon by his commander, Sgt. Krolev. He would need to wait until battle in order to learn to shoot it. There was little time for training and little need to waste the resources on a boy so young. The other soldiers humored the boy. Sgt Krolev started calling him 'Little Comrade' and told him stories of danger and victory in battle. The Sergeant wore a large scar running from his left ear, across his cheek and over the inside edge of his left eye. He had been struck by shrapnel from the 1939 invasion of Poland and held a deep grudge against the Polish, as well as the Germans, and perhaps, the boy thought, humanity itself, save for the Soviets. The other soldiers cared not that the Little Comrade would likely not survive battle. War was a game of odds and many were silently thankful that if Death were to come looking for payment, there was yet another soldier from which to choose. The train took the Soviet soldiers to East Prussia, where the Little Comrade and his fellow soldiers began their march through the countryside and toward distant Germany. The Little Comrade, although frightened, was eager to prove his worth, to glorify his Country and Company, and to defeat the savage enemy. It was 1944.

As the Red Army entered East Prussia and the soldiers prepared to battle, an Orthodox Priest gave a short prayer, reminding them that God was on their side and that evil must be defeated. The Little Comrade spoke briefly to his god. He was not a religious person, but felt a small prayer for honor and glory was appropriate as he envisioned a difficult fight against a capable, but morally bankrupt, enemy. Hitler's armies had decimated the occupied territories, enslaved its citizens; famine, disease and the whispers of genocide of the Jews filled the Russian boy with an anger that fueled a righteousness of action. As the troops neared the edge of Nemmersdorf, the Little Comrade spoke naively to his fellow soldiers of justice and right and revenge, of the glory of the Soviet Union and the evilness of the enemy. He looked over at the Father and smiled. He had been comforted by Father's words and emboldened by God's presence. Victory and righteousness were on their side.

As the battle began, the Little Comrade felt his courage build and he proved himself to be an asset in battle. After many hours, the fighting became sporadic and he was pulled by a fellow soldier into the nearest home. What the boy saw shocked him. The Soviets had started breaking into homes and rounding up all the women. Almost no female was too young. None were too old. The men of the house who were not already dead were beaten and tied and forced to watch as the soldiers formed lines, sometimes 12 to 14 men long, to rape the women, the elderly, the girls. The cries from the women, especially the young, would rise above the noise of battle still raging outside. The brutality of the Red Army struck the boy as inhuman, and witnessing the horror, he began to reel backwards, stumbling toward the door. *Where was the glory? the righteousness? the Honor?* the boy wondered. Daily he had heard of the atrocities of the Nazi enemy, the soulless evil that had marched in from the West and had to be destroyed for the sake of the Motherland. Yet now he wondered if his eyes betrayed him, if he was drunk with battle and fatigue. No, before him stood Evil itself, dressed in the uniform of the Red Army. He felt his dinner, eaten so many hours ago, rise in his throat and leave a burning sting and bitter taste. He moved to leave this horror, this aberration but was grabbed from behind.

"Little Comrade," one of his fellow soldiers said. "We have crossed thousands of kilometers through blood and fire and death. We are allowed some fun, some trifle, no?" The boy did not respond. It was Sgt. Krolev. His face turned down, eyes aglow with a fire of hatred. "You have not joined the enemy, Little Comrade, have you?" The boy shook his head back and forth. Sgt Krolev looked down at the Little Comrade. He grabbed the young boy by the scrotum and began to squeeze. "You are not homosexual, I hope? The Red Army does not allow homosexuals." The Little Comrade felt the grip tighten. He tried to call out a denial, but his voice had left him. He shook his head more violently than before. The grip relaxed and Sgt Krolev brushed off the shoulders of the Little Comrade's coat, straightening out his collar. "Good, Little Comrade. Now, go have some fun for the Motherland." His lips curled into a wry smile and he turned the boy around and shoved him to the end of the line. The old woman had died before it was his turn and, Sgt Krolev, expressing sympathy for his Little Comrade's loss, grabbed the Little Comrade and led him to house after house after house.

The boy's mind raced and his body became numb. He used what strength he had to stop himself from retching. This was not honor. This was not glory. He could not bring himself to participate in this crime, but he was yet unwilling to die. He devised a plan to avoid the defilement of these women, to try to prevent his own culpability. Because of his age and small stature, he was able to position himself at the end of the lines. This way, by the time his turn came, the women were usually unconscious or incoherent, or worse. If they were not yet dead, he had determined to climb on top of them and feign penetration, his victims unable to reveal his secret, to give him away as a traitor to the Motherland. Fifteen... twenty... he lost track of how many women in the homes he was forced to demean. His charade allowed him to avoid raping these women, his antics less an abomination than his Comrades' crimes. He thought once to raise his gun against his Comrades and stop the horror, but fear of knowing the moment of his own death stopped him.

After pretending to rape an old woman in the ninth or tenth house—he could not remember—he stumbled out into the street in a daze, at last free from Sgt Krolev and his seemingly insatiable appetite for horror. The sound of gunshots continued intermittently. He heard the sound of a bullet pass by, but he was unable, and unwilling, to even raise his gun. Another shot and a bullet grazed his right temple. He wished for a brief moment that it had struck it's target, but his lingering fear of death would not let the wish fully form, would not let him take action to bring an end to his journey through this nightmare. As he was trying to build the courage to act, whether to kill, to die, or to run away—he was not sure which—he was pulled into yet another home.

The room was dark and barren, except for the soldiers and the sounds of defilement. He was pushed to the end of a line, which had only two men before him, and then one. As he stood there, numbly awaiting his turn, he caught sight of the face of the victim. A young girl, a child not more than a year or two older than he, lie there in defiance. She had neither tears nor defeat on her face, but a resolute determination to survive, to take whatever it was the soldiers were forcing upon her and not give in to fear or despair or humiliation. She was struggling to retain her humanity in a world of madness and beasts. The soldier in front of him finished and the boy stood for a moment. The girl, positioned awkwardly on the floor, one arm sprawled on the floor above her head, the other behind her back, legs spread, looked him in the eye, as if to challenge him to cause her harm, to do what the others had not yet been able to accomplish, but quickly turned away at the sight of his youth. The Little Comrade, mechanically, dropped his pants and fell upon her. As his face approached hers, he saw tears well up in her eyes. She had turned to stare at the fire, to avoid looking at the young Russian soldier, and the tears began to run down her cheek. The cruelty of man, the horror of war. A world is created where men abuse and torture and rape and kill. These the young girl could fight, these demons she could defy. But she was unable to face another world, a world in which young boys become monsters, where even children willingly dance in the garden of evil. The boy began his act, once again undertaking his role as beast, as a player in theatre gone mad. His performance was meant to entertain no one, but had, nonetheless, played before him all the days of his life.

The young girl became confused. It struck her that perhaps God had abandoned this world and she felt the dread of a world where humanity had finally been lost and Evil, at last, had triumphed. She succumbed to the fact that the Devil had nothing better to do than to reveal the true depravity of the world and place not only a child monster upon her bosom, but also add insolence and contempt, by placing one who mocked her, one incapable of even performing his act of defilement upon her. This filled her with anger, and pain, and loss. She slapped him and the other soldiers began to laugh.

"The Little Comrade has got to her!" Sgt. Krolev shouted, hitting the soldier next to him. She raised her free hand to strike him again but stopped. His cheeks, too, were covered with tears and his eyes were closed, face turned slightly down as if the act was causing him more pain than her, and she recognized it was not cruelty or incompetence, but design that prevented his violation; deception was the essence of his performance. She brought her arm down behind his head and pulled it close to hers. She whispered in his ear, German and unintelligible to the young Russian. *"In diesem Irrenhaus ist der Glaube das Einzige, was bleibt"* As she did so, she slid her other arm from beneath her back and then carefully between their bodies. He felt a brief chill of steel on his stomach before he felt the oozing warmth. Confused at first, he continued his charade and the young girl let out a gasp. The other soldiers standing in the room, mistaking the reaction of the young girl, shouted out mixtures of praise and contempt. The young Russian aware of the unnatural warmth at his belly put his lips to her cheek and gently kissed her.

"Ahh, his first love! Let's leave the young couple alone," Sgt Krolev joked as he pushed the others out of the house, pausing to turn back and smile toward the young Russian. "Let us find our own fun, Comrades!" He continued to laugh. When the room was empty, the young Russian stopped moving. The warmth beneath him continued to spread as the young girl let out her final breath. He lay atop her for many minutes, his body convulsing in sorrow. He wiped the tears from his face, unsure if the salty taste left behind was from his tears or her blood. It did not matter. He despised the uniform he had so recently worn proudly, ashamed of the lies he made to secure it. The excitement of war, the glory of battle was pooled beneath him. The pride of the Red Army nothing more than a darkening stain, and the echo of her final words, still meaningless, ringing in his head.

The Russian got up and, leaving his weapon behind, walked out the door and into the night. He wandered for days, weeks perhaps, stumbling around the countryside, unaware of where he was or where he was going. He was picked up by Soviet forces, incoherent and suffering from exposure. It was three weeks before he spoke, and then, only in broken phrases, nonsense. He woke up screaming one night, shouting out in German: *"In diesem Irrenhaus ist der Glaube das Einzige, was bleibt."* It was only by chance that one day he was overheard by one of the attendants, repeating *Pikalyovo*, the name of a small town located southeast of St. Petersburg. He was returned to his home and placed in the care of his mother, who had long-since given up on seeing him alive again. She cried and held him close and thanked the Lord for his safe return. In her care and comfort, he was able to face life again; to return to the factory and help support his family, marry and have a daughter of his own. But he had never spoken a word about what had happened.

As the years between the War and the present had increased, the Russian had eased into a life of work, family and simple pleasures. His daughter grew into a young woman and spent her time studying and helping her mother around the house. One evening, while she was reading her books, she paused and turned to her father.

"Is it true, Papa, what I am reading about the East Prussian Offensive?" she asked, her expression one of disbelief. "It says here that the Germans claim the Red Army raped 100,000 women... girls."

"No, my Sweet," he gave her a kiss. "It may have happened, of course, but not like it's written there. Not so young. Not so many. These claims were part of German propaganda," he lied.

"You were too young to have fought, weren't you Papa? I am glad you were not there," she smiled up at him. He smiled back at her.

"Yes, my Sweet. Me, too," he lied again. It was best she did not know the truth. He wrapped his arms around her. He forgave his lies to protect his little girl from the horrors she need not know. He released her and looked carefully at his daughter, not much older than the young Prussian had been so many years ago. Both, so young.

A tear rose up in his eye as it all came rushing back to him. He had lied to protect those women, feigning coitus to protect them, the young Prussian, just as he was lying now, to protect his own daughter. He could not speak the truth to her. *I am sorry, my Sweet, it is true. It is all true.*

"I did not commit these horrors," he said to himself, aloud.

His daughter looked up at him, confused. "Of course not, Papa." He forced a smile, reassured he was innocent of these crimes. He had not forgotten.

Many years later, the Russian sat alone. His wife had died of influenza the previous winter. His daughter had married and moved to Moscow. He, himself, had grown tired and thin, but the blankets on his lap and the fire roaring in the hearth had kept the chill of the winter away, kept the warmth in his bones. As he sat before his ham radio and recounted his tale that night—to everyone, to no one—a chill crept through his body. He pulled the blankets a little closer and turned to see if the fire had, by some unfortunate mishap, gone dark. It had not, but the crackling flames seemed to him to have ceased emitting heat. A darkness passed through his thoughts. He had lied to protect the young Prussian. Yet it occurred to him at that moment that he had not protected the young Prussian. She had suffered the same fate as the others, had been made a victim of revenge for sins not hers. He tried to think thoughts of comfort— how he had stood before the moral abyss and, while faltering, did not fall in. Yet he could not shake the thought that he had not, in fact, done anything at all, other than lie. *And for whom?* The question popped into his mind. And it struck him then that his lies were not meant to protect her, but only to protect himself. His eyes grew wide and his voice faltered. He shivered. He wondered at the boy he had left behind that night, the person he had been. *Where was that boy now?* At this moment, he had forgotten. The phrase that had haunted his nightmares came back to him. He spoke them aloud. "In diesem Irrenhaus ist der Glaube das Einzige, was bleibt." He repeated the German phrase, so familiar, but as he did so his voice changed from hope to despair, and he realized he had sinned.

The signal weakened and as it faded into static, Clay heard the Russian repeating his hollow prayer, crying to himself, "In diesem Irrenhaus ist der Glaube das Einzige, was bleibt."

\* \* \*

Clay pulled the ham radio out from where it lay and took it up to the study. The antenna connection plate was still in place and he plugged the equipment in. It hummed to life. As he spun the dial up and down, silence had replaced what were once a myriad of frequencies crackling with life. He dialed up 7.0 MHz and depressed the microphone button. "This is America calling. Hello? Hello?" The airwaves responded with silence. "This is America calling. Is there anyone out there?" Again silence. He moved the dial up, and continued his plea for notice. The progress of man responded with silence.

## CHAPTER EIGHTEEN

*News Flash: Tuesday. 4:45 p.m. Potentially dangerous technology has recently been released into the environment, causing government concern. The activist group, Red Star, is believed to be behind the release of nanobots designed for the self-repair of inorganic materials. The Governor of New York says it is not safe, and several members of Red Star have been arrested on charges of public endangerment.*

Clay was stretching out his left knee, which was stiff after a hard racquetball match when his iMeme had interrupted his thoughts.

"More," Clay muttered.

*Today, a group of open-source developers have once again shown that cutting-edge technology is rapidly moving from the world of corporate giants to the everyman. Oleg Breznikov, a member of Red Star Open Source Guild—the hacktivist group that developed the new nanobot called InFIXstructure—describes this technology as, 'of the people, by the people, and for the people' and argues that 'technology and knowledge are not commodities to be bought and sold. They are the right of every individual in the world and should be freely accessible to all.' Mr. Breznikov was one of four individuals arrested today by the New York State Police.*

*Unlike Genesis technology, which creates new materials, InFIXstructure are free source code nanobots that use a variety of technologies, including GPS technology, satellite imagery technology, access to public records and basic mathematical laws of probability, to repair non-organic materials and structures.*

*Members of Red Star published the InFIXstructure App on the Cloud over three months ago and users have been spreading InFIXstructure nanobots into the environment since then. Areas where InFIXstructure is in use boast pristine roads and bridges, and like-new buildings and improvements. But some government officials worry of the unknown side effects of such actions.*

*Agent Kelsey Parker of the Bureau of Alcohol, Tobacco, Firearms, and Nanobots, who has been working in cooperation with the New York State Police explains: 'What we have here is the unauthorized distribution of unlicensed, self-replicating nanobots. While we admit that there are advantages to self-repairing bridges, roads and structures, there is the danger that these nanobots may not continue to behave as intended. Given that Red Star Open Source Guild has a history of anti-corporate and anti-government activities, we are warning all citizens to refrain from the procurement and use of InFIXstructure until further testing can be done. ATFN has reliable information that InFIXstructure may also contain codes which, if activated, would result in a complete disruption of government and corporate services.'*

*While it is suspected that persons outside the Red Star group have learned about and also used InFIXstructure, the Group states that it had consciously refrained from publicizing InFIXstructure's availability due to fear that the government would attempt to stop its introduction into the environment. Red Star alleges that any government ban is an attempt to keep ordinary citizens reliant upon corporate and government services and that such reliance is merely a pretext for the continued control of our society by money interests. Says Breznikov, 'We know that the powers-that-be wish to prevent self-repairing products in an attempt to artificially support the corporate interests and retain power for themselves. But we have won — the code is in the Cloud. Nothing can stop its spread. The people shall be empowered. Arresting me will not stop our work.'*

*The New York Governor's Office has denied its actions are a conspiracy meant to favor the rich. 'Any reference to a conspiracy is wholly misplaced. The Governor is simply concerned about the safety of this product and the danger it may pose to the public. These nanobots have not been tested. Members of Red Star are releasing untested and unregulated nanobots out into the environment and the State of New York has a strong interest in ensuring that these nanobots will not result in serious harms. We have been hampered in our efforts to discover the true nature of InFIXstructure by Red Star members' refusal to release the encryption codes for the operating system,' said Jackson F. Stevenson IV, division chief of the New York State Police. Several other states are following New York's lead and outlawing the use of InFIXstructure.*

*A small group of protesters have gathered outside the home of Oleg Breznikov. Says Tom O'Neil: 'This stuff is fantastic. Sidewalks repair themselves, streetlights never burn out. I'll pretty much never have to do any home repairs ever again. It's truly amazing.' Another man, who wishes to remain unidentified, states: 'You'll never need to wait for the government to come out and fix the roads again. I've used some of this InFIXstructure stuff on my house, my driveway, even my clothes. Watch this!' The man then ripped his shirt and when he held the torn edges together, they rewove themselves like new. 'Why the hell would I want to spend money on a new shirt from the Genesis when this one is still perfectly good? And free?' The government is warning all persons to refrain from replicating these nanobots and disbursing them into the environment…*

"Off," Clay stated. He sighed as the iMeme went silent. *Christ. Now even the roads will stay young,* he thought. He had always felt his age after a workout, but with everyone now having been inoculated with PreVentall, he became the slowest and weakest member of his gym, or any gym for that matter. Still, he wasn't sure he wanted to be young again. Not like that, anyway. Lillian was a good sport about it, but he knew she was becoming frustrated with his inability to keep up with her newly acquired youth. His kids loved him, but unanimously thought he was a fool. Hell, he was beginning to believe them. He took a quick shower and jumped on the El to go downtown. He wanted to walk around the city to clear his head a little. He had not been downtown in a long time. He could not remember the last time he was in his office and he could barely remember what he used to do.

A large number of people still no longer worked, but for different reasons. Unlike the pre-Genesis days when a vast number of Americans were unemployed due to the Great Depression II, now most Americans simply did not need to work. Congress passed legislation repealing the tax code and replacing it with a system of tariffs on out-going products. These tariffs on the foreign purchase of American engineered products created a positive revenue stream for the U.S. Government which then paid its citizens (much like the State of Alaska had paid dividends to residents from the Alaska Permanent Fund) in an amount equal to their pre-Genesis salary or government subsidy. With the introduction of Genesis, those previously receiving government assistance saw their lot in life improve greatly. The vastly improved purchasing power of the dollar coupled with their familiarity with an austere lifestyle, resulted in the formerly unemployed masses being able to sustain a comfortable lifestyle, albeit without too many frills. Some people, however, still desired to move up the economic ladder and find employment that would provide the opportunity to secure additional income and the opportunity to purchase bigger and better apps for their Genesis. But one of the unintended consequences of Genesis was the loss of thousands of jobs that became obsolete with the development of molecular manufacturing. Clay wondered how easy it was for those interested to actually find jobs and move up the economic ladder.

Clay had found that his previous salary allowed him to live the lifestyle of the new middle-class, a lifestyle that rivaled those of the upper-class only a few years earlier. Life in America had become what the Old World had once imagined—a nation with streets paved in gold, where a chicken could be found in every pot, and where, at last, man was able to drink from the Fountain of Youth.

As Clay walked past his office it struck him that the gaping hole in the sidewalk was repaired. He looked around and suddenly noticed that many of the roads and sidewalks were in like-new condition. And many of the nearby buildings, even those built at the turn of the 20th century, looked like new. It was then he noticed several building maintenance engineers with salt spreaders and several others with what appeared to be pressure washers, disbursing a fine mist of white powder as they worked alongside a building on the other side of the street. Clay noticed an almost instant change in the areas sprayed—the building and sidewalk transforming before his eyes. He stood and stared and one of the men, noticing Clay's gaze, stopped what he was doing and called out something to his co-worker. The two men looked toward Clay and huddled together, speaking animatedly. Clay had only heard of

InFIXstructure earlier that morning, but it appeared that many building owners must have been aware of it for some time. He wondered, *How long?* He tried again to remember the last time he had been downtown. *Had any of the buildings been treated then? Had I simply not noticed?* Fear of government reprisal for using InFIXstructure apparently did not trump the monetary interests of property owners in eliminating the cost of maintenance from their properties. The men across the street continued their conversation, faces hard and cautious.

The men's glances made Clay uncomfortable and he looked around again. The city was nearly empty. It was not an uncommon event during the day since most people no longer worked. Clay remembered when the city was full of crowds during working hours. Now, such activity was reserved for the evening, when people got together for dinner, theatre, movies, drinks, or whatever escape from the monotony of retirement they sought. Even the museums were generally closed at this hour, opening in the early evening and staying open until the early hours of the morning. Although Clay had turned away, he felt the continued stares of the men across the street and his pulse rate rose slightly. It suddenly struck him why they made him uncomfortable. He looked toward them again and recognized an expression on their faces, shared by his own countenance, to which most people had grown unaccustomed; the look of nervous uncertainty, of guilt and paranoia. As Clay recognized his own fear, he also was reminded of his age, which no longer lent itself to the natural and necessarily urgent need to choose fight or flight. He was reminded that his outward appearance was now an anomaly and it must have made the men across the street fearful. Rumors had circulated that certain people in the government and among the elite had refused to be inoculated because it was known among them that PreVentall was unsafe and that it was only a method of deluding the masses and calming the anger that had been growing during the Great Depression II, before the introduction of the Genesis. That the elite had long ago adopted the battle cry of the now-deceased CEO of Berkshire-Hathaway, Warren Buffet, when he stated that there was a war between the rich and the poor, and that the rich were commencing the war and winning, and it was only a matter of time before the rich made their final move. These rumors were dismissed by almost everyone as conspiracy theorist paranoia. The sight of the elderly could not be found among the many congressmen, corporate CEOs, and powerbrokers who regularly appeared on the news. But, even so, some people could not help but wonder. Clay's age must have initially made the men fearful he was someone of importance, someone in with the government—proof positive the rumors were true. He chuckled to himself and started on his way again but not before the men must have had decided Clay was not a top ATFN agent or other figure of authority and returned to their work.

As Clay walked on it struck him that he could not remember the last time he has seen a policemen, or even thought about needing one. It was not surprising. One consequence of the rapidly increasing standard of living was the reduction of criminal activity. Given that every person had what he or she wanted, crime, in its traditional form, was practically non-existent. Assaults and batteries were ineffective intimidation practices against people immune to harm or fear of harm. A stab wound was healed almost as quickly as it was inflicted. PreVentall nanobots were able to quickly stop the neural transmission of pain senses shortly after being triggered, making any injury only momentarily painful. Scientists had originally programmed the PreVentall Nanobots to stop all neuro-transmissions associated with pain, but experimental subjects suffered an alarming rate of injuries resulting from their inability to sense and react to stimuli. Over 60% of the initial test subject group suffered third-degree burns or lost digits from mishaps in the kitchen. While the body was able to quickly heal itself, scientists quickly determined that the regular severe damage to or loss of body parts was not conducive to a healthy lifestyle.

Murder also disappeared, no one having figured out how to prevent PreVentall from repairing any serious wounds. Beyond the physical ineffectiveness, the simple fact that everyone had most everything they needed, generally deterred anyone from resorting to a crime for personal gain. It made no sense to steal what was free for the asking. Burglary or theft, like all property related crimes, was fruitless in a society in which one need only command the Genesis to create what one wanted, provided it could be replicated. Likewise, crimes of power, such as rape and spousal abuse, also waned. Would-be victims empowered by PreVentall deterred perpetrators.

Many white-collar crimes also disappeared. There was little need to develop and execute a plan to accept bribes, misappropriate funds, or defraud investors when money could not buy you anything you couldn't already get for free or for very minimal cost. Greed had devolved into a psychological issue to be medically treated. Some people still possessed greed, but it ended up simply being a need to replicate hundreds of the same item in an attempt to satisfy some unfulfilled desire. It did not affect innocent parties like it had in the past. No longer did greed require the afflicted to deprive others of goods in order to satisfy their urges. There were endless amounts of everything for everyone, so the greedy ended up simply struggling against themselves and the need to find a place to store their vast amounts of "wealth."

Even crimes of passion disappeared. People began to look upon their relationships in a new light. Given the possibility of living forever, even happily married couples needed to assess the idea of remaining together for an eternity. The number of divorces jumped after the introduction of PreVentall as people realized that they had time to seek out partners who matched their ideal. Others remained in their relationships, but adopted open lifestyles, agreeing that an eternity with one partner was too much to ask. Just as many others renewed their marriage vows or committed to their significant other, as they realized that life was long and that shared common interests mattered most in their relationship. They argued that with the introduction of virtual reality into the bedroom, their sex-lives would be no different than those who determined to have many multiple relationships throughout the ages, but they retained the advantage of a shared life with someone they knew and loved.

The new paradigm which arose after the introduction of molecular manufacturing found many people, unaccustomed to the freedom arising from minimal labor hours and endless recreational time, bored and in need of an escape from reality. The manufacturers of PreVentall foresaw this dilemma and in an attempt to avoid a massive shift in public use of drugs, both licit and illicit, programmed PreVentall nanobots to neutralize the chemical processes of certain chemicals entering the body. As a result, most drugs no longer provided the user with any type of high. PreVentall was also able to correct the physical and chemical reactions associated with withdrawal, so those previously addicted to drugs were able to stop cold turkey and be cured of their addictions. All drug and drug-related crime ceased as a result of PreVentall neutralizing the effects of drugs in the body, eliminating all demand for drugs. PreVentall did allow limited normal processes to occur with the introduction of alcohol and THC into the bloodstream. Use of these drugs would produce the pleasant buzz in users, but prevented the negative feelings and traits associated with excessive use. Because of this, alcohol and marijuana use continued to be popular, but mostly for social, rather than physical reasons.

But not everyone cared for a chemical path to nirvana or was old enough to partake in drug and alcohol use. In response, the scientists offered escape in other, non-harmful, ways. Innumerable new gaming systems and virtual reality environments were created which allowed individuals to transport themselves to the worlds of their desire. Much like the Sims games of times past, users were able to adopt alternative identities. Unlike virtual games of the past, however, these games were no longer played on computer screens, but in real life, in virtual emporiums. Millions of empty warehouses, once responsible for storing the commerce of the nation, but now made obsolete by Genesis, offered an endless number of alternative worlds where participants interacted on a real level — fantastical worlds created by nanobots capable of mimicking any environment, both real and imagined. One offered a foreign planet circling two suns where participants battled in hovercrafts with lasers and conquered newly discovered species, and was populated with mostly boys using alias such as Han or Luke or Obi-Wan. Another provided a seedy inner-city neighborhood where the law changed with the whims of the then-currently strongest player — a kind of free-for-all reminiscent of the Mad Max films. Yet another, an unnamed world where participants lived alternate lives amongst strangers also seeking comfort in anonymity.

But power did not seem to be equally affected. While it was true the many power struggles that naturally arise between individuals of differing socio-economic classes disappeared, the power struggles between the U.S. and other nation-states continued, and, in fact, increased. The United States was, once again, the only true Super Power. And it had become clear to Clay that, unlike the past, the U.S. seemed willing to take advantage of that power, to flex its collective muscle and impose itself upon other nations. If such action had been taken by the U.S. when Clay was young, there would have been a huge outcry — not only from other nations (Clay was sure that protests were being made against current U.S. policy, but access to independent news sources had become difficult, if not impossible) but also from within. Mass gatherings of the young and socially conscious coming together to fight social wrongs, to stand up in order to attempt to bring justice to the world, and to meet like-minded others who were also willing to share a sandwich, a police beating, or a bed. Viet Nam. G-8. WTO. Occupy Wall Street. Yet the streets in American cities were relatively silent. Except when the government attempted to curtail means of amusement (by closing down a virtual theater for failing to limit user participation time), the youth and the aged alike, were too satiated to lift a picket sign, to lift a finger, to lift even a voice. Clay was not tech-savvy enough to protest against the inequalities he sensed America was visiting upon the outside world. But there were others who were more than capable.

# CHAPTER NINETEEN

*News Brief: Thursday. 9:15 a.m. Protesters against New York State's prosecution of Red Star, the hacktivist group responsible for the development of InFIXstructure, have gained a surprising new ally: the U.S. Government. President Browning ordered the dismissal of all charges against Red Star, stating that the EPA Nanomaterial Division scientists have analyzed InFIXstructure and have determined that it is safe for public distribution. In addition, President Browning signed Executive Order 16415, which places control of all criminal justice activities in the United States into the hands of the federal government. As the new Top Prosecutor, President Browning declared that all local legal action against Red Star for development and distribution of InFIXstructure is to cease immediately. In response to fears that InFIXstructure could compromise American scientific superiority, the President assured the public that the National Science Labs have developed a protocol to prevent the unlawful delivery and distribution of InFIXstructure to foreign nations, thereby negating any perceived risk to our National Security. While the use of InFIXstructure is now approved, the President emphasized that any suspected attempts by Red Star, or any other subversive organization, to implement or continue activities which are deemed to pose a threat to our Nation's domestic or economic security will be punished to the fullest extent of the law.*

Clay scrolled through the news section of the *Chicago On-Line Times*. While he still found himself yearning for the physical page to peruse through while eating breakfast, he had long ago become accustomed to reading the news on his iMeme holographic reader. As he ate a bowl of cereal, he surfed the Cloud for more details about the recent Presidential Order nationalizing all law enforcement agencies:

*Pursuant to Executive Order, current state, county, local and municipal law enforcement personnel, including local states attorney personnel, shall become employees of the Federal Government. The reduction of criminal activity — outside the arenas of Genesis-App piracy and national security — to near zero has meant that most law enforcement personnel have had little to do. Untrained and lacking the resources needed to prevent Genesis-App piracy and national security tasks, local officers have welcomed the news. Officer Patrick O'Donnell, a sergeant with the Chicago Police department for over thirty years expressed his opinion. "While it's great to see that crime has disappeared, it's been difficult coming to work each day with absolutely nothing to do. I joined the force to make the city a better place to live, but I don't see why I'm putting on my uniform twice a week only to do nothing. It's pointless." Once Executive Order #16415 is implemented, most police departments, including all 25 Chicago Districts and the O'Hare Airport Police District are expected to be eliminated.*

Clay turned the holographic reader off. He sympathized with Officer O'Donnell and all the law enforcement personnel who were showing up to work only to sit around and do nothing. Clay himself only went into the office a few hours a week because he found it a quiet place to sit and read without interruption from his family, as well as a good location to avoid questions from others who wondered why he was not reading on his iMeme. Clay no longer practiced law. Between his government paycheck and his access to Genesis, he never seemed to be in need of money or the necessary obligation to do something to earn it. Nonetheless, there was something about the disappearance of local law enforcement that made Clay uncomfortable.

Clay had always feared that advancements in technology would result in a police state, a nation dominated by Big Brother and populated with some form of thought police. But recent events seemed to have turned that whole notion on its head. The slow disappearance of police from the streets of cities and towns made sense to Clay; it accurately reflected the reduction of crime in

American society. But the complete and utter abandonment of local law enforcement personnel did not ease his misgivings.

Clay sat and contemplated the situation. *Was there not some scenario in which something broke down in society, whether it be the Genesis itself or the Virtual Worlds or some other piece of society that was so depended upon by a large number of citizens that its disappearance would, and only could, lead to rioting or other public rebellion? Was it expected the government could assume this role more adequately than local officers? Would federal police, soldiers really, retain that element of community connectedness that enables local law enforcement, being familiar with their community, to extend those professional courtesies that allow, for example, an otherwise innocent teenage law-breaker to be released with a warning, thankful for avoiding the hassles of arrest, but knowing all the while that he will still need to go home and confess to his parents — better they should learn of the transgression from their son than their friendly neighborhood police officer?* Clay did not think so. Especially since living in a paradise did not mean crime disappeared altogether. It simply stalked the streets, threatening victimless horrors.

Clay had just recently witnessed one such victimless crime. It was the men Clay had seen spreading InFIXstructure in clear violation of government direction. Their actions created no harm, yet, at the time, it had been illegal nonetheless. Another, more notorious example was the increasing number of pirated Genesis-Apps available. These crimes, too, had no individual victim, but they did cause economic harm to large corporate entities. It troubled Clay that the government was undertaking such a massive effort to protect corporate interests here in the Land of Plenty when so many non-Americans were denied the benefits of Genesis. It reminded Clay of the days before Genesis, when the government waged its War on Drugs, when recreational drug users whose activities only harmed themselves were subjected to mandatory minimum sentences which were not designed to rehabilitate or provide needed social services, but rather simply to punish without regard to the consequences of such action.

Clay got up to clean his bowl when Lillian walked into the kitchen.

"Large Diet Coke with McDonald's straw," she said to the Genesis.

"Hey Sweetie, how was the workout?" Clay asked, giving Lillian a puzzled look.

"Fine. And what's with the face?" she responded.

"I didn't know Coke had an Genesis-App."

"They don't," she said as she smiled. "It's a pirated app. I downloaded it this morning from the gym. I figure that as soon as Coke finds out, they'll shut it down, so I wanted to jump on it right away." She pulled a paper cup from the Genesis and took a long sip from the straw. She smiled. "That's Diet Coke! No more jumping in the car and driving to McDonald's just for a Coke anymore," she said grinning wide.

*Breaking News: Thursday. 9:53 a.m. Coca-Cola pirated! App freely available on the Cloud for over one hour!*

*That sure didn't take long,* he thought to himself as he heard the iMeme report. "More," he said to his iMeme.

*Coca-Cola spokesperson Rhonda Benzinger admitted that pirates managed to make an application available early this morning, but has confirmed that the illegal app has been removed from the Cloud and is no longer available. Ms. Benzinger assured shareholders that fallout would be minimal. Experts have contradicted Coke's statements and believe that the app was available for over two and one-half hours and estimates place the number of downloads at almost 100 million. Investors have responded negatively to the news this morning and Coke shares, which closed yesterday at $41.23 per share rapidly fell to sixty-seven cents before trading was temporarily halted.*

By the time Clay arrived at the gym the following morning, the Cloud was buzzing with stories about Coca-Cola.

"I fully understand the anger of Coke in this whole mess, but I can't believe the Government is going to come down so hard if anyone is caught being involved in this," Clay said as he hung his pants in his locker.

"Are you kidding? Coke's a major company, Clay. That little prank practically brought down the whole company! Those assholes," Miguel responded.

"Companies go out of business all the time, Miguel. It happens. Are we supposed to believe that Coke is too big to fail?" Clay countered. "Don't get me wrong, I'd hate to see such an old corporation just disappear. But it's more of a nostalgic thing. I mean,

Coke's a private company and I don't think it's the government's business to start charging application pirates with espionage."

"Jesus, Clay. Can you hear yourself?" Miguel asked, pulling his t-shirt over his head. "These pirates are a threat to our whole country! Sure, Coke is a drink. But Coca-Cola was a major player, a huge corporation. If pirates can bring down Coke, what's to stop them from bringing down other companies, the whole economy? The CEO is right, these guys need to be found and they need to be punished, to be made an example of, if only to protect the economy."

"That's nothing more than a slippery slope argument. Coca-Cola is still around. Maybe not worth what it was yesterday, but there's certainly still a market overseas. What they're doing is using the power of the State to punish someone for what amounts to an economic harm. It should be a civil matter. These guys weren't giving secrets to anyone—they were publishing apps like the thousands of others out there. It may be illegal, but it's certainly not espionage." Clay said.

"You're wrong about that, Clay. These guys are breaking into Genesis programming. What if these assholes at Red Star want to deliver some of this technology overseas? Can you imagine if some terrorists were able to get a hold of it?" Miguel paused for a moment and gave Clay a long stare. "I think the government is right to come down hard. It is a matter of national security."

"I think that the government is bored and looking for something to do. The Government is putting together a team of the best U.S. Attorneys in the country and expending tons of money to capture these guys. And while their actions were certainly illegal, I can't say that it rises to the point of espionage," Clay said, as he finished tying his shoes.

"You're too lenient. These assholes are criminals and they deserve what punishment they get." Miguel added.

*Breaking News: Friday. 9:07 a.m. Two suspects have been arrested in the Coca-Cola piracy case. Both members of Red Star, they have been identified as Noah Finkelstein and Joshua Landsburg.*

"I guess these assholes now have names." Clay said softly.

As information began to surface about the two men accused of the Coke piracy and the government began to build its case, the whole affair began to take on the atmosphere of a World's Fair. The two accused's every action was televised across the country and many watched in rapt attention. The public, having been raised on reality television, made certain to tune into what became the most-watched program in television history. While Clay was not a fan of reality television, he was aware that part of the allure was the lack of scripting, the possibility the completely unexpected can take place at any moment and present some bizarre and entirely entertaining act. And the Finkelstein-Landsburg trial delivered in aces.

Initially, the court had assigned the defense of the Finkelstein-Landsburg matter to a seasoned attorney by the name of Albert Cottingham, a man who was light-heartedly referred to as Old Codgerham by his colleagues. Old Codgerham was an ancient man who had been practicing criminal defense for as long as anyone could remember. No one, not even Magistrate Gutierrez who had been appointed to the bench three decades earlier, could remember a time when Old Codgerham was not an old man. And he remained so. After having been inoculated, Old Codgerham still had the appearance of a man in his mid-sixties. The running joke was that his current appearance was what he looked like when he was thirty, and Old Codgerham did not dispute it. When questions started being asked, the scientists openly theorized that due to a lifelong love affair with expensive cigars, rich foods, and expensive scotch, Old Codgerham's DNA was so damaged that the nanobots were unable to determine his ideal genome and his current appearance was the best that could be expected. Secretly, the scientists were concerned. They could not believe anyone with DNA so damaged by lifestyle choices would have survived so long prior to inoculation. They wanted to run tests to figure out why he seemed immune from the full benefits of PreVentall, but Old Codgerham refused to allow any physicians to do so. Some of the pubic believed that Old Codgerham had paid an engineer to modify the nanobots to retain his appearance as an old man, to secure his persona as the old codger, which had long won over the hearts (and verdicts) of many juries.

His appointment had caused some concern among the prosecution team. The prosecution held many press conferences in which they confidently promised to deliver convictions against the defendants, but knew that the case would be a difficult one to get the jury to understand. The main charges hinged upon applying a complicated interpretation to an early 20th Century statute designed to prevent spying and applying that statute to the 21st Century hacking and pirating of a private patent. The prosecution team feared that Old Codgerham's natural charisma, coupled with the fact he was an oddity for having been inoculated but still looked like a sixty-something year old, would distract the jury from understanding the evidence necessary to convict. His appointment ended up causing the court even more concern. The defendants refused to cooperate with Old Codgerham. They argued they had the right to counsel of their own choosing and demanded the Court appoint an attorney known not to have been inoculated. The defendants espoused the commentary of a well-known media personality who argued that PreVentall allowed the government to control the minds of those who were inoculated. The defendants demanded an attorney who could not be controlled by government manipulation. The Court denied their request, given their chosen attorney's complete lack of criminal defense experience.

The prosecution team, realizing the removal of Old Codgerham would make their job much easier, sided with the defendants and, covertly, cooperated with the defendants in disrupting the hearings to such an extent that it took nearly two days for the Court to even extract a not-guilty plea from the Defendants. Magistrate Gutierrez could not prove that the prosecution's actions were a conscious effort to disrupt the proceedings. Gutierrez also began to realize that any conviction brought down under the background of non-cooperation by the defendants with counsel would raise appealable issues — something that was made clear to him that must not occur.

The preliminary hearings were all held outside of public view and when news broke that Old Codgerham would be second-chairing for the Defendants, the question of who would take lead on the case was the topic of a multitude of conversations. When the Court unsealed the hearing and released the name of lead counsel, no one was more surprised than Clay to learn that the attorney chosen by the Defendants was none other than Levi Clayton Furstman.

"I just can't figure out why they want me to represent them," Clay said, exasperated.

"You've seriously never met these guys before?" Lillian asked. "Maybe they called you for advice at some point. The children of an old client of yours?"

"No. Nothing. I've gone through my computer files a dozen times. I've Googled their families and friends, and nothing. Just this crazy claim they want someone not tainted by PreVentall. I can't even figure out how they know I'm not inoculated or how they came up with my name!" Clay let out a sigh.

"So what are you going to do?" Lillian asked.

"What the hell can I do? I'm going to represent them to the best of my ability. For whatever that's worth," Clay added.

"You can't do that! You don't even like defending your friends for traffic tickets. Now you're going to defend the biggest trial in years?" Lillian said.

"What choice do I have, Lill?"

"Get inoculated. Go tomorrow. You'll be blemished and they'll dump you." Lillian said.

"Tainted," Clay replied.

"What?" Lillian asked.

"Tainted. They wanted someone who was not *tainted* by PreVentall." Clay corrected her.

"You asshole," she said softly. "You won't do it, will you?" Lillian asked a little louder. "You're not going to get inoculated, are you?"

"This isn't about me, Lill."

"The hell it isn't, Clay," she shouted. "It's all about you. You and your crazy notions of... of... Oh, hell! I don't even know what goes on in your head. Why are you doing this to me? To the kids?"

"What are you talking about?" Clay asked.

"I'm talking about the future, Clay! In case you haven't noticed, I'm not the same person I was before PreVentall. I'm young again. I'm healthy and alive. The whole country's young and alive, except you. And nothing's going to change that." She took a deep breath and lowered her voice. "What are you planning on, Clay? You know, for the future?"

Clay looked at her but remained silent.

"Are you just going to keep growing old?" Lillian asked. "In a few years you'll be sick, and then incapacitated, while the rest of us will go on... without you. Christ, Clay. I love you. Do you think I want to watch you waste away when you don't need to?"

"But I—" Clay started.

"You? You! What about me? What about the kids? Jesus, Clay. Climb out of that little world you live in and think about us!" Lillian said as she ran out of the room, crying.

News broke later that morning that Congress had passed legislation which amended the Espionage Act to make the pirating of any patented product that resulted in serious and irreparable harm to the nation, including severe economic harm to public corporations, eligible, in the most extreme cases, for PreVentall disablement and capital punishment. While the collapse of Coca-Cola was certainly significant, Clay was comforted by the fact that the defendants' actions did not rise to the level of capital punishment. It was, however, cold comfort, as Clay still had no idea on how to defend these men against what was beginning to look like certain long-term prison sentences.

Clay made an appointment with Old Codgerham to plan their defense strategy. Instead of buoying his spirits, the visit caused them to sink even lower. Old Codgerham sympathized with Clay, but admitted that even with some public sympathy for his clients, any defense would be difficult at best.

"We all know Finkelstein and Landsburg are innocent. No one seriously believes the stories the government is reporting. I mean, even if they are both geniuses, there's no way they could disassembled a Genesis in their apartment. They would need a university lab to pull that off, even if it could be done, which I don't think it can," Cottingham said.

"And yet the Cloud is filled with stories of both men having criminal records. Surely the prosecution will raise that," Clay began.

"Criminal records?" Cottingham said, his eyes opening wide in surprise. "Surely you've reviewed their rap sheet."

Clay looked down. "I wouldn't even know how to access them," he admitted sheepishly.

Cottingham shook his head in disgust and pulled a small stack of papers from his desk and tossed it at Clay. "Their rap sheets have nothing more dangerous than misdemeanor arrests for disrupting the flow of traffic and assembling without a permit," Cottingham said, raising his voice. "Now stop playing the martyr here and look at the facts. You've got two guys who may sympathize with Red Star, but who have no real connection to the organization. We both know the alleged hacking documents found on their computers are fabricated. The files don't match the Cloud back-up files, not to mention the government searched the computers before they had obtained warrants. And with all the alleged hacking files they did claim to find, not one of them relates to Coke. Hell, they didn't even have the Coke-App on their own Genesis!"

"I know," Clay said softly.

There was a pause in their conversation. "I won't lie to you, Clay. You are at a disadvantage that even you cannot comprehend."

Clay gave Cottingham a puzzled look. "What do you mean? Of course I understand. I've never defended anyone in a criminal trial in my life. Hell, I don't even know where to begin."

"And that simply proves my point. The fact that you've never defended a criminal case is irrelevant. We all have to take that first step. You are in a position no different than I, the first time I set foot in a courtroom. No, you don't understand at all."

Clay gave Cottingham another harsh look and then spoke. "No disrespect, really. But if I'm so dead in the water, why were you willing to take this case? It seems to me that rather than beating me down, you would — at least out of professional courtesy if not out of a sense of compassion to protect two innocent men — sit down and fill me in on your defense strategy. We have two clients who are looking at serious jail time and you don't seem to be providing much assistance." His voice had risen a little more than he had anticipated. Cottingham sat before him in silence. "I'm sorry, I don't mean to — "

"Listen, Clay," Cottingham interrupted. "I know you're frustrated here. And believe me, I am too. I'm sure you're a bright attorney, probably as well qualified as anyone out there, but — "

It was Clay's turn to interrupt. "But I'm no Old Codgerham." He flushed a little, not meaning to have called Cottingham's by his nickname.

"No Clay, you're not me. But that is not meant to infer that I'm a better attorney than you. It's only to point out the obvious — and it's the obvious that oftentimes is the most overlooked — I have an advantage that no other attorney has: the advantage of confounding science and the public. How do you explain my appearance? How do you put that aside? Unlike you, who simply has chosen to avoid inoculation, I publicly underwent a second inoculation, before a live camera, and I look like this." Here, Cottingham smiled. "What do you suppose a jury will think upon seeing me in person for the first time? What do you imagine a subtle wince when I stand, a brief closing of my eyes upon shifting my weight in my chair, a slightly staggered walk as I approach the bench would do? The jury would tune out the trial and spend the rest of the time trying to figure out if I'm for real or not. I am the famous 'Old Codgerham' and that fact alone, in this case, may be the only hope these two fellows have. It's not much, but there is a certain amount of sympathy out there for these two."

Clay sat for a moment. "Then why not take that tack? You'll be second chair at the trial. You can certainly attract attention, enough to throw off the case." This was, perhaps, the best idea that Clay had heard on this case yet.

Cottingham shook his head. "I didn't want to give this to you until after the weekend." He handed Clay a small stack of paper. It was a Motion to Withdrawal as Counsel.

"What the...?"

"I'm sorry Clay. I had met with the defendants earlier today and they said that if I remained on board, they would change their pleas to guilty. I think that's where this case is headed anyway, but they deserve a chance."

"But why me?" Clay pleaded.

"I don't know. But I certainly don't envy you. You're up against some stiff competition."

The prosecution team was headed by Philip Crenshaw. Crenshaw had been with the U.S. Attorneys office for more than two decades and had a reputation as a strictly-by-the-books attorney. He had won a number of big exposure cases against foreign companies suspected of attempting to transfer Genesis technology out of the United States. It was well known he believed all the government's dire warnings that the spread of molecular manufacturing technology outside the borders was a matter of the upmost importance and any breach would bring about chaos. Prosecuting those stepping over the line was oftentimes more than a job for Crenshaw—it was a way of life. He could not hide his pleasure when he finally received the written order granting Cottingham's motion to withdraw as defense counsel.

"We will eat this Furstman fellow alive. These god-damned Red Star people think that they will save the world. Spread Genesis technology and the whole world will be happy. Don't they realize the enemy is just waiting for a chance to get a hold of that technology and destroy us? Do they really think that the Chinese will use it to better their people? Fools!" The other members of the prosecution nodded in agreement. They knew Crenshaw too well to open their mouths in disagreement. The only person in the room willing to speak out was Col. Leeds.

"I want these men found guilty by a trial of their peers. No guilty pleas, no directed verdicts, no mistrials, but guilty nonetheless. We need to set an example here. Their demand to use the services of Mr. Furstman is an attempt to frame this trial as a sham, as a set up, with Landsburg and Finkelstein playing the role of scapegoats. We cannot allow them to succeed in this plan."

"Sir, you have no worries there. Their attorney has no criminal experience whatsoever. I'm not even sure he's ever even tried a case. All corporate and transactional work as far as I can tell. He probably can't tell the difference between an opening statement and witness testimony," Crenshaw assured Col. Leeds, smiling.

"Don't underestimate this man. While he may be uninoculated, he's no fool. He's going to come across as sympathetic to the Defendants' position, and if he can connect with the jury, they may transfer that sympathy to the defendants. Notwithstanding, I trust you will succeed. I would hate to think what may happen if you fail."

Crenshaw's smile faded.

Col. Leeds was familiar with Crenshaw's beliefs. And while he shared Crenshaw's concern of the technology falling into the wrong hands, it was for vastly different reasons. Unlike Crenshaw, Col. Leeds was certain that worldwide adaptation of molecular manufacturing technology would, in fact, lull the world into peaceful bliss, that nations would stop warring and the world's citizens would unite and dismiss all vestiges of government and military.

\* \* \*

"But this is not the way of man," Col. Leeds explained to President Browning. "Such actions give spark to illusions of fantasy but stoke the fire of nightmares. The Father-god made it clear government is necessary for the peaceful co-existence of man, and the military ensures those who fail to obey the rules of a civil society are properly punished."

"But we don't seem to have any real crime taking place, Colonel. In fact, the population seems quite capable of harmonious co-existence," Senate Minority Leader Robert Helig, interjected

"But Senator," Col. Leeds said, turning his attention away from President Browning, "this is not sustainable. It is a dream," he continued, again turning towards the President, "a fallacy waiting for collapse to prove it wrong. Mankind begs for the rule of law, for commandments to dictate the way they live and eat and even sleep."

"It sounds to me like you're simply trying to keep your relevancy here, Colonel," the Senator suggested.

"Not so fast, Robert. Let Colonel Leeds finish," the President said. Helig frowned.

"Thank you, Mr. President," Colonel Leeds continued. "The Genesis, like the Arc of the Covenant, is a means to complete and perfect order. And a way for men such as ourselves to rise above the masses, to use our God-granted abilities for the benefit of ordinary men without the necessity of becoming mired in their petty problems. The common man is free to pursue bliss, to frolic among his chosen path of glee, while those of us possessed of greater ability can concentrate on matters necessary to achieve the primacy of man through law and order."

"Are you suggesting, Colonel, that this is some type of Divine Providence? That we are doing God's work by preventing the sharing of Genesis technology to our European allies?" Senator Helig questioned. "No disrespect, but I believe the common good dictates that we share this technology immediately."

"Sometimes the common good is not the proper course, Senator, if we are to follow the true path," President Browning added. "I believe the Colonel is correct. Greatness does come at a price. Altruism is a dangerous character trait. People are best served by doing those things for which they benefit, using their own independent reason to gain personal happiness. To act altruistically is to act neither rationally nor for one's self-interest. America can only be as great as its citizens and the citizens can only achieve greatness if they are true to themselves."

Senator Helig looked down and shook his head. "I don't know what I hate worse: the Tea Party's insistence on cramming their self-righteous religious morals down everyone else's throats or their worship of Ayn Rand," he mumbled to himself. He lifted his head. "Mr. President—" he started, but Colonel Leeds interrupted him.

"The President is right. Men do not rise to lofty heights solely for altruistic purposes. Inasmuch as our actions benefit others, they provide certain advantages upon us, too. It is the cost which society must, and does, willingly pay for great men to undertake the task of leadership. And leadership is essential. I have no doubt that the spread of Genesis technology would result in society demanding an end to governance, a breakdown of civil society itself. This mistake would destroy all that we have worked for centuries to achieve, throw civilization back into the Dark Ages. Mankind has finally mastered nature itself, yet mastery of this knowledge can be used to undo everything we've learned to this point. What good would Genesis be if others used it to destroy society itself? It is our duty, as the world's sole superpower, to ensure the continuation of the government, of the military. If, as the case may be, America, and its leaders in particular, are also achieving personal advantages, then so be it. It is because of these advantages that we have been able to advance to where we are today."

"So we're just going to tell our European friends to get screwed?" Senator Helig's face grew red as he stood in anger. President Browning and Colonel Leeds remained seated and said nothing. "I apologize, Mr. President. Please excuse my outbreak," he said as he sat back down.

"Listen, Robert. I'm happy to throw the Democrats a bone here and there," Browning said, "but I'm not going to start a damn 'feel-good' program for the world. Genesis has too many potential military uses. Right now, we do more for the world than it has ever done for us and I will veto any attempt to allow the spread of Genesis technology to any other country, friend or foe. Don't push me on this. You don't have the votes to override a veto and I can make the lives of you and your Democratic Party a living nightmare." The President opened a wooden box on his desk, removing a Cuban cigar and handed one to each Helig and Leeds. "It's a real Cuban. Hand-rolled. Not a Genesis replication."

Senator Helig took the cigar and passed it under his nose taking a deep breath.

"One of those advantages I was talking about," Leeds said as he lit his cigar.

## CHAPTER TWENTY

*Breaking News: Tuesday. 12:38 p.m. Apple to be delisted by the end of the week! Debunking rumors that Apple, like hundreds of other companies in the past several months, had fallen victim to Red Star Application pirates and would be unable to turn a profit, Apple CEO Charles Redman announced that Apple had been bought out by Replicator, Inc. and would be privatized by week's end. While Replicator, Inc. has purchased a number of high-tech companies over the past several months, the purchase of Apple is by far its largest to date, exceeding the combined total costs in acquiring both Intel and General Dynamics. Shareholders will receive $973 per share, a significant increase over Apple's closing price yesterday of $277 per share, which has been falling over the past week as a result of continuing rumors of pirating. "Apple technology is highly protected and we are certain that no individual or organization is capable of pirating an App that could duplicate our products. Replicator, Inc. has agreed with our assessment and its buyout of our company will be good for it, our shareholders and the consumer," Redman stated.*

*In other market news, another dozen companies today have declared bankruptcy resulting from application pirates, and rumors swirl that Blue Chip company McDonald's Corporation has been pirated. "McDonald's has been a household name since the middle of the 20th Century," declared McDonald's CEO Les Birkshire. "It has survived economic downturns and government attempts at legislating the eating habits of Americans. It will survive rumors of piracy." Birkshire's comments failed to slow the downturn of McDonald's shares, which have dropped from a 52-week high of $152 per share to a close price today of thirty-seven cents. McDonald's can ill afford piracy. Its decision to retain higher-than-average menu prices overseas has negatively affected foreign* *growth and any damage to its domestic earnings could spell the end for McDonald's.*

*In related news, Government law enforcement agencies, including ATFN agents, have discovered evidence linking Finkelstein and Landsburg to the piracy and failure of not less than 163 companies this month. As with earlier pirated applications, the Government claims that these pirated versions were created prior to the arrest of Finkelstein and Landsburg and were programmed to be released at specific dates in the future in order to maximize damage to the American economy and present foreign adversaries ample opportunity to steal American Genesis technology.*

Almost nine months had passed since Finkelstein and Landsburg had been arrested. Over that period, more than 3500 corporations became victims of piracy and the public's opinion on the culpability of Finkelstein and Landsburg largely depended upon whether they were financially harmed as a result of being a shareholder of one of the victim companies, or financially benefitted by owning one or more of the pirated Genesis-Apps. With opening arguments scheduled to begin in two days, the rumor of a McDonald's piracy-App could not have come at a worse time for the defendants.

Clay sat in his basement office, struggling to develop a sympathetic opening statement. He had long ago given up hope of freeing his clients, and instead had taken the tact that keeping his clients imprisoned for only a matter of decades would be a victory, albeit not a very satisfying one. Clay took heart in knowing much of the public agreed with his assessment that Finkelstein and Landsburg were stooges, being set up for committing a crime executed by others. That, along with the simple fact that most Americans were enjoying the pirated Genesis-Apps, had given Clay some hope that his clients would fair better than the government had planned.

Clay awoke the next morning still sitting in the chair in his basement office. As bad as it had gotten, he never before failed to make it upstairs to bed for the night. He must have fallen asleep while going over papers in one of the many stacks of various sizes that littered his office floor, looking for ideas for his opening statement. He took this as a bad omen.

"What time is it?"

*It is 9:27 a.m.,* his iMeme responded. And then quickly,

*Breaking News: Wednesday. 9:27a.m. McDonald's piracy-App is confirmed.*

*Oh shit!* he thought as he turned his television on.

"Hi, Honey," Lillian said as she came downstairs. "Are you okay? I thought..." but she stopped herself mid-sentence. Clay was sitting on the edge of his chair, eyes fixed on the television, flipping from one station to the next, his mouth agape, like a man possessed. "What's going on?"

Television station after television station showed scenes of the floor of the New York Stock Exchange. Multitudes of people wearing colored vests were shouting in panic while the stock ticker at the bottom of screen rolled past an endless stream of red numbers and downward pointing arrows. Several people in the pits had become violent and were thrashing out at others in an apparent melee. The shouting filled the room with a myriad of tones and pitches, but among the chaos, two words kept being repeated. A feeling of dread passed over Clay. What transpired next, however, was nothing less than catastrophic.

Lillian let out a slight scream and Clay, noticing her for the first time slowly turned his gaze towards her, his face ashen.

Like most disasters, no one was able to pinpoint when it all started. But all the same, too many people lost their heads at the same time and panicked. Unlike Coca-Cola, which managed to continue to market its products overseas and remain financially intact — although with a significantly weaker market value — the piracy of McDonald's delivered a deathblow to the company as a result of its decision to weaken overseas markets and place its faith in domestic revenue. As word of McDonald's Corporation's collapse quickly spread, the fallout first impacted other players in the fast food industry, but soon thereafter infected all sectors of the market. Investors, fearing continued piracy would affect the entire American market and would drastically reduce the value of all equities, began to place sell orders. As more investors saw what was happening to the market, more and more began to sell their shares. Within 30 minutes, every American exchange was dead. The American economy collapsed in real time; the exchanges, all of them, ceased business as chaos and fear in the market devalued every stock of every publicly traded company to zero. Shares were worth nothing because the products were worth nothing. Everything was free — the energy to run the Genesis, the materials to build the products, even the technology to program the Genesis, all freely available on shareware portals across the Cloud.

What began as a bad omen in Clay's eyes became a firestorm. Lillian grabbed the remote and turned the volume completely down on the television to talk to Clay, but it did not stop the display of images flashing across the screen. Scenes of anger and rage, mouths forming the unheard shouts that by now, even in such short a span of time, Clay could discern.

"What's going on, Clay?" Lillian asked, breaking the silence.

Clay was instantly aware the tide of sympathy on which he had pinned his only hopes had turned. "I can hear it now, Lill. Can you hear it?" Clay tilted his head slightly to the side as if to listen better.

"I don't hear anything," Lillian said, straining to listen.

But Clay heard it. He heard it as sure as he heard the pounding of his pulse in his ears. "Listen. I hear it louder now."

"Are you okay, Clay? I'm worried about you," Lillian said, moving closer and placing her hand on Clay's forehead.

"No. I'm certain now. There it is. Surely you heard it that time? Finkelstein and Landsburg," he said, a slight grin on his face. "These guys blew it. They were folk heroes, Lill. Folk heroes! But now..." Clay grew silent momentarily. "Now, they're Public Enemies Number One. We had it, Lill. The public was on our side. But now, I can hear it. Can you hear them? They want blood. They want sacrifice. The Plebeians want justice. And justice shall be delivered, swiftly and harshly." Clay leaned back in his chair and stared at the ceiling.

Lillian sat on the desk in front of Clay and looked at him as if she did not even recognize him. Clay was a changed man. It was not that long ago that he had been appointed to this case, yet in that time a certain change had occurred in Clay. Once possessed of an energetic spirit, eyes glinting with a hint of cunning. Now, at the doorstep of the trial and with the collapse of the economic system, Clay had taken on the look of a deranged genius. During his last press conference he failed to even complete his sentences. It had been obvious to many for the past few weeks that the court should have assigned the defendants new counsel (Clay seemingly unable to properly defend the men), but no such action had taken place.

The morning slipped into evening and Clay remained motionless on the chair. Lillian had grown weary of his silence and spent the day straightening the house, though she dared not disturb the piles of paperwork in his office. Clay did not even seem to notice the knock on the door in the late afternoon. A clerk from the Federal Prosecutor's office dropped off an envelope which Lillian had brought down and placed on Clay's lap, and there it still remained. When her iMeme alerted her it had reached the hour of six p.m. Lillian came back downstairs.

"Honey," she said as she shook him slightly. "You've got an appointment to meet," she stopped herself. She could not bring herself to say the two words that so haunted Clay earlier that day. "The trial starts tomorrow. They're expecting you."

Without a word, Clay stood up. He took only enough notice of the envelope on his lap to toss it onto his now vacated spot on the chair and he went to upstairs to get dressed. When he reappeared, Lillian again noticed the change in Clay. His suit hung off his body like it, too, wanted to distance itself from the person of Levi Clayton Furstman. His eyes appeared cloudy and his cheeks sunken as he left the apartment, still not having spoken a word.

Lillian was half-asleep on the basement couch by the time Clay returned. He avoided the stacks of papers scattered across the floor that revealed no signs of order, no evidence of reason. He sighed heavily.

"Hello," Lillian said, hoping Clay had at least spoken to his clients rather than sitting silently before them. She noticed he had a nearly empty glass of vodka in his hand.

Clay looked over towards the couch. "You're still down here, huh?" He picked up the envelope and sat back down. "It's kind of crazy. I'm a failure even before the trial has started."

"Don't say that," Lillian scolded as she got up off the couch.

"It's true." He sighed again.

"No one would be able to defend these guys. No one will hold it against you. You'll give it your best and carry on."

"You're wrong. Other lawyers would defend these guys. They may not win, but they would defend them. But I've got nothing. No strategy, no argument, no legal footing to even raise an objection, let alone put on a valid defense."

Clay, who had been holding the envelope absent-mindedly, flipped it over and opened it. He pulled out a small stack of papers.

### MOTION TO SEEK THE DEATH PENALTY

> NOW COMES *Plaintiff, the United States of America, by and through the Office of the Federal Prosecutor and does hereby move this Honorable Court to enter its Order allowing the Government to seek the Death Penalty against the Defendants in this Matter, pursuant to Espionage Act of 1917, 18 U.S.C. § 793 et seq (as amended) and in support thereof states as follows: ...*

Clay flipped through the remaining pages of the Motion. The Motion argued that the defendants, by reason of their involvement in the demise of the entire financial system of the United States, had caused severe and immediate harm and were thus eligible under the Statute for the capital punishment.

Clay let the document fall from his hands and it fluttered to the floor. He stared across the room.

"You know, the funny thing is that I never really wanted to be an attorney. I thought it'd be a good degree. Something to open doors. And yet, it's been nearly thirty years and I'm still a lawyer," he said quietly.

Lillian remained silent as she looked around at the scattered piles of notes on the floor. Clay watched her eyes scan the room, stopping at each stack of notes and a sad expression, like someone whose dreams had become disconnected and lost, crossed her face. He tried to imagine what he would have done with his life had he not gone to law school. Whether they would have continued to date or even been married.

"So, give up the practice. Find something else to do. We're all going to have to find something to do." She finally said. "I would think the Genesis will continue to replicate things until our subscriptions run out. Maybe longer, I don't know how that works. And we do have some pirated Apps, they should still work forever, I would think. We'll figure out a way to make things work out," she said, sounding as broken as the world in which they now lived.

Clay did not answer. He did not need to. They both knew the answer.

Clay loosened his tie and headed towards the stairs. Lillian followed him. At the top of the landing, Clay paused. "I need another fucking drink," he sighed. Clay turned towards his Genesis. "Genesis, Johnny Walker Blue, splash. Waterford Lismore tumbler." The drink would not help, but it would not hurt either. He had purchased the app on a whim one night. It was late. Lillian had gone to bed and he was drinking with a friend who was talking about the joys of fine whisky. Clay was buzzed at the time and life had seemed so simple, PreVentall had not yet been released and the Genesis made him feel rich. *So much hope,* he thought. Clay had decided to splurge and purchased the Johnny Walker and Waterford Crystal Genesis Apps. They were expensive, but his friend was right, there was something spectacular about drinking a Johnny Walker Blue out of fine crystal that could not be matched.

He stepped to the counter and turned on the small television they kept in the kitchen. A mindless reality program faded into view. A young woman was vying for the opportunity to date a handsome and rich railroad heir, when the program was interrupted.

*U.S. markets will remain closed indefinitely. Senator Dunkin of Massachusetts has sponsored legislation meant to lessen the impact of the market crash by authorizing the Government to pay each and every registered shareholder one dollar per share for every outstanding share they own. "Americans are bleeding to death," the Senator explained. "I recognize that this is a band-aid when what the patient really needs is a tourniquet, but this move will provide some compensation to American citizens until things can be worked out. While I do not expect the dollar amount given to each individual will fully compensate them for their losses, our hands our tied. This seemingly minor act will obligate the Government for trillions of dollars of compensation. In times like these, every little bit of assistance can help."*

Clay took a sip of his drink and he felt the anger inside start to rise. "These bastards want a defense?" he asked out loud. "Why the hell should they get one? They sure as hell don't deserve one!" he shouted.

Lillian tried to keep her calm. "Clay, these guys didn't do it. You know that."

Clay did not let this detail deter him. The alcohol allowed his anger to grow, prevented him from hiding his hate and despair any longer. "But they did!"

Lillian gave Clay a puzzled look.

"I never told you. Never told anyone, in fact," Clay said, his voice lower. "They're the original pirates, they know how to program the Genesis."

A look of disbelief crossed Lillian's face.

Clay stood up, his eyes filling with rage. "Do you realize what they've done? They've wiped out industry. No one's worked very hard lately, but at least they worked. What will our children do? No more jobs, no more money, no more future whatsoever! Those bastards destroyed it all! Everything!" He raised his glass to take a drink and instead threw it as hard as he could. Lillian jumped as it shattered against the wall. "Genesis! Johnny Walker Blue, splash. Waterford Lismore tumbler!" He retrieved the drink and smashed it, too, against the wall.

"Clay, what are you doing? Stop that," Lillian begged, tears beginning to fill her eyes.

But Clay continued. It felt good to release his anger and he continued to call forth drinks and watch as they smashed against his kitchen wall. "Fuck you, Finkelstein!" The sound of fine crystal shattering echoed in the room. "Fuck you, Landsburg!" Another glass shattered.

Lillian tried again to stop Clay but he pushed her aside. Clay continued retrieving drinks from the Genesis and smashing glass after glass against the wall. She slowly turned to go, tears running down her cheeks.

"What are you doing! What's going on?" Katie screamed as she stepped into the kitchen followed by Matthew and Elizabeth. The two younger children's eyes widened as they saw their father seemingly out of control.

Lillian grabbed Katie and pushed her and the others out of the doorway. "Your father is having a rough evening." She flashed an angry glare back towards Clay through the doorway. "The case has taken a turn for the worse. It's okay, he'll be fine." She tried to comfort them all.

"Fine?" Matthew shouted. "That's bull! Nothing's fine! I just heard that everyone is out of business for good. That Dad's clients have screwed everything!"

"Now, Matthew," Lillian started.

"He's right, Mom. I heard a rumor that even colleges are shutting down. That's it. My life is over. Done." Katie's eyes were filling with tears.

"Why is Dad even defending these guys? They should be un-inoculated and die," Elizabeth added.

Lillian hugged her kids and then stepped part way into the kitchen. "Clay?"

He did not even seem to hear her. She opened her mouth to speak again, but then did not. She slipped her wedding band off her finger. Clay continued to smash drinks against the wall, mumbling to himself. She paused and then removed her car keys from the hook upon which they hung and put the ring in their place. "Come on, kids. We're going to grandma's."

Clay did not acknowledge their departure. Glass after glass was turned to shards, a small pile forming at the foot of the wall which was now soaked in single-malt scotch. And that is when it hit him. As he grabbed his keys from the hook he noticed Lillian's wedding band. He paused momentarily. He could deal with her later, right now he needed to speak to Finkelstein and Landsburg.

As the trial started, there was no escape from the barrage of images and stories emanating from the courtroom. Across the nation iMeme holographic screens glowed in the streets while computers around the world were hooked into the Internet and Cloud to display the events. Even an old RCA black and white console flickering in the heart of Africa picked up the live images of the courtroom as the proceedings got underway. As the jury was being led into the courtroom, the cameras scanned the multitude of faces in the crowd. The two defendants were accompanied by several Federal Policemen who were supposed to protect them, but it was clear from their earlier comments and body language that little effort would be used to suppress the crowd if it decided to lose control. Both Finkelstein and Landsburg wore the expressions of dying men who had been told by their doctor that their disease had advanced beyond the help of medicine and nothing now could stop imminent death — an expression that seemed to accept fate, but hinted at the fear that the end would be more painful than hoped. The members of the prosecution team were smug, failing, perhaps intentionally, to suppress their smiles. Clay could not help but imagine that this was the look of Southern prosecutors of the early twentieth century who, being charged with the condemnation of a black man accused in the rape of a white woman, were well aware the judge and jury had already reached a verdict before the opening arguments even began and that the trial was little more than theatre, a chance for the prosecutor to impress the jury with his thespian skills. The courtroom was a chaotic murmur.

"Oy yez! Oy yez! This session of the U.S. Court for the Seventh Circuit, Northern District of Illinois is now in session. The Honorable Judge Ronald O'Malley presiding," the bailiff stated as Judge O'Malley took his place on the bench. Everyone in the courtroom was standing. The bailiff signaled the audience to be seated, but even counsel, intimately familiar with the protocol, remained standing. The tension in the room was palpable as the crowd leaned in, awaiting the spectacle about to unfold like a crowd of Romans awaiting Caesar to proclaim *To the beasts!* Judge O'Malley was a large man who had sat on the bench for the past thirty-five years. He was not fond of high-profile cases and had warned the press that they would be on a short leash. As he surveyed the courtroom his face remained expressionless. "Please be seated!" he boomed. This time, the crowd obeyed.

Crenshaw gave a small nod to Judge O'Malley and stood to deliver his opening speech to the jury—a well-rehearsed and emotional appeal detailing the undoing of an entire nation, one sure to arouse the passions of the jury. Crenshaw had rewritten it not less than a dozen times, toning it down as of late so as to still retain its dramatic effect, but not so much as to incite a riot in the courtroom. While he, too, had every desire to see Finkelstein and Landsburg suffer a slow, painful demise, he was too dedicated to his profession to want vigilante justice to be carried out, at least not before he was able to deliver his closing statements and rejoice in victory. He took another look toward the Federal Officers standing watch over the defendants and recognizing that they would do little to uphold their duty to protect the defendants, made a conscious note to keep his eye, not only on the jury, but also the packed courtroom. Crenshaw faced the jury and audibly cleared his throat as he approached them.

As he was about to begin, Crenshaw glanced over at Clay and nodded (the gesture meant to convey to the jury that Crenshaw, regardless of what he may say in this courtroom, held the capacity for compassion). His eyes grew wide and he nearly stumbled at the sight. In the time that had led up to this moment—the presentation of the jury, the defendants being led into the courtroom in shackles, the entry of Judge O'Malley—no one had paid much attention to Clay. Now all eyes in the courtroom were turned toward him and a general gasp rose from the crowd's collective throats. Clay's face showed no signs of stress or worry. Although it was well known he was not inoculated, several in the courtroom swore he looked younger than he had at his last press conference. As Lillian watched from her mother's house, she was most surprised by his eyes. They were clear and bright and no trace of despair was evidenced on his countenance. He simply sat, a faint smile across his lips.

"Ladies and gentlemen of the jury, your Honor, friends and citizens of the United States," Crenshaw began. He had regained his composure and felt the need to draw attention back to himself, where he could begin his methodical dissection of the guilty parties. "The State is prepared to show you evidence of a crime so heinous, so wrapped in moral perversion, so depraved that I can only pray that the good Lord Himself will find it in His abundant heart to absolve these two men for what we here on Earth will never forgive." Crenshaw moved his eyes to the crowd and back to the jury, carefully assessing the levels of anger and passion that rose in each and every pair, conscious of his need to temper the crowd's anger and avoid a mob scene. "These two gentleman—if you will kindly permit me to use a term generally forbidden to such creatures as these two—have willfully and wantonly brought forth upon this proud Nation a pestilence so vile, it has poisoned our country to the very core!"

Not once did Clay attempt to reign in the inflammatory statements leveled at his clients. Crenshaw's opening statement promised and threatened and accused, and Clay thought he saw several members of the jury lick their lips, like hungry jackals, in anticipation of the forthcoming trial. On several occasions, Crenshaw's remarks prompted even Judge O'Malley to grab his gavel in anticipation of sustaining any objections. None ever came. The increasingly despondent Finkelstein and Landsburg sat in stark contrast to the calm reserve of their attorney, whose smile never faded.

But Clay's demeanor was not the only peculiarity. Every few minutes, he would reach into his suit coat and pull out an expensive cigar, which he would place under his nose as he inhaled deeply. He would then place the cigar neatly on the desk in an ever-growing pile. Later he began reaching into his briefcase, and then into file boxes he had brought into court. The courtroom cameras were trained on the impassioned monologue of Crenshaw, but increasingly they cut back to the view of the rapidly growing structure of cigars being built by Clay. Lillian watched in dismay as Clay appeared to be uninterested in anything Crenshaw was saying, as if the opening arguments of the prosecution were no more than the background soundtrack to a play that held no interest for Clay.

When at last Crenshaw completed his evisceration of the defendants, he thanked the courtroom and sat down among his peers. It was clear throughout he was unaware of the actions of Clay, and he gave a brief expression of surprise when he noticed the pyramid of cigars that had risen during his speech.

"Does the Defense have an opening to present to the jury?" Judge O'Malley asked.

Clay stood slowly, placing the most recent cigar upon the now impressive pile. He buttoned the coat of his suit and cleared his throat.

"Ladies and gentlemen of the jury. Regardless of what you may hear here during this trial, the facts will show that my clients have committed no crime against Coca-Cola, corporate America, or the citizens of these United States." A buzz arose among the crowd and Judge O'Malley called for order. Clay continued, "Before this trial is complete, you will discover that you have no recourse but to find them both not guilty." He stood a moment longer and then, unbuttoning his suit coat, removed another cigar and placed it on the pile before sitting back down. Judge O'Malley sat briefly motionless and stared at both Clay and the pile of cigars before he asked the prosecution to call forth its first witness. By the time Judge O'Malley dismissed the jury at the end of the day, Clay's pile of cigars had grown to take over almost the entire table at which he sat. As the crowd from the gallery stood to leave, Clay passed out the cigars to anyone willing to take them.

During the next eight days, the Prosecution brought witness after witness to the stand to prove their case. And over the course of those eight days, Clay never said anything other than, "I have no questions for the witness, your Honor." Eight days during which twenty-three witnesses came and went and Clay did nothing, other than continue his bizarre behavior of producing items from his person, his briefcase or his always present file boxes, setting them on the table before him, and passing them out at the end of the day. On day two, Clay substituted the cigars with expensive fountain pens. Throughout day three he produced Breitling watches from his file boxes, which he continued to bring into the courtroom by intermittently seeking leave to hold a brief recess; almost two hundred watches had emerged by the time the court recessed for the day.

By day four, the press pool started placing bets on what Clay would bring in an obvious attempt to distract the jury. No one had correctly guessed Robbe & Berking silver cocktail forks, which those in attendance found useful as they made their way out of the courtroom where a buffet of whole steamed lobsters, oysters on the half-shell and boiled shrimp awaited anyone who so desired. Nor did the press guess the Oakley sunglasses, Bollman hats, or Redwing boots brought on days five, six and seven. While the jury had been sequestered during the trial, the press reported it was likely that at least a few members noticed that some of those in the gallery on day eight wore the watches, boots, hats or sunglasses that Clay had previously laid out, en mass, during the course of the previous week. And some surmised that while Clay's tactics may have distracted the jury, it did not win him many friends among jurors who were unable to partake in any of his apparent generosity.

On the eighth day of trial, Clay walked into the courtroom with only a large brandy sniffer. The press and crowds seemed disappointed, having expected more large boxes of gifts. Their disappointment was short lived, however, as Crenshaw's presentation took place to the backdrop of Clay periodically placing diamonds into the brandy sniffer.

Tweeters in the courtroom observed and commented on Clay's activities.

*Furstman filling glass w/ diamonds! Who can blame? Finally cracked this week! #trialofcentury*

*Furstman continues bizarre behavior with diamonds. Task too big. Defendants sure to get death penalty!*

*Furstman joins party. No interest in helping criminals escape justice. Playing with diamonds today!*

*Furstman sees the dark. All roads lead to failure. We are doomed and F&L to blame. #finklelandsburg Lynching soon!*

By the time the prosecution rested its case, Clay had nearly filled the brandy sniffer with dozens of diamonds.

"Is the Defense ready to present its case?" Judge O'Malley asked. Clay appeared not to hear and had continued to place diamonds, one by one, into the glass. Judge O'Malley banged his gavel on the bench. "Ahem! Is the Defense ready to present its case?"

Clay looked up, surprised. "Pardon me, your Honor," he said as he stood. He buttoned his suit coat and approached the bench. "If it please the Court, your Honor, I move for a directed verdict and ask that this entire matter be dismissed and the defendants released immediately," he stated with a steady voice.

Crenshaw, was so taken aback by Clay's request he momentarily stood frozen, his mouth slightly ajar, before he regained his composure and shouted to the judge. "Your Honor! I recognize the difficulty facing the defense in this proceeding, but I will not allow this Court to be insulted! The defense has chosen to sit idly by, bringing forth favors and passing them out to the gallery while the State has set forth evidence sufficient to convict the two accused!" Crenshaw opened his mouth to say more, but Clay interrupted him.

"Your Honor. I have the right to be heard. The State has failed wholeheartedly to show any wrongdoing by my clients under the Espionage Act," Clay stated calmly.

The courtroom, sensing Clay was going to attempt some trick to secure the release of the two guilty men, burst into chaos. Crenshaw turned in time to see the guards snapping to life. While they had little desire to protect the safety of Finkelstein and Landsburg, they recognized at once that much of the crowd's anger was directed at Clay. While they did not think very kindly of his clients, they respected his position as an officer of the court, and not an accused, and vigorously attempted to settle the crowd down. Judge O'Malley was beating his gavel on the bench so hard it split in two, while screaming at the top of his lungs for order. The Bailiff, suddenly aware that he was witnessing the beginning of a riot, pulled out his sidearm and fired a single shot into the ceiling. The entire courtroom fell into silence as all eyes turned toward the Bailiff. Judge O'Malley threw a stern look toward the man but seized the opportunity to take control over his courtroom once again. "Order in the Court! Order in the Court! You will be seated at once!" The crowd settled down and slowly began to retake their seats.

"What in the God-damn hell are you talking about, sir?" Judge O'Malley questioned Clay. A murmur began to rise among the gallery again, and Judge O'Malley quickly pulled off his shoe and beat it on the bench. "And there will be no outbursts in this Courtroom or I will have the offending persons arrested immediately," he shouted to the crowd.

Clay, who had been standing behind the defendant's table, walked around and faced the jury. "Ladies and gentlemen of the jury. We have been gathered here these past several days to determine the guilt or innocence of these two men." Clay motioned to Finkelstein and Landsburg. He paused briefly before he started speaking again. "The prosecution has been tasked here with showing that by pirating the Coca-Cola App, these two men have potentially transmitted replicator technology into the hands of foreign persons and by such acts have caused a grave and terrible injury.

"Let us, however, be clear from the very start. This case does not revolve around the question of the transmission of replicator technology. While the Coca-Cola App was not authorized, its dissemination through the Cloud is no different than any other Genesis App available to the public for consumption. There are no Genesis secrets that can be obtained from a pirated application that cannot be obtained from a legal Genesis-App. In fact, I will stipulate here and now that the defendants disseminated replicator information in such a manner that the subject information could be obtained by foreign nationals," Clay said confidently.

Crenshaw, who had been jotting down notes, looked up and flashed a grin. *This is going to be too easy*, he thought as the courtroom threatened to slip into chaos again. Judge O'Malley preemptively banged the shoe he still held in his hand.

"No," Clay said, continuing his argument. "This case has nothing to do with dissemination. This case is about *harm*. And the question that has been set before this jury, this courtroom, is whether the defendants have inflicted harm upon this nation."

Crenshaw tossed his notebook down and leaned back in his chair. "On a silver platter, no less," he whispered to his co-counsel.

"This case started with the collapse of Coca-Cola," Clay said. "A little over a week ago it escalated with the collapse of the stock market. Not of any single company or industry, but the collapse of the entire stock market, the entire financial system, really. In the blink of an eye, the net value of all American citizens plummeted by... how much? A trillion dollars? Ten trillion dollars? A hundred million trillion dollars?" Clay looked around the courtroom. An anger simmered among the crowd gathered inside. Clay continued, "Who can tell how much was lost? My in-laws have been investing for years. They lost an entire lifetime of investments. How much did they lose? Ten thousand dollars? One hundred thousand? A Million? Who can say?

"I can tell you what I lost. I had a few shares of Huber, Inc. and Galaxian, both penny stocks. A few more Blue Chips as well. I, of course, was not a rich man. Just a simple attorney scratching out a meager living. How much did I lose? Ten thousand dollars, twenty thousand, maybe? Not much more. But it was all I had. Now the market is dead. The shares worth nothing and my personal wealth, as I'm continually reminded by the press, is zero. I'm broke. You're broke. Hell, we're all broke. And to add insult to injury, our prospect for employment in this country is slim to none. Most of us don't work very hard, but we were able to rely on government subsidies from overseas export taxes. But now what? There are no exports to tax because there are no more companies. We're broke, with no prospects for future income. But what does this all mean?" Clay looked around the courtroom and then back to the jury. "What does it mean that the economy has been destroyed? That you lost ten thousand dollars," he pointed at a random member of the jury, "and you lost a million?" he said pointing to another juror, "and I am, after today, soon to lose my job?"

Crenshaw smiled again. It was clear to him that Clay was throwing in the towel. Perhaps trying to distance himself from the two criminals and attempt to protect his own reputation. Attempt to keep some semblance of normalcy when this was all over.

Clay continued. "Over the past eight days you have sat there watching this trial unfold, listening to Mr. Crenshaw detail how my clients, single-handedly, destroyed America while I played with my cigars, and my boots and my pens. And today, with diamonds." Clay stepped over to the table, grabbed the glass of diamonds and tossed them into the gallery. A rather large woman in the front row fell to the floor to collect the loose stones.

Judge O'Malley stood up. "Order in the court!" he bellowed. "You will return to your seat! Now!" The large woman, whose head was under the seat of the gentleman who had been sitting next to her, looked back at Judge O'Malley, sheepishly. She flushed as she rose slowly to her knees, apologizing to the people sitting around her but holding tight to her cache of diamonds.

"Don't you see?" Clay continued. "It doesn't mean anything. We've been living in a world of capitalism and limited resources for so long it seems no one recognizes the Genesis has made money and investment and even net worth entirely without meaning! So, the stock market crashed. But where is the harm?

"You," he said pointing to Crenshaw. "Maybe you lost one dollar or maybe you lost one hundred million dollars, yet you, and every other person in this courtroom, has everything they ever need, or, if not, you can replicate it at will! This whole idea of classes and socio-economic strata is a lie. No one in America is in want; no one is in need. What does it matter if corporations are ruined? They're not living, breathing beings. They're merely pieces of paper supported by laws, but without any real substance. The shareholders, the citizens of this Nation, are no less rich today than they were nine days ago when their stock shares had a dollar amount attached to them. Don't you see? With the Genesis, each and every one of us has infinite wealth! McDonald's may well have disappeared, and along with it the few employees it required to churn burgers out from the Genesis. Yet where is the real, tangible loss?

"Even Les Birkshire's loss of his position as CEO of McDonald's is not a tangible loss. Sure, McDonald's can no longer pay him, yet he does not need, nor could he even spend, the money even if he did receive it. His account, like all of our accounts, is nothing more than a collection of promises—the banking system nothing more than a game of Monopoly. Money comes in and goes out of our accounts, but there is, in fact, no real transfer of value because money itself is worth nothing. It is nothing more than an electronic binary code that records transactions. When we go out for dinner or purchase a new car or a new home, our individual net value remains the same: infinite!

"The day Genesis was delivered to your household was the day you could have possessed ten billion dollars or ten cents, and it did not matter. In either case, your true value was not based upon your assets, but on the simple fact of whether you had access to a Genesis, with which you could create anything and everything. And in America, everyone has access to Genesis, which, like Death itself, is the Great Equalizer!

"What is it Finkelstein and Landsburg did, but to open our eyes? What *harm* did they commit? What *injury?* The statute requires that the State prove intent or reason to believe the prohibited act will cause *injury*. But no harm was suffered. In fact, no harm could be suffered. What harm to a nation that has absolute access to any resource at unlimited quantities and at no cost? What injury inflicted upon a nation with everything that was, is, or could ever be? No one in their right mind can reasonably believe we are any less rich than we were before this alleged calamity. The State can show no injury. It cannot prove its case!"

Judge O'Malley sat momentarily, absorbing Clay's speech while the crowd held silent. He looked up. "Would counsel please approach?" Clay and Crenshaw walked toward the bench.

"Listen, counsel," Judge O'Malley whispered, staring at Clay. "You may be right here, but there's no way that I'm going to grant your motion now." He looked out at the crowd in the courtroom. Many were engaged in quiet conversations, some nodding their heads slightly as they spoke, other animatedly disagreeing. "Some of these folks may have understood," he said, "but I'd bet my Genesis it'll take a number of them a while longer to comprehend what you just said. I'm going to continue this trial for a couple days. Then, if you are correct, I can have Finkelstein and Landsburg released without causing a firestorm." A barely perceptible slump had washed over Crenshaw's body, briefly, before he straightened his tall frame again and nodded slightly. Judge O'Malley stood, his full height on the bench rising high above everyone, causing everyone to stop speaking. He reached for his gavel and raised it to his shoulder before he remembered that it was broken. He gave a brief sigh. "The Court will take this motion under advisement. Court is now in recess!" He turned to the bailiff. "The defendants will be escorted back to their cells." He turned toward chambers, and stepped off the bench.

In the several days following, Clay noticed a change in society. It was as if the Country had awoken from some horrible nightmare. It was, Clay thought, as if mankind had been compelled, mindlessly racing toward the edge of the abyss like a mass of

Botticelli-like human-lemmings, and upon taking the plunge, discovering that they were not falling, but flying, free from the bounds of gravity and physics, from the chains of history, the bindings of human suffering. In taking flight, society's eyes were opened to the triviality of economy, of supply and demand, of the need for a government. With Genesis, all was good and all was possible. Mankind, or at least Americans, could live in peace and government could serve no purpose other than to protect the nation's borders and the secret of molecular manufacturing. While the citizens of the United States rejected the Monroe Doctrine and ideas of nation-building, and moved into the cocoon of isolationist thought, government itself was reduced to its basic and colonial roots. Professional politicians were replaced with statesmen, who dealt with the needs of society on a part-time basis. The Government concerned itself with only matters of public protection and the pursuit of happiness.

"Do you think it's odd now," Clay asked, "that we don't go into the office anymore? I mean, I've worked most of my life and now…"

Miguel smiled at Clay. "Come on, Clay. Just enjoy it. Did you really like going downtown and pretending you actually did something?" Miguel asked.

"Perhaps not. But it did give me something to do." Clay responded. And then more thoughtfully, "Don't you sort of feel like life has become a little less meaningful?"

"Less meaningful? What do you mean? I've got everything I need," Miguel said.

Clay was at a loss to explain. Miguel seemed to accept with a shrug that in the grand scheme of things, he had no need to do more than what he had already accomplished.

*Perhaps,* Clay thought, *Miguel had felt he had already achieved his life's goal, had fulfilled his youthful dreams, when he had managed to play professional baseball, albeit briefly. But what of others? What about those who had not yet made their mark on the world? Was it all now meaningless since Genesis provides all of one's needs and PreVentall endows one with immortality? Did it even matter any longer that a person would not make a mark in the world, had no means by which he could, as Beowulf so urgently sought, achieve vainglory, when one is immortal? When one's legacy would be one's very existence, not merely some memory or shadow of his old self, but the living, breathing being that he is?*

Yet the lack of any real consequences on Americans did not mean that the collapse was unfelt. The remainder of the world, those who were ensured of mortality, was now at the mercy of the U.S. government. As a result of the payouts by the U.S. Treasury to compensate shareholders for the stock market collapse and a liberal reading of the Commerce Clause, the U.S. Government now owned and operated all American corporations and continued to replicate and distribute products around the globe. This was done under the auspices of the Department of Defense and headed by the newly appointed Foreign Commerce Chief, Gen. William B. Rutheford. In addition to being in charge of all international trade between the United States and foreign nations, the Foreign Commerce Chief was also responsible for ensuring any trade undertaken would not include the dissemination of any classified technologies. In order to achieve this goal, the Foreign Commerce Chief was named as the head of the National Police Force as well as that of the division of the regular army responsible for protecting Genesis technology.

The whole situation struck Clay as ironic. So many folks who were only a few years earlier so radically conservative they would have the nation believe that any government interference with business was un-American and worth preventing at any cost were silent. President Browning had been elected as a Tea Party candidate. His promise of smaller government and laissez faire capitalism was responsible, through the use of publicly funded research dollars, for producing Genesis. And Genesis was responsible for the destruction of capitalism. Americans no longer needed money. They lived off government largesse in the form of the Genesis—lived on the dole, so to speak. The Twenty-First Century brought about a perverse form of socialism whereby from each came nothing, and to each went everything. A form of socialism where the entire country joined the ranks of what was once reserved for the downtrodden—public welfare—and lived off handouts. No longer did prosperity and happiness require independence and individual achievement. Sloth was rewarded as richly as productiveness. Mankind's drive to create and prosper had been diminished as labor held no benefit. Atlas had at last shrugged, and yet the world continued turning.

Yet the government continued to insist that the global spread of Genesis technology could only lead to destruction of Western society. And so the machinations of capitalism prospered outside the gates of America, perverted by the simple fact that America had unlimited supply regardless of demand. The American government began to collect the wealth of the world, not in dollars, but in power. There was nothing any foreign nation could offer that could not be duplicated one hundred-fold by the Genesis at no cost. There were, of course, certain non-tangibles that were desired by some, including Gen. Rutheford's second in command, Col. Leeds, who's position allowed him to set his own price.

Col. Leeds enjoyed his position as Assistant Foreign Commerce Secretary almost as much as being Deputy Commander of the National Police. As Assistant Secretary, he was allowed to travel abroad at will. While such trips included the obligatory meetings with foreign dignitaries, there were always opportunities to find time for leisurely activities, which Col. Leeds always found more interesting because of foreigners' desire to rub elbows with an American, especially one in a position to grant a temporary visa into the United States, and the chance to be inoculated. The desire for immortality was strong, and it was to his great delight that many people were willing to pay almost any price to obtain it.

* * *

Col. Leeds set down his glass and looked around the room. The Barcelona Toro Club was slow for a Friday afternoon. It was good that there were few witnesses to Spanish Prime Minister Balboa's anger as he left the table. The trade discussions had not gone as well as Balboa had hoped. They had gone exactly as Leeds had planned. He smiled as the waiter approached his table with the bill.

"Señor. Por favor, send those two ladies another round on me," Leeds said as he nodded towards the de Goya sisters sitting across the room. The younger, Maribel, was a famous Spanish model. The other, Inés, the wife of a wealthy businessman. The two sat at the bar drinking martinis in a bored and almost disdainful manner, as only the most privileged women can do. He watched from across the room as the waiter approached them and, after a brief conversation, pointed toward Col. Leeds. The two women looked over and caught his eye. Without so much as a smile, they waived the waiter off, the drinks rebuffed. Col. Leeds stood up and straightened out the jacket of his William Fioravanti suit and walked toward the women, his mouth twisted into a slight smile. They ignored his approach. He had not interested them with his thinning hair and thin frame. Like most Europeans, they believed that PreVentall not only restored one's youth, but also corrected those natural faults, such as premature graying or, in Col. Leeds' case, early male pattern baldness.

"In many cultures, it would be considered impolite to refuse a gift, regardless of its source," he said. The women continued to ignore him. "In others, an insult worthy of drastic measures."

At this, he pulled out a switchblade knife from his pocket and snapped it open. He then placed the blade in his hand and sliced the flesh open from the base of his index finger across his palm. A crimson line followed the blade. The women watched as the blood began to ooze from the open wound. He calmly set the knife down on the bar and pulled a handkerchief from his pocket. He wiped the blood from his soaked palm and revealed a completely healed wound. The women's eyes opened wide and they smiled. "Ooooh. Americano?" the one on the left cooed.

Col. Leeds smiled again, his cold eyes not softening at all.

"It is quite a wonderful thing, this ability to heal wounds, to remain healthy and young. Forever." He had their rapt attention now. He motioned the waiter to return with the previously rejected drinks. "Can I offer you a gift?"

"A drink?" Maribel questioned, her eyes seeking more.

"A drink now, yes. Perhaps more, later," he replied. He paused for a moment as he picked up his knife, wiped the blood from its blade, and replaced it into his pocket. "I have the ability to offer much more, if you are willing." The women looked toward each other than then back at Col. Leeds, smiling.

Inés spoke up. "We are very willing... Mr... Mr..."

Leeds did not respond. He motioned to the bartender. "Uno más, por favor," he called. "So, Señoras, shall we share a drink?" he said as he sat down beside them.

Maribel's apartment was located in Diagonal Mar, on the shores of the Mediterranean. The apartment encompassed the entire 25th floor. As Maribel poured them each another drink, Col. Leeds made his way through her apartment, seemingly unimpressed by either the panoramic views of Barcelona or the opulence of Maribel's taste in art and furnishings. When at last he entered her bedroom, the smile crept back onto his face. The room was dominated by a massive four-poster bed, 16th Century Habsburg, covered in silk sheets and, in Col. Leeds' opinion, too many pillows. On one wall was a tapestry depicting what appeared to be a group of naked people crawling up a hill, following several soldiers riding on horseback. Several of the naked people were tied to the horse by ropes, their bodies appearing to have suffered injury, perhaps, Leeds thought, from having been earlier dragged by the noble beasts. Col. Leeds smiled wider, recognizing a similarity between it and the movie poster for a film he had seen many years earlier, and many times since. Pasolini's *Salo*. He had found the film in his father's belongings shortly after his death. Even as a youth, Col. Leeds had admired the two young soldiers dancing at the end of the film; their fortune to have participated in the entire affair, yet remain beyond reproach as merely soldiers following the orders of those more senior.

The de Goya sisters met up with him, laughing to some joke between themselves, both slightly unsteady with the amount of alcohol they consumed. Maribel was holding a bottle of Barrique de Ponciano Porfidio tequila, one strap of her dress having fallen off her shoulder, allowing the front to fall down far enough to reveal the dark pigment of one areola. Col. Leeds had dominated the conversation all evening, inserting now and then a vague reference to being able to arrange a visit to the United States for inoculation. This kept the women entertained, as well as him.

Col. Leeds continued his assessment of the bedroom, to size up the surroundings. He contemplated his possibilities, knowing that the evening had progressed as the sisters had expected and the two were not surprised to find themselves at Maribel's place, standing at the threshold of her bedroom. Maribel stepped inside and set the bottle down on a table with the jerky movements of someone who has clearly had too much to drink. With the downward movement of her arm, her dress fell further, exposing her entire breast. She turned to Col. Leeds. "Does the Americano like?" she teased as she slipped the other arm from its sleeve, exposing both of her breasts.

"Yes, the Americano likes very much." Col. Leeds stepped toward her and pinched one of her nipples hard. She struggled to free herself but he did not let up. She slapped him across the face and he released her.

She looked down, ashamed. She was aware there would be a cost involved in securing immortality. "Forgive me, Americano." She turned back toward him, silently offering him her breasts again. "You caught me by surprise." He was smiling, a small glint in his eye. "Do not apologize, Señorita." He saw the redness of a welt forming above her nipple where he had pinched her. "I sometimes forget that you are still able to be hurt, you are still able to feel pain."

"It is nothing," she said through watery eyes.

Inés had already made her way to Maribel's bed and was lying upon it. Her dress was tossed on the floor and she was clothed only in a pair of white lace panties. He walked toward the bed, Maribel following.

"You will join me?" she asked, looking at Col. Leeds and patting the bed beside her.

"Yes, she will," Col. Leeds replied, turning to Maribel. She paused momentarily, but quickly understood. She slipped her dress down over her hips, revealing her flat stomach. As it fell to the floor at her feet, Col. Leeds admired her long legs. She had not been wearing any panties, only black thigh-high stockings, which she did not remove. She joined her sister on the bed.

Leeds pulled a small bag of white powder from his coat pocket and tossed it onto the bed between the women. They giggled as Maribel reached over to her bedside desk and pulled a mirror from the drawer. He pulled a chair to the foot of the bed and took a seat. The two women finished and were wiping their noses, watching him, unsure of what he expected. He stared at them with his cold eyes, silently. He bobbed his head slightly. The sisters looked at each other, awkwardly at first. The Americano made no move. Maribel reached over and caressed her sister's arm. This brought a slight smile to Col. Leeds face and Maribel kissed her sister on the shoulder.

"Yes. It's quite a thing to live forever, young and healthy. To be inoculated."

The sisters looked at each other, nervously. Inés closed her eyes and, reluctantly, kissed her sister on the mouth, briefly. The alcohol helping dull her discomfort and inhibitions while stoking her desire for immortality.

"Young and beautiful. Forever," Col. Leeds egged them on. Each time the possibility of inoculation was dangled before them, he was amazed at what the two women, sisters, were capable of doing to themselves and to each other. They had, Col. Leeds imagined, expected him to be the main character in their charade, and he had enjoyed their occasional queried glances, their expectation that he make a move to join the happenings. He never did, and when the women had finished, he sat there, bemused at their expressions portraying a mix of guilty satisfaction and narcotic intoxication. Col. Leeds stood up and pulled another small bag of white powder from his coat pocket. They pounced upon it and he sat back down, smiling broadly.

Maribel lay upon the bed, staring at the ceiling, while her fingers absent-mindedly stroked her thigh. Col. Leeds noticed a soft expression of victory in her expression, of having satisfied a powerful ally and achieved her goal. He added his smile to hers— aware that neither yet understood the full cost. Maribel removed her gaze from the ceiling and looked at the Americano. He noticed that it took her a moment to focus on his face, and, once focused, a continued effort to remain. "Come, my love. It is your turn. Let me spend my love on you this time," Maribel said, getting up on all fours. She slowly crawled toward where he was sitting near the foot of the bed. When she reached him she grinned a seductive smile. She raised herself to her knees, and, almost falling over, steadied herself by grabbing his shoulder. She wrapped her other arm around his neck and kissed him hard, pressing herself against his chest. He kissed her back and slapped her hard on her behind.

"Yes, you are the one I enjoy the most. And I did mention, didn't I," he paused as he glanced over at Inés, who was bending over to snort another line of coke, but stopped and cautiously eyed her sister, "that I can only accommodate one of you... that only one of you can be inoculated?" He had kept his gaze on Inés and flashed a wicked smile as he saw a fire rage in her eyes. He kissed Maribel again. Inés felt her opportunity slipping away, her chance at immortality. She stood up and threw herself at Col. Leeds, knocking her sister to the floor.

"I know a few things, Americano, that she has not even thought of," Inés moaned as she reached down and began to unzip his trousers.

"Do tell, my dear. Do tell." He smiled at her. At this, Maribel let out a small scream and leapt upon her sister, knocking her over to the floor. Col. Leeds started to laugh. "Yes, ladies. Which one shall it be? Which one wants to come to America? To be...

inoculated?" The darkness rose in his eyes. He always enjoyed the violence, usually inflicted by him. But tonight he would play spectator and participant and instigator all at once. He finished slipping out of his trousers, aroused by their catfight, and pulled the top sister off the other by her hair and placed his foot on the chest of the other, lying on the floor, not sure which sister was held by hand and which by foot. It did not matter to him anymore. "Which one should I choose?" he asked as he set them both free. They immediately pounced upon him and each other, in turn, trying to win his favor, trying to stop the other.

Col. Leeds awoke the next morning, showered and dressed before the sister lying on the bed roused. She rolled over and moaned as she opened her eyes. The sheets were streaked in blood. He smiled as he recalled the brutality, the savageness, at which the sisters had attacked each other, each more desperate than the other to attain immortality.

"Good morning, darling," she moaned.

*It is Inés*, he thought, but then paused. *Or is it Maribel?* Her left eye was swollen. She tried to fluff her hair, but her body ached and she realized that it would do little good. She tossed the covers aside, inviting him to seduce her, to have his way with her. Her naked body was covered in cuts and bruises. Col. Leeds made no move. She half-ashamedly pulled the covers back over herself and smiled. "I am yours darling. Take me."

He laughed out loud, motioning toward the corner of the room. "Gracias. But I imagine you'll be preoccupied." She looked over to where Col. Leeds had indicated. She let out a short scream as he picked up his jacket and headed toward the door. He paused at the threshold and turned back toward her. "I'm afraid I can't tell you and your sister apart. Forgive me for not knowing your name. Whichever you are, enchanté, I'm sure." He laughed again and left as she leapt out of bed to where her sister lay motionless. She hovered over her sister's body, momentarily, then sat down and rested the lifeless head on her lap. She began to weep tears of sorrow and shame, as she stroked the hair of her dead sister. "¡Oh Diós mío! Goddamn you Americano!" she shouted to her empty apartment. She cried for some time before it occurred to her that she did not know his name either.

# CHAPTER TWENTY-ONE

*News Brief: Monday. 8:30 a.m. The Iranian President today declared that his government would no longer stand by while the "American aggressors and their Zionist puppet-masters" threatened the safety and security of the Middle East. To counter the "Great Satan," he announced that Iran's Nanotechnology Initiative Council had developed its own molecular factory and would be providing its friends and neighbors with free goods in a matter of weeks. U.S. Military sources close to the matter have indicated that Iran has a long history of making unsupported statements in an effort to build its influence in the region, but confirm that recent intelligence indicates that Iran may, in fact, have developed, or more likely, stolen, replication technology advanced enough to threaten the safety of American interests in the area.*

Clay rolled out of bed and went to take a shower. As he turned on the water, the television above the showerhead came to life. The station changed automatically from *Healthy Lifestyle,* the station preference of Lillian, to *CNN.* Clay recognized General David H. Fallsworth, Chairman of the Joint Chiefs of Staff speaking to an audience of reporters. The camera panned the room. An American flag stood near an Israeli flag in a makeshift pressroom. Several IDF soldiers stood around the room, but General Fallsworth was flanked by two American soldiers, standing at parade rest on either side of the podium stage. Clay paused from applying soap to his body to listen. Since the Finkelstein and Landsburg trial there were often reports of other nations making threats against U.S. interests, but other than some mild retorts by U.S. officials, nothing much ever seemed to come from it. American citizens continued to be increasingly isolated from the rest of the world. While travel outside the United States was prohibited, the multiple advances in virtual reality allowed people to 'travel' to foreign countries without actually leaving U.S. soil. Given the increasingly hostile attitude of foreigners towards Americans, most were happy to take virtual trips, even if it made the world a much bigger place by making it increasingly difficult to know what was really happening elsewhere in the world.

Clay had heard rumors of American soldiers aggressively seeking to overthrow various nations but he was unable to verify them. Clay did not know anyone serving in the military and, in fact, no one Clay was acquainted with knew of anyone serving in the armed forces. What stories Clay had heard were always from a friend of a friend, all just hearsay and conjecture. Most Americans, by and large, had lost interest in world affairs and those who had not simply could not access any real information.

The television screen zoomed into a close up of General Fallsworth. He began to speak.

"Our intelligence indicates that Iran has performed an underground test of a 5-kiloton nuclear device. Our data also indicates that it is likely in possession of 3 similar-sized warheads, all believed to be mounted on the Maleki-Moat-3 missile, which has a range of up to 2500 km, well within the range of American Forces in the region and the entire state of Israel. While no specific threats have been issued, Iranian leadership has demanded that the Ankara Treaty be voided and the Palestinian people rise up against, and I'm quoting here, 'the American and Zionist presence on Arab lands and expel all Jews from occupied lands.'" The General looked around the room and continued. "This recent development is likely to complicate matters in the finalization of the Ankara Treaty, which, as you are aware, enters the final phase next week with the complete withdrawal of Israeli forces from East Palestine. Israeli forces are already on high alert and the Prime Minister has asked that, as a precaution, all Israeli and foreign dignitaries avoid travel to either East or West Palestine. Our government continues to press the Hamas leadership to abide by the Ankara Treaty and warns that any attempt to violate the terms would result in serious repercussions. We will keep the American public informed as these matters progress." Gen. Fallsworth looked up from his teleprompter and stood up straight. "I will now take questions from the press."

A general clamor arose as reporters sought to have their questions answered. The General pointed to a middle-aged man in the second row. A dark-skinned man with black curly hair looked at the small computer tablet in his hand. "Thank you, General. Rumor has it that Hamas leadership in West Palestine has privately admitted it accepted the Ankara Treaty only as a first step in a plan to liberate all of Palestine, from the Jordan River to the Mediterranean Sea. Can you comment on this?" A murmur arose in the room as the question clearly upset several members of the press corps from Hamas.

"The United States intelligence is not aware of the veracity of any such rumors. It is our understanding and hope that all parties to the Agreement have been acting in good faith and in the spirit of cooperation," Gen. Fallsworth responded.

The press corps hands were again raised and the General pointed to another reporter. "David." David Ben Raffi was of the right-wing Israeli nationalist paper, *Makor Rishon*.

"Thank you, General. Is the United States finally prepared to confront the Iranian threat to peace in the Middle East? Many have suspected the Iranians of possessing a nuclear device for some time, but now that they have performed a test while also announcing perfection of replicator technology, will the U.S. be in a position to act effectively to keep all parties in check?"

The General paused for a moment and then spoke. "The threat to the world by any nation possessing nuclear capabilities raises concerns. In the case of a rogue nation such as Iran, the concern is even greater. That said, we have reason to believe its actions will be rational. There has been no confirmation of Iranian boasts of mastering replicator technology. If they do not possess it, then any act of war would amount to nothing more than assured destruction of the Iranian nation. Iran simply does not have the resources to compete with an American military force equipped with Genesis technology. If Iran has secured replicator technology, then we would expect its people will rapidly enjoy the successes and benefits that American citizens have been enjoying for some time and any governmental action toward violence would be deterred by the acts of its people. The Iranian threat has always originated from the extremists and our data shows that a majority of the Iranian people do not support the destruction of the State of Israel, given the creation of East and West Palestine under the Ankara Treaty which will provide the Palestinian people with self-determination in a land of their own." As the General finished speaking, more hands went up and the clamor returned. The General pointed to a man sporting a beard and wearing a lapel pin bearing the colors red, white and green. "Mr. Aziz," the General said, making eye contact with the man. He was Mohammed Aziz from the FARS news agency.

"General, wouldn't it, in fact, diffuse the entire situation if America simply allowed replicator technology to be shared among all nations of the world? America is sharing this technology with the Zionists and placing its Arab neighbors at a distinct disadvantage—"

"Sir," the General interrupted. "America has repeatedly discussed the dangers of allowing Genesis technology to be spread across the globe and the instability, even if only temporary, that would be created by the sudden abundance of wealth, especially among the non-democratic nations. America is continuing to develop a plan by which the technology can be shared among all nations. Furthermore, at the present time America is not sharing this technology with any other nation. The world, including the Arab world, benefits from the greatly reduced cost of acquiring American replicated products. Even Iran has benefitted from access to cheaper food supplies and clean water—"

"And yet we remain at the mercy of Zionist and American interests," Mohammed Aziz interrupted. "America allows the world to suffer to further its own imperialistic goals."

"Mr. Aziz," General Fallsworth said, looking straight into the eyes of the Iranian. "I have not come here today to discuss American Genesis technology with you or any other person. Rather, my message—and let me make it infinitely clear to you—is that your nation is advised in no uncertain terms, that should it engage in, or encourage, any act of aggression, whether against American interests or not, it will be dealt with in a harsh and swift manner heretofore unseen in this world. This is not a threat. Should you have any doubt, sir, I would welcome the challenge." He smiled as he nodded to the soldier standing to his left. The soldier and his partner stepped forward as Mr. Aziz began shouting accusations at General Fallsworth. Without a word, the two soldiers lifted Mr. Aziz by his arms and carried him out of the room as he struggled helplessly against their superior strength.

The television turned itself off as Clay finished his shower and stepped out. It struck Clay that the apparent lingering need to remain a Superpower was nothing more than a remnant of a bygone time. Those in power perhaps had not realized the true transformation that would take place across the nation when Genesis replicators were distributed to all American households. Their desire to create cheap products to lift America to the peak of its power, to show off the true power of capitalism and provide America with supreme power, ultimately, brought forth the ability to create an entire world of peace and egalitarianism, a world where greed is meaningless and power is for naught. Rather than create the penultimate capitalistic society, they brought forth the means for the implementation of true social and economic equality. And yet, it seemed there were those who were in power for so long they were no longer able or willing to spread knowledge and prosperity. They held their secret close and brandished their superiority to the rest of the civilized world. Clay recognized this failing in society, but was helpless to do much about it.

Clay sometimes felt he was a lone spark in a world of darkness. He had made attempts to discuss his thoughts with others, but he was almost always greeted with a clear lack of concern and the friendly advice to enjoy his life and be thankful for what he had. Clay dressed in silence, unsure of what he would do to occupy his day.

Clay found himself downtown, wandering around aimlessly. He felt old this day, too tired to hit the gym, too befuddled to partake in one of the many virtual amusements offering escape. He sat down on a bench in the Riverwalk, alongside the Chicago River. It had been quite some time since he took the time to simply sit and watch people on their journeys to and fro. Parents with children making their way toward the beach or the museums, business people hurriedly marching toward some meeting or appointment. Today he found himself disappointed. People passed by, alone and in groups, making their way toward some unknown destination, each one young and in perfect health. *What would happen to that old couple, having spent years together celebrating each other's successes, nursing each other's illnesses? Would they fall in love again, reignited by youth and vitality, or would they find that a lifetime spent together was enough, that, having been given a second opportunity, they would part ways, seek different paths that led, inevitably, toward vastly different destinations?* Clay wondered. He thought of Lillian. She was walking down some path that stretched forever, and he had refused to join her. *Selfish,* he thought to himself. A couple walked by and, upon seeing Clay, made a wide detour to avoid him, as if he had some disease. As if they could succumb to it. He felt out of place in a world that no longer aged.

Clay stood up and looked to the east, walking slowly toward Navy Pier. He was startled to see the Walking Man on the Riverwalk. He looked no different than he had before the Genesis changed everything. He looked odd to Clay, and Clay realized how odd he must appear to others. The United States had become a country of plenty, and yet, people like the Walking Man seemed to be left out — non-participants in the progress of man. Or perhaps he made a conscious decision, just as Clay had done. The Walking Man slowed his movement as he approached Clay and then stopped and turned to him.

"Do I know you?" he asked Clay.

The question startled Clay. The Walking Man spoke with a deep, rich voice that lacked any hint of despair or want. It was a voice that Clay did not expect to reside in one whose life was seemingly less fortunate than most. "Excuse me?"

"I'm sorry," the Walking Man said. "I do not mean to be abrupt, but have we met before?" He held out his hand and Clay instinctively reached out and shook it. The question was raised so naturally that Clay had almost forgotten that it was a seldom-used inquiry in a world of iMemes. Clay reached to his iMeme but was greeted with only the smoothness of the Spot.

"I'm Clay—"

The Walking Man turned away as he interrupted Clay. "Oh, yes, Clay. Levi Clayton Furstman." A hint of recognition crossed his face and he turned back to Clay and said, "I've heard much about you."

Clay pulled his hand back, looking for some hint of an iMeme on the Walking Man. "I'm sorry, I don't know what you mean. I don't think we've ever met."

The Walking Man stood silent for a moment, and then spoke again. "No, you are correct. We have not met. And you would have little reason, it seems at this time, to know much about me. But that may change. Yes, that may change. As for my acquaintance with you, let's just say I know about you from," he paused, "from a mutual friend."

Clay blinked several times trying to catch some fragment of understanding. It struck him that this man was, perhaps, somewhat insane and he took a step back.

The Walking Man recognized the look of confused fear in Clay's eyes. "I apologize for my forthrightness. It's just that you are... are..." He seemed to be trying to express an idea he couldn't quite articulate. "Well, it's clear you haven't been inoculated with PreVentall and, at this point, I am aware of only a few people who continue to live in our natural, human state. I am intimate with many of them, or, at least those who are not otherwise involved with, or working for, the State. I know you are not working for the State—you're appearance notwithstanding. But I have been told from our friend that you are a man who may think quite like the rest of us and who, at least as of yet—and perhaps always—shall remain untainted by the molecular bastardization that is rising around us all."

Clay moved to take another step back, but caught himself. This man seemed at once to be simultaneously both a raving lunatic and a man so articulate that Clay could imagine him giving oratory in a Shakespearian play. Yet this talk of the State and knowing Clay through a mutual friend—it made no sense to Clay. Perhaps he had once been a man of intelligence, but by ill-decision or misfortune, came to his current state of being. This man was outside the system, a remnant of a world long since gone. Yet he seemed to be in control of his faculties. Maybe not entirely sane, but clearly not insane, and certainly not dangerous, even to Clay in his un-inoculated state.

"There are others who are not inoculated?" Clay asked, before he could stop himself. Clay had recently come to believe that he had been the only American not yet inoculated, though standing there in front of the Walking Man, he realized that such a notion was absurd. Of course the Walking Man was not inoculated. Certainly there was no program to inoculate those outside society; better they should continue their lives as they had, slowly dying off and freeing the rest of society of pity or concern or contempt.

"A few," the Walking Man said, before pausing and then, more thoughtfully, continuing, "I'm sorry if I startled you. It is not often that one sees another aged person on the streets anymore. It is less often that I see one who I do not know well. Mortality is a bond shared with few amongst our population, and I make it a point to know those who share the bond."

Clay was unsure how to respond. "I thought I was the only one who wasn't inoculated, actually. The last of a dying breed," and then, almost to himself, "the last of the dying..."

The Walking Man turned to look over his shoulder. "You seem somewhat conflicted," he mused.

"Yes. My family members have all gotten their shots. I barely recognize my wife anymore. Lately, it seems, I recognize myself less. When we were all growing old, I suppose I held this certain illusion of youth." The Walking Man raised his eyebrows. "Sure, I understood that I was getting older, but I felt younger than my age. I always believed I looked younger than my age, as well. And I was comfortable with who I was and what I had become. But now, well... it's different. Now that my wife and all my friends *are* young, well, I guess I feel old... older than my age even. The crazy thing is that I don't, physically, feel any different than I did a few years ago, but my point of reference has changed. I am no longer healthy compared to others my age. Now I'm old and out-of-shape compared to my peers. And the crazy thing about it is that I'm still not sure I want to be inoculated. I—" Clay stopped suddenly. He realized that he had been going on with a complete stranger and he suddenly felt awkward. His face flushed slightly. "I'm... I'm sorry, I just..."

"You and I are not so different, Mr. Furstman," the Walking Man said, matter of factly. Clay looked quizzically at him. "Do not look so surprised. I may not appear to be a typical American—not that I claim to be—and my friends may not be inoculated, but I am well aware of the affront upon our very beings that you feel inoculation inflicts. We were not meant to live forever. Rather, we are programmed to grow old and die. It is a lesson that has been taught to us for thousands of years. It is a lesson we must not forget." The Walking Man started to walk and Clay followed alongside as he continued his discussion. "I fear we are making very dire mistakes, approaching those unintended consequences we will not be able to undo." The Walking Man paused. "I fear we may have dug too deep."

"You sound as if you think we're destined for some kind of eternal damnation," Clay said.

"I am not a religious man. And while I have not been able to decide on the existence of a supreme being in the universe, I have studied various religious writings. I believe these stories hold many important keys to the nature of man, to our place in the universe. These are shared stories that are reflected in the writings of all mankind's earliest civilizations. These stories were not written by any one person, but developed over centuries. They are tales of import. They are the result of generations of learning, of successes and failures, of survival. I believe these stories spread and were passed down among generations because they were understood immediately by all who hear them. They touch upon instincts that are hard-wired into our humanity and, as such, have a resonance in our very existence. These stories are the ancient wells of truth."

Puzzled, Clay looked at the Walking Man as he continued to talk.

"There is a meditation I'm familiar with: 'The sickness of our time will be healed by those who drink deep from the ancient wells of truth. From ancient wells of truth they will draw strength to keep faith with those who sleep in the dust.'" Clay nodded slightly, trying to comprehend all that the Walking Man was telling him.

"Death, you see, is one of those ancient wells of truth. All around us, nature contains the lessons of life. For centuries, man has asked: 'Why?' 'For what reason?' 'Is there a purpose?' And ultimately, the answer can only be: 'Death.' As a species, we live to reproduce and pass on our genes, to survive. But as individuals, we are born to die. Nature accepts this fate. The lioness kills the young wildebeest without remorse and the heard neither stops nor mourns at the death of one of its own. Nature understands that the group must survive, but the individual must die. Yet it appears man has not yet learned this lesson. He fights against nature to feel a little younger, to survive a little longer, to breathe one more breath. But this is not our nature." The Walking Man paused as they approached the intersection. He gazed up and down the street, as if looking for something. The street was empty, and as he moved to step off the curb, he stopped. It seemed to Clay that the Walking Man had suddenly changed his mind about continuing forward, and, instead, turned to his left. The Walking Man broke the brief silence with a question. "Are you familiar with the story of Adam and Eve?"

The question gave Clay pause. Had someone asked him this morning who the Walking Man was, he would have answered that the Walking Man was, if anything, at least a bit odd. Yet he now found himself mesmerized by the man, intrigued by his insight, his speech. And although his brain told him to be wary, his gut told him that perhaps he had been wrong, had been too quick to judge.

"Sure," Clay said. "God creates Adam and Eve. They live in the Garden of Eden until they eat the apple. Then God tosses them out."

"And why does God toss them out?" The Walking Man asked.

"Because they disobeyed God. He told them not to eat from the tree of knowledge, yet they did so anyway. I think it's taught that they were kicked out for sinning against God. Original Sin."

"Yes, a very interesting interpretation," the Walking Man said as he nodded. "Of course, it begs the question of whether any sentient being can achieve the apex of humanity without first having mastered the art of reason and free choice. While it has been argued that Adam and Eve had free choice *not* to eat the apple, it is a mockery of the tale. Free choice cannot exist without reason. The dandelion does not choose when to release its seeds to the wind, anymore than the monarch butterfly is capable of choosing to winter in Sierra Chincua, Mexico like its ancestors before it. These are not reasoned actions, but merely instructions followed by instinct, genetically wired into their lives. It is choice that makes us human, and choice requires reason—the ability to hear the primordial callings of our DNA, but to question whether such action is proper, or desirable, in a given situation. Perhaps Shakespeare said it best:

*What a piece of work is a man, how noble in reason,*
*how infinite in faculties, in form and moving how express and admirable,*
*in action how like an angel, in apprehension how like a god!*
*The beauty of the world, the paragon of animal.*

But Adam and Eve, they were created human in form only. They had not yet acquired reason. Before that first act of disobedience, they had no knowledge of good and evil, no concept of right or wrong. They had not yet developed those infinite faculties, that God-like apprehension. But upon their decision to eat thereof, they broke the chains of ignorance and became human. And it was the decision to eat thereof that brought about this change, the act of reason from which humanity blossomed. Eve tells the Shiny One that the Supreme Being warned not only against eating from the tree of knowledge, but that the prohibition was extended to merely touching the tree. That is, it is not the fruit which carried the knowledge, but the act of reaching for the fruit, the act of disobeying their God by exercising free choice—free choice of reason—that gives man his humanity."

"Are you suggesting that God wanted Adam and Eve to eat the," but Clay stopped short of saying *apple*. He knew the fruit was more likely to be one familiar to the Semitic people who wrote the Bible. "fruit? That this was some sort of set-up?"

The Walking Man did not answer, but only smiled at Clay as he continued. "The Supreme Being failed to set any boundary on his creation, or, at least, not much of one. He set Adam and Eve into the Garden of Eden and gave them dominion over everything they saw. The only rule was to refrain from eating of the tree of knowledge. It was the only rule they could break, and, to become human, they had no choice but to do so.

"Christianity has really made a mess of that one. It could not have been an 'Original Sin' for man to eat of the tree of knowledge— at least not from humanity's perspective. You see, it was only through that action that man became human. Had the Supreme Being wanted mindless obedience, blind faith, He would have, in all His infinite knowledge, created the microchip and have been done with it all. Program obedience and worship. Light, dark, the Sixth Day."

The notion of God sitting before a worshipping mass of computers struck Clay as odd as he wondered whether God, like man, would end up worshipping his electronic creation instead of the other way around.

"But getting back to my original inquiry of why man was expelled from Eden, your response is, in fact, not entirely correct. While the Supreme Being had directed Adam and Eve not to eat of the tree of knowledge of good and evil, it was not their newfound possession of knowledge, their emergence from the darkness of ignorance into the light of reason that barred them from Eden. Don't get me wrong, we are told God was angry about it, though not exactly why. Perhaps the Supreme Being, like any parent, lashed out at the lost innocence of their child, the recognition that along with knowledge and understanding comes the realization that one must leave behind the pixie dust of eternal youth, the notion we never grow older, we never grow old, and thus, never die. So for punishment, He introduced labor into the world. Labor, in the form of manual work if man wanted to eat; and Labor, in the form of childbirth if woman wanted to reproduce. But it was more than that.

"The Supreme Being actually placed in Eden two trees: the tree of the knowledge of good and evil and the tree of life. And when He placed Adam in Eden, the Supreme Being commanded him that he may eat of every tree in Eden, *except* the tree of knowledge of good and evil, warning Adam that 'on the day that you eat from it, it will become certain that you will die.' That is, on that day, death would be the natural and end state of man since on that day they would become truly human. Note the distinction. God did not tell Adam he would die at the moment he ate of the tree of knowledge. Not at all. Rather, only that death would become certain. We are told that Adam himself lived nine hundred and thirty years, certainly not evidence of instant death. So you see, God simply warned Adam that the wages of humanity were death." The Walking Man smiled at Clay.

"So why did God remove Adam and Eve from Eden?" Clay asked.

"Recall, prior to eating from the tree of knowledge, prior to becoming human, the Supreme Being placed no prohibition on Adam from eating of the tree of life. Why was that?" The Walking Man did not wait for a response. "By inferring to us that Adam was free to have partaken from the tree of life prior to eating from the tree of knowledge, we are meant to understand that Adam and Eve were not, could not have been, fully mortal, fully human. The freedom to eat from the tree of life, taken alongside God's original admonishment that eating from the tree of knowledge would make death a certainty, makes it clear that Adam and Eve were immortal, otherly beings, if you will."

A puzzled look crossed Clay's face but before he could speak, the Walking Man continued.

"I will revisit my original inquiry. Why were Adam and Eve expelled from the Garden of Eden? It was not, as some profess, for eating from the forbidden tree, or succumbing to Original Sin, but the Lord kicked Adam out 'lest he put forth his hand, and take also of the tree of life, and eat, and live for ever.' It would seem that man, in his initial, unnatural state of inhumanity—a state in which free-will did not exist and man was not man, but simply a being—was free to eat of the tree of life because, at that time, death had not yet been introduced to that particular species of God's creation. Recall, it was only after Adam ate from the tree of knowledge that 'it will become certain that you will die.' But in choosing knowledge, in choosing to become fully human, we must accept death. It is ordained, a life's journey's end.

"And death is, in a sense, ultimately, a human trait. Does an animal contemplate its own death? Its own mortality? To even the Great Apes, the contemplation of death is surely not considered except insofar as it is contrary to the basic instinct to survive. But man, having taken that leap from primate to human, from a creature fashioned in the image of God to a creature who is God-like in apprehension, knowing of good and evil, was then commanded to go forth, be fruitful, multiply, and die. We are not gods. We are not immortal, possessing that which is the last trait separating us from the gods. Death is what makes us human."

The Walking Man stopped and turned to face Clay. "So you see, what knowledge has been passed down amongst the generations, our communal understanding, that deep well of truth, dictates that we must die. It cannot be otherwise. I fear that a grave mistake has been made, and I — and others — do not want to be a part of this abomination, if I may regress back to the Biblical vernacular of my tale. Certainly, some evil will come of this. An evil that is great enough, that was feared enough, that warnings against it permeate the tales of old. A warning to all future generations."

"Wow!" It was all Clay was able to muster at the moment. He tried again. "I don't know… so you… you…" but Clay was at a loss to formulate the questions that were swirling around in his mind.

The Walking Man reached his left hand out and touched Clay's chest while he briefly placed his right pointing finger to his lips. Then he quickly nodded his head toward a gentleman standing across the street, staring toward the two of them. Clay moved his eyes to look at the man without turning his head.

"We can't talk anymore right now. We should talk again when we can assure privacy. I will contact you." The Walking Man started walking away, head held high and a blank look on his face.

"But, what do you —" Clay began. But the Walking Man continued on, seemingly unaware of Clay any longer. Clay looked across the street and the man who had been looking their way was gone. He looked back toward the Walking Man, and he, too, was gone. Clay shook his head, unsure whether their conversation had even occurred. He brought his hand hard to his head as he thought, *I never asked the Walking Man his name!*

## CHAPTER TWENTY-TWO

*News Brief: Tuesday. 10:30 p.m. It was announced today that PreVentall Version 2.0 will soon be available. The second generation PreVentall nanobots take advantage of recent advances to enhance the normal functions of daily living. Rather than merely return our bodies to their youthful state, Version 2.0 will provide strength and conditioning enhancements, vision enhancements, smell and taste enhancements, and a myriad of other options. Imagine having 20/5 vision, as keen as that of an eagle; being able to smell with the acuity of a canine; being able to hear notes you previously only felt. These enjoyments can be yours once you've received the 2.0 upgrade. Make your appointment today!*

Their lovemaking was bitter, almost mechanical. Lillian's young firm breasts raised slowly up and then down with her regular breathing. She didn't say anything, but Clay knew she was disappointed. His graying chest hairs, his slightly sagging muscles weren't enough to excite Lillian, he was not able to arouse Lillian as he once had when they were biologically equal. He had been aware for the past few months of a slight disappointment in her when they would undress. Of course, she loved him, but he knew that she also looked forward to a time when he, too, would acquire his lost youth, the firm muscle tone, the contours of a healthy, young man. Tonight, however, he had had difficulty rising to the occasion. And when he was finally able to accomplish an erection, her mood had changed. She had lost the initial passion and seemed to be thinking other thoughts as he spent his love inside her. He felt empty, alone, as if he had masturbated with the help of her body, but the absence of her being. As if he had used the Virtual Fantasy. She had asked him several times this past week what he was waiting for, why he refused to be inoculated, but he was unable to respond with any valid reason for not getting inoculated. Clay continued watching her breasts as they rose and fell in with her slow, rhythmic breathing.

*Why haven't I been inoculated?* He thought for a long while, and concluded, with some shame, that the answer was, oddly enough, *vanity*. His refusal to take the PreVentall was a conceited effort to remain true, to be pure and untouched, as if he were some chosen being, some blessed savior, meant to save humanity from itself. Yet his refusal to be inoculated mocked his conceit, obliging him to remain a frail and imperfect being, rather than a more ideal and more perfect man.

He thought back to the lecture from the Walking Man. What had sounded so right then, now seemed so wrong. He asked himself, *Why shouldn't man live forever? Why shouldn't we strive to be the best we can? Could we not become gods ourselves, masters of our own destinies? Hell, have I not been wearing glasses for all these years? Aren't they artificial enhancements to make my life easier, more enjoyable?* Wearing contacts did not make Clay any less human than people who did not wear them, he reasoned, yet somehow he had a visceral rejection to the notion of nanobots residing in his body. *Why were nanobots any different?* It was absurd. *Why?* he asked again. *Am I afraid to live forever, to be young and healthy again? Do I fear having to wake up for an eternity, with a family that will never grow older, in a house that will never fall into disrepair? Science had finally come close to creating a utopia, a world in which disease and crime and poverty were banished. What is it that prevents me from embracing this technology? From celebrating man's evolution to greatness?* He rolled over onto his side, determined to visit the clinic the next day.

Clay got off the train and headed to Dr. Ruberick's office. He did not have an appointment and hoped that the doctor would be in. And, more importantly, he hoped, that Dr. Ruberick would be able to inoculate him. The need for medical treatment had all but disappeared with the widespread use of PreVentall, initially leaving physicians with little to do except to inoculate their patients, and soon that too was complete. *What did doctors do now?* Clay asked himself. *Do any of them even practice medicine any longer?* Clay wondered if Dr. Ruberick's office would still be open, whether he still had a practice. He guessed that pediatricians would still have viable practices, inoculating the newborns, but as he thought about it more, he couldn't remember the last time he had seen a baby. *Do people still have children? Do they even consider it? What would happen to the planet if couples continued to have children, but no one ever died?* Yet he had read only last week (or was it last month) about the OB/GYN research field actively attempting to inoculate fetuses to ensure healthy newborns. Science was still attempting to overcome the difficulties of ensuring that nanobots allowed for normal cell differentiation during fetal development while also correcting genetic errors in those fetuses that would otherwise be born with birth defects. *People must still be out there having babies. Certainly species propagation was still taking place among the human race.*

As Clay continued up the street, he spotted the Walking Man on the other side of the street, approaching the Schubert Theatre. The Walking Man looked Clay in the eye briefly, and then stopped. He pulled out a piece of paper from his pocket and wrote on it before lifting it before him and briefly staring at Clay again. The Walking Man then set the paper down on the ledge of the box office at the Theatre, and without any further acknowledgment to Clay, continued walking down the street. The box-office was closed at this hour and the streets were otherwise empty. Clay stopped and watched the Walking Man continue his journey for a few blocks, before he turned a corner and Clay lost sight of him. Clay turned back toward Dr. Ruberick's office. As he passed the theatre, he looked toward the box office and saw the small sheet of paper the Walking Man had left resting on the counter, the slight breeze curling one corner and then releasing it, giving Clay the impression the paper was beckoning him over. He looked around to be sure the streets were still empty before he crossed. As he neared the box office a young couple appeared from around the corner and headed in his direction. They were engaged in conversation, but Clay felt awkward retrieving a scrap piece of paper from the box office window, and so not to raise suspicion, he placed both hands on the counter and placed his head near the window-glass, pretending to discover some information about the current show written on the posters hanging in the back of the box-office. While he moved his head left and right, he placed his fingers on the edge of the scrap of paper and worked it under his hand. As the couple walked past him, they suddenly stopped talking and stared at him. Clay pretended not to notice them, squinting his eyes slightly to read the information posted in the box office a little better. The couple walked by and Clay could hear the murmur of their conversation begin again. He looked down to his right hand, trying to determine if they had, perhaps, noticed him slipping the note into his palm when it struck him. *You stupid moron,* he thought. *As if they give a rat's ass what you're doing with your hands. They're simply taken aback at seeing a man in his mid-fifties wondering around the streets.* He paused for a moment. *Or am I now close to sixty?* he wondered, trying to remember what year it was; when he last celebrated a birthday. Clay had long since become accustomed to seeing young people everywhere he looked, but except for his friends, his appearance never failed to raise interest in others. He flushed at his silliness but having started this farce, he felt compelled to complete it in the event anyone else was watching. He waited a moment longer and lifted his head slightly as he opened his eyes wide, as if he had suddenly discovered what he had been looking for, and put his hands into his pockets, along with the Walking Man's piece of paper.

"*Young Frankenstein the Musical* tickets go on sale October 5th," he advised his iMeme, "and you, Clay, are the biggest dork," he mumbled to himself. He tapped his iMeme to put it to sleep. He removed it from the Spot and placed it in his pocket as he continued his journey eastbound. A group of people came out of the restaurant on the corner and paused briefly as they saw Clay.

"Sorry folks, nothing to see here. Keep moving, nothing to see. The freak show known as Clay is going to end soon," he whispered to himself. Clay quickened his pace, now more determined to find Dr. Ruberick's office open. He turned onto Michigan Ave. and entered the lobby of the building where Dr. Ruberick's office was located when he last visited. The concierge's desk was empty. There was not much need for concierge services in office buildings any longer. Nor, mused Clay, for office buildings themselves.

When he exited the elevator on the 25th floor, he saw immediately that the office was dark and empty. A yellowing note card on the door advised patients who had not yet been inoculated to contact Patricia Harmsfeld, M.D., pediatrician, and provided her office number. Clay looked through the glass doors into the vacant office. Empty chairs, a magazine rack filled with aging magazines, a notice on the wall asking that all patients turn off their iMemes while in the examining rooms. The floor was quiet and it appeared that all the other offices were also vacant. The air felt heavy compared to the fresh air outside. It struck Clay that the silence was what had been bothering him during his recent visits downtown. The buzz of people moving with purpose had been replaced with the leisurely chatter of people with no particular place to go and no particular hurry to get there. The entire city had become like a vacation resort, filled with the comings and goings of casual travelers heading toward their destinations, but unconcerned about detours on the way. Clay tried the door and was surprised to find it unlocked. He entered the waiting room and sat down on one of the leather and chrome chairs. He leaned back, closed his eyes and sat in the silence. The air was humid and smelled faintly musty. He let out a deep sigh. Again, he was disturbed by the silence. The ventilation system was off and the only sound Clay heard was the faint buzz of the ballast from a fluorescent fixture in the hallway.

*Dr. Harmsfeld, huh?* he thought. "I sure hope the hell she has office hours today," his voice split the silence.

He wanted to query his iMeme for Dr. Harmsfeld's address so he reached into his pocket to retrieve it when he was greeted with the roughness of paper. He had forgotten about the note from the Walking Man. He pulled it out and read the neatly printed text:

> *Please meet me at 159 W. Lower Wacker Dr. I would like to continue our conversation and introduce you to some of my friends. Tomorrow at 9:30 pm. BRING NO ONE. AND NO iMEME.*

He thought again about his conversation with the Walking Man. It had seemed so logical, so correct when the Walking Man spoke of Eden and the ancient wells of truth. His speech had touched Clay in a spiritual way, working its way to the root of his feelings. Yet, it also seemed to defy logic. *What is wrong with eternal life? Eternal health? Is it wrong to want to live forever?* he asked himself.

He wondered, though, if he truly wanted to live forever. Forever was a long time. *Perhaps PreVentall only extended our lives for hundreds, or perhaps thousands, of years,* he thought. *Even so, what would it mean to live a life of Methuselah?* Like the Walking Man, Clay was not religious, but he was spiritual. He believed in a greater power, some force that man, ultimately, would be answerable to. Clay recognized at that moment it was his spirituality that was bothered by PreVentall, his belief in something larger than himself. *If man were to live forever, to whom would he ultimately answer? Without the belief in death, in some final judgment, then our actions become meaningless, selfish. Religion had been teaching its followers for generations:*

The end is near!
Repent today!
Fear tomorrow!

*But immortality erases tomorrow, renders it without meaning and without fear. In the absence of death, there are no questions, there is no need to be able to respond with truths, no manner by which anyone could be held accountable. To whom would one's soul belong but to oneself? With the comfort and knowledge of an ensured tomorrow comes the freedom of answering only to myself today,* he thought. *I was, I am, and I shall forever be: the holy trinity all in one.*

It became clear to Clay: the Walking Man was right. *Man had to be kicked out of Eden in order to prevent his immortality, to prevent man from becoming a god,* he thought. *Without death, there can be no final accounting, no need to weigh the meanings of our lives or to measure the length of our weakness. We, and we alone, would be the arbitrators of our own lives.*

*Thank you, God, but we won't be in need of your services any longer. I appreciate the offer for life everlasting in the hereinafter, but I think I'll stay with immortality in the here and now. So sorry.*

*What could it all mean for humanity to, at last, evolve into gods?* Clay wondered. *No,* Clay thought. *PreVentall is not simply a prescription for poor eyesight, a prosthetic for a missing limb. It is much, much bigger. And, perhaps, much more dangerous.* He looked around, awakening from his thoughts. He suddenly realized he had no idea how long he had he been sitting there. He felt the need to leave, but not to seek out Dr. Harmsfeld's office. He was feeling much less sure about inoculation.

Clay reread the note before placing it back into his pocket. He briefly considered tearing the note into several pieces, but decided against it. He did not want to enter the appointment on his iMeme and he did not want to forget the address. His memory was not as sharp as it had been only a few years ago.

Lower Wacker at 9:30 p.m. was not a very inviting place, even with the current lack of crime in the city. The last time Clay was on Lower Wacker, it continued to serve as a shelter for many of the city's homeless population. But that was some time ago and Clay wasn't sure whether the homeless population even existed, having decided the Walking Man himself was likely not homeless.

Certainly, the advent of the Genesis removed many from the streets by the sheer fact that the generosity of people could sustain them at levels previously unattainable, and they, presumably, enjoyed the comforts of the present day. Perhaps not. Perhaps they were overlooked and continued their lives of poverty and exclusion. *Tomorrow at 9:30. Hell, I don't even know what day it is now.*

His iMeme startled him as it chimed in: *It is Wednesday. 11:03 a.m.* Clay stood up and the hair on the back of his neck followed suit. He was certain he was still alone, but he had the sudden urge to leave Dr. Ruberick's office quickly. When he stepped outside the sun was high in the sky. The day had warmed and the temperature was pleasant. Clay tried to remember the last time it rained, the last time he saw a dark cloud.

*Lillian calling.* His iMeme interrupted his thoughts.

*I'll take it,* Clay thought. "Hello?"

"Hi, Clay. I was just wondering where you are. You didn't leave me a message and I thought you might be home by the time I got back from swimming this morning."

"Oh, I'm sorry. I... I was going to..."

Clay stopped himself. *Going to what?* he thought. *Tell everyone that PreVentall is evil? That immortality is dangerous? That I'm beginning to believe what some half-crazed homeless guy told me?*

"Hello... Clay?"

"I'm sorry, honey. I wanted it to be a surprise, but... well, I came downtown this morning...

*Careful what you say, Clay. You don't want to screw this up. Don't tell Lill you're taking advice from a street person.* He tried to plan his next words, but everything started getting jumbled up in his head.

"to... to... I mean..."

*Think, damn it! To what? Don't get yourself in trouble here.*

"I was going to surprise you and... and finally get inoculated."

"You what!" He heard Lillian give out a squeal.

"But", he added quickly, "Dr. Ruberick's office is closed and I couldn't."

*Damn it! Too late! Why couldn't I think of something else to say?*

"Oh, Honey! Finally! I was beginning to worry about you. So did you go somewhere else? I'm so happy! What are you going to do?" In her excitement, Lillian was not waiting for answers.

"I guess I have to make an appointment with a Dr. Harmsfeld. I'll try to get in—" he paused again. He was no longer certain he wanted to get inoculated anymore—at least not until he met the Walking Man—but he was in too deep. He tried to recapture the excitement he had had earlier that morning.

"I'll try to get in at the next available appointment, maybe she could even do it today," he said, sounding less enthused than he had hoped. He heard Lillian scream again and he realized that it didn't matter any longer whether he sounded sincere or not. Lillian wasn't even listening. He could feel her excitement through his iMeme, feel the anguish and tension that had held her captive for so long spring free as the man she loved finally proved that he was not completely insane.

"Oh my god! The kids are going to die! They were beginning to worry about you. Honestly, so was I. Everyone was." Lillian paused to catch her breath. "Wait until the Diazs find out! Miguel and Jennifer are going to shit! We're going out with them tonight. Oh, man, oh man! Jennifer thinks you're never going to get inoculated. And I'm pretty sure Miguel thinks your nuts as well. Jesus, I can't wait. I... oh, I'm sorry. You know I love you, but I can't keep pretending that your age doesn't matter. I've got so much energy and I just want you to share it with me." She screamed in excitement again.

"I know. And I'm sorry. I don't know why I've been delaying this for so long. It'll be done soon enough and you won't have to hang out with an old fuck for much longer." Clay winced slightly. He could not help but cringe at the irony of the situation. Here was Lillian, worrying that if he did not get inoculated, he would die, while he felt that getting inoculated would, in a way, kill him, kill his humanity, kill the very part of him that was the essence of what it meant to be human. To live, and to die. To be flesh and bone. To allow evolution to determine his fate, rather than science.

"I can't wait to see you younger again! Maybe tonight we'll celebrate your final days as an old man." He relaxed a little, picturing Lillian grinning from ear to ear, her brain making plans.

"I can't wait. Love you," he said. His stomach was turning. He could not tell if he was scared, nervous, or excited. The emotions began to start getting mixed up.

"I love you, too, darling." She hung up.

Clay was alone on the wide-open street, but he felt trapped. The wheels were set in motion now and it would be increasingly difficult to avoid getting inoculated. At least he could try to push the appointment off until late in the week, or maybe even next week. Perhaps by then he will again want to be inoculated.

"Dr. Harmsfeld's office," he said. His iMeme began dialing. He figured he had better at least make the appointment if nothing else.

While Lillian was getting ready for dinner with the Diazs, she would steal glances at Clay and smile. The news that he was finally going to get PreVentall put a look in her eye that Clay had not recalled seeing since they first began dating. The kids were all out and she was standing before the mirror wearing only a black lace bra and thigh-high fishnet stockings held up with a garter belt. Throughout their marriage, she had always been modest, even when the two of them were alone. Clay loved Lillian. Her firm breasts always excited him and he loved her round, athletic curves. But Lillian was self-conscious and she would tell Clay that she did not like her body, and that he was crazy for not agreeing with her. But since she had been inoculated, she had a newfound confidence. True, she was able to workout more than previously, but essentially, she looked the same as she did when she was in her early thirties. Clay finished putting his shirt on and walked up behind her and placed his hands on her exposed behind and gave a squeeze. She slapped at his hands and stepped to the side.

"Uh, uh, uh. Not now. You're just going to have to wait until we get back here later, old man." She walked over to the closet and put on a black skirt. As she bent over to put on her shoes, her skirt raised up to reveal the tops of her stockings and the bare flesh of her upper thigh. Lillian was not one to forego panties, although Clay had suggested it on numerous occasions. She finished and turned to see Clay still staring. "A little something to think about at dinner," she smiled and walked out of the room.

Had the dinner conversation not turned to Eva's activities, his imaginings of the events of later that night would have been all that Clay would have been thinking about at dinner.

"You going senile, old man?" Miguel asked. "You don't seem to be fully engaged here, old friend."

"I'm sorry. It's just that—" Clay started, but did not know how to finish. He certainly was not going to share what he was thinking.

"It's just that Clay finally decided to get inoculated!" Lillian interrupted. She turned to Clay, "Sorry, I couldn't hold it in any longer."

"God damn! It's about time. I was getting tired of being seen out with such an old guy," Miguel declared, giving Clay a firm pat on the back.

"Jesus! She said I was *going* to be inoculated—not that I already had been," Clay said, wincing from the pummeling Miguel had given him.

"Sorry, Clay." Miguel said, still grinning.

"Oh, Clay," Jennifer said. "We're so excited for you! You'll absolutely love being young again."

Clay put on a smile, "Yes, I can't wait. I've got an appointment for Friday. Seems a lot of folks are going to be getting the Two-Oh upgrade and the office is going to be completely booked for weeks. The doctor is taking time off to prepare, but she agreed to get me in early to get the initial PreVentall inoculation." He tried to sound enthused.

"Yes, that Two-Oh is something else. But I think the really good stuff will be coming out with the Oh-Three. They're already starting to talk about what it will do." The excitement in her voice was palpable. "There have been rumors that they're Beta testing Oh-Three. I heard that it will allow information to be uploaded directly to your brain. It's going to make school obsolete. Children will simply receive uploads each year with all the knowledge they're supposed to know at that age and, *bang!* it's all in their heads, ready for instant recall whenever needed. They also say that instead of going to college, people will just upload the knowledge they seek. They think the human brain will actually be able to store all the discovered knowledge in the world. Imagine, everyone would know everything!"

Clay frowned. "I already know a few people who think they know everything—and that's a few people too much!" They all laughed.

"Speaking of interesting developments, Clay and Lill," Miguel interrupted. "Have you heard the latest on Eva? She's been involved in some pretty interesting work lately and it's going to lead to some pretty damn interesting possibilities."

Jennifer turned abruptly toward Miguel, her smile leaving her face. "I'm not sure we're really supposed to be saying anything," she reminded him.

"Oh, it's okay. Clay and Lill won't say anything, and besides, I'm sure Eva will be joining us out sometime soon, now that she's back in town. And it's all she's been talking about."

"She's not telling anyone other than us, but I guess you're right. She would certainly include Clay and Lill in any conversations she shares with us," Jennifer added, giving Miguel an excuse to continue.

"What's this about?" Clay asked, finally getting his mind off of his wife.

"Well, you know that Eva was working on replicating the California condor when DARPA stepped in, right?" Miguel asked. Clay and Lill both nodded. "Well, now it seems that they are replicating chimpanzees. They are taking well-trained animals — ones that have some communication abilities through sign language — and they are testing to see if the knowledge and characteristic are being duplicated. They're obviously working toward human replication. If it works, she says there are rumors that the government has already sent a Genesis to Mars and, rather than building a rocket and sending men to explore the planet, they'll teleport them, basically, by Replicating astronauts right on Mars. They are training folks right now to live and work on the planet. If human replication works, they will disassemble the astronauts here and reassemble them on Mars. And what's more, with the Two-Oh upgrade, the human body can work with less oxygen and gravity. The astronauts will be able to work up there without bulky spacesuits. They say in the next 10 years, folks will be able to vacation on Mars!"

"Wow," Lillian sighed. "That's fantastic! According to Clay's doctor, Two-Oh won't quite be out by Friday, but it's getting close."

"Well, I'm going to call my doctor to see if I can get in ahead of everyone else," Jennifer said. "We've known her for so long, and she did get Miguel into the early testing when he had his eye fixed. I'm going to see if maybe she can put me on call so I can just come over right when it's released."

"That'd be great, Jennifer! Do you think I could sneak in with you?" Lillian asked. Jennifer gave a shrug, and Lillian continued. "Boy, I just can't wait. I am so looking forward to the oxygen enhancement capabilities. I've heard that you can swim underwater for up to 2 hours without needing to take a breath. It'll be great for my swimming and would really add a new dimension to scuba diving." Clay's upcoming transformation and Two-Oh dominated conversation for the rest of the evening.

As they pulled into the driveway, Lillian reached over and rubbed Clay's thigh. She let her fingers run from his knee to his crotch, where she held it a moment to elicit a response from Clay. She leaned over and kissed him. Slowly moving her body between his and steering wheel, as she reached over and worked the seat adjustment button so that the seat slid backwards and the seat back reclined. As she straddled him, continuing to kiss him, she slowly began grinding her hips against him. He could feel her warmth through his pants. He reached around her waist and slid his hand up her skirt. He gave her bottom a firm squeeze. She let out a soft moan and kissed his neck, working her way to his ear.

"You'll be sorry you didn't get your shot today," she teased. She nibbled on his earlobe. "I'm going to try my best to kill you this evening, old man."

With that she opened the car door and slipped out onto the driveway. She walked several steps and then stopped and bent over to remove her high-heels, widening her stance to keep her balance. As she did so, her skirt rose up, exposing the flesh between her stockings, and the bottom hem of her skirt. The light shining from their front porch cast a glow around Lillian, and the glare from between her legs highlighted the slope of her thighs, the curve of her hips, cast her as a negative before the nighttime sky. The Dave Matthews Band's *Crash Into Me* popped into Clay's mind as he softly sang a few lines. She turned her head and gave him a sly smile, as she walked toward the front door, swinging her hips from side to side with exaggeration.

Clay pulled the car into the garage and had his jacket and tie off by the time he entered the house. He could hear Lillian upstairs and he quickly shut off the lights and went up to the bedroom. He entered their room slowly, smiling. Lillian was sitting before the mirror on her dressing table. She had removed her blouse and skirt and Clay stood there admiring the firmness of her body, the smoothness of her skin, the way the garter lay across against her lightly tanned hips. He could see her breasts, nipples erect, in the mirror as she continued to brush her hair. He walked up behind her and kissed the back of her neck gently, his hands lightly caressing her shoulders. She closed her eyes and let the brush fall to the floor, bending her head forward and pulling her hair aside so that her neck was more accessible. He continued to kiss her and let his hands slide down her arms, along her breasts, and over her hips. She stood up and let him embrace her with both arms, cradling her body close to his. She started rocking slowly, rubbing her body gently across his. She turned around and they embraced in a long kiss. Then she nudged him slowly across the room and as he fell onto the bed he caught sight of the two of them in the mirror. Her firm, young body pressed hard against his soft, graying frame. He instantly felt shame. In his desire to remain true to his own self, he seemed to have completely ignored Lillian and her needs. She was a part of his life, but lately, seemed to belong to another world. That, of course, he realized was his doing. He consciously chose not to get inoculated. It was he who chose to remain what he had become.

Or maybe it was her. Lillian had been inoculated without even mentioning the possibility to Clay, leaving him to struggle with their differences, making him out as the problem.

"What's wrong?" Lillian asked, sensing that Clay had become emotionally distanced.

"How did we get to this?" Clay asked.

"To what? What are you talking about, Clay?" Lillian raised her body off Clay's chest.

"You. Me. We're living in different worlds." Clay trailed off.

"I'm right here, Honey." Lillian kissed him.

"You are and you aren't." Clay tried to sort out his thoughts, but his brain was swirling with vodka. "I mean… ever since you were inoculated we seem to have headed in different directions. I down our original path and you down some fork in the road."

"Don't be ridiculous! Our lives are not set out. Life always presents challenges and opportunities and we have to make choices everyday. If your doctor told you that you had cancer, you would have to choose whether to receive treatment. And you would. Being inoculated was nothing more than another choice we both faced. I made a choice to improve my health, to be inoculated."

She was right. He tried again to clear his head but the alcohol was making it difficult. "I guess I'm just feeling old. And you're so..." he struggled to finish the sentence.

"So much in love with you." Lillian smiled and kissed Clay again. "Come on old man, I know how to make you feel young."

Clay woke up abruptly and sat upright. His head was throbbing. It was 3:47 in the morning and Lillian, sensing movement in her sleep, rolled over to her back and gave a soft moan before settling into a sound sleep again. The covers were wrapped around half her body, her right leg sticking out from beneath, revealing the smooth line of flesh from her hip down to her toes. Clay tried to remember what had happened. He knew, of course, it was not real, but he could not help but feel perhaps he was mistaken. Last night, he and Lillian had tried to make love, but age and alcohol had gotten the worse of Clay. But sometime later, Lillian had gotten up. Clay was still awake and he sat up, waiting for Lillian to come back to bed. But it was not Lillian who returned, it was someone else. He could still feel his excitement when he saw this other woman, this beauty, standing before him, naked, her body glistening in the soft moonlight shining from between the window blinds. He could not place her face or name, but he knew her, recognized her features. He had seen her before, perhaps in another dream. He didn't speak, but reached out to her and pulled her close. He laid her down on the bed and kissed her tenderly on the lips, down the neck, across her shoulder and down her arm, before working his way up her hip and waist to her breasts where he took his time before swirling his tongue around her nipples. As he worked his way down her belly she embraced his head with both of her hands and held his face close to her, legs spread wide, hips gyrating. Lying in bed now, in the pre-dawn light, he closed his eyes and could almost remember. Her smell, her taste, the way she convulsed when she finally reached orgasm.

Clay opened his eyes. The clock read 5:43 a.m. He lay there for a moment unsure of whether he had awoken earlier or whether that, too, had only been a dream. Lillian was asleep soundly beside him. He swung his feet over the side of the bed to stand and make his way to the bathroom when he saw it. There on the floor was *Virtual Fantasy*. The events of the previous night started to come back to him more clearly. His tryst with the stranger was no dream, or not completely. He had made love to another woman, or at least his wife in the form of another woman, a woman Clay felt was both entirely foreign and yet, intimately familiar. Lillian had gotten up to use the restroom and must have returned with the game. She had suggested it may be fun for a little change of pace, but he knew that it was due, in part, to her struggle to maintain the passion and eroticism of sleeping with a man who was, physically, twice her age. He didn't blame her. He tried to muster up the image he saw last night, the woman who he could now not dismiss from his thoughts, but yet eluded him. He tried to remember who it was that Lillian had become, who he had imagined, so enticing, that he was left feeling like he cheated on Lillian. He lay back down and fell into a deep slumber, dreaming of making love again, not to Lillian, but to her.

## CHAPTER TWENTY-THREE

*News Brief: Thursday. 8:45 p.m. In an unprecedented move, the Prime Minister of Canada has submitted a petition to the United States Congress to be admitted into the United States of America. The Petition states that by unanimous vote in the House of Commons, the Canadian people have denounced the Constitution of Canada and has granted its sovereignty to the Constitution of the United States of America. By unanimous vote in all the provinces, with the exception of Quebec where the measure passed by a slim margin, the Nation of Canada was dissolved earlier today. The President has called an emergency meeting of Congress to approve the admission of the Fifty-First through Sixtieth States, and the three territories, into the folds of the United States. The measure is expected to be approved almost unanimously, and the Prime Minister and Speaker of the House of Commons shall act as temporary Senators, while the Speaker of the House of both Quebec and Ontario shall serve as temporary Representatives, until the next national election, at which time the number of Representatives for each state shall be apportioned pursuant to the Constitution. General Thomas P. Rogers, former Chief of the Defense Staff of the Canadian Forces has surrendered his command to the Federal Police and has placed all troops at its disposal.*

Clay had just gotten on the train and was staring blankly out the window. The car was nearly empty. It was almost 9 p.m. and it was a little late for people to be heading downtown on a Thursday evening. Most people would already be at the restaurants or bars, or perhaps the virtual experience theaters. He was thinking of last night; of the woman of the Virtual Fantasy who Lillian had become. He could not shake her image from his mind, yet could not pinpoint her features, could not define her true image. He had the distinct feeling that if he could only step back for a moment and stop trying so hard to remember her, her true image of her would come to his mind as it sometimes happened when he was at a loss for a name or word. Clay could not stop thinking of her, could not calm his thoughts.

He had the folded note from the Walking Man in his hand and he was absent-mindedly rolling one corner of the paper. As the train pulled out of the station someone sat down beside him.

*The whole damn train is empty and you decide to sit right next to me*, Clay thought as he turned to see who would be so impolite as to not take an empty seat among those remaining in the car.

"How are you, old man?"

The fog of thoughts racing through his mind resulted in a delay in recognizing the face beside him. His mental haze receded with the lights from the last station as he brought the face into focus. Eva was sitting next to him, smiling at the success she had in surprising him.

He smiled back. "Well, I'll be damned. How are you?"

"I'm great, thanks. How about you?"

"Good... good. Lillian and I were out with your folks last night. Seems you've been pretty busy." Eva nodded. "Congratulations! It's great to hear that things are going so well with you. I imagine you're so busy you haven't even touched the last book you borrowed," Clay said. The hazy image of woman that had been haunting his thoughts tried to fight its way back into his brain.

"Yeah, work's been crazy," she replied, her smile disappearing briefly, but quickly returning. "But the book, no, it's great. I'm not as far along as I would have hoped, but it's incredibly entertaining and funny and thoughtful all at the same time." Eva was going to say more, but Clay seemed to be lost in thought. She sat silently for a moment.

Clay had his eyes closed tightly, concentrating on the woman from last night. The features of her face, her eyes, her lips, her cheeks, seemed to be coalescing. He struggled to bring the image into focus and as the image of the mysterious woman began to take shape, Eva interrupted. "You okay?"

The image faded again, like smoke: too soft around the edges and too thin to provide substance to the features. For a moment Clay felt disappointment rising but it turned to brief sorrow at having felt so close to discovering her identity, but failing once again. "Oh, I'm sorry. I was... I mean, I was trying to remember something. It's not important," he said. He put on a smile. "So, you out for a little R and R this evening?"

"Uh, no. I stopped at my parent's house a little earlier tonight and now I'm heading to a meeting," she replied. She gave Clay a curious glance.

"A little scientific pow-wow, huh?"

"You could say that. How about you?"

The question caught Clay off guard. He had not thought how to respond to why he was on the train. Certainly he could not tell Eva he was off to meet with a possibly half-crazed genius whom he hoped would shed light on the dangers of PreVentall and the meaning of life. His mind raced. "I'm... ah... going to the Palace box office to see if there are any tickets available for the latest Broadway Series play. I think they've revived a musical version of *Young Frankenstein*. I'm hoping to take Lill as a surprise, so don't mention anything if you should see her," he said. Clay enjoyed the comedy, and, in fact, enjoyed most of Mel Brooks' works. Lillian only liked comedies and musicals.

Going to the theatre now was easy for them. It used to be a challenge. Lillian did not enjoy dramas or serious plays because she didn't like walking out of the theatre unsure of the underlying message or theme, or the remaining unanswered questions that required thoughtful consideration. She was clearly a child of the sit-com, where all dilemmas arise and are resolved in 30 minutes. Over the past decade or so, however, Lillian became more and more willing to watch a play. When books started disappearing and universities stopped teaching liberal arts courses, the fine arts began to fade and theatre and other art forms no longer provided social commentary. The art politic was dead. Comedy, albeit mostly slapstick, survived because it required no thought process, it did not challenge one's beliefs or present problems that forced one to question.

"Of course I won't," she responded. "I wouldn't want to do anything to ruin any surprises," she added.

Clay looked over at her and smiled.

She smiled back and said, "I hope you don't think I'm strange, but I really enjoy hanging out with you. Of course, since

I've been out of college, I've always enjoyed going out with you and Lill and Mom and Dad, but since everyone's been inoculated... I don't know. It just seems very weird. But you're not changed." Clay looked down at his hands, which like the rest of him, showed his age. Scarred, slightly wrinkled, joints a little out of true. As the train pulled into the next station, Clay noticed that the few people waiting on the platform stared at him. He became uncomfortably aware of his oddity. Except the occasional foreign dignitary or people like the Walking Man, he was alone in physical age.

"Mom said you're scheduled to get inoculated Friday," Eva said frowning. "That's too bad." She placed a hand on his shoulder and looked at him seriously. "I mean, it's great that you'll be young and healthier again. But I'm going to miss you being... well, you being you, instead of someone else, like everyone else seems to have become."

Clay smiled at her again.

She looked into Clay's eyes. "I don't know, I guess it's a little awkward but... I've always had a kind of crush on you and, in a way, I'd... well, I guess what I'm trying to say is that I'm impressed you held out this long. I'm sure it's not easy, especially seeing everyone you know get younger. In the back of my mind, I kind of thought, maybe even hoped, maybe you would never get inoculated." Eva paused a moment as she collected her thoughts. "I don't know, it's silly, but I just hoped that somehow you would remain healthy, but just not be like everyone else."

Clay looked at her, unsure of how to respond.

Eva lowered her voice and leaned in close to Clay. "I've always felt very comfortable around you. You can't imagine how much I loved it when Dad brought me downtown for Book Club with you. It wasn't only that I got to dress up and feel like a grown up, it was your willingness to treat me like an adult. To listen to my thoughts and ideas of the books we read, to challenge them and make me think. I really loved those times. We were all so innocent back then. And now that everything's different, that everything's changed... well... it's nice to see you as you. I feel sometimes that when I'm with you, things are the way they should be. Somehow more... I guess I would say... natural," she continued. She shifted her body in her seat to better face Clay. "Maybe I'm just nostalgic, but I've always enjoyed your willingness to share..." she paused and looked around, and then continued, much more softly, "...to share your books and intellect and ideas. You really have enriched my life and I'm not sure I've ever thanked you. So, thank you." She gave him a kiss on the cheek. "Jeeze, will I ever shut up? I've been talking non-stop," she said smiling.

The train pulled into the Clark and Lake Street Station and Clay shifted his weight to get up when Eva quickly stood up. "Oh, this is my stop."

"Mine, too," Clay said too quickly. He realized he needed to go to this meeting alone.

"Fantastic," Eva said, exiting the train and heading left towards the Clark Street exit.

"Ah, I'm heading to the Wells Street exit," Clay said, recognizing an opportunity to part ways with Eva.

"Well, it's been great to see you. Oh, and I've still got your... ah..." again lowering her voice, "your copy of *Metamorphosis*. I'd love to get together with you sometime to discuss it. Fascinating, especially given that what must have been quite an incredible notion when it was written is now, somehow," she paused a moment, "a bit of reality."

"Anytime," Clay responded. He turned and began to walk to the opposite side of the station.

He questioned the time, but no response came. He remembered that he had left his iMeme at home. He consciously placed his fingers on the Spot, confirming the absence of his iMeme as he glanced up at the holographic displays which displayed the time. It was nine twenty-three. By exiting at Wells instead of Clark, he would have to walk a few blocks out of his way. He would definitely be late and hoped it would not cause a problem.

As Clay arrived at the Garvey Court entrance to Lower Wacker, leading down to the city's lower sections, he noticed some commotion below. Two men in military uniform were dragging a ragged man toward a waiting National Police van that was surrounded by four more uniformed men. As the soldiers forced the older man into the vehicle, they pulled his head back to avoid banging it against the vehicle's roof. Clay thought he recognized the man but he could not place him. His face was lined, and his grey hair was long and disheveled. Clay immediately assumed that the man was homeless, living in the relative protection of Lower Wacker Drive. But then he paused. He was not sure the homeless still existed in America, hidden from the rest of the world like parasites in the bowels of the city. Perhaps Genesis had done away with such sadness.

Clay and the man made eye contact, and Clay thought he saw the man shake his head ever so slightly, communicating some message, the meaning of which Clay was unable to grasp. One of the soldiers looked up at Clay, nodded to one of the others, and the two soldiers quickly began moving toward him. Before Clay had an opportunity to react, he was bumped solidly from the side and pushed back in the direction from which he had come.

"Clay!" The warm greeting was a little too loud, and Clay wondered for a moment if it were meant for someone else, turning his head to search for whom the greeting was directed. "Sorry I'm late, I thought we had agreed to meet at Dearborn and Lake, not Clark and Lake," the voice continued as an arm wrapped around his shoulder and pushed him along. "Hurry, we'll be late." By now, their heads were close enough together that he could hear the whisper, "Keep walking and don't say a thing. Let me handle this."

Clay turned and opened his mouth to say something, but was unable to respond. He was speechless. Eva looked him in the eye briefly and they only managed a couple more steps before Clay felt the strong grip of a stranger on his arm.

"Excuse me sir, but I need to have a word with you," the soldier said firmly. Clay turned and saw that he was standing before two of the soldiers, the one on his left retaining the grip on his arm. Clay recognized the similarities instantly. They were clearly brothers. They each stood before him, with tight jaws and steady gazes. "Sir, I'm going to need you to come with me," the first soldier said. "If you will just come this way," the second continued, his voice indistinguishable from the first. Clay looked closer. These guys weren't just brothers, they were twins. Identical twins. Exact duplicates. Eva stepped forward. "What is this about?" Her voice was strong and commanding. The two soldiers looked at her for the first time and both took a small step backwards.

"Do you know this man, Dr. Diaz?" the one on the left asked.

"Of course. Clay is a long-time friend of my family. What is your business with him?" Her voice was a little softer now, but still commanding.

"I'm sorry, ma'am. It's just that I thought..." The soldier looked to his brother, who continued, "There are some BAMF activities going on here and, well, given his OutAp," here he pointed toward Clay, "we have reasonable cause to believe that he may be involved."

"I'm sure I don't know what you're talking about. He is with me. If you'll excuse us, we are in somewhat of a hurry," Eva said firmly.

"I'm sorry, Dr. Diaz, but with all due respect, he is a BAMF and I will be required to investigate this further," the first soldier said as he pulled on Clay's arm, attempting to lead him down the Garvey Court ramp.

"I can assure you, he is completely innocent." She leaned closer to the soldiers and whispered loudly, "He's a nice guy, but not so tech savvy. He doesn't adapt to technology very well," she added, before returning to a normal volume. "If you complete your check, you'll see that he's perfectly innocent."

The other soldier pulled out an electronic device that Clay was not familiar with. He read the screen and then turned to the other. "No previous history. Class two job history, married, kids, all inoculated. No known contact with suspect. He has a two o'clock appointment on Friday with Dr. Kovak for inoculation," he said as he turned back to Eva. "I still think he should be brought in for questioning. Sir, if you'll just come with us."

"What's going on here?" No one had noticed a third soldier, an officer, had approached during the questioning. Eva looked over at the new soldier. Clay thought he saw a brief expression of disappointment cross Eva's face, but Eva was now smiling widely, eyes sparkling. The tall, well-built lieutenant's face immediately lit up when he saw Eva. "Why, Dr. Diaz. What a surprise to see you here!"

"Lt. Cobbs," she responded, grinning back.

Lt. Cobbs turned to the two soldiers. "What's going on here, soldier?" he asked.

The soldiers both wore scowls on their faces. "Sir. This man is a BAMF and we want to take him in for questioning."

Lt. Cobbs turned back to Eva. "Doctor, do you know this man?" He looked Clay up and down, apparently not very impressed with what he saw.

"Please Lt. Cobbs, I'm not in the business of hanging around with strangers." She recognized her tone as a bit too condescending. "I mean, of course I do," she said, trying to sound more pleasant. She turned to Clay and flashed him a brief expression of uncertainty.

"This, Clay, is Lt. Cobbs." Clay held out his hand, but Lt. Cobbs ignored him completely. Dismissing his rudeness, Eva turned back to Lt. Cobbs and continued, "Clay is a long-time family friend, very close to my parents. He's not very tech savvy, but he's no threat." She leaned a little closer to Lt. Cobbs. "Perhaps a bit of a no-techno, but I can vouch for him."

Lt. Cobbs turned back to Clay, still somewhat suspicious. "What are you doing around here, anyway?"

Clay wasn't sure how to respond. "I was meeting Eva here to…" he fumbled for words.

"To help me plan my folks' surprise wedding anniversary party," Eva interjected. "We were just heading over to the theatre so I could purchase some tickets as a present, and then we thought we'd have a drink to go over the guest list. Shoot! Listen to the time! The box office closes soon." Lt. Cobbs continued to stare at Clay.

Eva put on her best look of desperation. "If you could call your dogs off, I'd really owe you one."

This caught Lt. Cobbs' attention and he seemed to soften somewhat. "You'll owe me one, huh? I'm going to keep you to that, Doctor." He turned to the men. "Alright, he's okay," he snapped at them. "What are you doing harassing Dr. Diaz? Let's get back to our mission here!"

"I apologize, Dr. Diaz," one of the soldiers spat through his teeth. "You are free to proceed." Eva's face wore an expression of contempt. The soldier turned to Clay. "Apparently, I have nothing to detain you on." He leaned closer before he released his grip on Clay and threatened, "I don't recommend missing your appointment on Friday." The duplicate soldiers turned and started walking back to the vehicles still waiting below. One turned around. "I hope you enjoy returning the *favor* Doctor." He smiled and continued on.

"She will. Oh, she will," Lt. Cobbs smirked. He winked at Eva before turning and walking after the other soldiers.

"What the …?" Clay started.

"Shhh. Just shut up and start walking," she whispered.

They walked to the Ford Theatre in relative silence. Eva asked the ticket kiosk several questions about the various plays coming to Chicago over the next season, seeking Clay's advice on what her parents may enjoy. She purchased several tickets and then wrapped her arm around Clay's. Clay was trying to figure out what was going on, but every time he opened his mouth to speak, Eva tugged his arm to stop him. She started to lead him toward the South Loop where she lived on the 9th floor of an old print-house that had been converted to condominiums back in the early '90s. When they entered her apartment she walked over to the kitchen and opened a cabinet. "Vodka on the rocks, right?"

"That'd be great," Clay said, still leery to speak. Clay watched as she poured two glasses of clear liquid from an unmarked bottle. He gave her an inquisitive look and shrugged his shoulders.

"Don't worry, you'll like it. It's a 'secret' recipe a friend of mine made and gave to me. He actually distills it himself. Says he enjoys the process, but I think he's afraid that if he makes a Genesis-App, it will spread and the whole country will be able to drink his vodka. He enjoys sharing it with friends, but doesn't want it replicated." She handed a glass to Clay.

He took a sip. "Mmmm. This is good." He was surprised at the quality. Crisp, smooth, with just a hint of flavor, perhaps fennel, but very faint. He was watching Eva as she wrote a note.

"I thought you would like it," she smiled. "He makes it with homegrown potatoes. He says that the replicated potatoes ruin the taste." She handed him the note and gestured to keep quite.

Clay took the note. "I can't remember when I last drank a non-replicated vodka. It must be... let's see now..." He looked down at the note.

*We need to talk in private.*

Clay looked at Eva. "What the —"

Eva had spilled her drink onto Clay. "Oh, I'm such a klutz!" She gave him an imploring look. "I'm sorry. I didn't mean to spill my drink. Here, you can get out of those wet clothes in the bathroom." She pushed him into the bathroom and shut the door. "Just take them off and I'll throw them in the wash," she said, speaking from the other side of the door. "I've got one of those steam units, they only take about forty minutes to complete a cycle. Toss out your clothes so I can get them started."

Clay was dumb-founded. But he was also wet. He disrobed and grabbed a washcloth to wipe the vodka off his body. He looked at his body in the mirror. *Sagging and graying, but only a few pounds over my fighting weight,* he thought. He looked around the room. He had no desire to sit wrapped in a towel in front of Eva. She may be comforted by his aging carcass, but he was not comfortable displaying it in a world of young people. He spotted a bathrobe hanging on a hook and wrapped it around his body. It was too small, but would serve him better than the towel. He picked up his clothes off the floor and gathered them together. Eva was waiting outside the bathroom door and immediately grabbed them. There was music playing over speakers in the ceiling. "I'm so sorry," she said again, loudly, as she threw his clothes into the steamer. She closed the door and pressed the start button. When she heard the cycle begin, she turned back toward him. More softly she said, "I am sorry, but I need to speak to you in private."

Clay was still at a loss. "Aren't we alone here?" he asked, looking around.

"Physically, yes. But..." She let out a sigh and poured herself another drink. "I know you're aware of some of the work I do. But even Mom and Dad don't know the full extent. It's top-secret stuff, Clay. Classified. Take a look around. Do you notice anything strange?"

Clay took a quick look around the room. "No."

"Take a close look," she said.

Clay took the time to let his eyes wonder around the room. It was an open loft space. The kitchen, living room and dining room were one great room. The room was typical of a single woman. Counters clean and arranged, a china cabinet with decorative glass, soft pillows on the couches. A few plants scattered about the room. He caught whiff of something. *Was that a scented candle?* he wondered. *Or perhaps a hint of perfume from her robe he wore?* The walls were dominated by pictures of friends and family. Clay noticed all the family photos of her parents were pre-inoculation. They were a handsome couple, aging well. There was a photo of Clay and his family alongside the Diazs. It was taken a number of years earlier when both families rented a cottage in Galena one December. Everyone was rosy-cheeked, Miguel, Clay and the kids from having just returned from skating, and Lillian and Jennifer from having remained indoors drinking hot chocolate and schnapps. Clay finished his vodka and instinctively moved to put the empty glass in the Genesis for recycling. He looked around quickly again, and then looked to Eva.

"No Genesis," she said matter-of-factly.

"I don't get it."

"I'm working on top secret stuff. The people in my group aren't allowed to have Genesis. DARPA is worried that we will bring work home and classified information will be leaked, or worse, we'll intentionally export it overseas. We're off the grid, so to speak. They fear that we could be subject to sabotage, duplication, blackmail… torture. We're not even allowed to have iMemes." Clay looked at Eva's Spot. He quickly looked to her wrist, the absence of an iMeme explaining the watch among her other bracelets. "They're afraid the two-way communication systems can get hacked and secrets will be stolen. We are definitely alone here. But you have an iMeme —"

"I didn't bring it," Clay interrupted.

"I know. But I need to be absolutely sure here. No iMeme, no self-repairing clothing, nothing with any nanobots. Absolutely nothing that can be hacked."

"My god. Do you really think someone's out there trying to steal your knowledge? That some foreign agency has you targeted?" Clay turned his attention to the windows.

She stared at Clay and took a deep breath. "It's not the foreigners that I'm worried about."

Clay turned back to Eva. "What do you mean?"

"I mean Cobb's men, DARPA, the National Police. Whoever the hell is really behind all of this," she said.

Clay was really confused now. "But I still don't know what you mean."

"Clay, this place is clean. No iMeme. No Genesis. Nothing. Even the walls are painted with a special paint that prevents the InFIXstructure nanobots on the outside of the building from penetrating this space."

"You mean to tell me that there's not a single nanobot crawling around or inhabiting a single molecule in this entire place?" Clay was amazed. He suddenly felt free, unfettered. Safe.

"Nothing. Not one iota," she said, averting her eyes from Clay and biting her lip. Clay got the impression she was holding back something, but he let it go. She turned her gaze back toward him. "By putting your clothes in the steamer, I could guarantee that we would be truly alone."

Clay moved over to the freezer and removed the bottle of vodka to pour himself another drink. He wasn't sure whether to smile at the thought of knowing he could visit Eva and be truly off the grid or worry about whatever it was that Eva was frightened of, and why she felt it necessary to be 'truly alone.' In either case, he needed another drink. "I hope you don't mind. Do you need a refill?"

"No, thanks. I'm fine," she said, showing him her glass still nearly full. Eva was staring at him. He looked down and remembered that he was dressed only in Eva's robe. The belt had loosened and he being larger than she was to begin with, his chest was almost fully exposed. He became conscious of his physical appearance again and tried to wrap the robe around himself more tightly.

"I'm sorry," she said, still staring, but not as intently. "I don't mean to stare, but it's just that you're so... so..."

"So old?" Clay offered.

"No. So natural," she corrected him. "I don't see many people who are natural anymore, who are still real. Especially people I know and love. They've all changed into people I have a hard time recognizing. You wouldn't understand, perhaps, but when I see my parents now, I see them as I did when I was 9 years old. It's crazy, but when I'm with them, it's like my brain can't comprehend what's happened and I feel like I'm a little girl again. It's kind of nice to look at you and feel like I'm an adult, to be connected with my past in the present, in the here and now, rather than in some bizarre otherworldly, 'I'm the same age as my parents' way. And I'm going to miss you being old and me feeling my real age and living in the here and now."

"What?"

"I'm going to miss that connection when you get inoculated."

Clay looked at her hard. Inoculation. He had not had the opportunity to discuss matters with the Walking Man this evening. He had been hoping to get a better grasp of what the Walking Man meant. Of how other people were dealing with being human, in a world gone inhuman. He wondered if these others were in serious trouble for being human, for refusing to submit to technology. Whether this was not the America he remembered. An America where people had the right to choose, the right to self-determination. Clay's doubts about being inoculated grew stronger.

"Well, I may not get inoculated. You probably wouldn't understand, but I don't want to be young again. I want to be older, to slowly march toward my golden years like mankind has done for thousands of years."

He stopped for a moment, recognizing what he was saying was not exactly true. Certainly he did not look forward to becoming an invalid, but on the other hand, he was not yet willing to give up his humanity to PreVentall.

He continued, "Don't get me wrong, aging isn't something I've been looking forward to, at least not in the sense that I want to get old. I'm not ready for a nursing home, but I'm not in the same shape I was five years ago either. Add to that, everyone I know is young and can do things that I have to struggle with and it hits hard. It stinks, in fact. And I'm no fool. I don't want to die, and—I can't believe I'm saying this—I certainly don't want to die *hundreds* of years before Lill, before my kids and friends. But I don't want to be some semi-human, cyborg thing. I am a human being, with all my faults and all my shortcomings. But I am a human and I think that means something." He took a large swallow of his vodka. "I met someone just a few days ago who questioned whether inoculation was really the end of humanity."

"I know."

"You know what?" he asked.

"I know what you were doing. Didn't you think it was odd that I showed up right as you were heading to 159 W. Lower Wacker?" Eva asked.

Clay's mouth dropped open.

"Yes, I know about the meeting. I was headed there myself but the Niklases were already there. I spotted them in time to avoid being seen myself, but I had to be sure you weren't the new person joining tonight's meeting. Earlier tonight, when I saw you on the train, I felt certain it was you who was the new person Dr.—" but Eva stopped herself, thinking better to avoid the name she did not want to share with Clay, for his protection and Dr. Nakosh's. "The new person *he* said would be at the meeting."

Eva spoke with intensity. "But when you headed towards the Wells Street exit, I thought maybe I was wrong, that maybe you weren't the one. Once I saw the Niklases, I had to be sure. If it was you, I had to try to stop you from going down there and getting caught if I could. I knew it was too late for the others, but I was hoping it wasn't too late for you." She lowered her head and fell onto the couch, a mixture of frustration and relief.

"I'm beginning to feel like a broken record here, but..." Clay paused, recognizing that the phrase had no literal meaning to Eva, having grown up in a world of cd's and mp4s. "What the hell are you talking about? Niklases, BAMF, missing me getting old, the 'new' person?"

"Come over here and sit down. This is going to take awhile." Eva said as she patted the cushion of the couch next to her. Clay grabbed the bottle and brought it with him. He thought he might need another drink before this was through.

"Listen, I am part of a group of people who are, unofficially, exploring the dangers of PreVentall. Or at least I was. It is headed by a gentleman who is also 'off the grid,' so to speak. He's a brilliant man, but has he always stayed somewhat below the radar."

"You know the Walking Man?" Clay interrupted.

"Who?" It was Eva's turn to be confused.

"I'm sorry. The Walking Man. It's the name I've given to the guy who invited me to the meeting. I don't know his name, but I've called him the Walking Man for years. He has always interested me. He seems to just wander around the city, walking here and there, but never really seeming to have any particular place to go. You know him?" The idea that Clay was going to learn more about the Walking Man excited him.

"I do. And perhaps, given what's happened, it's best if you don't know too much about him. You probably shouldn't know anything I'm going to tell you, but I have to tell someone. And I know I can trust you, Clay." She let out another sigh. "God, this is difficult. I can't tell my parents, since they've been inoculated. I'm not sure I'd tell them even if they weren't. But you're different Clay. Besides you're not being inoculated, you understand things. You question things, analyze things. I can tell you anything and I know it's safe. It may sound funny, but you're my closest friend. The one person I can be completely open with, completely honest."

Clay was taken aback. He was not sure how to respond. He had known Eva all her life. They had shared many times together and while he admired Eva and was proud of her, and considered her a friend, sitting in her living room drinking vodka, wearing her bathrobe, and being told that he was her closest confidant before she was going to let him in on some heretofore untold secret was not something he had ever considered, and it struck him as disconcerting. Eva sensed his discomfort.

"I'm sorry. I shouldn't have brought you here. But it really is out of my hands now. I don't know what else to do." She turned away from him and started to sob softly.

Clay put his arms around her and pulled her close. She placed her head on his shoulder and continued to cry. "It's okay Eva, I'm sorry. I... I... it's just that... well, I care an awful lot about you. I value our friendship more than you could know. I'm not sure what's going on in your life right now, but I'll always be here for you, you know that." He held her close and tried to sooth her.

Eva pulled away from Clay, wiping her eyes. "I'm sorry. I didn't want to do that. But you can't imagine what went through my mind when I saw the Niklases and thought that you had somehow beat me to the meeting, that, maybe, you had been caught, too."

"I'm sorry. I still don't understand. What group was I invited to this evening?"

Eva took a large sip from her glass. Her mouth puckered up from the alcohol as she exhaled.

"Okay, listen," she said as she straightened her back. "About a year ago I was approached by an individual, a man I'd never met before." Clay raised his eyebrows, but Eva continued on. "Names aren't important right now. In fact, it might be best if you didn't know. Anyway, I was asked if I'd be willing to sit down with a few people and discuss some of the social ramifications of PreVentall and Genesis technology. At first I thought it was some kind of joke — some people from the office trying to get me to join them for a party or something. No one outside my work group knew my involvement in Genesis matters and discussing certain aspects of my work is a crime. I don't go out that often, certainly not often enough for a women my age, but by the time my day is done, I'm usually exhausted. I know they say no one works anymore, but there are a group of us who do. We're all working for DARPA and our jobs are real. Most of us continue there because what we do is important. Some stay for fear of what may happen if we stop showing up. There are some pretty scary people working there."

Clay gave her a stern look. "Like Lt Cobbs?"

"Oh, he's not so bad compared to some of the others. At least I can handle him," she said, forcing a laugh. "Anyway, I figured it was some of the guys trying to get me to loosen up and have some fun, so I finally agreed to meet down in Millennium Park during one of the free weekly concerts. I was expecting a few of the scientists from the lab to be sitting around having a few drinks and complaining about the military guys. I spotted the man who had invited me but when he saw me, he turned his head away and walked past me, dropping a slip of paper onto the blanket I was carrying. It advised me that there would be a woman on a purple and white blanket wearing a red beret sitting near the most southwest speaker tower. The note directed me to set up my blanket near her, close enough to dissuade any other person to sit between, but not too close. I did as I was told. The woman didn't even acknowledge my arrival. I tried to catch her attention a few times, but I seemed to remain outside her cone of vision. The concert was not scheduled to begin for almost an hour, so I laid down on my back and watched the clouds roll by, listening to people gathering in the park as the sky slowly changed from light blue to a deeper hue.

"Sometime later, I realized the music had started and the sky seemed to have jumped several shades darker without warning. I turned my head and saw the woman next to me was standing up. I thought for a moment that she was preparing to leave, but the man you call the Walking Man came up and gave her a hug. They exchanged some brief niceties and I turned away quickly. A slight fear began to grip me," Eva said. Clay gave her a quizzical look.

"It may surprise you, but the Walking Man's actually a brilliant scientist. It's not likely that you would be familiar with him, but when he was with the University of Chicago, he developed a lot of technologies that have been incorporated into much of what we use everyday. He worked with Dr. Chin Ho, the man who is credited with perfecting Genesis technology. He was eventually run out of the university by Dr. Ho, who was politically much more powerful than he.

"And there he was, not five feet from me. If I were to be seen with him, I'd... well, I don't even want to think about that right now." She paused a moment.

"What do you mean? What would happen?" Clay's voice carried with it a tone of concern.

"The Walking Man was deeply involved in the research leading up to the breakthrough in molecular manufacturing. But he soon discovered he and Dr. Ho disagreed on how Dr. Ho had been presenting his findings, and more importantly, Dr. Ho's seeming lack of ethical integrity. It started out with minor breaches, little things. He was representing that the theoretical output of his experiments were actual outputs produced in lab experiments, closing his eyes to certain data that raised questions about his findings or whether his methods actually worked. You see, early on in nanoscience, they were working on experiments that provided results that were sometimes hard to verify," Eva explained.

"I'm not following you," Clay admitted. A puzzled expression crossed his face. "If the experiment produced results, then couldn't other scientists see if they could replicate the results in order to prove the experiment as valid or not?"

"It's a bit complicated, but let me use an example here. Early on, Dr. Ho's lab published findings in *Nature Nanotechnology* basically stating that, using proprietary technology, Dr. Ho was able to induce various nanomaterials to self-assemble. He had begun work on fully-functional self-assembling nanochips. That is, he sought to induce silicon and gold to self-assemble into functional nanoprocessors. Although the lab was able to produce all the individual components of the nanoprocessor, when it tried to put it all together, the nanoprocessors did not perform. When Dr. Na—" She stopped herself. "I'm sorry. When the Walking Man was working in Dr. Ho's lab, at some point it became his assignment to show that fully functional self-replicating nanoprocessors could be produced using Dr. Ho's proprietary technology—technology that, by the way, had already been advertised for commercial application. Dr. Ho was in the process of marketing his technology to public and private investors—seeking to make some serious money at the time—when the Walking Man started his experiments. Contrary to Dr. Ho's assertions, the experiments showed not only that the materials would not self-replicate, but also that the original experiment was seriously flawed. While the original experiment self-replicated the various components of the nanoprocessors, these components contained flaws that prevented them from properly conducting electrons, as they would have had they been created by standard lithographic techniques.

"Dr. Ho's original research merely developed structurally correct components without regard to the conductivity and functionality of the nanoprocessor. The Walking Man determined that by modifying Dr. Ho's proprietary technology, rather than creating self-replicating nanoprocessors, it was possible to create scaffolding on which the nanomaterials could then be disbursed to promote self-assembly."

"Sorry, but you lost me," Clay confessed.

"Basically, the Walking Man showed Dr. Ho's proprietary technology would not perform as advertised. It would, however, work with certain modifications. When the Walking Man raised this issue, Dr. Ho refused to accept the findings, prohibited the Walking Man from performing further tests and assigned him to a dead-end project. The Walking Man's research was going to blow a huge hole in Dr. Ho's claims of nanoprocessor self-replication and put a serious damper on his attempts to market his proprietary technology. Not only would it affect potentially millions in federally funded grants, it would scare investors in Dr. Ho's private company away."

Clay leaned towards Eva, trying to be sure he understood what she was telling him. She continued on. "Dr. Ho's refusal to even entertain the notion the original research may have been flawed, and his continued marketing of the proprietary technology to public and private investors even after serious questions were raised, was enough to cause the Walking Man to leave Dr. Ho's research group. He ended up starting his own lab group at the Illinois Institute of Technology. I worked with some of his lab group when I was finishing up my doctoral work.

"Dr. Ho eventually gave up on the questionable technology, and, as we all know, pioneered the Genesis project. But a lot of Genesis was rooted in the research coming out of the Walking Man's group. There had been some disagreements on whether the Walking Man should have been credited with some of the Genesis research and whether an acknowledgment—which is what he was given— was adequate. Unlike Dr. Ho, the Walking Man had little desire to acquire fame or fortune for his work. He was a scientist, through and through. Lately, there had been a rumor that he had died a few months ago," Eva said.

Clay's eyes widened. "How the hell would he have died?"

"Age. Alcoholism. There were various rumors, but the long and short of it was that he refused to be inoculated," she responded. "Anyway, as I said, he was not interested in fame or glory. But as soon as he found out that Dr. Ho was going to be moving forward with the Genesis project in conjunction with DARPA, he did everything he could to try to secure some authorship of the research, some control to try to prevent, what he deemed, a marriage made in hell. There is no doubt that Dr. Ho is a brilliant man. But his ethics leave a lot to be desired."

"So the Walking Man is a great scientist?" Clay asked. "That doesn't even make sense. Why the hell is he wandering around like he doesn't belong, like he has nothing to do? What has he been doing with himself? Hell, why doesn't my iMeme even recognize him? He's got to be plastered all over the Cloud somewhere."

"He's not interested in fame. I've already told you that. Once DARPA got involved in the project, he left the university, dropped out of the scientific community and disappeared. Rumors circulated that he had gone a little nuts. I have to admit, the first time I saw him after he left the university, I would have agreed, had I not heard him speak.

"It was that night of the Millennium Park concert that I saw him again. When I turned and saw the woman next to me hugging him, I didn't even recognize him. He looked like one of the many unemployed people who used to hang out in the parks before Genesis. But there seemed to be something definitely out of place with him. It took me a few minutes to realize who he was, and that's when I felt the chill up my spine. I closed my eyes to try to think of what to do next. He was sitting on the edge of the blanket nearest me, not more than two feet away. I couldn't get it out of my mind that when he was hugging that woman, he was looking directly at me, smiling at me. I moved to get up and leave, but he spoke my name, almost in a whisper."

\* \* \*

"Eva? Please, just hear me out," Nakosh pleaded, his voice gentle and smooth.

The hair on the back of Eva's neck stood on end and she had the uncomfortable feeling that they were being watched. She took a deep breath and settled back down, keeping her head in the direction of the performers. She tried moving her eyes to see him better, but he remained outside even her peripheral vision.

"I apologize for my persistence, and my deceit in getting you to come, but I wanted to reach out to you." His eyes never left the stage, although now and then he would close them and gently sway to the beat of the music. "I understand the danger of you and I conversing. If you are not comfortable, please, feel free to get up and walk away. You can pretend this never happened. But if you are willing to hear me out, it would mean a great deal to me," Nakosh said.

"Listen, Dr. E," Eva paused. "I mean, Dr. Nakosh. I'm not sure this is a very good idea." She looked toward the stage as she spoke, hoping that her voice was loud enough for him to hear, but not so loud as to be overheard

He laughed softly. "Dr. E? Is that what Chin has you calling me?"

Eva hadn't thought about it. Dr. Ho forbade the mention of Nakosh's name, or even his work. If anyone did speak his name, Dr. Ho would have a fit. He had once physically struck a scientist who accidently mentioned the name. To attempt to avoid any transgressions, Eva and her fellow workers simply referred to him as Dr. E. It had become so natural that it rolled off her tongue before she had time to think about it.

"We should be safe," Dr. Nakosh assured her. "Don't make eye contact. I will do all the talking. You may have questions. I am sorry, but at this time you will need to hold on to them. I will do my best to reach out to you in the future, to help you with your inquiries, but tonight, I just ask that you listen."

Eva gave a gentle nod and then lay back down on her blanket. As Dr. Nakosh began to speak, it struck her that she was able to see Lyra high above. She moved her eyes to the east to espy Cygnus and Aquila flying overhead in the flowing sparkle of the Milky Way, and then she turned her head further toward the eastern horizon to catch a glimpse of Pegasus rising over the Lake. *When did the stars come back out? The Milky Way?* she wondered. It had seemed like only yesterday she had been a little girl, excited to see even Betelgeuse or Sirius on a cloudless evening. She let her eyes dart among the heavens as the rich tone of Dr. Nakosh's voice was carried by the music to her ears.

"Eva. I know you know, better than most, the incredible impact that Genesis is having on society, on American society. We hold in our hands the potential for greatness. I know you also understand that greatness can be used for good or ill. Have you ever wondered why DARPA seized control of Genesis? Of the California condor project? We are but men. It is our nature to reach for the skies. It is our destiny to remain firmly planted on the earth. From which we came are we obligated to return," he said. And then his voice fell silent for some time. Eva wondered if he had left. Just as she was going to risk turning her head, he began again. "Or not. We have been given new wings. Genesis holds the promise to raise humanity to the heavens — but, like Icarus, we make our ascent without thought of the consequences. To what outcome?"

As he spoke, the Walking Man continued to pause occasionally and Eva could hear the soft murmur of his companion's voice. Eva noticed he did this each time someone happened to walk within earshot of the two blankets. She was unable to make out any of the words spoken, but she recognized that it gave any passer-by the appearance that Dr. Nakosh and his companion were having a conversation. She relaxed a little, continuing to explore the Milky Way above.

"You're wondering why it was you with whom I wanted to speak to? It is because you are different Eva. You are special." He let his last words sink in. "No, it has nothing to do with your cunningness in perfecting living replication. No, Eva, that was no accomplishment whatsoever. If not you, I have no doubt someone else would have figured it out, if not at that moment, then certainly by now. The Law of Calculated Chance Methodology." Eva frowned, but Dr. Nakosh continued. "No Eva, it is your ability to reason, your ability to think and question and analyze. The scientists you work with are brilliant when it comes to known math and science, but they are lost if the answers they seek lie outside the realm of knowledge. That is, they are incapable of developing new thoughts, questioning existing theories." He stopped again and she heard the low murmur of he and his companion exchanging quiet conversation. It was only then that she caught glimpse of some stranger walking past them.

Dr. Nakosh's voice returned to an audible level. "You are able to grasp the subtleties of discourse, solve problems without first having been given the solution. And so I ask: Why is it Genesis is forbidden from moving beyond our borders? You and I both know that Genesis creates equality and soothes conflict between people, rather than raising fears and violence. Why do we have soldiers in the streets? We are certainly not in need of going to war, and should we choose to wage war, it can be done without the mess of human actors. Most importantly for a scientist, why PreVentall? Why remove genetic errors from the equation? Hasn't the history of life, the basis of evolution, revolved around variations in genetic code?

Where would life be today if those genetic traits that gave one creature an advantage over his fellow creatures were corrected, if those genetic anomalies were erased?"

Eva shut her eyes. The questions began dancing around in her mind. The music from the band began to rise and increase in tempo. With each beat of the drum, each chord of the keyboard, the questions multiplied, every one a step in a complicated dance, until her mind could not keep up with the movement, the beat. The music came to an abrupt end and Eva opened her eyes. She was lying on her back, the Great Square of Pegasus high overhead. From all around she heard clapping and cheering. She sat up and noticed others in the audience were beginning to rise and gather their belongings. She looked quickly to her left, but the space was empty. She felt disorientated, unsure of how long she had been lying there. She tried to remember what Dr. Nakosh had said, but his exact words eluded her thoughts. When he had stopped speaking she could not say. She considered asking the couple behind her if anyone had actually been sitting next to her at all, but thought better of the idea.

* * *

Eva stood up and moved from the couch. "When I first realized it was... the Walking Man, I was skeptical," Eva said. "I certainly didn't believe what Dr. Ho said about him, but you do have to wonder whether any of it was based in fact. I always presumed that he had become some sort of anti-science lunatic trying to uphold some crazy fanatical standard. I mean, who's on the leading edge of technology and then just leaves it all behind? Who wouldn't want to be inoculated? Eternal youth and unlimited supplies of everything you could wish for or imagine." Eva frowned again. "I mean, we're living in the age of Paradise, right? But he raised some serious questions. Before I met him, I defended the system and regurgitated the standard arguments about the whole world being better off even if Genesis wasn't being shared, about how the rest of the world was benefiting significantly from our progress. It's a win-win situation, right?"

"It would seem that way," Clay responded, neither sounding nor feeling convinced.

"Yes, that's how I started feeling. I guess I had never sat and thought about it much, but after that night, I started to notice things, little things, about what I was doing, how the government was handling it, and how it could impact the world. It all started to make me look at things a little closer. It was when the Niklases showed up that I really started to question what was going on." Eva finished her glass of vodka and poured herself another.

"The Niklases?"

"The two soldiers that wanted to question you. Did you notice anything odd about them?"

"Other than they were identical twins, no."

"That's just it," Eva explained. "They aren't twins at all. They're the same person. DARPA had been working with NASA on transportation technologies for putting men on Mars. But DARPA decided that rather than risking multiple lives, that they could disassemble a single astronaut and reassemble multiples of that same person, who could all work in perfect unison, being the same person, and should something go wrong, no one would really be lost because that person, in one of his other multiple reassemblies, would still live on. There were some serious concerns raised, but apparently DARPA decided to go ahead on its own and put the technology to use in the military. A soldier by the name of Niklas Mueller was selected as the guinea pig and, apparently it's been quite successful. They've now got several hundred of him operating across the country, and who knows where else. We call them the Niklases."

Clay found that his jaw had dropped once again. "You mean to tell me that our military is being staffed by a bunch of... of clones?"

Eva shook her head. "Not clones. Replicons. That was when I decided to go to one of the Counsel's meetings."

"What's the Counsel?" Clay asked.

"That's what we call the group you were invited to this evening, the Counsel." She sat back down next to Clay. "There were about a dozen Counsel members, all from various backgrounds, none of them inoculated. They all had their reasons for avoiding PreVentall, but they all shared a common fear of the technology and where it could lead.

"You know, if it weren't for you, I don't think anything they would have said would have affected me. But all those books you loaned me, all those discussions we had when I was growing up, and even now, I think they all helped me to really be able to think, to question whether what we're told is right or wrong and to think independently. I tried to raise some of these issues with friends before, but it all seems to go right over their heads. It's like they're incapable of imagining something that they didn't learn from the Cloud." Clay smiled in spite of the situation. Eva forced a smile in return and continued.

"Lately, some of the Counsel mentioned they thought they were being targeted by the government. They couldn't pinpoint any specific thing, but there were little things: a feeling like being followed, something not quite where they left it. A lot of things that they couldn't prove or deny, just gut-feelings. We all took extra precautions and we thought we were safe. I'm not sure who was arrested tonight or how they found out about the Counsel. But I don't want to think about what the Niklases may be doing to them now."

"This Niklas guy is trouble, huh?"

"I wouldn't know if I had ever met the real Niklas or not, but he had to be one royal asshole to begin with. With upgrades, he could only be worse."

"What do you mean?"

"The Niklases aren't running on PreVentall Two-Oh. The Two-Oh upgrade is peanuts compared to what advances they've developed and put into the Niklases. And they've been put on assignment to round up all the BAMFs."

"What the heck is a BAMF?"

"I'm sorry. A BAMF is a non-inoculated person. The government, or the National Police, anyway, think that some people are going to cause problems, are going to risk our national security. They figure that, at the very least, BAMFs are traitors or terrorists. Why else wouldn't someone get inoculated?"

Clay opened his mouth to object, but Eva stopped him.

"I understand why folks wouldn't get inoculated, I'm just telling you what they think."

"Why do they call them... I mean people like me, BAMFs?"

Eva blushed slightly. "I didn't make this up, so don't blame me. It stands for Basic Attribute Mother Fucker."

"What? Because I don't want to screw around with my natural self, I'm some kind of freak? Is that what they're saying?

Well, if they think they can make me do anything I don't want to, they've got something coming to them!" Clay had risen, but suddenly sat back down. Of course they could make him do whatever they wanted. He was no match for the National Police.

Eva tried to smile at Clay. "It's too late for that," she said. "If you would have been taken along with the other members of the group tonight, I'm not sure what would happen to you. You may not be aware, but the government is monitoring all people with an OutAp, I'm sorry, I mean outward appearance, suggesting BAMF sympathies. I don't know why, but they are. If I had been caught, well..." Eva trailed off. She took another long drink of her vodka.

"Thank God you have an appointment for inoculation. And that Lill and the kids are inoculated. If none of you were, they would have dragged your ass in—and Lill's and the kids'—so fast your head would still be spinning. At least now, you only seem a bit eccentric. But you are, and will remain, a marked man until you get inoculated. If you don't show for your appointment—and knowing the Niklases, they will check up on you—then... well... I don't know, but I can promise you it won't be good." Tears began to well up in Eva's eyes.

"And you?"

"And me? Well, I guess they'd come after me, too. I probably raised a lot of suspicion being in the area tonight. Thank God you were there. And we got lucky that Lt. Cobb was there too." She wiped her eyes and attempted a smile. "I guess we kind of provided the perfect alibi for each other." Her smile quickly faded. "But if you don't show up at your appointment, then... well... I think we'd both be in trouble." She held back a sob.

Clay was trying to get a handle on everything that Eva was telling him. They sat in silence for a moment before Clay broke it.

"Do you believe in the human spirit? That in each of us there exists something intangible that makes us, us?" Clay did not wait for Eva to respond before continuing. "It goes beyond nature and nurture. There are too many identical twins, too many people sharing the same genes, living in the very same environment that end up being every bit as different from each other as you and I. No, there must be something more than the collection of molecules that each of us is comprised of that makes us human, that makes us, us."

Eva sat quietly for a moment, thinking about what Clay had said, and then replied. "When I was young, I was afraid of death, afraid of the unknown and the uncertainty. But then I got older and I guess I entered that phase where you think you're immortal. It's not conscious, of course. But I think of all the things my friends and I did in high school and it's a wonder some of us weren't killed, or at least seriously injured. And now, well..." She paused.

"Now what?" Clay asked.

Eva opened her mouth as if to say something, but stopped. She turned away from Clay. "Well, now that immortality seems like a reality, I... I guess I haven't thought much about it. But, yes, I think that people do have souls." She turned back to face Clay. "Or at least I hope we do."

"I think we do," Clay said. "And I had been thinking about what the Walking Man had told me, trying to get my mind around it. I couldn't quite put my finger on it, but my whole body, my gut kept telling me that PreVentall was wrong, that inoculation violates some essence of our humanity. And now, after tonight, after seeing the Niklases, I think what's been bothering me is that we have souls. And I can't help but wonder, if there is a soul, then what lies beyond this world? After we're dead. I know some cultures believe in reincarnation, that the soul is on a journey of learning and we keep coming back here to try to acquire the knowledge we need to move on to the next level, the next plane of existence. And while I can't say I believe in reincarnation, I do think that we have a soul that moves on, an essence that must be accountable for our actions here on earth. We must."

Clay continued speaking, and Eva listened intently, as she always had. "If we have no soul, then life, somehow, seems without meaning. Every culture has developed some type of religion, which is, if you think about it, nothing more than an attempt to impart upon us responsibility for our actions, to hold us accountable to something greater than we are, something larger than life, something that transcends life. Otherwise, our actions here on earth are without any real meaning, no different than the mayfly; we are born, we reproduce and die in order to propagate the species, to keep our race alive. But why? Maybe it's because we are intelligent, but I refuse to believe that our existence has no real purpose."

Clay was reminded of their book club days as Eva began to pose her own questions. "But don't you think that our impact on other people, while we're alive, is purpose? Don't you think my actions affect those living in the here and now, and perhaps in the future, and that my happiness is directly related to my actions toward others? What about Milton's *Paradise Lost*? I seem to remember when we were discussing it that you suggested that Milton believed heaven and hell lay between the ears, that our actions while we're alive created the personal heaven or hell we live in, not when we're dead, but while we're still breathing? We don't need a god to hold us accountable. We all have to sleep with ourselves at night."

"I did say that." Clay thought back to his discussion with Eva, a little surprised she remembered that conversation. "But the fact that we choose our own heaven and hell here on earth does not mean that we don't have a soul. Even if we only answer to ourselves, that self which holds us accountable is more than a collection of organs and tissue and cells."

"You missed the point. We may have a soul, but who's to say that it does not end with our mortal existence?" she countered.

"It may," he admitted with some regret. "But if that's so, then we're just running on treadmills, continually moving forward but getting nowhere. What's the point of doing what's right, of acting responsibly... of... of anything? As a species, we've been around for, what, 200,000 years? And now, we'll presumably be around forever. But for what purpose? To simply be? Mankind has endured 200,000 years of joy and suffering simply to allow future generations to endure the same joy and suffering? Maybe it's my age, and my closer proximity to death, but doesn't that all ring just a little hollow to you? If we're here just to be here, then why do we even worry about the next generation? Let's just end it all here and now. If this is really all there is, then we're no different, really, than any beast of the forest, seeking shelter and avoiding pain. Intelligent, yes. But hollow."

"And if we have a soul? If it exists after our own death?"

"Then what we're doing, what humanity is doing is wrong. Genesis is supposed to free us, supposed to make everything better, but if we have a soul, if our earthly lives are just one phase of our existence, then we are trapping ourselves, trapping our soul, in the here and now. Rather than freeing us, it is chaining us to the physical world, binding us to our current state of being. Never will we be accountable for our actions, never will we be able to grow and improve. How can we evolve, as a species and as individual human beings? I can stick a knife in you and you'll heal immediately. No harm, no foul."

Eva grimaced.

"I'm sorry, that's a bad example. I would never do that. But the point is we have lost our ability to suffer consequences for our actions. We have moved beyond accountability into the realm of chaos. Don't you see, it no longer matters if we even have a soul or not. In either case, we're free to do as we please, to act as we please. If we are nothing more than creatures that possess time on this earth and serve no higher purpose, then we are left to our own devices. Even if I were able to harm you, what would it matter? You are simply another creature who survives only to procreate and continue the species. And you no longer even need to procreate since you'll live forever. If we have no higher purpose, your life is no more valuable than that of any other creature on this planet.

"If, however, we do have a higher purpose, if we do possess a soul that will continue on after our mortal death, that will be held accountable for our acts here on earth, it no longer holds any meaning if we live forever. Since we will put off the proverbial day of reckoning indefinitely, then, once again, my actions are without consequence."

"This whole thing is really turning out to be a mess." Eva looked tired, almost worn down.

"Are you alright?" Clay asked. "You look... I mean are you feeling okay?"

"No, I'm fine."

Clay looked more closely at her. "If I didn't know better, I'd say you look a little tired."

Eva let out a small laugh. "As if that were possible! It might be my makeup. I'm trying this new product and it seems to —" she stopped herself. "I'm sorry. I don't want to bore you. I'll just wash up quickly. Be right back." She stood up and went into her bedroom.

Clay looked around the room again. He was tired. Upset. He did not want to get inoculated, but neither did he want to cause harm. If it was only his life, he could act as he desired, could resist the pressure to be inoculated. But it was not only his life in danger. Tonight's events had raised the stakes, had placed his family in danger, had placed Eva in danger, too. When Eva returned she looked refreshed. No trace of weariness appeared on her face.

"Wow! You look like a different person!" Clay was surprised at the transformation. "No offense, but you should consider tossing that makeup."

"I just did. Thanks." She mustered another smile. "Your clothes are just about finished. You should probably leave as soon as they are ready. I've got a busy day tomorrow and I don't want to be late. Not after tonight."

Clay saw Eva tense up again. "What the hell do you do at work, with these people?"

"I really can't say too much. The less you know the better."

"Then why are you helping them?" Clay demanded.

"Listen, Clay. It's not really like that. I got into this mess trying to save the California Condor, remember? I didn't know that they were going to use my research on people. It wasn't like that at first. It was all pretty innocent stuff. But now… well, now I can't just walk away. There's too much at stake for me. I've got my family to think about. And now yours."

"Have they threatened you?"

"No, not directly. But you've met the Niklases. I'm not sure what would happen if I started to cause any trouble."

Clay thought about the Niklases for a moment. "It's that Cobb who I don't like. Who the hell does he think he is anyway, treating other folks like that?"

"He's just some asshole who thinks an awful lot about himself. He's been trying to fuck me for almost a year now, but…" She stopped herself. "I'm sorry, that was a bit crude." She paused for another moment before she went on. "He thinks he's some god's gift to women. That I should be honored that he wants to sleep with me, like he's some great prize and I should be a willing conquest. He makes me ill." She paused as she finished her drink. "But he did get us out of a jam tonight."

"Yeah, by eliciting a promise from you that you'll compensate him for his assistance?" Clay realized he was a bit more angry than he had expected.

"Oh, don't worry about that. I can handle him." She let out a sigh. "It's…" she stopped herself before she spoke Dr. Nakosh's name, "the others. I'm scared what may happen to them."

Clay had forgotten momentarily about the others. The group with whom he would now never be a part. "Do you think they'll be okay?" Clay was angry. "There's got to be something we can do to stop them..." Clay stopped himself. It struck him he didn't even know who he was up against, what perceived evil he was trying to prevent. He wondered how he could even help when he wasn't even sure what the problem was. Clearly, Lt. Cobb and his men had more power and resources available to them than the ragtag group that was arrested earlier. "Maybe they didn't arrest the Walking Man. Maybe he was delayed or managed to escape?" Clay wanted to meet him again, to discuss his fears of PreVentall with other people who shared his feelings.

Eva gave him a long steady look as she took a deep breath. "I hope he's okay." Another pause. "He used to say some of the most profound things." She began to tear up again, fearing the worst for those who were arrested. "From ancient wells of truth they will draw strength to keep faith with those who sleep in the dust."

Clay stared at her.

"It was something he used to say," she said softly. "And now... I don't want to think about it." She leaned over and cried on Clay's shoulder. He put his arms around her and tried to comfort her. He was upset too.

It had been decided for him. Just moments ago, Clay wasn't sure that he would be able to go through with the inoculation. Lillian surely wanted him to do it, as did, it appears, just about everyone else. Everyone else, that is, except Eva and himself, and maybe a man whose name he did not even know. But now he had to, not for himself—he was willing to die for his beliefs—but for the sake of his family. For the sake of Eva. His refusal could endanger them all, and he could not let harm come to any of them if he could prevent it.

Eva leaned back and tried to wipe the tears from her eyes. "I'm... I'm sorry, Clay. It's just that... I don't know. Things just don't feel right. It's like all these great things we've done, things we've invented that are supposed to make everything better, are making everything worse. It's like the whole world has gone topsy-turvy. Where are those wells of truth? How can we keep faith when we don't even know what's real anymore?"

"In diesem Irrenhaus ist der Glaube das Einzige, was bleibt."

Eva gave him a puzzled look. "What's that?"

"It's a phrase I heard a long time ago. It popped into my mind, just now. "'In diesem Irrenhaus ist der Glaube das Einzige, was bleibt.' In this Madhouse, Faith is all that remains," he said, softly, as he too, began to cry. For her. And for his lost humanity.


**The End**

## Acknowledgements

I would like to acknowledge and thank the many people who have supported me in this work, have pushed me along and have wished for my success. You have all been more valuable than you could know, and I thank you from the bottom of my heart. Much thanks to fellow author Shari Brady for her invaluable advice in the world of self-publishing. Thank you Oak Park Writer's Group for your support and feedback. I would also like to give a special thanks to Marcy McKay who was recruited (perhaps against her will) to provide the initial edit of this book (don't worry Jeff, I still love her). Mom, Dad, Lindy, Karen and David, I love you all! To Tom Brunner (Uncle Puff), for my favorite review of the book. To my many friends who read it and provided invaluable feedback: Jim Walter, Mark Buckley, Jorge Fragola, John Wakely, Maggie O'Donnell (I knew you'd like it), David Linde, Greg Sorg (Homey), Debbie Gamauf, Devin DiDominicus, Matt Weldon, Jeanine Hill-Fletcher (sometimes you just have to push forward), Detlef Schmidt, Everado Martinez and anyone else I may have failed to mention by name. Thank you Carolyn Schiffner of CMS Design for the cover and webpage design. Thank you Matt Larkin at Incandescent Phoenix Books for copyediting and your valuable insight. Thank you Jennifer Rice Epstein for providing editing assistance. Thank you Deb Ruff for your invaluable copyright advice. A special mention to the great folks over at Ice Nine for their quick and kind response (Thanks Alan Trist). A special thanks to Russ Burke who helped me begin my journey down the path of bioethics. I wish to acknowledge the Nanoscale Science and Engineering Center (NSEC) for Integrated Nanopatterning and Detection Technologies at Northwestern University under National Science Foundation Award Number EEC-0647560, which made studying nanotechnology my profession, albeit briefly. I also wish to acknowledge Miri Eliav-Feldon, author of *Nanotechnology 1, Assyrian 0*, which is mentioned in this book and can be found at: www.haaretz.com/weekend/week-s-end/nanotechnology-1-assyrian-0-1.306387. Lastly, I want to thank Laurie Zoloth, for introducing me to the world of nanotechnology, inspiring me to ask the important questions, and being a shining example of *Tikkun olam*, the idea that we have a duty to transform and heal our world.